THE PLACE BETWEEN

KIT OLIVER

PARROT CAT PUBLISHING

For P.
Thanks for getting me started. I miss you.

THE PLACE BETWEEN

CHAPTER ONE

THE BREEZE COMES off the harbor with all the salt and brine of low tide, and Ned joins the crush of students winding through campus to their first day of classes. He needs a coffee. He needs a briefcase so he's not hauling around his scuffed and worn backpack like he's an undergrad. He also needs his phone to beep with the message he's waited for all day, but when it finally buzzes in his pocket, he huffs out a sigh.

A favor, Chris has written in the newest email to arrive. Ned purses his lips, stepping out of the swirls of students under one of the quad's towering maple trees. Definitely not what he's waiting for, but he reads it anyway, Chris's explanation of a professor out on emergency leave, an open course and *Ned, if you could teach it, please.*

He tips his head back and stares up through the branches at the blue, brilliant sky. The leaves are just starting to turn with the first blush of red and gold on the highest limbs. The fall foliage comes earlier in Maine than he always expects it to, no matter that he's been on this campus for five autumns now.

A favor. It's an intro course, one Ned can teach in his

sleep. He did teach it in his sleep last year, those days when he'd roll out of bed after tossing fitfully all night, his eyes gritty and stinging. *Do it,* he tells himself. He can email Chris back, go get his coffee, and get on with his evening. Maybe even afford a briefcase one of these days. His thumb hovers over his keyboard, but he shoves his phone into his pocket instead of typing out a reply.

His phone doesn't buzz again as he jogs across the street, lifting a hand in thanks to a sedan that slows for him. He pulls his shirt from its neat tuck into his slacks and shoulders open the café door. The bells hanging from the knob jingle their cheerful peal over the chatter of students and summer's last groups of tourists with their beers and coffees. Ned's stool sits empty against the bar, and he drops his backpack next to it, hiking his elbows on the bar and leaning over it to catch Patrick's eye.

"Hey," he says. And then louder, "Hey, Pat, your phone, man."

"Jen didn't send you anything?" Pat asks. He dumps an inch of foam from the top of a pint glass, bubbles sliding down into a pool of froth on the metal tray beneath the taps.

"Let me just see it for a second," Ned says.

"What do we say?"

"And a coffee."

"We say 'please,'" Pat says, but tosses his phone over.

Leave it alone, she'll text you if she texts you, Pat'd said that morning, batting Ned's phone out of his hands, while Baxter snuffled at their feet, eager for his walk.

Now, Pat taps a finger on the bar to get Ned's attention. "How was your first class?"

"Fine." Ned types in Pat's passcode. Half the students hadn't shown up, and half of the ones who had will probably drop his course before it meets next. Ned will have a lecture hall full of new faces, and he'll have to go over the syllabus once again, but it was fine—and fine's been as good as it gets for so long that Ned's learned to not complain.

Jen may not have texted Ned all day, but she's no slouch about posting pictures. Ned's kid is cute as all hell. Ned scoots his stool closer to the bar and leans over Pat's phone, scrolling through the stream of photos. Peggy's got pigtails today, her bright purple backpack over her shoulders, and a grin that looks like it could split her face in two. She's the absolute most adorable thing Ned's ever seen, standing there on the front steps to their house.

Jen's house. Ned bites at the inside of his cheek. He has to remember that—it was their house and now it isn't because there isn't a *them* anymore. It's Jen's dark green front door, and Jen's front stoop, and Jen's stone walkway. The grass has grown up enough to tickle the bottoms of Peggy's pink Velcro shoes. Jen never did like weeding those stones. No, that was always Ned's job.

Ned sighs and Pat reaches over and plucks the phone away. "Enough of that, you depressing lump of a doctoral student you." Louder, he says, "Hi, what can I get for you?"

Ned wasn't done looking, but Pat tucks the phone into his back pocket, so Ned pulls his own out. The screen's still blank, no new notifications over the lock screen picture of Peggy smiling up at him, all dimples and dark brown hair and baby teeth she has yet to start losing.

She will, soon enough. And hell if he isn't going to be there to see it.

A newspaper hits the bar next to his elbow.

"Black tea with milk," says the guy who dropped it.

Ned rubs at his forehead with three fingers. On his phone, Peggy's wearing her teal T-shirt with a giant purple triceratops that he'd gotten her. It's too small for her now, only a handful of months since he took that picture.

"Milk's behind you," Pat says.

Ned locks his phone, pressing his fingers into his temple. First day of kindergarten. What kind of father is he to miss her first day of kindergarten?

"Steamed milk," Newspaper Guy says. "No foam. Please."

"Righto, steamed milk, very fancy. Two percent okay?"

You have work. Put on pants, go finish your PhD, and you'll be done before you know it, Pat had said, smacking Ned on the top of the head just hours ago.

"Skim," the guy says.

Ned tucks his forehead into his palm. He should go upstairs. He should definitely not ask for Pat's phone again so he can stare down at Peggy grinning, the morning sun catching on her round cheeks, and the stuffed triceratops sticking out of her backpack. He should let it be. He knows what searching through the pictures Jen's posted will lead to —Ned's own kid, balanced on Jen's new boyfriend's hip, grinning her grin for the camera.

Pat deposits a cup of coffee in front of Ned. He stares at it. He needs to pour milk into it. He doesn't have the energy to pour milk into it, and he needs to because that's how he drinks his coffee. *Do it,* he tells himself. *Just get up and do it.* This semester is going to be good. Quick and painless, get up here to campus, do his work, graduate, and get back home to Boston. Milk in his coffee is a good first step toward that. *Do it, do it, do it.*

Pat leans across the bar, pours a splash of milk into his cup, and then spins the jug so Ned can see the label. "Move your butt, or I'll put more in." Pat gestures to the *skim milk* printed in large letters.

Ned sighs. He shifts, pulling his forehead out of his hand. Stands too, and reaches behind to grab the pitcher of whole milk.

I'll teach that class, he texts Chris. Typing takes more

energy than it feels like it should. He's going to have a bear of a semester, teaching three courses. He chews at his lip and adds, Thanks. Before he can rethink it, he hits send and opens his email.

A couple of comments on your dissertation draft, Chris has written in the first one. *Come see me.*

Ned's stomach dips. *Come see me.* Ned's written that to students before. It's never good.

"Shit," he mutters into his wrist. He drops his hand and blinks his eyes open and—

Shit.

The sight of Ned's former statistics professor makes a headache pulse in his temples. Of all the people to run into, freshly back to campus, facing Chris's critiques to his dissertation, and the semester stretching before him.

"Hi," he says as politely as he can manage.

Ned gets a stiff nod and a glance from behind black-rimmed glasses. Well, that's two of them who aren't interested in a chat. Typical.

"Hey for your tea, can I get a name for the cup?" Pat asks, brandishing a marker.

"Professor Abbot."

"Professor Abbot," Pat says, his tongue between his teeth as he writes, the name a bold purple flourish that Pat underlines twice. "Professor—oh!"

"Pat," Ned mutters. He shakes his head, though it only turns Pat's surprise into a huge delighted smile.

"*That* Professor Abbot?" Pat laughs and draws a loopy, lopsided star on the cup.

Doctor, Abbot had also allowed himself to be called when Ned took his class. That had been four years ago and Ned still remembers the weight of that thick syllabus with *Doctor Charles Henry Abbot, PhD* printed across the top.

"Ned's a big fan." Pat grins. "I've heard so much about you."

Ned ducks over his coffee. An entire semester of statistics with Abbot, and Ned doesn't exactly want to get caught in a conversation. No, he quickly learned to steer well clear of Abbot and the austerity of those glasses, the perfect, precise part in his dark hair, and the exacting tailoring of his shirts.

Back before he'd known any better, he'd thought Abbot attractive, when Ned had newly joined the sociology department as a first-year doctoral student, and he'd spotted Abbot at the lectern that first class on regression analysis. He'd been happily married to Jen still, but hey, he could look—and slim, tall, and dark haired, Abbot had been something to look at. *Like he walked out of a Brooks Brothers catalogue*, Ned had thought, excited to get to work with a professor roughly his same age who openly dated men. What a treat it had seemed to have a colleague with a boyfriend.

Now, Ned hunches over his coffee and tries not to grimace.

"Good, uh, to see you," Ned says, fitting a lid onto his cup. He'll bring it upstairs to his and Pat's apartment. He needs to take Baxter for a walk anyway. Whatever intrigue Ned once felt about Abbot, he's long since decided he just looks stuffy, overdressed, and too straitlaced in those perfectly creased slacks and dress shirt, buttoned neatly at the cuffs.

"Anything else for you today?" Pat asks Abbot.

"Hot chocolate."

Ned pauses, his hand looped under the strap of his backpack.

"With whipped cream," Abbot adds.

All those years ago, Pat had taken to calling Abbot

Chuckie H., after enough nights of Ned poking at his keyboard or pacing the café, a hand in his hair and a crinkled, creased problem set in his hand. Now, Pat grins at him, his purple marker hovering over the side of a new cup.

"Please," Abbot says. "And sprinkles."

"Sprinkles?" Pat's mouth spreads into a wider smile. "Rainbow ones?"

"If you have them."

"Sure do," Pat says. "Hot chocolate with whipped cream and sprinkles? That's Ned's favorite drink."

"It's not," Ned says.

"He always asks for extra sprinkles." Pat winks at him. *Smile,* Pat's taken to telling Ned, *you've forgotten how.*

Ned's headache beats behind his eyes. "I don't." He tugs his bag higher on his shoulder. Pat's ridiculous on a good day, and Ned hasn't been having many of those lately. "Have a nice evening, Professor. Bye, Pat."

"You're not coming to the meeting?" Abbot asks.

Abbot's got that clip to his words, an accent to how he speaks, though Ned's always privately thought the guy's voice is all the more stilted when aimed at him. *And your chosen control variable?* Abbot used to ask, standing at the front of the lecture hall, his eyes fixed on Ned's. It's been years since those classes and still whenever Ned sees him, he wants to tug at his collar.

Ned shrugs his bag higher, knowing it's wrinkling his shirt. He's done at the office until tomorrow, and if Abbot wants to wear a tie and keep it tightly knotted at this point in the day, that fits with his whole overly prim and proper schtick he seems to never let rest.

"I don't have a meeting," Ned says. He has Baxter to take for a long walk, an evening preparing for tomorrow's classes, and hours to spend fretting over Chris's email. *Come see me.* Ned's stomach drops again. *A good semester,*

7

he'd told himself just the other day as he packed his car and settled Baxter into the back seat next to Peggy's empty car seat, his throat thick at the fact of driving away.

"Hmm."

Just that. Just a low noise in Abbot's throat, and then he's collecting a giant cup topped with whipped cream and a frightening number of sprinkles. It should look ridiculous, the creases in Abbot's slacks and that tower of cream threatening to slip down over his hand. It does look ridiculous, but still Abbot manages to aim a glance rife with dislike at Ned as he turns and leaves.

Ned fumbles for his phone. He clearly should've actually read his email because *meeting tonight* tops another message. Apparently, Abbot reads his email on the regular. Of course Abbot read his, he's probably fundamentally incapable of failing any type of professional obligation.

Even while holding a hot chocolate covered in whipped cream and garish, flashy sprinkles.

Which Ned so very much wants to know the story behind, but he apparently has a meeting to get to. And he still has a dog to walk.

As he makes his way up the narrow, dark staircase to his and Pat's apartment above the bar, their door rattles in its frame. Ned eases open the lock and eighty pounds of black and white fur barrels into him, wiggling and panting, a tail thumping against his knees.

"Easy there," Ned says, a furry, fluffy head shoved into his hand to be petted as he drops his backpack. He steps back from the paws that land at his waist, carefully balancing his coffee. Baxter drops down and circles, tongue hanging from his mouth. "Where's your leash? Go get your leash."

Baxter scrambles to the coat rack and Ned's sure the scratch of nails on the old wood boards can be heard downstairs in the café. Probably Baxter's galumph back again too, his leash skittering along behind him, clutched in his teeth.

"You're a genius," Ned tells him, clipping the leash onto his collar. He gets his chin licked and he scruffs up the long fur behind Baxter's ears. "Chris wouldn't make you meet again about your dissertation, now would he? Yes, you're a good boy."

Baxter hurries down the staircase, and Ned opens the door onto the street for him, warm late afternoon air rushing in. This time last week, he was bringing Peggy down to her favorite park, Baxter trailing along and sniffing at the base of the slide. The park's probably crowded right now as evening edges into Boston, everyone spilling out of work and the neighborhood kids celebrating their first day back at school. He rubs at his eyes. He should be there with Peggy tonight, reminding her again and again about waiting her turn for the swings instead of just bum-rushing them like Baxter when he sees a squirrel.

Knots of freshmen clog the paths of campus, and when they part there're still crowds of tourists on their way to get a happy-hour drink and enjoy a late summer evening out on the town. Baxter dodges this way and that, sniffing bike racks and parked cars and a hapless baby in a stroller before Ned can quickly pull him back.

"Enough." Ned tugs at his leash again when Baxter squirms his way into the crowd waiting to cross at the light. Ignoring him, Baxter manages to wind between pairs of legs. And of course, he zeroes in on a pair of shiny dress shoes that don't look like they belong to anyone interested in being examined by an excitable dog.

Ned looks up and—no. No, not at all. Because it's Abbot who Baxter has managed to find.

"Sorry," Ned says. *The Chuckster, Charlie Horrible, C. H. Asshole,* Pat had called Abbot as Ned received his midterm grades that semester in Abbot's course. "Baxter, no, leave it."

Abbot blinks at him from behind those black-rimmed glasses, his hands still full of his tea and that hot chocolate topped with its tower of whipped cream. That must be distain coloring his expression. That or pure disgust that Baxter's still sniffing so enthusiastically over his shoelaces.

Ned grabs for Baxter's collar and pulls him back. "Heel, you hear?"

"Ned," Abbot says in greeting.

Mr. Coppola, Abbot'd called him once, that one and only time Ned had thought it would be a good idea to go to his office hours. *Edward*, it had been next and even now Ned wants to cringe. Ned shifts his weight, eyeing the red light across the street.

This isn't as bad as that afternoon stuck in Abbot's office, Ned's midterm on the desk between them and a pen in Abbot's hand. Ned had spent that hour finding anywhere in the room to look besides Abbot bent over and writing until red ink had spilled across the margins in tidy, neat rows of corrections and hardly any of Ned's original work was visible through the shine of it.

"How was your summer?" Ned makes himself ask as the orange hand gives way to the white walk figure.

Anyone else in the department would make small talk on the way to the building that houses the sociology department, but this is Abbot—*Professor* Abbot—and he just crosses the street and says, "Fine."

"Mine was good," Ned says half a block later when Abbot still hasn't asked in return. Of course he doesn't ask—as far as Ned knows, the guy's head is filled to the brim with statistical analyses and there's no variable in there controlling for professional courtesy.

Ned glances at the hot chocolate again. All right, statistical analyses and rainbow sprinkles. Apparently.

Ned slows his pace as Baxter stops to sniff at a bench, letting Abbot get ahead of him, rolling his eyes at that straight, stiff back.

"Be good," Ned tells Baxter, leaving him a bowl of water and looping his leash around a tree near the sociology building. *And don't get stolen by a homesick freshman*, he should probably add. It wouldn't be the first time Ned's returned to find Baxter sprawled on his back, paws in the air as a huddle of students take turns scratching his belly.

With that tongue flopped out and tail wagging, Baxter's inherent lack of dignity is an odd sort of look against the university's white-trimmed brick buildings and the manicured grass of the quad. Ned had thought it beautiful when he'd first seen the campus, all of New England's grandeur and Portland's picturesque streets. He turns away from the sight and heads inside, halfheartedly shoving his shirt back into his pants in some semblance of professionalism. Lately, that same view of campus just makes him tired.

Ned plucks at his collar and tries to smooth out his slacks as he joins the professors filling the conference room. He's always hated Chris's insistence that Ned's possibly on equal footing with them, as if Ned teaching a handful of classes is at all equivalent to being tenure-track faculty. He smiles and nods back greetings, his back itching as he lingers near the door, but Chris waves him in as soon as he spots him.

"Ned," Chris calls out, smiling under his cap of white hair, his round cheeks as rosy as ever. He hugs Ned over the bulge of his stomach and then steps back, holding Ned by the shoulders. "You'll really teach that course?"

"Yeah," Ned says. *No*, he'd so much rather answer. "And I got your email about my dissertation. Do you have a minute to talk?"

"I'll give you two minutes after this." Chris nudges out a chair and pushes Ned toward it. "Come, sit, we'll get started."

Half of the faculty are on their phones and the rest are chatting with each other. Ned sits slowly, still trying to straighten his shirt. Maybe this won't take long and he can get out of here. Or maybe what he needs to hear will be quick, and he can slip out and leave the real faculty to their evening here. Which would be all the better, so he doesn't have to sit here with his committee members knowing his dissertation is still unfinished.

Come see me. His stomach clenches.

"Real quick," Ned says, leaning across the table to catch Chris's eye. "'Cause that last draft I sent you, you had said it was good, and I'm really hoping to be finished this semester, so—"

"It is good." Chris's smile only makes his cheeks redder as he turns on the projector. "That's just it, Ned. We're going to make it great."

"Great." It doesn't need to be great. It needs to be finished. He tries for a smile of his own. "I'm trying to graduate this semester, and I've got some job applications—"

"Exactly." Chris spreads his arms out, expansive in his cheer. "We're going to get you hired by the best, Ned. Just the topic we're discussing tonight."

"We're discussing my dissertation?" *No, please.*

"We're talking about competition in academia."

"Right. What?"

Ned's phone buzzes against his thigh and he grabs for it, bumping his elbow against the chair next to him.

"Excuse me," Abbot says. Ned looks up. Abbot had his hand resting on the back of that chair and Ned's elbow is precipitously close to him.

There are other places the guy could choose to sit.

Maybe this is what Abbot does for fun: stockpiles all the ways in which he can ruin Ned's life, just as soon as Ned's resolved to get himself back on track. *A good semester*, Ned had promised himself, and look at him, hours into it and stuck in this damn meeting already.

"Sorry," Ned mutters and shifts his chair farther from Abbot's.

"Sit, everyone. Henry, hi, hey, you two stay afterward, all right?" Chris points between Ned and Abbot, still smiling.

Ned's stomach plummets. "Us?"

"Just for a quick second," Chris says.

"Me and him?" Ned glances at Abbot. *No*, he wants to say. "Yeah, sure."

Life Outside of Academia glows on the laptop Chris opens, and then up on the screen when he plugs in the projector. Abbot sets his tea in front of himself, the garish, bright purple of Pat's writing marring the side, though that hot chocolate isn't anywhere to be seen. Ned moves his chair to the side, trying to give him more room. Maybe he chugged it in his office. Maybe he runs on a steady diet of whipped cream, sprinkles, and sugar that fuels his haughty disdain whenever he sees Ned. The thought might make Ned smile, if his heart wasn't going too fast, Chris's *Come see me* banging through his mind.

Chris gives him a wink. "Ned, this talk will be just the ticket you're looking for."

Working to Make Work in Academia Work for You, reads the subtitle to Chris's talk. Ned tries not to frown. The ticket he's looking for is a graduation cap, robe, and doctoral hood, Portland in his rearview mirror, and a life where he gets to see his daughter every week—not stuck in a city two hours north of her. He slumps in his chair and rolls it farther away from Abbot. One of the wheels sticks, and when it gives out a squeak, Abbot glances at him from behind those glasses.

"We want to be the best," Chris says to the room, his hands rubbing together as he bounces on his toes. "Nationally, internationally, student recruitment, graduation placements, research initiatives, all of it." Another bounce. "And how do we do that? How do we stand out from the crowd, lead the pack, and show them what we're made of here at Callahan University?"

Silence. Across the table, Aliyah's phone buzzes.

"Get back to work?" she asks, winding a long thin braid through her fingers as she taps at her phone.

Beside her, Lee snorts a laugh. Doctor Kerr, she'd introduced herself the first day of the seminar Ned took with her. Back then, her blonde hair had been shaved on one side and she'd held class on the quad in the warm sunshine. She glances at Ned and rolls her eyes. He tries to muster up a grin for her, though it feels more like a grimace.

"People, people, no," Chris says. "That's exactly why we're here: we're going to mix things up. Take a new approach. Do what no other top university is doing. We"— Chris holds up his hands, palms out, his face lit up—"we're going to revolutionize academia."

Aliyah's phone buzzes again. Next to Ned, Abbot takes a sip of his tea. Chris grins around the room.

"Can we talk about research funding?" Lee asks.

Chris drops his hands.

"We're tackling the problem from the bottom up," he says and clicks to the next slide. "The number of academics leaving the field for other jobs, faculty's dissatisfaction with personal lives, the shift away from viewing academia as an attractive career—there's a fix for this. And it's called: balance."

Ned's chair squeaks again. Aliyah scrolls through her phone.

"This is going to be a department-wide initiative, starting this semester. We're talking hobbies, we're talking time with family, we're talking weekends away from the office, nights without computers, evenings with friends, all of it. No more feeling like you should be working all hours of the day. Go outside, live your life, and work smarter, not just harder."

Someone clears their throat. Aliyah's phone buzzes again and Lee purses her lips, her arms crossed. Chris grins at them. Ned spins his chair back and forth slowly, scratching at his eyebrow with his thumbnail. *Yikes*, he would mutter if it were anyone next to him other than Abbot.

When Chris finally clicks through his last slide, it's late enough that the evening's a dark, deep blue. *Baxter*, Ned thinks as Chris finally starts to wrap up. He glances out the window as everyone scrapes their chairs back from the table. Baxter's there and sure enough, someone's sitting with him, a long, dark brown braid down her back and her hands scratching over his belly. Well, good. At least between Ned and his dog, one of them is having a nice enough evening.

"My dissertation," Ned says, leaning across the table as Chris folds his laptop closed. "Can I just get an idea of what you want to talk about?"

"More analysis," Chris says. He's still grinning.

Ned cocks his head. "I'm sorry, what?"

"Your work is perfect. We're going to make it even better." Chris points at him. "I want you to go back and add in a really thorough analysis of big-picture numbers. We're going to knock the socks off everyone clamoring to hire you."

"Me?" Ned asks. As far as he knows, exactly zero people are clamoring to hire him. And no, Chris isn't pointing to him, Ned realizes too slowly. He's pointing at Abbot.

"You'll help him out," Chris says, that finger leveled right at Abbot's chest.

Ned blinks. "What?"

"I'm sorry?" Abbot asks.

"Ned doesn't have a quantitative researcher on his committee." Chris waves toward the back of the room, where most of the faculty have already made their break for freedom. Of course Ned doesn't have a quantitative researcher overseeing his work—it's not quantitative work. He did hours—*hours*—of interviews, which he then transcribed on his weekends, Peggy sitting at his feet with her stuffed dinosaurs, begging him to play with her.

"Chris," Ned says.

"That will take months," Abbot says. *No*, Ned can so clearly hear.

It echoes his own thoughts. No, no, no—he's done. He's supposed to be *done*.

"Oh, no it won't, Ned's a smart cookie." Chris jostles Ned's shoulder. "Look at you, the only grad student in the room with us, top teaching evals, and you're so close to earning your degree. You'll sail through this."

Ned stares at him. He's the only grad student here because everyone else had the sense to take research positions, rather than have to work for Chris and his overbearing, unbridled enthusiasm.

Ned clears his throat. He doesn't look at Abbot beside him. "That type of statistics really isn't my strength."

"Which is why Henry here will be helping you," Chris says. "You'll do great."

Henry, Ned thinks. Apparently not everyone has to follow Abbot's strict, uncompromising rules about calling him *professor*. Ned's stomach turns over and he pushes his hand back into his hair. "Chris—Chris, wait, this isn't—"

"Gotta get home." Chris tucks his laptop under his arm. He gives Ned a smack on the shoulder and then pushes past him. "Setting an example, you know? I'm off to dinner with the wife."

"Chris," Ned tries again, but Chris is gone and it's just Ned and Abbot left as the door swings closed.

Ned stands quickly and his chair squeaks again. Abbot glances down at the wheels.

"I'll, uh—" Ned starts. He stops. *Talk to Chris*, is maybe what he was going to say. *Be in touch*, he could finish that sentence with. *Get us out of this*, is what he wants to blurt out. He's not working with Abbot all semester—no. *No.* There's no way.

He grabs his backpack and pushes his way out of the room. Outside, whoever was petting Baxter is gone, and he jumps up when he sees Ned, two leaves stuck to his bushy tail and his tongue hanging from his mouth.

"Chris is fucking absurd," Ned says to him, dumping out his water.

What a waste of an evening that was. Baxter stretches his back legs one at a time, and then bows down to stretch his front legs too, long tail held high in the air. Whatever. Chris's initiative will fade like every new idea introduced at the beginning of a semester: rampantly discussed for a week, and then lost to the mire of approaching midterms.

Last year, Chris had wanted them to mentor high school students, and the year before was a fitness challenge. That had at least lasted until the beginning of October, but only because Chris had ponied up for Celtics tickets for the winner, and Lee had wanted to take Minori to a game. This round of "work hard, play hard," as Chris's final slide had read, would wither away soon enough.

Ned's phone buzzes halfway across campus, and he pulls it out of his pocket to find a series of pictures sent by his mom. His dad swinging Peggy around, a hand under each of her arms. Them kneeling in the backyard, surrounded by a plastic T. rex and Peggy's triceratops. The two of them outside her new school, a stegosaurus in his dad's hand, and Peggy waving to what must be her teacher.

Peggy and his dad have the same smile, one Ned knows is on his own face as he grins down at his phone. Same easily tanned skin, same brown hair, though it's gray now on his dad. If Peggy had been the boy they thought she'd be, it would've been the three of them nearly identical at any age, none of Jen's blonde hair or freckles. Peggy's even gotten the beginnings of the family's height, half a head taller than her friends, though time will tell if she'll grow into the foot-baller's frame Ned got from his dad, or if she'll take at least some delicacy from her mother.

Ned's smile fades as he keeps looking. Peggy's ecstatic. She'll have gotten graham crackers as a snack after school, eaten at the same kitchen table Ned sat at when he was a kid. It was the same snack he'd eaten for years, though he'd had toy cars spread across the table, as his parents still like to remind him, not the collection of dinosaurs Peggy's amassed.

Thanks, he sends back to his mom, his throat thick, knotted up tight and hard. Love you, he adds, and shoves his phone into his pocket. He's got time enough to stare at those photos later tonight, and he'll probably have a mess of a time preparing for tomorrow's classes with the temptation of them there.

And now he's got his dissertation to work on. Again.

"C'mon." He tugs at Baxter's leash. It's going to be a better semester than the last one. Better than last spring, better than last fall—better than all of it. Somehow.

CHAPTER TWO

THE SANDWICHES in the break room are squished on one side, and when Ned bites into one, the bread's grown soggy. He sticks half of it in his mouth anyway. There's no food like free food.

"If you've got an appetite like that, you haven't checked your email," Aliyah says as she pokes through the fridge.

"Don't check your email," Lee says. "Chris has funding for this—this *thing*."

"What thing?" Ned sticks another bite in his mouth. The sandwich isn't half bad, though maybe that's just being sick of the food Pat serves at his café. Ned needs to go to the grocery store. Vegetables, he'd told himself, not the steady diet of coffee and department leftovers he's already back to. He looks down at the sandwich. It's got lettuce on it and a thin watery slice of tomato.

"Chris isn't fooling around," Lee says. "Did you try to log on to the department server last night?"

Ned chews and shakes his head. He was poring over his scribbled notes from Abbot's class, scratching his fingers through his hair, and tapping his pencil on the table until Pat had thrown a sock at him. *Done*, Ned had crowed when he'd turned his final in for Abbot's class. The grade he'd gotten had felt like a victory, passing the course even if it tanked his GPA. What a nightmare to crack open that notebook again.

Aliyah sighs deep in the back of her throat. "He's got the entire network shut after the workday, and there's no logging on at home, 'cause he's blocked the VPN too. We need to"—she holds up two fingers of each hand—"'enjoy the evening off.' It's bullshit if you ask me."

Ned sticks the last of his sandwich in his mouth and frowns around it. "He shut down the network?"

"We're his little guinea pigs." Aliyah closes her eyes. "Copy all your university files to your hard drive, don't let anyone know you might actually want to get your work done."

Ned swallows. "Can't that get you fired?"

"Goody Two-shoes over here," Aliyah says. She sighs again. "Yeah, don't copy them, you'd definitely get fired."

"Chris is locking the building too," Lee says. "I don't know how he convinced the university, but he's not kidding about this one."

"Good luck to us all," Aliyah mutters.

A better semester than last one, he reminds himself as Aliyah and Lee head back to their offices. He takes a deep breath and lets it out slowly. He'll be good and done here, soon enough. He'll run into Chris at conferences and the occasional visit to see Pat, but the eccentricities of the sociology department under the guidance of Chris Hausman won't be Ned's to deal with.

Just as soon as he graduates. He wipes his palms on his thighs and rubs the back of his hand over his mouth, leaving with a lingering glance at the rest of the sandwiches.

"Chris?" he asks, knocking his knuckles against Chris's door.

It's every inch an office for a department head, with its windows overlooking the quad, the rich colors of the rug, and Chris's giant wooden desk. Upstairs in the office Ned shares with Sameer, they have a single window that warps in its frame each year. Sometimes they can even get it open —a counterpoint to when they can't get it shut again, come the cold weather.

"Come in, come in," Chris says, and Ned sits in the chair at his desk, the same one he'd sat in last fall, a fading tan from his wedding ring on his finger and his dissertation proposal between them.

The proposal they'd both agreed to, and that Ned had presented to his committee, and they too had signed off on. Ned clears his throat.

"I wanted to talk to you about the changes you're suggesting," Ned says.

Chris spreads his hands out on his desk. "I'm not throwing you to the wolves here, Ned. Henry will help you."

Henry again. Chris's buddy "Henry" is exactly the issue. Ned shifts in his chair. "I'm basing my career on qualitative analysis."

"Showing your range will impress universities looking to hire you."

"I've already completed my analysis."

"All research can continue to be improved."

I can't do it, Ned wants to say.

"You've got this," Chris says before he can. He leans across the desk. "And we'll get you graduated this semester. A couple weeks of revisions and then you can defend your dissertation in early October. I already emailed your draft to Henry and he's ready to meet with you."

Ned blows out a breath. His stomach turns over at the

idea of Abbot reading his work. Didn't Ned already have to suffer through enough of that?

"I'm pushing you to do this because I care," Chris says.

The pulse of irritation inside Ned's chest softens. "I appreciate that, but—"

"You're going to knock it out of the park."

Behind Ned, the door opens. *I'm not*, Ned wants to say. He glances over his shoulder, expecting Lee or Aliyah here to complain about Chris's pet project. Maybe even Abbot, showing up out of the blue again to ruin Ned's day. It's not any of them, though the older man standing there certainly has the same haughty, overly polished look about him as good old *Henry*.

Ned stands and straightens his shirt. Given the way the guy's looking at him, Ned's still got crumbs stuck to his face. There's a certain glare to the eyes behind his glasses that goes with the austerity of his salt-and-pepper hair in its close short cut, and Ned's suddenly all too aware that he never irons his clothes, just gives them a good shake after pulling them from the dryer.

"Ah, is Henry available?" Chris asks.

Why the hell that guy would know, Ned has no idea, but the man nods.

"Go on and meet with him now then, Ned," Chris says. "And let me know how it goes. I'm interested to hear what you two find."

"Course," Ned says. It's more of a mumble than any real attempt at words, and he backs out of the office, trying to ignore how the guy glances over him.

In the hall, he digs his fingers into his eyes. Chris cares about him. Ned knows he cares. And it's probably for the best. But it'd be great if he just cared a little less.

Ned steels himself outside of Abbot's door. Maybe Abbot can talk Chris out of this. He presses his lips together and knocks. And waits. And then knocks again, shifting his weight. *Chris*, he thinks, frustration rising through his throat. Of course Abbot's not here. That'd be too easy. Or maybe he's here and he somehow knows it's Ned in the hall and he's ignoring the tap of his knuckles. Ned knocks again, louder.

He finally steps back and looks at the door. This is definitely Abbot's office, a tidy nameplate hanging on the wall. And it is his office hours right now because it's posted right there, and the times match Ned's watch. So no, he's not wrong. Abbot's just skipping out on his own office hours.

Asshole, Ned thinks at the varnished wooden door.

His phone buzzes in his pocket and he reaches for it quickly, like it might be Chris calling to apologize and say he'd gotten Abbot's schedule wrong, he's rethought Ned's dissertation, he wants Ned to go ahead and graduate, he found someone to teach Ned's classes and he should move home immediately.

"Hey, Dad," Ned says into his phone.

"Kiddo, what's good?"

"Nothing's good." Ned leans his shoulder against the wall next to Abbot's annoyingly polished nameplate. "I'm back up here, living with Pat, and Chris wants me to keep working on my dissertation."

"Pat's an angel. You're an angel too. Absolute perfection. Jury's out on this Chris character."

Ned rubs at his eyes. "I'm as far from perfect as anyone can get."

"If you look it up in the dictionary, it's got your picture, kid."

"I crashed your car into the garage door. You remind me every time I drive back home."

"Like I said, model child, without a fault. Probably got it from your old man."

Ned rolls his eyes. "Thanks."

"Just make sure you check behind you before you reverse," his dad says. "That's the trick to it, you know—figuring out whether the door's actually open before you drive through it. What you did definitely works as a way to get out of the garage, but it's just a bit messy."

"Is that what it was?"

"Stick with me, kid."

Ned tries to smile. That was a hell of a long summer, saving up from mowing neighbors' lawns to buy lumber and hardware and paint, and then figuring out how to rebuild a garage door. It hadn't looked like much in the end, but his parents had kept it, his dad patting it proudly now and again, with his usual teasing how he was glad Ned went into academia rather than construction.

Though look where that's left him now. Ned tips his head back and blows out a breath.

"Listen," Dad says. "Tomorrow evening—you got plans?"

"I'm a doctorate student, I've always got plans." Though, well . . . no. He doesn't, not this time around, thanks to Chris, not if he can't log onto the network or even access the building. He shifts his grip on his phone. He's going to have to figure out how to make this semester work, without his evenings and weekends available to get anything done.

"Didn't know if you'd found yourself a lady friend," Dad says. "Or man friend. Guy friend? Dude pal? A companion—how's that, gender neutral. See? I can be hip."

"Dad." Ned shakes his head. *Dude pal*. His father is one of a kind. "That's the opposite of hip."

"Jennifer's gotta work late and your mom has tennis, so Ms. Margaret and I have the afternoon and evening together. Plus, no school for her the next day she's supposed to be easing into Kindergarten or something fancy like that."

Ned straightens. "Yeah?"

"Peggy suggested a tea party, but frankly her T. rex is always spilling the cream with those little arms. So I thought I'd drive her up? If you're around."

"You don't have to do that. I don't have a class to teach then, I'll get the bus down."

"I'm happy to. We're on our six hundredth round of listening to 'Puff the Magic Dragon,' and I'm pretty sure we can break a thousand there and back."

"That's four hours in the car."

"No, it's four hours for me, five minutes each way for Nappy-Mcgee once we hit the highway. I think there's a permanent drool stain on her car seat. Anyway, you hate the bus."

Ned does hate the bus. Can't work on it or he'll get carsick, and it's always crowded enough that he's not quite able to relax and enjoy the ride, even with headphones in and a seat to himself. He could drive down, though it's no mistake his dad's offering to be the one making the trip—Ned's car has seen better days. A rattle-trap, his dad had declared the last time Ned dropped it off at his auto shop.

"You don't want to spend all of your afternoon in the car," Ned says.

"I want to drive your mini-me up so you can see her. Anyway, I'm a grandfather, I think I'm contractually oblig-ated to spend my time leaf-peeping."

"The trees have barely started changing."

"Then I'll get my hours in ahead of the crowds," Dad says. "How's that for a plan? I'm always thinking. I'm bringing a book—your mother signed us up for this book club. Keeps the brain young, or something like that. Frankly, I think she thinks Susan's husband is rather handsome—"

"Dad—"

"But she swears it's not that. Though he is rather handsome. I'll admit it even if she won't."

"Oh my God, Dad."

"So you'll have Little Miss Peggy to yourself 'cause my dear wife is keeping a page count of how much I actually read. Well, Baxter will have her to himself, but maybe they'll let you play with them. I just got twenty-five pounds of bones for him, you know. Grass-fed marrow bones, straight from the farmer. You cannot get better than these. Premium quality, Baxter's gonna love them."

"Dad . . ."

"We'll see you tomorrow. I'll bring some food for you and your tiny dino daughter. Or your mother will probably pack some—watch out, it'll be healthy. She's on a quinoa kick."

"You really don't have to do this."

"Acai berries too. Is that how you say it?"

"Dad."

"You're right I don't have to, but I want to. You love having Peggy up there. The prodigal daughter returns to the land of her birth, reunited once more with the streets of Portland, a return heralded by—no, I'm talking to Ned. Ned, your mother says 'hi.'"

"Hi, Mom."

"Ned agrees Susan's husband is quite the looker," his dad says, his voice muffled. Ned shakes his head. Louder, his dad says, "Bye, champ. I've got a new idea for how to organize the Tupperware, and I've got to show it to your mom before she makes a break for it. I'll see you soon. And hey—I love you, Ned, you don't even know how much."

"I've got an idea," Ned says. "Love you too. Thanks, Dad."

Ned stands there for a long minute, staring down at his

phone before he pushes it back into his pocket. His dad is something else. That's what Pat has always said, even as far back as when Dad had lobbed them underhanded baseballs and they'd swung bats nearly taller than themselves. Spending his day off driving from Boston to Portland. . . Ned shouldn't bother to be surprised.

Do anything for you, his dad had said, roughing up Ned's hair the day he'd helped him move out of his—Jen's— place. It had been brutally hot for late spring, and even Pat's good cheer had faded by the end of the afternoon.

Ned rubs at his forehead. That was a shitty day. A shitty week, a shitty month, and it has turned into a shitty year and change since then. Staring down the hall, Ned's eyes grow hot. *Let it out*, his dad had told him when Ned had tried to work his house key off his key ring, his hands shaking. Dad had just rubbed at his back: *I've got you, kid.*

If his dad could, he'd probably analyze the data for Ned's dissertation. He'd do it with his bare hands through some sort of sheer stubbornness and force of will. Hell, he'd carted around boxes of books in the heat of that moving day —he wouldn't balk in the face of regression analysis, not if it would help Ned.

Though the only person who can actually help Ned is behind a door that won't open. He raises his fist to knock on Abbot's door again, but stops, turning as footsteps approach. A girl jogs up the stairs. An actual kid, only a handful of years older than Peggy, not a newly minted freshman. She's eleven, maybe. Or twelve, but not older than that.

She must be lost. Probably the kid of some faculty member. He'll help her find their office, though before he can catch her eye, she opens the door in front of him and disappears into Abbot's office.

"What?" Ned asks.

"Ned?" Abbot asks.

He's got a coat draped over his arm as he comes up the stairs. It's blue and clearly too small for him. Not his, Ned registers so dimly that he shuts his mouth with a click.

"I came by to see you," Ned says, which sounds better than *When the hell did you get a kid?*

"Clearly." Abbot brushes past him.

Ned turns, still staring, and then follows him through the door. Abbot's office is the same as the last time Ned was in here, a smaller, neater version of Chris's with the books arranged by subject, and his desk clear of any stacks of papers or stray pens. Though a phone sits on the edge of his desk, and it's not Abbot's because Abbot's phone doesn't have a PopSocket, let alone a case with an octopus. A cartoon octopus that's bright green with red spots on its cheeks.

What the hell? Ned thinks.

"Is this a good time?" Ned asks. He's blinking too fast. He clears his throat, like the girl will disappear instead of trying to tug her jacket away from Abbot.

"No." Abbot pulls the jacket back away from the kid, holding it up higher than she can reach. "Not right now."

"But the dog's out there."

"Chris sent me," Ned says. He blinks again. Abbot wasn't talking to him.

And he's not talking to Ned now, either, launching into something that sounds like German. Maybe. Ned knows his mouth is open again. Abbot's from . . . somewhere. Somewhere in Europe. Ned never asked after the slight accent behind his words, and it's not like Abbot's the type to offer up details, regaling the rest of the department with tales of his life outside of work.

The kid answers him back, tugs at the jacket again, and points to the window. And Ned so, so wants to know now—where he's from, what the hell he's speaking, and who the kid is. He can feel the questions sitting in his mouth, ready to be blurted out.

"He said to wait," Abbot says.

The kid sighs. Dramatically. And sits herself in the chair that Ned once sweated in, wiping damp palms over his thighs. He should be sitting in it now, too, by all rights, not watching Abbot drape the coat over the back of it and then pass that phone over to this . . . this . . . child, who has appeared out of the ether.

Abbot sets his own phone on his desk. It's got a plain thin black case on it.

"Um," Ned says. *What's happening?* he wants to ask. "Don't you have your office hours now?"

"I'm not available today." Abbot shakes his mouse to wake his computer.

The kid sits up straighter. "I'll go."

"No."

"I'm going to," she says.

"You're not."

"I'll just be outside."

"You won't."

"I'll be back before Dad is."

"He'll expect you to be here."

"I'll just be down there," she says, and Ned knows that look on her face, the moment an idea crystalizes and becomes action.

Peggy's still small enough to scoop up before she can dash away, but she won't be for long. No, she'll be this age soon enough, grabbing her coat, scooping up her phone, and making for the door.

Ned maybe should stop her as she darts past him.

Abbot stands and says, "Liesl—"

But she's gone, her steps retreating down the hall before they're swallowed by the staircase. Abbot crosses to the window, hands pressed to the windowsill and his forehead against the glass as he peers down into the quad.

"Is that your daughter?" Ned clears his throat. That's not what he was going to say. "Chris sent me."

"He did." It's not a question. Abbot straightens, still looking outside. "My sister."

"Oh," Ned says. Like that clears anything up. She's young. A lot younger than Abbot. A lot, a lot younger. "How old is she?"

"Twelve."

"Oh," Ned says again. He's blinking too much. He's glad Abbot hasn't turned back around. "How old are you?"

"Thirty."

"You're thirty? How the fuck do you have tenure at thirty?"

Abbot turns enough to look back over his shoulder.

How do you have a sister young enough to technically be your kid? might've been a better question. At the very least, it wouldn't have involved cursing. Ned's probably the first person to ever say "fuck" in Abbot's office.

Not the first to think it, he's sure. He shifts his weight to his other foot.

"I'm here to talk about my dissertation," Ned says. That sounds right. More professional. Though his mouth just keeps moving. "You're two years younger than I am."

Abbot turns back to the window. "I told you, I'm not available right now."

"It's your office hours."

"I'm watching my sister."

"Chris sent me."

"You've mentioned." Abbot straightens slightly. "Dogs shouldn't be left unattended."

Ned opens his mouth again. He shuts it. Dogs are fine.

Ned can leave Baxter by himself, no problem. Hell, he's alone right now. He's—

Ned steps up behind Abbot and cranes to see past him. "That's my dog."

Abbot just looks at him. They're standing too close. Way, way too close. Close enough that Ned can smell hints of aftershave and see the darker shade of stubble on Abbot's thin cheek, where there's already the brush of a five o'clock shadow on his pale skin.

Ned takes a step backward. "Sorry."

"You shouldn't leave your dog out there," Abbot says.

That's not what I was apologizing for, Ned thinks and steps back again. Abbot's an attractive guy, Ned remembers all over again. An asshole, but a good-looking one, with that jawline and those eyes. "Chris said he sent you my dissertation."

Abbot turns back to the window. "I haven't read it yet."

"Well, can you read it now?"

"No," Abbot says, short and curt—and yep, there it is, the reason Abbot fills Ned with boiling ire rather than any simmer of interest.

He clears his throat loud enough for Abbot to hear. "I'm trying to finish up edits this semester so I can graduate."

"I have my sister," Abbot says, his shoulder turned toward Ned.

Ned raises his eyebrows. He looks at the window, then back at Abbot.

"She's down there," Ned says.

"With a dog."

My dog, Ned thinks, *who is better behaved than some professors in the department.*

"You can't read it right now?" Ned asks.

"No, I can't read a several hundred-page dissertation right now."

"The chapter on my results is only fifty pages."

Abbot's eyebrow twitches. "How concise."

Ned huffs out a breath. He can't tell if Abbot's joking.

No, he isn't joking. Abbot's probably not capable of joking. Though whether he means that chapter should be longer or shorter, Ned can't tell.

"Well, can we go over the plan, then?" Ned asks.

"I have some work to finish," Abbot says. "Perhaps afterward."

Perhaps. What an ass. They all have work to finish. That's the whole goddamn point.

"Chris said you'd help," Ned says.

"Chris also has greatly reduced our working hours."

Chris calls you Henry, Ned wants to say. *You have a sister, and she has an octopus on her phone, and where along the way did she get that, while you got an enormous stick up your ass?*

"I can go over my results with you now so you don't have to read the entire thing," Ned says. The least Abbot could do is bother to turn around. "Or I can go hang out with your sister, if that helps, and leave you in peace to read it now."

"No, we're leaving soon."

"It's your office hours," Ned says again. He knows he sounds like a broken record.

"Which I'm unfortunately not available for."

Because no one comes, Ned's sure. It's still no excuse. They're here to help students. That's their foremost job, to teach and to support students, and their research happens outside of that. It's how Chris runs his department and how the deans run the college. And technically, Ned's a student, and technically, Abbot's the professor who is supposed to be working with him, so technically—

"Henry."

Ned twists around. It's that guy again. The one who already interrupted him once today in Chris's office and now is doing the same in Abbot's. Abbot finally turns, pockets his phone, and takes his jacket off the coatrack set next to his perfectly, painfully neatly organized bookshelf.

"Liesl is waiting for us downstairs," Abbot says.

Ned wants to scoff. That's a hell of a lie. She's downstairs with Baxter laid across her lap. And Abbot's just . . . Abbot's just leaving Ned here. This is absurd. Their boss sent Ned here and Abbot's abandoning his work because this guy wants him to, this guy who just showed up and—

—and is Abbot's father.

They've got that same look to them, a face that could be handsome if it weren't so pinched, dark hair and glasses and a haughtiness that's apparently genetic. At least the sister got spared from that preternatural stiffness. *Jump*, the older Mr. Abbot could probably say, and Abbot would ask, *How high?* given how he's already brushing Ned aside and shrugging into his coat.

The two of them are the same height, have the same lean, spare build and the same god-awful way of walking, like it's imperative they get to where they're going as stiffly and efficiently as possible. It'd be graceful on anyone else. On them—on Abbot especially—it just looks so damn stuffy.

So that's where he gets his attitude, Ned thinks.

"Thanks for the help!" Ned calls after him. Abbot doesn't turn around, and Ned just stands there watching the two of them walk down the stairs, twin footsteps echoing back toward him.

CHAPTER THREE

THE PROJECTOR SHINES a blank blue light on the screen, and when Ned shifts in his seat, the wheel on his chair squeaks again. At least there's no Abbot around to glare at him, and Ned rolls backward a couple inches, kicking his legs out beneath the conference room table.

"Turn your computer off and back on again," Lee says.

"It worked yesterday." Sameer leans over the projector, fiddling with the cord.

"It's your computer, it can't read that cord," Ned says. He takes another bite of his salad and wakes up his laptop. This lunch talk is dragging, and that's saying something considering how these typically go. He's got a minute or two —more if he's lucky—and he can get some work done.

Anticipated date of graduation, reads the job application on his screen, the Adams University logo staring back at him from the top of the webpage. Ned pulls the inside of his cheek between his teeth. Last spring, he'd once thought. And look at him now. *December*, he types. He deletes it. *May*, he writes and erases that too. If he defends his dissertation in October, he'll be out of here this semester. *December*, he writes again and hits next.

Another page of questions loads. He sighs. All of this is on the résumé he's already uploaded, and he's now retyping it.

"Give your talk without the presentation," Aliyah says.

Ned pushes his chair back from the table. Sameer worked all week on this presentation, crowding their small office by pacing back and forth, mumbling as he practiced, and Ned doesn't really want to fill out yet another job application that he won't hear back from.

"I've got a cord upstairs that should work." He takes a last bite of his salad. *Vegetables*, he thinks as he chews quickly. And he went running that morning, before Chris turned the VPN back on. He can do this. Is doing this, job applications be damned.

The halls are quiet, classes in session, and everyone else probably outside enjoying the autumn sunshine. Ned checks his email on his phone as he walks toward the stairway. There's a picture from his mom of Peggy sitting at the kitchen table, her tongue poking out the corner of her mouth and her hand wrapped around a crayon. He grins, zooming in on the photo.

"Excuse me," Abbot says, a mug of tea in his hand.

Move, Ned wants to say. He tugs his shirt straighter. Who the hell just stands there in the middle of the staircase and doesn't make any space for someone coming the other way? Abbot does. And also doesn't return emails. Ned tucks his phone back in his pocket.

"I emailed you," Ned says.

Abbot just stands there, right in Ned's way. "I know."

"When can we meet?" Ned asks. Healthy food, exercise, and his dissertation. He's got a list and damn it, he's going to see it through.

Abbot takes a step toward him, like he's expecting Ned to move to the side. "I haven't had time to finish reading it."

35

"When will you?"

"I have a conference proposal due Friday morning."

Ned raises his eyebrows. "Great, let's pick a time in the afternoon then."

"No."

Ned stares up at him. He has half a mind to walk farther up the stairs so he can be looking down at Abbot, though hell if it'll make any difference.

"No?" Ned lets out a laugh. This isn't fucking funny. Peggy's coming tonight and it was supposed to be a good day because of that. Though Abbot was also supposed to return the email Ned sent him, and look how that's gone. "I have a big old project to complete too, as it so happens."

Abbot brushes past him. "I'll be in touch."

"When?" Ned calls after him, but Abbot just keeps walking.

That afternoon, Ned sits slouched at the bar with a coffee in front of him. His laptop gives a beep and a window from his VPN client pops up.

"Let me save it, at least," he mutters and stabs a finger at the keyboard. "What the actual hell."

Pat runs his towel over a beer glass. "I can see it now: extended happy hour for the sociology department starting early on weekends, faculty flocking over here in droves, looking for a cold one to cap off the week. Free to socialize, available to stay after the cheap drinks end, the sound of the till chiming as I ring up—"

"This is absurd." Ned clicks again and again at the connect button and just gets an error message each time. "I can't work on anything now."

"Is it anarchy over there?" Pat asks.

"It's going to blow over. There's no way Chris is really doing this." Ned pushes his face into his hand. He doesn't even have a copy of his work on his computer. Of course he doesn't—it's all backed up to the university server that Chris just locked him out of. "I'm going to quit. All the other grad students aren't even stuck with this, it's just for anyone teaching."

"Didn't you spend, like, four years waiting to get offered classes to teach so you can put them on the old CV?" Pat asks.

"Five," Ned groans. His plans never work. Isn't that the hell of it—for so long now, Ned thought he knew what he was doing, but the damn rug keeps getting pulled out from under him. What a joke his life has become, trying to bumble through the best he can and foiled at every turn.

"Five," Pat says. Through his own fingers, Ned can see Pat holding the glass up to the light, inspecting its shine. "Good job, bud."

"I'm going upstairs." Ned smacks his laptop closed.

Pat grins at him. "Hey, I meant to tell you, your Mr. Abbot. Damn."

"Bye," Ned says.

"Just saying." Pat shrugs. "Wouldn't kick him out of bed if I played for both teams like you do."

"I'm quitting and I'm moving out." Ned pushes out the door and lets it fall shut behind him.

At least Chris can't take away his actual books. With his feet up on the arm of Pat's old gross couch and his head pillowed in the crook of his arm, Ned flicks through the reading for his morning class. Baxter scratches at the door and lets out a useless whine of hope. Ned'd had a house with a yard. They had. Him and Jen and Peggy and Baxter, when they'd all lived together across Portland in the house they'd been renting. He swears Baxter can still remember that, being let out to play under the birch trees, Peggy toddling after him.

Well, it's been a shitty adjustment for all of them. Jen

got the best shake of it, moving back to the house they'd bought together and rented out at the beginning of Ned's program; though to hear her tell it, Peggy's got a hell of a hobby of being up at all hours of the night, and single parenting isn't exactly the gem of a situation that Jen was apparently aiming for.

Ned scratches at his hair, probably making a mess of it. Peggy sleeps when he's got her at the very least, and he'll be done here at some point. Soon, hopefully. And he'll be back again like he was this summer, and when Peggy was little: there for the day-to-day, not just every other weekend. He'll have a job that pays the bills, Baxter can have a yard again, and Ned won't be cowed under the weight of a dissertation that still isn't done.

Footsteps clump up the stairs, and Baxter's tail moves faster. By the time Pat's got the door to their apartment open, Baxter's a wriggling mess of excitement, turning this way and that as Pat wrestles his head back and forth.

"You're gonna break him," Ned says. Spoil him, more like. Baxter stares up at Pat, panting in adoration, his weight propped on Pat's knees and his feet sliding with the click of nails on the hardwood.

"Ned's an old stick-in-the-mud, isn't he?" Pat asks in a too-high voice. Ned rolls his eyes. "Yes, he is."

"M'working."

"No, you're eating this cookie I can't sell because the new kid broke it in half," Pat says and tosses it so it lands on Ned's stomach.

Ned looks down on it. He should probably care that it's there, butter and chocolate against his shirt. He turns back to his book.

"I got a question for you," Pat says. His palm thumps against Baxter's side. "Can we have a horribly awkward conversation?"

"I don't want to know if it burns when you pee."

"That new kid? The cookie breaker? Well, the espresso machine isn't working, courtesy of him." Pat settles himself on the arm of the couch. Ned waits, eyeing him over the top of his book and socked feet. "And the summer rush is winding down. So."

Ned licks at his lips. "Yeah?"

"I kinda need you to pay rent this month."

Ned lowers his book. "Okay," he gets himself to say.

"I'm sorry, I know it's—"

"No, no, of course, I—" Ned shakes his head. "I get paid next week, it's no problem."

Pat rubs his hands down his thighs. "I'm sorry."

Ned picks up his book again. With his thumb, he flips to the next page. "Not at all."

Pat grimaces down at his lap, his face scrunched up until he relaxes again. He smacks Ned's foot. "I'm sorry about Chris and your dissertation. It going okay?"

"S'fine." It's not. Nor is scraping together rent money. It's Ned's fault though, too complacent when Pat only asks him to pay every once in a while. He should've saved up. He flicks to the next page. He's getting good at this—ruining everything he touches.

"You still gonna be able to finish this semester?" Pat asks.

"I dunno." Ned turns another page. *You never want to talk about anything*, Jen used to tell him. He rubs his thumb and forefinger into his eyes. "I'm not sure. No. I don't know."

"Sorry," Pat says again.

Ned drops his hand. "You looking to rent out my room?"

"What? No, no, I—Ned, you know I love having you and my main man Baxter here."

"I get it, if you want someone who can actually pay—"

"No." Pat grabs his foot. "Stop, no. I was just curious."

"I'm trying," Ned says.

"I know. Hey, it's all good."

"I'm supposed to be finished, but I can't get Abbot to meet with me."

"A hard no from Mr. Charles Henry?"

"He won't meet with me and won't return my emails." Ned presses the heel of his hand into his eyes. "I can't believe Chris actually wants me to work with him."

"Can you try him again?" Pat shakes Ned's foot back and forth. "It's like a horse, see. You fall off, you get back on. Into the saddle again, etcetera, etcetera. And you've taken some tumbles, my dude, but we're going to get you back out there. It's a metaphor."

"It sounds like a bad sex joke."

"It's a metaphor and you're the rider and the horse is a horse, which is also your PhD and Chris and your handsome Professor Abbot and your dissertation."

Ned tips his head back. "And where does my daughter I never see fit in there?"

"Focus on the horse, my dude," Pat says. "Ask Abbot again. Turn on the old charm, don't just give up after one try, you know?"

Ned scrubs his hand over his face. All any attempt at charm got him was a wife who left him and then months sleeping with too many men and women in the direct aftermath until he'd just given up, so exhausted by having to actually make nice with anyone to even begin to bother. *A waste of those abs on you*, Pat had said when Ned had stopped going out, smacking him on the stomach and shaking his head like it really was a crying shame.

"I'm sure he's immune," Ned says.

"Look, he's just busy, right? Doesn't he want his

students to actually learn from him? Do it outside of work hours."

"Chris is locking the damn building." Abbot probably doesn't give a shit if anyone learns anything. Who else would dodge his own office hours?

"Listen to you, you have so many reasons to not even try. Do it outside of the building. Hell, do it downstairs in the café if you want. Just—Ned, just get it done. You're going to be a mess if you don't get rocking and rolling on this." Pat leans over and grabs Ned's wrist, pulling his hand away from his face. "You're kind of a mess already, bud. Peg's gonna be here soon, right? Cheer up, you giant depressed lump."

Ned turns back to his book and breaks off a corner of the cookie as Pat heads back downstairs. He sets the rest on top of his laptop before he can undo the run he went on. It's some sort of genetic miracle that his early thirties haven't ruined the body he worked so hard for, back when he had the energy for it. Ned crosses his ankles and tries to keep reading. Fucking Abbot—thirty years old and living the life Ned's killing himself to achieve.

By the time Ned's phone buzzes with a text from Pat, Baxter's already barking. Your lovely lady's here, Pat wrote, and Ned clips on Baxter's leash, grabs the cookie, and shoves his feet into his shoes.

Downstairs, Peggy blinks awake as his dad shuts off the car. It's a hell of a thing that every ounce of excitement of unbuckling her car seat and lifting her out for a hug is going to be tempered by saying goodbye to her in a few short hours. *Don't think about it* has been his rule since Jen loaded Peggy into the car and drove out of the city.

"Hey, monster," he whispers. Her arms wind tight around his neck. He cups the back of her head, pressing his lips to her forehead and swaying her back and forth. He loves her so fucking much. It should be impossible to hold this kind of hard, happy joy in his chest, right next to the mired drudge this semester has been.

"Grandpa says there's only one real kind of bowling," Peggy says when he pulls back.

Ned kisses her forehead again. Her cheeks are red from her nap, and there's a crease along the side of her face that matches her car seat.

"I missed you," he tells her. Misses her even now, in a way that he's never been able to sort out—how it's possible to be holding her and still be gnawed at by the ache lodged up in his throat.

"Candlepin bowling," his dad says. Ned swings Peggy to balance on his hip and hands her the cookie. "We discussed it, she's ready for her debut on the lanes. Hi, kid, you doing all right?"

"Yeah." Ned nods, and if it's too quick and firm, his dad doesn't ask. Ned's all right. All the better that his day has moved along from how it started. He kisses the top of Peggy's head. She's already got crumbs on her face and a smear of chocolate on her cheek. "Hey, thank you. For driving."

"We had a good time," his dad says. "Hello, Mr. Baxter, yes, hello to you too."

Peggy squirms down from Ned's hold on her. She gets her face licked, every inch of it, laughing. It's pretty gross, considering where the mouth on that dog has been. Ned's grinning, he knows.

"Pegster, you ready?" he asks. God, that always gets him, how readily she holds her hand out for him to take and that tiny palm tucked into his, holding her cookie away from Baxter's eager, searching mouth with the other.

"Sandwiches," his dad says, handing over a paper bag.

"Dinosaur chow for Miss Peggy and boring old chicken salad for you, Ned."

"Thank you," Ned says again.

His dad waves him off. "Go have fun, forget about work. Pat's inside? I'll be here when you two are done."

Ned squeezes Peggy's hand. He's got a game of bowling —or however much Peggy will make it through—a picnic in the park, and probably a playground to explore. Whatever it is that she wants to do. What an excellent, perfect way to end his day. He'll happily leave the drinking and dating and ostensible excitement of a late summer afternoon and evening to the rest of Portland—he's got what he needs.

Outside of work, he thinks as they start down the street, Pat's voice ringing in his head. Well, as if Ned's really doing anything else with his free time, all those nights he doesn't have Peggy to spend with. It's not the single worst idea Ned's ever heard.

"C'mon, Pegasaurus," he says and squeezes her hot little hand. She squeezes Ned's hand in return and he smiles, his chest warming straight through. He'll do whatever it takes to move home to her as absolutely and unreservedly quick as he can, even if that involves one Charles Henry Abbot and Ned's evenings.

CHAPTER FOUR

"The, um, paper?"

Phil, Ned reminds himself. The kid's name is Phil. Ned nods for him to go on.

"Can I turn it in late?"

Ned keeps his chair spun toward Phil but leans over to hit print on his computer, coaxing the ancient crappy printer to spit out yet another article.

"Why?"

"I've got, like, a thing."

"You've got, like, to be more specific," Ned says. He taps a stack of paper straight on his desk, staples it, and adds it to the growing collection in his backpack. Chris is going to have to plant some trees at the end of this initiative if this is what Ned's reduced to in order to get his work done.

Though, no—what he's really reduced to is begging. He eyes the clock. Five more minutes before the bell rings for the end of the class day, and then it's game time.

"A soccer thing." Phil hooks his thumb into his backpack strap.

"No."

"Please?"

"Oh, okay, then."

"Really?"

"No, not really." Ned squeezes the stapler shut again. "It's in the syllabus—no late papers."

"But I'm busy all weekend."

"Well, good thing that paper isn't due for two weeks, then," Ned says. He adds another article to his printer queue. "Gives you plenty of time."

"But like . . ."

Ned taps another handful of printed pages against his desk. "Like?"

"Maybe I could get you a rough draft on time?"

Abbot, Charles Henry. "Socioeconomic Trends in Educational Attainment." What the actual hell is that, cited right in the introduction of the paper Ned's holding? Abbot could've mentioned once or a dozen times that he's written a goddamn journal article on Ned's research topic. He shoves the paper in his bag harder than he needs to. "No."

"Geez," Phil mutters. He leaves in a scuff of flip flops and the door hanging open.

Ned rubs his palm down his face. He loves teaching. Loves his students. He blows a breath into his palm. Kids these days. And goddamn but does that thought make him feel old.

His backpack is heavy when he shoulders it. An entire printed-out dissertation will do that, though. He shrunk the font at least, to save on paper. Hopefully Abbot has good eyes, what with those glasses.

The hallway's crowded with students, freed from their last lecture of the week. Ned winds his way to the stairwell, jogging to make it to the next floor before the knot of kids with their phones and coffees can clog up his path and ruin his plan. Because this is going to work. *Peggy*, he thinks and pushes against the flow of students into his least favorite lecture room in the building.

Only Abbot's left behind in the lecture hall, unplugging his laptop from the projector and sorting through a stack of papers since his students apparently had the good sense to flee. Ned takes a deep breath and starts toward the front of the room. Abbot probably made the class turn in an essay already, no matter how early it is in the semester. Hell, he probably gave them a reading assignment to complete before the very first class.

Ned drops his dissertation on top of Abbot's keyboard. It lands with a thump. "Brought this for you."

"Excuse me?"

"Figured you hadn't gotten to it yet or I would've heard from you," Ned says. He tips his watch toward himself and lets Abbot see him checking it. "Five o'clock on the dot. Look at that, you now have all weekend to read it."

"I'm teaching," Abbot says.

"You were teaching." Ned gestures to the empty class-room. It's a show, all of this. His heart is hammering. Back on the horse, Pat had said like this would be a breeze, when Ned really just wants to crawl into the dark, shadowy spot behind the lectern and stay there until the day's over. "And now it's Friday evening and this was your last scheduled commitment of the week. I checked."

Abbot just looks at him from behind his glasses, his face hard and a certain sternness around his mouth that Ned's sure he got from his dear old dad. "You checked."

"Uh-huh." Ned makes himself put on a grin. There's a benefit to department-wide scheduling and that annoyed crease at the corner of Abbot's eyes is it. "And since it's Friday, there's no talks going on right now, no meetings this evening, and it's not like you have office hours to get to." *Or that you'd go to them*, Ned wants to add. He bites back the words. Snapping at each other isn't going to get this finished. He tries for another winning smile. That charm, like Pat had said. "So, let me buy you a beer, we'll get some dinner, and we can hash this out."

Abbot nudges Ned's dissertation aside so he can fold his laptop closed. "No thanks."

Ned steps in front of Abbot before he can push past him. "We have to do this."

"I told you, I have a conference proposal—"

"It was due today, I remember. I am going to graduate this semester, and I will tell your buddy Chris exactly how helpful you've been in getting that accomplished."

"I could have plans this evening," Abbot says.

"Yeah, you could. And in that case, I would just do the work on my own and let my committee know that you did indeed help me, which will look especially great for you, considering how horribly I'll mess it up."

Abbot lifts a slim shoulder. The cloth of his shirt looks annoyingly nice and expensive. "You have your notes from my class."

Which aren't exactly helpful, Ned knows full well, given how little he understood that semester. Abbot probably knows that too. *Just say you think I'm stupid*, Ned wants to snap. Less beating around the bush that way, and it's not like Abbot's one to pull punches. He takes another breath, trying to calm that flash of hot irritation in his chest.

"What a shame, though, if that's what your teaching amounted to," Ned says as coolly as he can looking over him. *Brooks Brothers*, Ned thinks again. For his part, Ned's sure he looks like he stumbled out of a flea market that was running a special on plaid shirts. He straightens. It's no matter—Ned has a point to make, and the creases in his shirtsleeves from rolling them up all day aren't going to make a difference. "Chris especially. He'd be so disappointed."

Abbot turns to look at the blank projector screen. His jaw flexes. Ned has him, he's nearly certain. Abbot's the type of guy to care what his boss thinks of him. And sure enough, Abbot blinks once and then he says, "Fine."

"Then let's go before Chris can lock us in here," Ned says.

Ned pushes his tongue into his cheek as they walk. Peggy. Building forts. The way she jumps with both feet onto crunchy leaves in the fall. How she gets jelly from her sandwiches all over her round cheeks and strands of her hair stick to it. This is all going to be worth it, and he'll be back to her before he knows it, leaving behind this university, this campus, and most especially the icy thick silence between him and Abbot.

Ned holds the door to Pat's café open for Abbot and for a moment, he's sure Abbot won't walk through it. Ned lets out a breath when he does and leads them through the crowd toward a booth in the back.

"Here okay?" Ned asks. The café is more crowded than Ned would like, though maybe it's some small blessing that the chatter at the nearby tables works to dull the silence between them. His skin pricks under the cold look he gets, but Abbot sits. Next to the espresso machine, Pat props his chin on his hands, elbows on the bar, smiling at them. Ned squeezes his eyes closed. "Shut up, Pat."

Pat's still grinning. "Didn't say anything."

Ned dumps his backpack beside him in the booth and sits, rubbing two fingers over the corner of his jaw. He's sore there. Probably ground his teeth all night.

"Want anything?" Ned asks. Pat leans farther over the bar, that smile on his face, and Ned tips his head toward him. "Ignore him."

"I'm fine," Abbot says.

"Dinner?" Ned asks. "I'm going to eat. My treat."

Because Pat's food is free food, Ned doesn't add. Abbot turns and looks at the chalkboard hanging behind the bar. He's probably never been in a place like this, except for when he's buying hot chocolates with sprinkles. Pat serves pub food all night, and most of the time, their apartment smells like the deep fryer. Nothing on the menu seems like it'd be Abbot's speed. They should've gone to some sort of place with fancy lettuces and tofu marinated in wheatgrass, though screw it—it's been a bear of a day already and Ned's going to get nachos.

"The spinach salad," Abbot says finally.

The salad's on the lunch menu. The kitchen doesn't make it once happy hour starts. Ned nods. "One spinach salad coming right up."

"You're killing me," Pat says when Ned tells him.

Ned glances over his shoulder. At least Abbot hasn't made a break for the door with Ned's back turned; he's just unfolded a newspaper across the table. It's going to get sticky, Ned's sure. Abbot really, really doesn't belong in a place like this.

"You love me," Ned says to Pat.

"I'm not sure I love you more than making that dumb salad."

"Please," Ned says. He leans over the bar. "Also, this was your stupid idea."

"It's not a stupid idea, it's a stupid salad, who even likes spinach?" Pat sighs far more dramatically than any grown man probably should. "One condition."

"Anything."

"You spend the evening here."

Ned lets out a laugh. "I'm always here."

"No, you come in, grump around, then go upstairs and sit alone with your dog."

Ned blinks. "Don't take that tone about Baxter."

"I'm taking that tone with you," Pat says. "One salad in exchange for an actual Friday evening outside of the apartment. With people. Interacting."

"I went bowling yesterday. That was with people."

"It was with your five-year-old," Pat says.

"Who is a great person." Ned tosses his hands up. "Fine, whatever, just get the damn man his salad so he doesn't abandon me in statistical hell."

Pat's smile is too big when he keys the order in, but Ned's long-learned to ignore him.

"Ready?" Abbot asks when Ned slips into the booth across from him. *Finally?* Abbot doesn't add, though Ned hears it all the same.

Ned blows out a slow, steady breath. He's not going to get annoyed. He's going to get his work done, and if he needs to toss back some free beers from Pat to do so, then so be it.

"Chris was pretty specific." Ned roots around in his backpack. The printout of Chris's email is wrinkled from how Ned has shoved it in his bag, but he hands it across the table anyway. "He wants me to take my findings and contextualize them in the broader trends of college attendance across the nation."

Or something like that. Ned runs his thumb and forefinger over the corners of his mouth.

"And what have you done so far?" Abbot hasn't folded his newspaper closed yet.

"Um." Ned opens his laptop. He's got a spreadsheet on his computer. Ned stabs at the keyboard with one finger and *shit*, that's right, he can't open it until Monday morning when Chris turns their network access back on. Dammit.

Ned scratches at the back of his neck. "I was comparing state percentages with national averages."

"Percentages of what?"

"College attendance."

"And you compared them to what averages?"

"Ah, first-generation student matriculation."

"Which will reveal what, precisely?"

"The—how the broad trends of admittance reflect shifting . . ." Ned clears his throat. "Shifting trends."

"I see," Abbot says.

Ned works his tongue into his cheek. "I'm not—this analysis thing, I'm not really good at this."

"I'm well aware."

They could be back in Abbot's classroom, what with the tenor of gaze Abbot levels across the table, Ned sweating at the fact he could be called on at any moment. He'd always felt like he was back in high school again, terrified of his own teacher. Instead, he'd been watching a guy his own age click through slide after slide as all the other students, younger than Ned by half a decade, had nodded along, their fingers tapping over their keyboards as they took notes. Ned would sometimes type too, just for the look of it.

"I'm a qualitative researcher. People. I do people, not numbers," Ned says. Got awarded a fellowship for it too, not that Abbot gives a crap. "I can send you my publications."

"No thanks."

Ned leans back in the booth against the cracked, peeling vinyl. Abbot probably wouldn't read them anyway. Quantitative researchers never do, sitting there with their surveys and data files and spreadsheets, as if they hold some inviolable answer to the questions of the universe. *Breathe*, he tells himself.

"Look." Ned reaches into his backpack. "I know you're

familiar with my research. I found this paper that you wrote on the socioeconomic trends of university attendance."

Ned drops it on the table between them, half of it falling over Abbot's newspaper.

"My father wrote that." Abbot's mouth tightens.

Great, Ned thinks. It should be impossible for Abbot to hold his face like that, pinched and stern. Don't bring up dear old dad, apparently. Well, Ned can add that to the list of things guaranteed to piss Abbot off, like being in Ned's presence, having to work with Ned again, being reminded of Ned's incompetence and ineptitude, Ned in general. All the more reason Abbot should be helping Ned on this project—he can graduate and leave Abbot to Callahan University and Portland and the entire state of Maine, and Ned will be safely, finally back in Boston, never to bug him again.

Abbot doesn't even glance at the paper, just straightens his newspaper like he's about to start reading it again. "You do understand the concept of contextualizing your study, don't you?"

"Yes." Ned nods. Theoretically. As in, he gets it when he reads papers where it's done. Reads right along and doesn't bother to wonder how the researcher did it.

"Food!" Pat yells toward him. Ned stands too quickly, his thigh knocking into the table. Abbot straightens his paper again and brushes away his father's article, pushing it back over to Ned's side of the table.

"Fuck me," Ned whispers over the bar.

"No thanks," Pat says. He pulls at one of the taps and pours a beer for Ned. "What does your Charles Henry want to drink?"

"Straight lemon juice. Orange juice with toothpaste mixed in."

"Yum."

"Water," Ned says. He rubs his palm over his face.

"Cheer up. The night's only going to get better from here." Pat winks at him.

Ned groans and collects their plates. He has to go back for their drinks and when he does, Pat's already moved down the bar, chatting with two women as he pours more beers, though he tosses another grin Ned's way.

"So," Ned says as he slips back into the booth. He jerks his napkin smooth, settling it on his lap. He can do this. He has to do this. *Peggy.* He shifts his laptop to the side to make space for his plate. "Is it worth it to break down college attendance generationally? To look at trends now, versus maybe a decade ago?"

"Generations in the US are typically considered spans of fifteen to twenty years, not ten," Abbot says. He finally folds his damn newspaper up and pulls his salad in front of himself. "That's your friend?"

Ned glances over to where Pat's still chatting. "Unfortunately."

"I didn't realize you two knew each other so well."

Ned scrubs his fingers into his hair. "I have the poor luck of living with him."

"I see."

"Which is why I need to finish my dissertation and move. He's awful." Ned dumps his fork and knife next to his plate. It's not true at all, though there's no sense in detailing the particulars of his life for Abbot. Pat's his only friend here. His only friend at all, really, which is just depressing, but Ned loves the hell out of him and has since they raced their bikes down their street, skinned knees and grass stains. He jerks his napkin smooth, settling it on his lap. "Did you want a straw?"

"No."

"Okay." Ned grabs a chip from his plate. He should've

ordered something he could eat with a knife and fork. Abbot actually slices his salad into a smaller, neater pile of leaves before taking a bite, and here's Ned, eating with his fingers.

It's fine. It has to be fine because Ned has to get this work done, and this is apparently the only way he's going to do it, sitting here across from Abbot. Wasn't enjoying their evenings Chris's whole point? That they'd have time away from the office, not stuck in a booth together, their work printed out? Ned glances at his watch. Maybe this will be over soon, if Abbot can find it in himself to be helpful.

"You've worked with Chris," Ned says. "What is it that he's going to want to see from me?"

"Your work situated in the greater context of—"

"I mean specifically." Ned picks up another chip, cheese dripping off the edges as Abbot neatly pierces a carrot with his fork. "You must have an idea."

Abbot's lips press together. For a moment, they just stare at each other before his brown eyes shift away behind his glasses. "Probably not multilevel modeling or any other type of analytics expected of a quantitative study."

"More specifically than that," Ned says.

"Regression analysis controlling for socioeconomic status and geographical location. Two-mean factor analysis. A chi-squared table." Abbot presses his fork into a spinach leaf. "It's not onerous."

"Says the statistician."

"It's not," Abbot says. *You're just dumb*, Ned hears all the same. "The principles are simple enough."

"You're not helping your case."

Abbot spears a disk of cucumber. Ned feels a little bad for it, stabbed by the tines of that fork.

"Your final project could be useful," Abbot says.

"The one I did for your course?" Ned leans back in the booth and laughs. "No."

"It'd be better than entirely starting over. It's related enough to your research. If you're already investigating first-generation college students here in Portland, you can just extrapolate the same tendencies nationally."

"Huh." Ned cocks his head. "So you did finally read my dissertation."

"I did." Abbot takes a sip of his tea. "It didn't take very long."

Abbot's face is completely straight. No hint of a smile around the corners of his mouth, no twitch of his eyebrow. Coming from anyone else, that might've been a joke, but from Abbot it just stings.

This is like pulling nails. And that's being generous. "You know, qualitative work isn't the be-all and end-all of research. There's a lot to be gained through interviewing. More, if you ask me."

"Are you asked often?"

Ned squeezes his eyes shut. This is so painful. Maybe they can just call this quits. Ned can send Abbot off with a list of questions; and if Abbot really doesn't get back in touch with him soon, Ned will go to Chris. It'd give Ned the rest of the evening off, at the very least.

He can dodge Pat and go to the gym or take Baxter for a run. And he really could make a break for it, because Pat's not looking his way, instead leaning across the bar and chatting with the crowd that's gathered. There's another couple there now and the folks Pat was talking to before, one of them laughing as Pat gestures broadly. He points, too. Right at Ned. And . . .

Ned ducks his head over his plate. "Shit."

"Pardon?"

"That's Lee. Oh, dammit, Pat."

"Lee?" Abbot asks.

"Don't look," Ned says.

Abbot looks. "That's not Doctor Kerr."

"That's her wife," Ned says. Minori waves at him. He grimaces out a smile and lifts a hand. "Lee's next to her."

"Ah."

Ned rubs his fingers over his forehead. When he looks up, Pat's halfway to them. *Don't*, Ned so wants to say. Wants to hold out a hand like he can stop all of this from happening, Pat's giant grin, Minori already bending down to give Ned a hug, and Lee, her hand around a glass of beer and her eyes wide, staring at Abbot.

"Call the department police, you two have work in front of you," Lee says. She leans over and taps Ned's laptop. "I'm telling Chris."

Well, fuck. "We're having dinner," Ned says.

"Oh, is that what we're calling it?" Lee asks and grabs for the paper in front of Abbot, making a show of shaking it out and reading the abstract. "'Cause this looks a lot like your research topic."

"We're eating." Ned points to their plates. He's even got a beer in front of him.

Lee swats him on the shoulder with the article. "I'm just giving you a hard time, you look terrified. Shove over."

"No, we're—" Ned starts. Abbot's eyes move between Ned and Lee, his fork in the air and a piece of orange pepper speared on it. Ned quickly shakes his head. "We're just finishing up."

"You said you were eating, so you're eating." Lee slips into the booth next to Ned and scoots toward him, forcing him to shuffle down the bench. "Otherwise I might just think you two met up to get some work done. Abbot, what's good?"

Abbot sets his fork back on his plate. *Some help here,*

Ned thinks at him, but he just tucks his hands into his lap. Abbot's so damn stiff, sitting like that. *Relax*, Ned wants to say. It's all the more horrible how unnaturally still and reserved he is.

"I didn't know you came out to this." Minori slides into the booth next to Abbot.

"To Pat's?" Ned's tongue thickens in his mouth, too big to get the type of words out he needs to, the ones that will get the two of them out of the booth and open up his and Abbot's escape route. This isn't how this was supposed to go —a quick chat about Ned's work and then he and Abbot would both be on their way. Ned glances at the door. He'd have to climb over Lee to make it there.

"To trivia," Minori says.

Pat hooks a chair with his ankle and pulls it over, dropping into it, elbows on the table, and a giant awful grin aimed right at Ned. "Oh look at that, it *is* trivia night! Who knew? Oh shucks, and if I recall correctly, you made me a promise. You're staying for the entire thing, Mr. Ned."

"I—" Ned stares. Pat just grins wider and starts nodding. "No."

"You two are eating, definitely not working, no sir, so it's no problem, right?" Lee asks. Her grin is nearly as wide as Pat's. "'Cause if you were working, I'd absolutely, one hundred percent take a picture of this table and email it to Chris. You know what, I might take it anyway. Insurance, as it were."

And she does. Ned grabs for his laptop and the paper, but it's no use, because his dissertation is right there and why the hell else would he and Abbot be out at dinner together?

"We're not staying for trivia, we were eating and we're almost done," Ned says. Which is a bald-faced lie because their plates are full, and sure enough, across the room a speaker crackles. "Since when have you even done trivia here?"

"Since forever you've just become allergic to fun." Pat smacks his palms lightly on the table. "We need a team name. What're we going to be? The academics? I'll have you all know that I did in fact complete high school."

"There's no 'we,'" Ned says.

"Oh, you never come out, Ned." Lee pushes her shoulder into his, then points across the table at Abbot. "And you never, ever come out."

"Like you go out, Lee?" Ned asks.

"No, she doesn't," Minori says. "I, for one, am in favor of this department-wide experiment."

"What fun," Pat says. *Stop*, Ned mouths at him. "I'll get the answer sheet."

"Get a pitcher, too," Lee calls after Pat. "Ned, another?"

No, because Ned's going home. He and Baxter can put on a ball game, and Ned can try to scrub his brain of this night he's gotten himself into. Minori takes off her coat and pushes it between herself and Abbot. Maybe Ned can just hitch himself over the back of the booth, apologize to the folks behind him, and make for the door before Pat can catch him.

"Yeah." Ned rubs at his temples. "Why the hell not."

"Minori." She holds out her hand to Abbot. "I don't think we've met."

"Oh." Lee gestures toward Abbot. "This is Henry. Doctor Abbot, from the department. This is my wife."

"A pleasure," Abbot says softly. Ned slouches into the corner of the booth. It's anything but, he's sure.

"Have you been at Callahan long?" Minori asks.

Abbot licks quickly at his lips. "Eight years."

"I see." Minori raises both eyebrows at Lee. "Excellent job introducing us, hon."

"I wasn't—" Lee waves toward herself, then toward Abbot. "Not my fault."

"Were you at the holiday parties?" Minori asks. "The one last year? Lee forgets herself."

"I wasn't," Abbot says.

"See?" Lee asks. "And you know Ned."

"Of course I know Ned." Minori leans across the table and rubs Ned's arm. "How are you? Are you also planning to murder Chris, just like my dear spouse is?"

"I wasn't thinking murder," Ned says. "Doesn't look great on the résumé."

"Lee's got all sorts of plans to make it look like an accident," Minori says. "How's the job search going?"

"Fine," Ned says. Awful. Slow as anything. As tedious and drawn out as this damn evening feels. Abbot's still got his hands in his lap, his eyes flicking at Lee and then away again.

"And the pipsqueak?" Minori asks.

"Good, yeah," Ned says. Peggy was a toddler when Lee started at Callahan. Ned had brought her to the department building exactly once and let her spin around in the chairs in the break room as she laughed her little head off. Trust that Abbot would've steered clear of anything so adorable as that.

"All right, all right, all right." Pat swings his chair around and drops into it, sitting backward. He puts five glasses on the table, a pitcher of foamy beer, and a piece of paper. "Ready? Are we ready? I'm ready. Ned, look alive, man."

"I really wasn't planning to stay for this," Ned says. *We weren't*, he could say, but Lee's looking between him and Abbot again, and there's no *we* that Ned particularly wants to toss out there for her to pluck out of the air and run with.

Pat grins as the sound system crackles. "That's what we call, 'too fucking bad.'"

"Welcome," the announcer says. He sounds bored. Pat should be running this himself, not sitting here, delightedly ruining Ned's evening. "First up for the night: there are fewer of these real-life animals in the world than there are fake ones."

"You coming down to the game?" Minori asks.

"What game?" Ned asks.

"Gnomes," Pat says.

"It's going to be fun." Lee pours herself a beer. "That's what I'm telling myself."

"Gnomes aren't real," Ned says.

"The department baseball game," Minori says. "Well, typically, the faculty retreat, but Chris apparently replaced it this year with a new tradition because he's ridiculous. Yankees versus Red Sox, next Sunday, down in Boston."

"Can't," Ned says. He'll watch it on TV. He has Peggy that weekend and dinosaurs to play with, a birthday party to shuttle her to, and books to read together. If Pat were closer, Ned would kick his ankle under the table. Ned has fun—he has lots of fun, and it's not his problem Pat doesn't think so.

"Henry?" Minori asks. "You'll be there?"

"Yes." Abbot adjusts his fork on his plate.

"Stuffed bears," Pat says. "Oh! Beanie Babies!"

"Ned, you're not going to spend your Sunday with your coworkers?" Minori asks. "Unimaginable."

"I don't think I'm invited," Ned says. Whatever retreat this is, he's never been on it. It's maybe the one single benefit of still being a student and not pulling in the salary of an actual faculty member, that he's not stuck spending his Sunday as part of Chris's experiment on them.

"There're a lot of real bears out there," Lee says.

Pat holds up a finger. "And a lot of Beanie Babies."

"Beanie Babies freak Pat out," Ned says.

The booth is too crowded. It was already, and now only the more so. He drops his backpack onto the floor and slides into the space where it was sitting to give himself some more air to breathe. He and Abbot should've been done with tonight already. Ned should be upstairs by himself right now. *No, the gym,* he reminds himself. He's going to be healthy this semester. Get his life back on track. He pokes at his cooling, congealing nachos.

"I'm not freaked out," Pat says. "I need a pen. Who's got a pen?"

"You have pens at your own damn bar, Pat. Walk two steps," Ned says.

"Barb! Barbara! A pen!"

Pat gets an exasperated scowl from the bartender. His backpack's still in the way, so Ned nudges it to the side with his foot and hits something harder than the soft side of his bag. Across the table, Abbot looks up.

Ned's cheeks flush. "Sorry," he mumbles.

"Next," the announcer says. "What coach came off the bench to play for his team in the Stanley Cup Finals?"

"This is my moment." Pat smacks the table with a palm. "Lester—wait for it—Patrick. Goalie. 1928. A pen?"

"Ned, you got dragged into this whole initiative, and Chris won't even pony up tickets to the game for you?" Minori pours herself a beer and pushes the pitcher into the middle of the table. "For real, or are you not roped into this thing the way the faculty are?"

"Oh, Ned's roped in," Lee says. "Ned, you're coming."

"I have a family thing," Ned says.

"We have a stupid work thing," Lee says. "Nice try. Also, that interdepartmental conference we're supposed to do this fall? Chris changed that too—weekend away. Don't think you're leaving us to deal with that man on our own."

"I really can't," Ned says. "Have fun, though."

Lee groans. "We're so, so not going to have any fun. Join us in our misery, Ned, so we can get our lives back all the sooner. Chris loves you, it'd work wonders."

"You know what?" Minori asks. "I like it. This whole thing. You wouldn't be here tonight without it, Lee. And Ned too. Would you, Henry?"

Lee frowns across the table. "Don't take Chris's side."

"Just saying." Minori shrugs.

"He's dragging us to Boston and then to the wilds of Maine's seashore," Lee says. "What's he going to do, make us sleep in tents and get trampled by a moose?"

Abbot shifts slightly. "He has a house up north."

"Great." Lee tosses her hands up. "He has a house. He's ruining my life."

The sound system crackles again. "Name five dinosaurs in the movie *Jurassic Park*. For a bonus point, name the one dinosaur that actually lived in the Jurassic period."

"Ned!" Pat leans across the table and smacks his arm. "This is you, my dude!"

Ned sighs. He tops up his beer. He wants to go home. Home to Peggy and her dinosaurs, though at this point he'd happily take the retreat of the apartment upstairs. Across the table, Abbot looks like a deer in headlights, crowded into his corner of the booth, his salad and water still in front of him.

"The brachiosaurus lived in the Jurassic period," Ned says.

"And?" Pat asks.

Ned sighs again. "And the T. rex, velociraptor, gallim- imus, triceratops, and all the other dinosaurs in the movie lived during the Late Cretaceous."

"A pen," Pat says. "Barbara!"

"She's going to ban you from this bar and be completely justified," Ned says. "Whether or not you own it."

"I have a pen," Abbot says.

"You let Peggy watch *Jurassic Park*?" Lee asks. "Isn't it scary?"

"Peggy is made of tougher stuff than that," Pat says. He leans right across the table to pluck the pen from Abbot's fingers. "Thanks, man."

"It is too scary, she has nightmares every time and yet she's obsessed. Hey Pat, how did Peggy first watch *Jurassic Park*? Want to remind us who thought it would be a brilliant idea to let her see it?" Ned asks. "And now, they keep making sequels. I can recite them from memory."

"See, there's that too," Minori says. "We can actually go to the movies, Lee, if you're not working every night."

"Work can be fun," Lee says. "Look at Henry and Ned, out to dinner with their laptops and journal articles."

"We weren't working, we were just eating," Ned says.

Lee laughs. "Sure."

"That doesn't count, hon," Minori says.

"Work is great. Abbot's all about work and the old personal life." Lee turns in the booth to look at Abbot. "How is Louis doing these days?"

Abbot shifts in his seat. "We broke up," he says.

"Oh." Lee jumps slightly, then frowns at Minori. "Ow."

Minori just shakes her head. "Nice, sweetie."

Any other night, Ned might smile. He rubs his fingers over his forehead, then plucks at a soggy chip. An olive rolls off it, onto the table, and falls to the floor.

"Final speed questions of this round, folks," the announcer says. "First team to answer both correctly gets the points. What's the only state that can be typed on one row of keys on a standard keyboard? And second, what's the only number whose letters are in alphabetical order?"

"We'll get you a ticket to the Sox game, Ned, come with us," Lee says.

"Eight," Pat says.

"I really can't," Ned says. "I have a family thing."

"Eighteen," Pat says.

"Pat, if eight wasn't it, eighteen isn't going to be either," Ned says.

"Ned, you have to come with us, you and Henry are the only two in the department who Chris actually likes," Lee says.

Ned shakes his head. "I have to drive Peggy to a birthday party."

"Ooh," Pat says. "Neighborhood drama. She got invited? This is Timmy's party next Sunday. This—okay, back home," Pat says and waves Abbot's pen around. "We've got these neighbors and they have this grandson, Timmy, and it's this thing about birthday parties for kids, right? So Peggy gets invited, 'cause everyone likes Ned of course, but then half of the block doesn't get an invite and—"

"Pat," Ned says. "Nobody cares."

"Um, false. Everyone cares," Pat says. "My mom cares. My dad cares. Your mom and dad care, and I know, 'cause your mom told my mom that—"

"Pat."

"Sunday?" Lee asks. She leans back in the booth, a grin spreading across her face. "Sunday afternoon? That happens to be when the game is."

Ned licks at his lips. "Well, sometimes, they want the parents to stay and give a hand."

"Is this sometimes?"

He should just lie. He bites at the inside of his cheek. "Um, no."

"Please," Lee says. She clasps her hands and knocks them against his arm. "Please, please, please."

"No," Ned says.

"Henry?" Lee asks. "Can you convince your dinner buddy here to come?"

"You can type Alaska on one row of an American keyboard," Abbot says. "And the answer is forty."

"Well, damn." Pat scribbles on the paper. "You, professor man. You're not leaving. There's two rounds to go."

"Didn't think trivia was your thing, Henry," Lee says, giving Ned one last light punch.

Abbot's got his hands tucked into his lap again. "It's not."

The night's cooler when they finally push outside. It's a relief from the heat of the bar and the noise in there. Ned shrugs his backpack on. He should've brought a coat. Or gone home when he meant to. Or not tried this plan at all, unless he and Abbot were going to drive out of Portland, where they wouldn't run into anyone they knew, though that would've meant being stuck in a car together, and given how his life is going, his beater of a car would've broken down halfway there.

"Awesome," Pat says, hugging Lee and then Minori. "Awesome, awesome. And hey, good to see you, man."

Pat shakes Abbot's hand with all the enthusiasm that Abbot lacks, going as far as to clap Abbot on the arm. It's amazing that Abbot never simply climbed over Lee to escape. Ned might've, too. Or army crawled under the table, just for the chance to rescue any part of his night.

"We're parked down here," Minori says. Lee glances at Abbot and then Ned and back again, then raises a hand in a wave goodbye. "Night!"

"Night," Ned calls back.

Pat grips Ned's shoulders and spins him a step to the side.

"I'm going to give Barb a hand with the dishes," Pat says. "Don't wait up, if you know what I mean."

"I don't want to know what you mean," Ned says.

"What I mean is Barb's boyfriend is stopping by later, and he plays a mean game of D&D. I'm trying to get in on it."

Ned tries to shrug him off, taking a step away. Abbot's just standing there, listening to this. "You're the worst."

"Hey." Pat drags Ned back in front of him. "Listen. I'm glad you came out."

"You hijacked my evening. This was done under duress."

"I'm serious," Pat says. "When was the last time you did anything other than watch TV and then go to bed at a frankly embarrassing hour?"

Ned tries to twist away again. "Watching the Sox game tonight like I meant to would've been plenty of fun."

Pat squeezes his shoulders. "You're allowed to do stuff with other humans, you know. Actually enjoy yourself for once."

"You know what, I never asked." Ned jerks a step backward, Pat's hands finally falling away. "I hope Baxter peed on your bed because I didn't get a chance to take him out after work."

"Baxter loves me." Pat reels Ned back in and gives him a too-hard hug, ruffling his hair. "And I love you, man."

Pat disappears back into the bar, and Ned ignores his last wave. It's awful, having Abbot standing there, listening to Pat. He's Ned's goofy friend from home, who just ended up in the same city as him, and the person Ned is around Pat is a far cry from the way he tries to be at work. Ned smooths down his hair. These two parts of his life were never meant to crash together, and he wasn't supposed to have to suffer through the look Abbot gives him as he pulls the strap of his briefcase higher on his shoulder.

"Well," Ned says. "That was horrible."

"I didn't realize you and Doctor Kerr were so close."

Ned shrugs. "She's pretty cool. But sorry about all that. Pat's . . . Pat."

"It's fine."

It was something a lot less than fine. Even Ned's got the beginnings of a headache and Abbot spent most of the night folded neatly into his seat in the booth, silent as anything. He'll be the same during the game, Ned's sure, and all the worse without the distraction of trivia or Pat's boisterous, loud joy. And Ned . . . God, Pat's an ass. He's so right. Ned's going to be flopped on his parent's couch, clicking through their TV stations, the ones he and Pat won't shell out money for. Maybe his dad'll have some work for him to do down at the shop, or he can give his mom a hand with something around the house.

"I'm going to see Chris on Monday," Ned says when Abbot just keeps standing there, looking at him. "What am I supposed to tell him about the analysis?"

Abbot shifts slightly, glancing down the street. "I have a paper to finish for that conference."

"Right," Ned says. Abbot has said that. Repeatedly. "Of course you do."

He turns his back to Abbot and unlocks the door behind him. The stairs are rickety and old and Ned tosses the door shut before he has to look at Abbot again. Baxter's nails skitter over the floor, and Pat must've left the light on because Ned can see the shadow of Baxter's paws working beneath the door at the top of the stairs. Ned rubs at his forehead. Pat's fucking horse that Ned was apparently supposed to climb back on. He imagines it giving him a solid square kick in the chest.

Onward, he makes himself think. Keep going, head down, and someday, this will be over. Maybe he'll just sort through his final project from Abbot's class. It's not the worst idea in the world. Or at least not any worse than sitting through trivia with the man—if Ned can survive that, he can survive revisiting the project, sprucing it up, and handing it in to Chris.

He blows out a breath.

Probably.

Maybe.

CHAPTER FIVE

"You've got this," Pat says, a hand on each of Ned's shoulders. "You're a genius, you're awesome, you're incredibly handsome—even I can see that—and you are going to knock Chris out of the water."

Ned closes his eyes. "Don't hold your breath."

"You just have to go in there and sell it." Pat pokes Ned in the chest. "Smile that smile of yours. Show him the old razzle-dazzle. Get that dimple working for you."

Ned rubs at his chest. "Ow."

"You tried once, Chris shot you down, so you're going to try again and blow him away. Show that guy what you're made of, and what you're made of is statistical genius."

"I think I'm made of stress, caffeine, and pizza," Ned says.

"And genius." Pat spins him around. "Go get 'em."

Ned's not quick enough to dodge the smack on the ass Pat gives him, though he does firmly shut the door on Pat's laugh. What had he told Abbot? That he and Pat were friends? *Brothers or as close as either of you will come,* Ned's mom had said, a hand on each of their heads the day they'd knocked over the bookshelf as they'd wrestled. They'd taken a lamp with it and a small porcelain vase, one Pat had replaced in arts and crafts at summer camp and still sits on Ned's parents' mantel, lumpy and misshapen.

Ned's palms sweat more than they should as he makes his way across campus and into the sociology building. It's only Chris. He's at least nice, unlike some other certain professors in the department. He's always nice, even when he's making Ned redo his dissertation. *Breathe*, he tells himself and knocks on Chris's door.

"Hey," Ned says, sticking his head inside. "Is this a bad time?" *Say yes, say yes, say yes—*

"Come in, come in." Chris waves him inside. "I've only got a minute, but it's yours."

Ned sits on the very edge of the chair. *Go*, Pat had said this morning, knocking Ned's phone out of his hand when he'd been happy to put it off another day.

"I just sent the file over to you," Ned says. *Under duress*, he could add, Pat's finger hovering over Ned's keyboard with the threat he'd email over all sorts of files Ned kept on his laptop if Ned didn't hurry his ass up and show Chris the work he'd done.

"Yep, got it." Chris shifts toward his computer. "Well done, Ned, putting this together so quickly."

It wasn't quick. It was an entire weekend of work, sorting through Abbot's comments on his final project and the messy mire the paper had been. He puts on a smile. "Of course."

"Chris?" A knock on the door. Lee pokes her head in. "Everyone's ready for you. Hey, Ned."

"Right, right." Chris stands, an eye still on his computer. "Sorry, Ned, faculty meetings call."

Ned leans forward in his chair. "Super quick, can I get an idea if this is heading in the right direction?" Or if it's enough? If there's any chance it's finished, and Ned can be done and he can graduate and get on with his life? And if this nightmare of his dissertation still—*still*—not being up to snuff can be over?

"Hmm, let's see. Histogram, multivariate—oh. You switched your dependent and independent variables, kid." Chris grimaces and gives Ned an apologetic look. "Henry didn't catch that?"

"They were too busy eating dinner." Lee looks like she's going to start laughing and she winks at Ned.

"Funny," Ned says to her. *I told you that you should've helped me*, he wants to say to Abbot next time he sees him. Maybe stick a finger in his face too. Chris might've come up with the most annoying initiative on the planet, but he's no dummy.

"Dinner?" Chris scrolls through Ned's work even as he gathers up a folder and his phone. "Let me just finish this meeting real quick, Ned, and I'll get back to you."

He won't, because Chris is teaching this afternoon, and after that, his stupid initiative will cut off his network access and he won't be able to email Ned later today. Ned makes himself keep smiling. "Can we meet again tomorrow?" he asks.

"You know what, before we do, go ahead and fix those variables. Let's also get a write-up on these tables before we go over this again, all righty?" Chris claps him on the shoulder. "Good first steps, but give it another shot, okay?"

Ned lets out a breath. It's not okay. "You're sure we can't talk about it first?"

"Get that write-up done, and we'll definitely chat," Chris says.

Ned drops his voice. He doesn't need Lee to hear this. "I really, really don't know what I'm doing."

He has no clue what he's doing in so, so many ways. The only thing he knows is how unfair this is, and it burns through his chest, Chris pulling the rug out from under him the very moment Ned thought he was done with his dissertation. A knot rises up through his throat and lodges there. *This is academia*, he tells himself. It's not fair and it's not supposed to be.

"Download the state education data and start there," Chris says. "And tackle your research questions with those numbers in hand. You've got the interviews and they're great. Your work is on point so far, now just do that again and back it up with some hard facts."

"All right." Ned's stomach flounders and then sinks. "I'll do that."

"Henry will help you," Chris says.

Say something, Ned tells himself. He can explain to Chris exactly how much help his buddy Henry has been. "Great," he says instead. Telling Chris that would involve drumming up a reserve of energy that ran dry a long, long time ago, and the fumes he's been coasting on are puttering out.

"It's basic stuff, you can do it." Chris thumps him on the arm with a smile.

Ned's throat squeezes closed. The statistics are basic. That's the entire problem—it's simple analysis, and Ned's so awful at it that Pat could probably do it better than him. Hell, Peggy could and she's just mastered counting to one hundred.

"All righty?" Chris asks. He's still smiling.

"All righty," Ned echoes. Fuck.

Ned trails Chris and Lee into the hallway, where Lee glances up at him. "Dissertation not going well? You've got that look about you."

"Just trying to get it done," Ned says.

She rubs his shoulder gently. "It'll be over soon."

Most of the faculty is in the conference room and

Professor Li waves to him. *How's it going?* she'd asked just yesterday when she'd found him pouring himself coffee in the break room, and Ned had only managed a mumble.

He should've forced out more of an answer for her since she's on his dissertation committee, but he was out of energy then and he's out of energy now. Fucking switched his variables. He's not surprised he messed up. No matter how many hours of work, bent over the kitchen table, his notes from Abbot's class in front of him, his final project on his computer screen, and Abbot's comments printed out, it hadn't been enough. Abbot's *lengthy* comments. Ned rubs his palm over his face.

"Chris," Lee says. She catches Ned's eye and motions to him to wait for a moment before he can continue down the hall. "Your plan is working great. Perfectly. Can we be done with it?"

"It is? How's the wife?" Chris asks.

"She's wonderful, we had a lovely evening at Ned's buddy's bar. Very fun." Lee grins at Ned where he lingers in the doorway.

Ned's stomach jumps. She really did take that picture of his and Abbot's work on the table. But she wouldn't show it to Chris and rat on them—Lee's cool. She's awesome, really. Ned's always gotten along with her no matter the divide of grad student and faculty, and she's not one to throw him under the bus.

"Guess who was there?" She pokes her tongue into her cheek, still grinning at Ned as she takes a seat. He frowns. She's awesome but she has a wicked, impish sense of humor. It's what he likes about her. It's also making the back of his neck prickle.

"This one?" Chris tips his head toward him. Ned edges slightly farther away. This isn't his meeting; he doesn't need to stay for this.

"And," Lee prompts. She looks like the cat that got the canary, wagging her eyebrows at Ned.

"Glad you got some free time in." Chris glances at Ned as he takes his seat at the head of the table. "And? Aliyah, did you make it over?"

"Some of us have kids," Aliyah says. She levels a look at Chris. "And work that we should be doing. That we want to be doing, even. And can't."

"Say hi to the little tykes from me," Chris says. "All right, who was it?"

Lee's grin could split her face in two. "Doctor Charles Henry Abbot, PhD."

Footsteps come to a stop next to Ned. Maybe Abbot didn't have enough of torturing Ned in his class, let alone Friday night at the bar, for him to show up just now. Well, this is some comeuppance at least, Lee grinning at Ned, and Abbot looking from her to Chris and back again, clearly not expecting to walk into the room hearing his name.

"Henry?" Chris tips his head, his mouth opening in a small smile. "You were out at a bar the other night?"

"Guess what they were doing?" Lee asks.

Stop, Ned mouths at her. She just grins. She's baiting him. She's not going to say anything about their work. It's fine. It's all fine, it's just Lee having some fun.

"Having dinner together," Lee says.

Ned doesn't let himself close his eyes. That's worse, how she said it, that tone, than if she'd up and told Chris they were working. It makes it sound like it was *something*, like it was a—a—

"You two went out to dinner?" Aliyah asks, spinning her chair around to look at Ned and Abbot.

Like it was a date.

"Really?" Chris's smile spreads. Widens. Splits his face and he claps his hands together.

Ned stares at him. *No*, he thinks. He clears his throat. "No, we were—" *Working*. He shakes his head too quickly. That's the one excuse he can't give. "We weren't—it was just—"

"Just dinner?" Aliyah asks. "Just having dinner?"

"Wait, really?" Chris looks between Ned and Abbot more slowly. Ned touches his fingertips to his forehead. Abbot's no help here. And he just has to go and sit in the chair nearest to where Ned stands in the doorway. It doesn't make this look any better. What a goddamn downside to having a department he felt comfortable coming out as bi to —it's actually a reasonable assumption to make, him and Abbot seeing each other. Dammit.

"We ate dinner," Ned says. "We weren't—it wasn't like that."

Very funny, Ned and Abbot, ha fucking ha. Ned puts on a smile. Another day and he might find this amusing. Maybe Chris's initiative is working, if everyone's in such a good mood about this. They all have their families to see, kids to spend time with, spouses to connect with. Ned has a dog that snores and a missing wedding ring that he used to try and spin around his finger, before remembering all over again that it was gone. He takes another step backward.

"Oh," Chris says. "That's too bad."

"Too bad?" Ned echoes. Chris actually looks disappointed. Ned wants to rub at his eyes to make sure he's seeing that right.

"You? Out to dinner?" Chris shoots a small fond smile at Abbot. "You know what, Henry? If that had been something serious, I might have given you your network access back."

Aliyah jerks her chair back around. "What?"

"No fu—" Lee claps her hand over her mouth. She drops it and clears her throat. "No way."

"That's all he has to do?" Aliyah asks. "I'll eat dinner with Ned, can I have mine back too?"

"Or maybe a key to the building at the very least," Chris says. He chuckles a little. With his red shiny cheeks and his belly, Ned's always thought Chris looked a bit like Santa Claus without the beard. Maybe instead, all this time Ned should've been picturing him in a straight-backed wooden armchair, stroking a cat on his lap and laughing maniacally.

"You're not serious," Lee says.

Chris grins again. He's having so much fun with this. That's the real rub, isn't it? He loves them all and makes it so hard to be angry at him for this, no matter the irritation on the faces around the table.

"I might be serious, it'd mean the whole initiative is actually working, but he'd have to find out." Chris points from Ned to Abbot and back again. "You know what, I can kind of see it, the two of you dating."

"No," Ned says and the word comes out louder than it should've.

"You two are cute together." Chris grins again before he holds up his hands. "Enough, all right, let's get started so you can get back to your work. But, remember, everyone, enjoy your evenings at home tonight!"

Lee tips her chair back and raises her face to the ceiling. "Fuck."

"First impressions, feedback, thoughts on this whole thing," Chris says.

Aliyah straightens in her seat. "That's what this meeting is about? This entire hour?"

"Yes." Chris sits down. "Let's hear it."

Aliyah leans forward in her chair. "You want to cut our workday short, and also keep us here for an hour of our actual work time to talk about our shorter workday?"

Chris grins around the room. "That's the plan."

Fuck, Lee mouths again.

Ned turns and makes for the door before he can get stuck in there too.

Upstairs in his office, Ned sets out his laptop, his notes from Abbot's class, and a pen. One of his best ones, with the ink that flows nicely, and the heavy weight that feels good in his hand. He sits in his chair, rolls it in toward his desk, and sets his hand on his mouse.

State data. He can download state data. And he has his research questions thumbtacked to the bulletin board above his desk, next to Peggy's picture from preschool and the Red Sox schedule. He flexes his fingers over his keyboard. He looks at his notes and then at his screen. Types out, *The results show that first-generation college students tend to*, and then stops.

They tend to . . . go to college and be the first generation in their family to do so. Hence the phrase *first-generation college student*. Ned clenches his teeth. *Feelings around inadequacy and stress transitioning to campus life*, the note tacked to his board reads. He lets out a breath and bends over, setting his forehead on the back of his hands. *First-generation college students tend to not know how to fucking finish their fucking dissertations*, he types without looking at the screen, his knuckles bumping into his forehead.

The smartest one of all of us, Dad had said, helping Ned move into his dorm his first day of college. Dad had already been wearing the ball cap he'd bought at the bookstore. Ned had met Jen later the same day, blonde and gorgeous and laughing, as he stared around campus, sure someone would come out of the woodwork and escort him away from the rest of the freshmen, reminding him he didn't belong there.

Ned stands and shoves his chair aside. It's a beautiful day outside. A sea breeze blows in through the window screen, warm autumn air breaking the hot stick of summer and the smell of the ocean, clean and crisp and clear. A Frisbee sails across the quad, and a figure teeters across a slack line strung between two trees. Ned leans his forehead against the wall of the narrow dormer beside the window. The trim is old and worn with too many layers of paint, probably some sort of metaphorical testament to the endurance of academia and all the scholars who have come before him and will come after.

He closes his eyes against the happy, cheerful sight out the window. He shouldn't have started this PhD program. No, he should've stayed where he was with his new wife, a job with retirement savings, dental insurance, and a salary large enough to afford a house. He'd been happy. Maybe he and Jen could've stayed that way. Maybe if he hadn't come to Callahan, they'd be onto their second kid by now and planning visits to pumpkin patches and apple picking, and he wouldn't have ruined their entire lives and Peggy's too.

Footsteps tap down the hall toward his office. He doesn't turn around. Hopefully it's not a student of his, looking to say hi, to ask him a question, to talk about an assignment. He'll lie if it is, tell them he's sick, not feeling well, under the weather. He can't handle them right now. Not his students, not any of the faculty, not even Pat.

This is why he sits at home so much with Baxter. He's not fit for human company. Maybe it's some blessing that Peggy doesn't live up any closer, if this is the type of father he's turned out to be, slumped against the window in his office and not smart enough to do the basic, elementary analysis that any doctor of sociology should be able to handle.

"Ned?"

He rubs the heel of his hand into his forehead. He knows that voice. "What?"

"Can I talk to you?"

Ned turns enough to see the shine on Abbot's fancy-ass, expensive-as-hell dress shoes.

He shrugs. Abbot can do whatever the hell he wants. Ned doesn't have it in him to play at being nice.

Ned crosses to his desk and reaches for his backpack. He should go. He's going to go. Back to the bar, back to the apartment, hell, maybe back home to Boston. He can climb into his childhood bed, pull the covers over his head, and just stay there until enough of life has passed on by that he doesn't have to deal with this shit anymore.

Abbot catches his wrist.

Ned stares at Abbot's hand, there on his own forearm. Long fingered, veins running along the back, a smattering of dark hair. A heavy nice-looking watch peeks from the cuff of Abbot's shirtsleeve. It's a nice hand. An attractive hand. Ned jerks his arm away.

"I wanted to talk about what Chris said," Abbot starts. He licks at his lips and then he pauses.

Anyone else and Ned would gesture for them to continue. Maybe smile, help them feel more comfortable. The corners of Abbot's eyes crease and his gaze drops from Ned's. Ned wants to rub at his skin where Abbot touched him, the spot too warm.

Instead, Ned huffs out a breath when Abbot doesn't continue. "I have work to get to."

"I know," Abbot says. "I do too."

"Yeah, you mentioned."

Abbot has his work and that damn meeting downstairs. Which he apparently just walked out of. That's a very Abbot thing to do—he probably stood up and just left, no matter how rude it was.

"I think Chris was serious," Abbot says.

"About his god-awful plan?" Ned drops his bag into his desk chair and sorts through it, pretending he's looking for something. Maybe if he digs down far enough, he'll find a damn clue about how to do this analysis. State data. He should be able to take a handful of spreadsheets and turn them into something coherent. He should've never shown those graphs to Chris. Switched his variables. Undergrads do better at statistics than Ned does. Hell, high school students do too. Maybe he can hire one of them to come sit with him and hold his damn hand through this.

"I think he was serious about the network access."

Ned jerks a stack of papers out of his bag. "What network access?"

"Giving me back my VPN if I—" Abbot shifts his weight to his other foot. "If I were to start dating."

Ned flicks the first page of the article in his hand over, like he's really reading it. If Abbot were to start dating. He looks up. Slowly, he lowers the papers.

"Dating?" Ned asks. "Dating who?"

Abbot shifts again. His mouth opens. Closes. And then opens again, and he says, "Well, you."

"Me?" Ned wants to look behind himself as if someone else is going to be there. He doesn't need to—it's the window and an old radiator that makes awful squealing noises the moment the heat comes on. There's no one standing back there. Just Ned. With Abbot looking right at him.

Abbot's thumb rubs across his first two fingers. "It was a thought."

"A thought?" Ned's voice rises too high on the end of the question. His knows his mouth is hanging open. "You want to date me?"

"No, I don't."

"Oh, thank God." Then, he shakes his head. Wait, no— that was rude. Abbot's rude. Who says that? That he wouldn't want to date someone so baldly and plainly? Who says he had a *thought* that—that—*dating* would somehow convince Chris that—?

Ned touches his fingers to his forehead.

Abbot takes a deep breath and steps farther into Ned's office. Ned moves backward, clutching his papers.

"If Chris were to think that his plan was working, and if I had access to the VPN, I could finish my paper." Abbot gestures toward him and Ned watches that hand move, the one that had touched his wrist, now waving between them. "And you need my help. So."

"So," Ned says. He really needs to stop repeating Abbot's words. He needs Abbot to leave. He needs to stick a finger into his ear and work it around until he's certain he never heard any of those words. "You're kidding."

"I'm not."

"This is a joke."

"It isn't."

"You're suggesting—" Ned coughs out a laugh. The papers crinkle in his too-hard grip. "You're suggesting that you"—Ned points at Abbot—"and I"—he pokes his finger into his own chest—"convince Chris that we're seeing each other?"

Abbot's tongue touches to his lower lip. He nods, just once. "Yes."

Ned tosses his papers onto his desk. "The fuck, man?"

"I know it's unconventional—"

"It's *absurd*."

"Especially given our professional roles—"

"You were my goddamn professor."

"And our—" Abbot's mouth purses "—rapport."

Ned shoves his hands into his hair. Clutches his fingers tight, like the pain will bring this moment into a sharp enough focus he can make sense of it.

"Our rapport," Ned echoes slowly. "You mean, that you don't like me. You can just say it."

"That's not true."

"You think I'm the dumbest student to ever be accepted into this program."

Abbot's forehead furrows. "I don't think that."

"You wrote on my first exam *Try again*. That's it. Nothing else. You didn't even grade it."

"You did try again," Abbot says.

"Well, I really fucking regret it." Ned drops his hands. His hair is probably sticking straight up. "You cannot possibly be serious about this."

"I am."

"He also said we would make a good couple, so excuse me if I'm not taking pointers from someone as off his rocker as Chris Hausman." Ned points between them again, his finger moving fast enough to blur. "This? Us? No."

"I was thinking we could go to the department baseball game," Abbot says as if he can't possibly hear Ned in this tiny stuffy office he's invaded. "You like the Red Sox. It would be one afternoon."

"You want me to go that?" Ned's voice rises on a horrible cracking squeak. "With you?"

"Together, yes. Ostensibly."

Ostensibly. Ned huffs a laugh.

"It would only be a couple hours," Abbot says, "and that's it. If I could work on my paper, I would have time to help you with your analysis."

"And if I don't?"

Beneath his dress shirt and tie, Abbot's chest rises slightly on a breath. "Then I still have a paper to finish."

"You already have tenure, you can submit your paper whenever you want. Wait until next semester. Hell, wait until next year," Ned says.

Abbot's probably got a sabbatical coming up, and he can roll around in all his free time and finish his paper whenever he feels like it. Ned will likely still be here, and Peggy will be in Boston, and he'll get pictures of her occasionally as she grows bigger and bigger without him.

He grabs his backpack and jerks the zipper closed.

"I have to submit this paper for that October conference." Abbot's eyes shift. He's lying, Ned's suddenly sure. "I have a deadline for a grant."

"I have a deadline for graduation, but you don't particularly seem to care about that."

"I do. I will." Abbot steps closer to him. Ned draws back, his hip bumping into his desk. "I won't write the analysis for you, but we can get it done."

Ned hates that little spark of hope that flickers in his chest. "You're as ridiculous as your buddy Chris."

"It's an afternoon. We go, we sit together, we leave." Abbot spreads his hands out. "That's it."

"That's a lot. A lot, a lot."

"I, of course, understand if you don't want to." Abbot finally—*finally*—moves toward the door. "But I hope you'll consider it."

Ned slumps into his chair, listening to the door shut and Abbot's footsteps fade. Fucking absurd. Absolute absurdity. He scrubs his hands over his face, hoping when he drops them, Abbot's ridiculous proposal won't have just happened.

On his desk, his papers are wrinkled. Ned smooths them out. Then, he stands and grabs his bag. He can't sit here, so close to where Abbot was standing. Rubbing his hand over his wrist where Abbot touched him, Ned makes his way out of the building, jogging down the stairs until he can pull in a deep breath of fresh air.

"You okay?" Pat asks when Ned pushes into the café. "What did Chris say?"

"I messed up everything I worked on over the weekend." Ned's hands are numb. He leans across the bar, grabs a glass, and holds it under a tap. It's an awkward pour from this angle. He probably shouldn't be using beer to cope with today.

He downs a big foamy swallow and sinks onto a barstool. Wild. All of this is wild. Ned opens his mouth to spill everything to Pat, then closes it again with a click of his teeth. He's not going to repeat what Abbot said. He's not going to even think about what Abbot said.

"Cool, just gotta fix up your charts, then, right? Or hell, plan B," Pat says. "We'll come up with plan B, and we'll knock it out of the park. Chris won't know what hit him."

"Yeah." Ned takes another sip and lets out a hard laugh. Abbot sure as hell came up with a plan of his own, didn't he? His words ring through Ned's head, a loud crazed pealing of a too-insistent bell. "Plan fucking B."

"And we'll get you back home to Peggy," Pat says. "Back on that horse, right?"

"I hate your horse."

And Abbot. And the department. And his dissertation. Ned swallows another long drink of beer.

"The horse is proving slightly more ornery than I originally thought," Pat says. "But my dude, you can do this."

Ned leans his forehead into the heel of his hand. "That's what you said this morning."

"And it's what I said at the start of this term, and this summer, and when you and Jen—" Pat makes a fizzing noise and mimes an explosion. "And I mean it. Look at you, you're doing it."

Ned closes his eyes. "I'm literally, actually, failing at everything."

"Ned." Pat leans across the bar, looking far more serious than he has any right to. "You've come this far. You can't back out now."

"Sure, I can. I can move home, see my daughter, find a damn job and a place to live, and get the hell out of here."

"And then have Peggy grow up with a dad who almost but not quite got his dissertation done?"

Ned frowns. "People quit doctorate programs. It happens."

"A father who gave up when the going got tough?"

Ned sits up on his stool. "Screw you. Don't bring her into this. The going's been tough."

"And you're tougher than the going is." Pat leans over and rubs his palm across Ned's hair. "You got this, my man. We're going to get you through this, all right?"

"I wish you didn't care," Ned mutters. And that his dad didn't care. And his mom. And Ned himself.

He tips his head back. Abbot's offering him a way out. A way that would mean he'd be done this semester. He doesn't really want to quit, no matter what he lets himself say. If he had, it would've been long before now that he backed out of the program.

Peggy, he thinks.

Building snowmen together in the park this winter, only a couple months from now. Tossing snowballs for Baxter, and drinking hot chocolate, and searching for Peggy's mittens before school, in a rush to get out the door. Day in and day out. Week after week. No dissertation hanging over his head and his future finally there for him to step into.

He's so close. So, so close.

Pat wouldn't even have to know. Nobody would. One afternoon—that was all Abbot wanted.

"Fine," Ned says, squeezing his eyes shut.

Back on that damn horse. In so many more ways than Ned would've ever thought to guess.

Pat holds out his hand for a high five. If he's surprised Ned slaps it instead of just glaring at him, he doesn't show it, just takes Ned's glass and tops it up as the foam subsides.

Ned pulls out his laptop. *Fine*, he writes to Abbot. No subject line. He doesn't even add his name. Just that. *Peggy*, he thinks again and tamps down the nervous flutter through his stomach at the thought of Sunday as he hits send.

CHAPTER SIX

Ned crosses the ribbon over itself. "I need your finger."

Mouth pursed and ink already staining the side of her hand, Peggy wraps her fist around her marker. Ned glances at the clock on the stove, and yeah, they've got to get a move on. His stomach flips over.

"Pegster. Hey." He slides the present and its stegosaurus wrapping paper closer to her. "One finger, right there. Nope, press harder. You've got it, just like that."

"You have to curl it," she says as he pulls the knot tight.

"Finish up your card." He pats at her chair where her butt should be, instead of in the air, her weight on her knees and her elbows on the table. He could just stay here with her all day, Timmy and his party be damned. And Chris and his ball game, too. "And sit right, hon."

"You have to curl it with scissors, like Grandma does."

"Well, Grandma's an expert," Ned says. "Peg, sit on your bum, please."

She does, but one carefully crafted g later, she's back on up on her knees. "Sarah had cupcakes at her party."

"She did?" He has no clue who Sarah is. Probably

another of the myriad of Peg's classmates he can't keep track of. He taps her chair again. "Sit, you pterodactyl of a child."

"Pterodactyls aren't even dinosaurs," Ned's dad says as he pulls open the fridge. "See, I'm up on all that sweet, sweet dino knowledge. Ned, did you get lunch?"

"M'fine," Ned says. He's not. And a stomach full of food isn't going to help anything. "Peg, you gotta finish that up, we have to get going."

"Cake is better than cupcakes." Peggy finally moves on to the *y* awaiting her.

Ned checks the clock again. She's still got her shoes to put on and the entire journey from the kitchen table to his car parked in the driveway. And besides, Timmy's house might be just down the street, but Bouncetacular or whatever the place is called that Ned's supposed to get Peggy to is clear across town.

"Cake is delicious," his dad says.

"You're a terrible influence." Ned tips his chair backward and stretches to reach the scissors on the kitchen counter. "Promote carrot sticks, why don't you?"

"You going to bring me a piece, Pegadactyl?" Dad asks.

She shakes her head, already kneeling on her chair again. "M'gonna eat it."

"Carrot sticks are passé anyway," Dad says. "It's like Twitter. They already reached their peak, we're onto julienned vegetables now. It's all the rage."

"Do you know how to even use Twitter?" Ned asks.

"I can tweet," Dad says. "I've tweeted. Twote. Twotten?"

"Dad."

"And I'll have you know that my sole aim as grandfather is to undermine all your hard work parenting. I take my job seriously, so no, we shall not speak of carrot sticks."

Ned rolls his eyes as he fits the ribbon between the

blade of the scissors and his thumb. "At least you're honest. Peg, make a move toward your shoes."

"I have to fold it," she says.

Ned shakes his head as he stretches the ribbon and releases it to curl back on itself. That's another few minutes at least, Peggy carefully putting a crease in her masterpiece of a birthday card. He should care more than he does, letting himself linger here as the afternoon stretches on.

"Fold it and I'll tape it on, and then we're going," he makes himself say.

"Hey, have fun," Dad says. "What a game to get to go to."

"Yeah." Ned should try to put more cheer into his voice, but over the flutter of his stomach, it's a tall order. "Quite a game."

"Your whole department's going?"

"All of them," Ned says, trying to keep his words even. All of them, including Abbot.

Ned shifts in his chair. Then he stands, as if that'll help ease the burst of nerves shattering through him.

It's sunny outside. Sunny and hot, summer still in full swing down here in Massachusetts, regardless of what the calendar says. Ned squints through the windshield and pulls his hat lower on his forehead against the glare, his phone perched in a cupholder so he can keep glancing at the map, the street signs unhelpful, at best. Everett Street . . . there's no damn Everett Street.

"It's a bouncy place?" he asks.

Nothing. In the rearview mirror, Peggy's walking a plastic apatosaurus over her thigh. Well, it's better than getting carsick as Ned weaves through the tiny streets. Half of which are one way. Or inexplicably closed.

He pulls into a gas station to turn around again and mutters, "Geez."

"Louise," Peggy says.

Despite the garish sign that Ned finally spots, the damn place is tucked in the corner of a strip mall, and now not only is Peggy late but he's going to be too by the time he parks at the T station and catches a train to Fenway. That'll go over real well.

Ned quickly unbuckles her car seat and ushers Peggy inside. Maybe Abbot'll get the same look on his face as when Ned showed up a few minutes behind schedule for one of his classes. Like the damn sky was going to fall in because Ned had slipped into his seat at the very last peal of the campus bell.

"Love you," he calls after Peggy. "I'll pick you up from Timmy's house, okay?"

Not even a wave goodbye as she's swallowed up by the shrieking pack of her friends. Yeah, Ned'll pick her up all right—exhausted beyond anything, and stuffed full of pizza, ice cream, and cake. She'll be a mess when he drops her back at Jen's.

Though a cute mess. Ned lingers for a good long moment, watching her laugh. She'll be all the cuter later, rubbing at her eyes and tired after bouncing her tiny adorable brain out. He so wishes he could text Abbot, Sorry, they want parents to stay. With a sigh, he gives her a last wave and ducks back out into the sunshine.

The streets outside of Fenway are packed when Ned steps off the T. He tugs his ball cap down against the shine of the afternoon sun and weaves his way toward the stadium between crowds of college students and families, kids perched on shoulders or ushered along hand in hand with their parents. Ned had brought Peggy here only a couple weeks ago. They'd had hot dogs and she'd dripped ketchup on her shirt. He'd carried her into the house that evening, passed out on his shoulder, the brim of her hat poking into his neck.

He and Peggy can have that type of day again as often as he wants to, when he finishes his degree. They can be back here this coming spring, when the next season opens, all summer long, and this time next year, too. They can go to the science museum, the aquarium, and the Cape to see the whales. Ned draws in a deep breath. Not so long from now, they can go ice skating on the Commons and curl their hands around cups of hot chocolate, the day stretched before them without Ned needing to get in the car and make the long trek back to Portland.

There's just this damn game between him and all of that.

Ned tucks his hands in his pockets and hunches his shoulders, forcing himself forward. He's never once dreaded walking into Fenway Park. He didn't even know it was possible, and look at him now.

Among the food trucks and their sizzling sausages and the vendors hawking hats and shirts, Abbot stands, a pillar of stiff aloofness. He's alone, unmoving, and looking the other way, his profile angled toward Ned. No navy-blue cap with a red *B* sits on his head, no shirt with *Red Sox* lettered across the chest—he probably doesn't even have a key chain stamped with the Sox logo, let alone knows who's pitching today.

Ned pulls in another deep breath. Abbot keeps looking the wrong direction. Ned could still back out. Give in to the sick twisting in his gut and slip backward into the crowd before Abbot spots him.

Peggy, he thinks and makes himself walk over.

"Way to get into the spirit of things." Ned waves his hand over Abbot's outfit. If Ned knew Abbot any better, he'd pluck at the sleeve of the button-down Abbot has on.

It's green too, not even a dark blue to match the rest of the crowd.

"You're here." *Finally*, Abbot doesn't say.

Ass, Ned thinks. "Nice to see you too."

Maybe Abbot doesn't really want to do this either from the sour look on his face. They can call it off. Go hit up a bar and avoid the entire pretending-to-be-on-a-date thing. Though somehow Ned can't quite imagine Abbot throwing in for an afternoon of day drinking.

"Everyone went in." Abbot hands Ned a ticket.

"Traffic was bad," Ned says. Abbot should try to get a five-year-old, two shoes, and a birthday present into a car, and then through the maze of Boston. Belatedly, he tacks on, "Sorry."

Abbot's silent as they make their way through security. Silent and tense as all hell. Pushed together by the knots of people weaving through the concourse, Ned's shoulder bumps into Abbot's.

"All right." Ned glances down at his ticket and then the sign above them. He smooths down the front of his shirt. Through the short hallway that leads out to their seats, Ned can make out the bright green of the grass and the players dotting it. "You're sure this is a good idea?"

"No."

"Great." He tucks his hands into his pockets and rocks back on his heels. *Go out there,* Ned tells himself. His feet don't move.

"Nedster!" He turns and there's Lee, a beer in each of her hands and a grin on her face. "You made it!"

His stomach flips over and cartwheels with a tight, sickening clench. "Hey," he gets out.

He wants to step away from Abbot. He wants to interrupt the glance that Lee shoots first at Abbot and then him.

Wants to stop her before she can tip her head, grin, and say, "Nice of you to wait for him, Henry."

Abbot shifts his weight. "It was no problem."

"Huh," Lee says.

Don't, Ned wants to bark out as she looks between them again. This is absurd. This is his professional reputation. His career. They shouldn't do this. He should back out. He should just turn and leave before the thought clearly about to form behind Lee's eyes coalesces into something irreversible.

He doesn't. Takes his third deep breath. A fourth. Watches how Lee looks between them again, and watches her grin spread over her face—the grin that made Ned sure they'd end up friends the first time he saw it. Mischievous and playful, and now, aimed at him, causing his heart to hammer in his throat.

"You know what?" Lee asks. Ned wants to close his eyes. He can nearly hear her words before she says them. "You two are kind of cute together."

We're not, Ned wants to scream.

He looks at Abbot. They didn't talk this through; they have no plan, and Abbot—he's so awkward and stiff and just stands there, rubbing his thumb across his fingertips and not looking back at Ned. At least that itch that sat under Ned's skin when he was younger at the thought of standing with another man where anyone and everyone could see them has long since faded into a dull echo. But it's *Abbot*, of all people. Ned tries not to grimace.

Peggy, Ned thinks.

He will do anything for Peggy. He will walk through fire for her, and he will sit through this baseball game with Abbot, and he will convince Chris that Abbot has indeed gone on a date. He wants to rub at his forehead. Instead, he shifts his weight closer to Abbot and makes himself smile.

Abbot, who'd marked his midterm until it was covered in red ink, who'd given Ned the worst grade he'd ever received in high school or college or his masters or his doctorate, and who'd written that damn *Try again* on his exam.

Ned sets his teeth and reaches for Abbot's hand. His palm is warm and dry against Ned's.

It's weird. It's so, incredibly weird. Abbot laces their fingers together, and Ned's standing there in Fenway holding the hand of his statistics professor.

"Wow." Lee laughs a little. Her eyes are wider than Ned's ever seen them. "Did we really interrupt something the other night?"

Ned shrugs. He's sure he's holding Abbot's hand too tightly.

"Told you we were eating," Ned says.

Lee's mouth drops open. "Shut up."

Ned squeezes Abbot's hand harder than he needs to. His mouth is too dry.

"You two—" Lee points between them. "You two . . . oh my *God*, Minori!"

Ned would laugh at Lee's tone, how she heads through the crowd toward the rows of seats, calling out her wife's name. His stomach climbs into his throat and his palm sweats against Abbot's. He yanks his hand back.

"Well," Ned says as Lee disappears, and for a small respite of a moment, they're left alone in the mass of fans moving around them.

Abbot stares somewhere past Ned, a stiff, solid pillar against the buffeting swirl of the crowd.

"Thank you. For doing this," he says.

"Yeah." Ned's voice sounds like a croak. His tongue is far too big for his mouth. He's shaky, the adrenaline draining from him. Or maybe ramping back up. Nine innings to sit through, and all their colleagues out there in their seats, waiting for them. *Have fun*, his dad had said. If he only knew.

Ned exhales. Well, the milk can't be unspilled. Or beans, as it were. He has an idea of what Lee's doing with the rest of their coworkers, and it's certainly not keeping this whole thing quiet.

"Ready?" Abbot asks.

Hell no, Ned thinks. He nods. "Sure."

Fenway looks the same as ever with perfectly mowed grass, rows of red seats, and Boston's blue sky hanging over the stadium, cheerful with the white puffy clouds dancing in the breeze. They've missed half of the first inning, and Ned examines the score board, catching up on strikes, balls, and the current batter, as he follows Abbot down the concrete steps past seated strangers until they reach the group Ned so unfortunately recognizes.

Chris jumps to his feet when he sees Ned and Abbot. "You made it," he says, leaning across Aliyah's husband, Tom, to grab Ned in a hug.

Peggy, Ned thinks.

She's probably already halfway to being all sorts of sticky and cranky, caught in that special kind of euphoric delirium that birthday parties can so aptly induce. He loves her. He's doing this for her.

He makes himself smile. He could really go for a good shot of joy, the type that the Sox typically stir in him. Lee stares at Ned, both eyebrows raised. He's still got a lump in his stomach.

He ignores her, avoiding the hand Lee reaches out as he edges past her to the empty seats beyond Tom, and she misses trapping him there by the hem of his shirt. He can all too well imagine her questions as it is. Aliyah's too, when she leans around Tom and tries to catch Ned's eye.

Tom just hands him a beer, either unimpressed or uninterested in the stares Ned and Abbot are eliciting. Ned always did like him.

"They're starting Hernandez as pitcher," Tom says as Abbot settles on Ned's other side. Tom pushes his glasses up higher. "Hayer's batting like shit this season."

"Course he is."

Tom grunts in agreement and slumps back in his chair.

Ned gets a look from Aliyah before she turns back to her conversation with Minori. He can do this. He's doing this. He takes a sip of his beer, forcing his shoulders down. The lager's good. Already warming up in the September sun, but Ned's not complaining. Tom's a good egg. Always has been. Ned can sit here between Tom and Abbot, and make his way through this game. Aliyah and Minori both look at him, then turn back to their whispering.

Breathe, he tells himself.

Ned kicks his legs out as far as he can. These seats don't leave much room for his knees. He balances his beer on his thigh and pulls his hat down against the shine of the sun. Abbot's just staring through his glasses, no sunglasses in sight, and apparently, he doesn't much go for hats.

Act like you're dating him, Ned instructs himself. Like he's here with an attractive guy, and it's a treat to be together on a Sunday afternoon. Abbot's not bad looking, but the flutter in Ned's stomach isn't the butterflies of a burgeoning relationship, but a raging pterodactyl trying to burst out of his gut.

"You know what's going on?" Ned asks, pointing his chin toward the field. He can feel Lee watching them.

"It isn't overly complicated," Abbot says.

Ned snorts and raises his beer. "Sure."

Abbot shifts in his seat. There's really not enough room between them and his sleeve brushes Ned's arm.

Ned tries to edge away as far as he can without ending up in Tom's lap. "Ever been to a game before?"

"No."

Ever been on a date before? he so wants to ask next. Abbot's hand rests on his own thigh, just sitting there. Ned could take it again, but instead he sips at his beer, staring at the field with more attention than a foul ball flying past the third baseline warrants.

Hands fall onto his shoulders and squeeze. Careful with his beer, Ned tips his head back and puts on a smile. "Hey," Ned offers.

Chris looks entirely too happy, perched on the edge of his seat in the row behind him. Ned's pretty sure today is going to end with a headache. "Good game, yeah?" Ned says.

"You made it," Chris says. Ned gets a clap to the shoulder that sloshes his beer against the sides of the cup. "Look at you two."

Maybe he and Abbot should thank Lee for spreading the gossip, as it saved them the trouble of telling Chris themselves. Though Ned's not exactly sure this is better, Chris beaming at the two of them. Ned works to keep his smile on his face.

"How long has this been going on?" Chris asks.

"Not long," Abbot says.

Ned's cheek twitches. Or maybe that's his eye. *Not long.* What the hell does that mean? Abbot could've let him know if he'd come prepared with canned responses, maybe put them on the same team here, not throw out an ostensibly shared history while Ned's left to flounder and nod along.

Chris shakes Ned's shoulders again. He feels like a bobblehead. "The two of you here together, it's just so wonderful."

It's something, all right. Wonderful is not it, though.

These seats are too small, and twisted around like that to talk to Chris, Abbot's face is too close to Ned's. If Ned moves at all, their shoulders will knock together and their knees too. They'll be sitting like Tom and Aliyah, thighs pressed against one another. Tom even has his hand on Aliyah's knee, pale against her dark skin.

Ned looks at his own knees, thankfully covered in his jeans.

And then Abbot's standing and Ned jerks back before his face can get too close to the guy's belt buckle. Jesus, warn him first. Though of course Abbot didn't, just turns to the woman sitting beside Chris, and to Ned's shock, hugs her. Tightly. Ned twists farther around, staring. Abbot's really hugging her. Arms around her, her hand rubbing over his back, and when he straightens, she kisses his cheek.

"Henry, so good to see you, sweetie," she says.

Ned wants to rub at his eyes or maybe ask her to repeat herself. *Sweetie.* Ask both of them to repeat themselves when Abbot says "You as well," and does something with his face that might just be approaching a smile.

"And you're Ned," she says, turning her smile on him.

Ned's beer drips over the side of his cup. He wipes his fingers on his pants. Abbot's not exactly helpful when Ned glances at him. No explanation, no introduction, just his stony brand of silence.

"Nice to meet you." Ned sticks out his hand.

"Susan." She shakes his hand firmly. "It's so nice to finally meet you."

"Susan," he repeats back. He should maybe know her, from her tone. He takes her in, the silver hair pulled back to the nape of her neck, her neat sweater and slacks. Which might make her . . . "Oh. Chris's wife."

"Chris is my husband."

That's right, she's a professor—no, a dean at the university, since last year sometime. Chris had invited them all to her promotion celebration, but Ned had been with Peggy and hadn't gone.

But Abbot probably went. Abbot knows them. The two of them, not just Chris. *His father*, Ned remembers, stopping by Chris's office. Abbot knows their family—Abbot's family knows their family, beyond the congeniality of a professor and department head.

This is a hell of a lot more complicated than Ned wanted to sign up for.

"Nice to meet you," Ned gets out and sits again. He waits for Abbot to sit down too, then leans over and mutters, "Next time you get a brilliant plan, try not to involve any university deans."

From the back, they hopefully look like they're whispering sweet nothings, especially when Abbot turns to him. They're still too close, and Ned can make out Abbot's eyelashes behind the lenses of his glasses, and the different shades of brown in his eyes as the sun catches on them.

"And this had better work," Ned adds. He knows his voice sounds hard. He squints out over the field so he doesn't have to stare right into Abbot's face. "'Cause it doesn't look like my dissertation is any more finished than before this damn game."

"I'll talk to Chris when we get back to campus," Abbot says.

"Good," Ned grunts. He hated being in Abbot's classroom, but at least there were rows of seats between them, the lectern that Abbot stood at, and the distance of student and professor that's worn off since then. Ned shifts in his seat.

Chris claps him on the shoulder again. "You teaching the good professor a thing or two about baseball?"

"Trying to," Ned says as brightly as he can.

"How'd you swing this, Henry?" Chris ruffles Ned's hat on his head. Ned smooths his cap back down with his palm, knocking his elbow into Abbot's arm, and he quickly drops his hand. "Ned's quite the guy."

Abbot eyes him. Ned raises his beer for a long drink.

"I was extraordinarily lucky," Abbot says dryly. Ned lifts his eyes in a long roll that behind him, Chris can't see.

"Makes two of us," Ned says. He gets a laugh and another pat on the shoulder. He keeps his hand in his lap as the next batter steps up to the plate, careful to not let his elbow touch Abbot's again.

Tom stands as he takes the last drink of his beer. "Another?" He shakes his empty cup at Ned.

"Sure." Anything for a chance to get the hell out of here. He makes himself glance at Abbot. "Want anything?"

"No, thank you."

Lee's going to try to grab him if Ned slips out of their row. He tips his head toward Abbot and catches Tom's eye. "Let's head that way, it's less crowded."

It's not, but Tom follows him all the same, and Ned brushes in front of Abbot when he stands to give them room.

"Aliyah wants me to get the details," Tom says as they pick their way past the last people in the row and reach the concrete stairs that lead back up into the concourse.

"Oh."

"I'm not going to," Tom says. "I'm getting a beer."

Ned smiles, and for the first time, it feels genuine. "Thanks, man."

Ned lets his shoulders relax. Tom is such a good guy and so wonderfully uninterested in departmental gossip. They can get their beers and maybe kill some time up there, grab a bite to eat and chat about Tom and Aliyah's kids and

100

Peggy, in an idle, easy conversation. There'd be no weight behind it, no need to think too carefully; Ned can just lament increasingly elaborate kids' birthday parties and Tom can throw in his own grievances. This'll be so much better than sitting down there with Abbot, and hell, it's Ned's Sunday, he might even get to enjoy a couple minutes of it.

"Ned?"

Ned glances behind him. That's not Abbot's voice calling his name. Familiar, but not Abbot, so Ned can continue on his escape. He keeps walking.

"Ned, hey!"

Tom turns too, and Ned stops. That voice is familiar. Way, way too familiar. His stomach drops.

"Ned," Jeff calls, jogging up the stairs to reach him. "Hey, man! Long time!"

Jeff sticks his hand out. His other arm comes up, ready for a back-clapping hug. Ned stumbles back a step, knocking into Tom. His hands go cold, and he doesn't lift one to return Jeff's offered handshake.

"Hey," Jeff says again, softer, though his grin doesn't fade and his hand is still held out toward Ned. "Crazy running into you here."

Ned's heart hammers in his ears.

Slowly, Jeff lowers his own hand. "I'm Jeff," he says to Tom.

"Tom," he grunts back. *A man of few words*, a high-shrieking part of Ned's head thinks.

"Ned and I are old friends," Jeff says, and Ned takes another step away from him, crowding Tom out of the way. "Is Peggy at that party? She was talking about it all week."

Ned turns. There're some college kids on the steps ahead of him, and Ned shoulders past them into the shadowed, cool interior of the stadium. His hands are shaking. His whole body is. He shoves into the crowd.

"You okay?" Tom asks, jogging to catch up with him.

Ned nods. He keeps walking, past the line for hot dogs, past a stand of T-shirts, and past the crowd outside the bathrooms, where Ned slips past a group of middle schoolers and leaves Tom behind.

He's fine. This is fine. He's going to be fine.

The staircase is cool and dark, and only a trickle of people move up and down it. Ned wants to sprint to the top. He makes himself sit and fumbles for his phone.

Jeff's here, he texts Pat.

His phone lights up immediately. Fuck.

Ned presses his shoulder to the side of the stairwell, refreshingly solid. *Breathe*, he tells himself.

Go deck him, Pat writes. Right in the nose.

Another breath. Another. He pushes his hand down his thigh.

Yell that he's a Yankees fan and fuck him up, Pat adds.

"Ned?"

He jumps. His phone skitters from his grip and lands on the concrete. Abbot picks it up. He wipes his palm over the screen and hands it back. *Take it*, Ned tells himself. He doesn't move.

Abbot gently sets it next to Ned's foot. "Are you okay? Tom said you were over here."

Ned picks up his phone. It's not broken. The screen's in one piece and showing a string of emojis Pat's texted him of a boxing glove and cartoon explosions. I'll help, appears next. Ned forces a slow breath in and out. Pat would help. He does help. Did help, popping apart framed pictures and tossing them out—Ned's college graduation, his bachelor party, his wedding. So many damn wedding photos of Ned and Jeff there in their suits, a new ring on

Ned's finger, and Jeff's speech for the reception in his jacket pocket.

Ned sets his elbows on his knees and pushes his face into his palms.

"Ned?" Abbot asks again.

"I'm fine," he says from behind his hands.

"What happened?"

Stay the fuck out of my life, Ned wants to snap. There's no force behind it, even in the storm of his mind. "Ran into a guy I used to know," Ned mumbles.

"An ex?"

That pulls his head up. Abbot's looking at him, a hand on the railing and his eyes on Ned.

Go away, Ned wants to say.

"No," Ned says instead. Abbot probably wouldn't budge, and Ned doesn't have the energy to argue. His hands are still trembling, but less so than they were. "My, uh—" He clears his throat. "He's my ex-wife's current boyfriend."

"I see."

Abbot looks so calm. That railing's dirty as all hell, though he hasn't let go of it. Maybe Abbot carries hand sanitizer with him wherever he goes.

Ned cups his shins in his hands. His head is swimming, dizzy and sick. "I didn't expect to run into him here."

"We can leave," Abbot says. "Or you can, if you need to."

Leaving would mean getting on the T and heading back to his car. His phone lights up again. Dump a beer on him, Pat texts. Ned closes his eyes and rubs at his forehead. This sick slick of hurt in Ned's chest has existed for so long. He's so tired of it, a constant, heavy companion that sits inside of him and twists awake whenever he thinks of the whole mess his life has become.

It's the Yankees and the Red Sox. And his coworkers

might drive him up the wall, but besides Pat, they've been the only consistency in his life since Jen packed up and left.

He can get up and go. Or head back out there. He rubs at his face.

"I'm okay," he says. He is. Or he will be, some version close enough to fake it, at the very least. It's not the first day of Ned's that Jeff's ruined and sure as shit won't be the last. At some point, he'd better get used to it. He stands and grabs his phone with a shaky hand. "But I do want that beer."

When Ned gets back to his seat, he balances a beer on his knee and pretends to study the field, ignoring Tom's glance. He can see where Jeff is sitting now, a handful of rows down and over, sandy hair under his hat. At least he's not here with Jen. Hell, at least he's not here with Peggy. Ned pulls in a breath through his nose and lets it out again, shifting to get more comfortable. He can do this. Jeff's been carrying on with Jen long enough that Ned's certainly no stranger to what it takes to get his mind back off of it.

At the bottom of the ninth inning, Ned pulls his phone out of his pocket to check the time. He doesn't exactly have to rush to go get Peggy, but he's not going to linger either, not with their colleagues still there and precious few hours of his Sunday remaining. And Jeff down there. He stays rooted in his seat until Jeff passes by him, resolutely staring at the field until he's sure Jeff's good and gone. He's blocking Abbot's way out, though if Abbot cares, he stays quiet about it, only rising when Ned does.

Still, Lee manages to grab him anyway, looping her arm through his as they file out of their seats and into the shaded, cooler interior of the stadium. Ned blinks in the sudden darkness. He could probably twist free of her, but there's not room to go anywhere in the press of the crowd around them.

"So," she says.

"Don't want to hear it."

"Oh, you're gonna." She squeezes his arm. "Charles Henry Abbot? And you? Really?"

"C'mon, don't do that." He's so tired, but it only makes her grin all the wider.

"You like him," she singsongs.

No, Ned would so like to tell her.

"Is this what the other night was at the bar? I think I owe Minori ten bucks. How long has this been going on?" When he doesn't answer, she smacks at his forearm. "I want the details."

"Quit it."

"I apologize for her," Minori says and drags at Lee's other arm.

"Details," Lee calls back as Minori steers her away.

Ned closes his eyes for as long as the crush of the crowd will allow him to before he has to look around himself again. And there's Abbot next to him, like he has been all afternoon. Ned lifts his cap, runs his fingers through his hair, and sets it back on his head again. Thank God this is over. They made it through, and it's behind them now. He rolls his shoulders, waiting for his stomach to unknot with the ease of knowing this is good and done with.

"Are you okay?" Abbot asks him. His head is tipped to the side. Probably concerned that Ned can't put on a damn show for Chris.

"You, ah—" Ned glances around them. No Jeff to be seen. Chris is nearby though, standing there with Susan as Lee and Minori head off after Tom and Aliyah. "You ask Chris about the network yet?"

"I will soon."

"Think we sold it?" he asks before Abbot can ask him if he's all right again.

"I don't know," Abbot says. He glances at Chris. "Hopefully."

"Yeah." Ned rubs his palm over the back of his neck. Hopefully. "It wasn't that bad."

"I'm sure that's not true."

Ned gives him a small smile. "I'm not going to argue that."

"For once."

Ned looks at him. That was nearly a joke. Or it was Abbot being his usual asshole self. Annoying that Ned can't tease apart Abbot's sharp, biting humor from him just being a jerk. He opens his mouth to ask, then shuts it. There's no use. Ned doesn't care and it doesn't matter, since they're done here.

"You driving back with them?" Ned asks, gesturing toward Chris and Susan.

Abbot's shoulders rise and fall on a sigh. "I am."

"Ready for all of Chris's inevitable questions?"

"I think I should've thought this through more thoroughly."

If Ned had any more energy, he might laugh at that. Instead, he just shakes his head.

Ned's out of here. He's going to pick up his kid, eat dinner with his parents, and make his way back to Portland in his own time. Hopefully late enough that even if Minori and Lee have the energy to go out for a drink, they'll be gone from Pat's.

He tips his hat up a bit, his palm on the back of his head. He can enjoy the rest of his afternoon now, the warm sunshine and a good few hours left in the city he loves so much before heading back to Maine.

"So nice to meet you," Susan says, and Ned shakes her hand with enthusiasm that for the first time today feels genuine. He can wash his encounter with Jeff off of himself, too, and get back to forgetting all about him.

"You too," he tells her. "See you around campus."

"Oh, I certainly hope so." She gives him and Abbot a smile that Ned tries to politely ignore.

"Later," he says, giving Chris a handshake too. "Thanks for putting this together, it was fun."

Or something like fun. More like horrible and interminable, but Ned's willing to be a bit more generous now that the day's over. He lets out a breath as Susan turns away. *Take that*, he thinks to Pat's imaginary horse.

"Thanks for coming," Abbot says softly.

"Had worse," Ned says, even though Chris is still standing there and he has to drop his voice. "The Sox won, at least."

Chris still doesn't move. Just grins toward them with that smile of his, round cheeks and shining eyes. "That's not a goodbye," he says.

Susan shakes her head and pulls at his arm. "Oh Chris, don't torture the poor boys."

Chris holds up his hands. "Just saying."

"What's not a goodbye?" Abbot asks.

"C'mon," Chris says. "I'm not even watching."

"Chris," Susan says again.

"They're just so cute together," Chris says to Susan. "And I know you think so too."

Ned blinks. And then he realizes what Chris is waiting for and his stomach drops. "Oh God," he mutters.

If they were really dating . . . Ned presses his lips together. Of course, Ned would give Abbot a proper goodbye. Two people in the throes of the excitement of a new relationship don't part after an afternoon together with a handful of words.

Ned shifts to put his back to Chris and Susan, catching

Abbot's eye. "It's fine, let's just ignore them," Ned says. *Chris wants us to kiss*, he doesn't say, can barely even think it.

Still, Abbot must get it loud and clear because he looks over Ned's shoulder. "Chris is still watching."

The T stop is right there. Ned's neck pricks with Chris's eyes on him.

"I volunteer to let them know I have some sort of horrible disease. Outrageously contagious. Extremely gross, all sorts of nasty," Ned says.

Abbot glances over him. "And here you are, looking fine."

Ned closes his eyes. "Chris is just messing with us."

"I'm fully aware of that."

"Is he still watching?"

"Yes, but Ned, I don't expect—"

"I told you, it's fine, do you ever listen?"

Abbot blinks behind his glasses, those damn long lashes of his looking like they're nearly brushing the lenses. "I do listen."

Ned huffs out a breath. It's a good thing Chris can't see his face. "Doesn't seem like it."

"You said it was okay." Abbot's eyes shift from Ned to where Chris is surely still standing, or Abbot would've had the good sense to step away and put some damn distance between them. "And I heard you."

"Good."

Abbot looks back at him. "So is that permission to—?" He gestures between them.

"No," Ned says quickly.

Abbot draws back. Ned didn't realize he'd even moved forward. "Sorry."

"No, I mean—it's . . ." Ned clears his throat.

"What?"

"Just—" Ned draws in a quick breath. Abbot thinking about kissing him is just—no, Ned can barely even imagine it. "Um, yeah."

"I don't know what that means."

"It means I want to get the hell out of here," Ned mutters.

Abbot nods. "Me too."

A pinched, high laugh wants to work its way out of Ned's chest. This is so absurd. All of this. The conversation they're stumbling through, Chris standing there—being here together at this damn game, that any of it was Abbot's idea. Abbot, of all people, dreaming this entire thing up. And being willing to kiss Ned.

That giggle nearly worms its way out. Ned presses his teeth together against it. Panic sits high in his throat. He really does want to get out of here. And there's exactly one way to bring that about quicker.

Ned touches Abbot's jaw. Sandpaper stubble and soft warm skin. *Never mind*, Ned nearly says, faced with the reality of Abbot's cheek under his fingers. Though, he doesn't get the word out before Abbot's eyes meet his, a soft clear brown behind his glasses. Where Ned should turn away, he hesitates instead, and the pause opens into a long unwinding moment of invitation Ned isn't quite sure he means to give.

Lips press softly against his. Two fingers touch Ned's elbow. The smell of Abbot's skin up close, the quiet smack of their lips parting—and before Ned's caught up to it even happening, the kiss is over.

Abbot blinks against the sun. Ned drops his hand. Clears his throat.

"Later," he says, and he digs his hands into his pockets, rubbing his thumb against his fingers where he can still feel Abbot's cheek.

Ned doesn't look back at Susan or Chris, just shoves his way through the crowd toward the T. The train is busy as all hell. Ned balances with a hand on a stanchion and stares out the window, the dark tunnel rushing past. Air pushes into the car when the doors slide open and aftershave that isn't his wafts past him. Ned rubs at his nose with the back of his hand. Someone close to him is wearing that aftershave, he wants to be sure. It's not Abbot's. With a lurch, the train starts again and Ned braces himself, staring out the window and trying not to breathe too deeply.

CHAPTER SEVEN

NED PURSES his lips as he scrolls through his email. Nothing. Not a single reply from a single university.

Hire me, he wants to start emailing all of them, day after day, until he gets at least an interview. With a tap at his mouse, he flicks back to the window of job postings. He's applied to all of them, even the one at Adams.

He sighs. His coffee's empty. But if he walks downstairs to get more from the break room, he'll end up running into someone, and he'll likely stop to chat. And if not that, then just returning to his desk will prompt yet another round of checking his phone, his email, and then his phone again, and he should be grading if no other job applications are going to pop out of thin air.

He leans back in his chair and covers his face with his hands. Of course this is how this semester is going so far. Fucking figures.

"What the actual hell?" Sameer says from the door.

Ned jumps. "Give me a heart attack, why don't you?"

"You're fucking dating Doctor fucking Abbot?"

Oh *no*. Ned drops his hands to his keyboard. "I'm working."

"How long has this been going on?" Sameer asks, his chair squeaking as he sits. Ned gets a foot pressed into the back of his chair. This office is too damn small if Sameer can kick him while seated at his own desk. "Why didn't you tell me?"

Ned hunches forward over his laptop. There has to be some other job, somewhere in Boston that he's qualified for.

Another shove at his chair. "I thought we were friends, man."

"We are," Ned says. "And office mates. And, as one does in an office, I'm doing work."

"Did you, like, ask him out? Oh my God, did he ask you out?"

Ned pulls a stack of articles closer to him. It's a good thing he had to print so many out to take home with him, since the papers give him something to shuffle through. "I'm not saying."

"Please." Ned hears him clap his hands together. "Please, please, please."

Ned rubs at his eyes. Dragging himself into the office on a Monday is bad enough—but this morning was nearly impossible, even with dodging all of his coworkers and holing up in here. Of course, Sameer was going to find him, having heard the entire story. Ned had steeled himself for showing back up to work with the news of Abbot and him flying through these halls as he lay in his awful lumpy bed, Pat snoring through the too-thin wall and Baxter flopped over Ned's feet.

He makes himself sit back from his keyboard. "All right. I'll tell you exactly what happened."

Sameer leans forward, already nodding. This room is too damn small. "I'm ready. I've never been more ready."

"Here's how it went." Ned turns his chair fully around to face Sameer. "You listening?"

"Yes. Absolutely."

"It's none of your goddamn business." Ned spins back to his desk.

Ned gets a paperclip thrown at him. He leaves it where it falls on the floor next to his shoe and refreshes his email again. Sameer grabs the back of his chair and shakes it.

"Ned, please, I need this. I just got sent yet another stack of interviews to transcribe, and I'm pretty sure I've lost my fingerprints from all the typing."

"Hands off, I'm busy." Ned's computer beeps with a new email, and he lurches forward and grabs for his mouse. There, staring back at him from his screen: New message from Abbot, C. H.

Ned lets out a low, reflexive groan at the sight of the name as he clicks on it. He scans the handful of lines there and the groan tapers off. Huh. Look at that.

For the first time in what's surely too long, Ned grins at his inbox. *We can meet Thursday evening*, Abbot's written. Which Ned can't do because he's teaching, but still, his smile widens. It worked. That awful, dragged-out day at the game worked. Even running into fucking Jeff was worth it, if Abbot can meet with Ned.

And moreover, they don't have to keep up this farce. Ned wants to pump his fist into the air. *I can do anytime this weekend*, Ned sends back. He doesn't have Peggy, doesn't have any conflicts at all, and can speed through this damn analysis and probably have time to get his grading done too. He wants to cheer.

"Job interview?" Sameer asks.

Ned springs up from his seat. This calls for some celebratory coffee. "Just a meeting I've been trying to schedule."

But Sameer follows him into the hall and down the stairs, no matter how quickly Ned jogs down them. Someone finished the coffeepot without brewing more. Ned can't bring himself to care, dumping the used grounds in the trash and running the carafe under the faucet.

"We're not done with our discussion," Sameer says, leaning back against the table set in the middle of the room. There are never enough chairs, with them being pilfered for seminar rooms more often than not, and today's no different, leaving plenty of space for Sameer to perch on the edge.

"It's not up for discussion."

"When did this start? Was it over the summer?"

The real question is when is it over, and the wonderful answer is right fucking now. "We're not talking about it."

Sameer leans closer and drops his voice. "What's he like?"

"What's he like?" Ned shakes his head. He's Abbot. Sameer knows exactly what he's like.

"You know," Sameer says, waggling his eyebrows.

Ned's brain catches up and he grimaces. "Aw, c'mon man, no."

"No, Jesus, not like that." Sameer holds up both hands, though his eyebrows just start wagging again. "Okay, maybe like that, but outside of work, you know?"

Ned pours water from the carafe into the coffee maker's reservoir. He shrugs. Ostensibly, he should be gushing over Abbot or at least trying to hide a smile. That's what people do when they're in new budding relationships—chatter on until their friends have had more than enough of them.

But, oh so thankfully, they're done. One ball game, one afternoon, and they're finished. Ned doesn't have to come up with any type of an answer at all. "It's private," he says.

"Ooh." Sameer kicks his legs. "That's the single cutest thing I've ever heard."

Ned frowns down at the coffeepot and shoves a filter in harder than he needs to. "Shut up."

"And look at that, speak of the devil."

Ned pauses in digging his spoon into the coffee grounds. Closes his eyes. He turns. Abbot's standing in the doorway, a mug in his hand, and Sameer, with his tongue pushed into his cheek, grins between them.

Sameer jumps down from the table. "I'll leave you two lovebirds to it."

Stay, Ned so wishes he could say so he wouldn't be stuck here alone with Abbot. Instead, he manages to get a smile on his face. It drops off again as soon as Sameer's turned down the hallway.

He and Abbot really kissed, didn't they? That fact hasn't changed, no matter how much Ned's tried to ignore it.

Whatever. It's fine. Ned's kissed plenty of people in his time. He turns back to the coffeepot. What's one more? Even if *this* one more is standing in the doorway, all creased slacks and perfectly parted hair.

"Hey," Ned says. The coffee's only starting to gurgle. *Faster*, Ned would urge it if he could. Maybe he can just take the first cup that brews and leave the rest of the pot weaker than it would be—the karma he'll get for that would probably mean spending the rest of the semester finding the carafe as empty as he did today, but it'd be worth it.

"Good afternoon." Abbot opens the refrigerator, pulling out a container packed full of salad.

"Spinach?" Ned gestures with his mug toward it, the last dregs of coffee swirling around the bottom. He should rinse it out, but Abbot's next to the sink, setting his lunch aside and filling the electric kettle with water.

Abbot looks down at his salad. "It is."

"Cool." *Cool.* He wants to wince. That's not what he meant to say—he should've led with *Let's celebrate never ever spending an afternoon together again.* He clears his throat. Coffee was a bad idea. He should've just stayed where he was, clicking through his inbox again and again until his mouse gave out.

"So you talked to Chris," he says. That's better. Or at least less horrible than *cool*.

"I did. He gave me the VPN access code last night."

"You get your paper done?"

"I've been working on it. I actually wanted to talk to you."

"Yeah, I got your email. I teach Thursday nights, but I'm around all weekend."

"I wanted to talk to you about the game." Abbot opens a tea bag, sets it in his mug, and looks over at Ned.

"What about the game?" Ned asks slowly. *No*, he thinks. He's not thinking about the game. He hasn't been thinking about the game since he left—didn't read the sports section, didn't watch the replays on TV, and dodged Pat's questions. Jeff was at the game, and Ned's an expert in not thinking about Jeff. "Let's meet this weekend, all right? When works for you?"

"We have our faculty retreat this weekend. Ned—"

"When're you back from that? Sunday?"

Abbot shakes his head. "No, I can't on Sunday. But Ned, I wanted to say—"

"You're gone all weekend?" Ned interrupts.

"Chris is taking a number of us to his house. That retreat, like I said." Abbot purses his lips. He doesn't exactly look pleased. "Ned—"

"I'm doing what?" Chris asks from the doorway. He must've just gotten out of his car because his coat is draped over his arm and his briefcase is slung over his shoulder. "Afternoon, Ned. Oh! You're making coffee, don't mind if I do. That was fun yesterday, wasn't it?"

Ned makes himself nod. It was something, all right.

Nauseating is one word for it. He'd slept poorly most of last night, waking up sure he was back in Boston in that house with the green front door. When he'd let Baxter up on the bed, he'd gotten his face licked and lost half the real estate of his own mattress, but at least he'd finally been able to sleep.

You look like shit, Pat had said when Ned had stumbled out for breakfast. No wonder Ned hasn't gotten anything done today—he needs a nap. Or more coffee. He glares at the pot slowly filling drip by drip.

"You were looking for me?" Chris asks.

"Looking for you for what?" Abbot asks.

"For the form. You two signed it, right?" Chris asks. "I can take it now."

Abbot's forehead creases. "What form?"

"For the university, of course." Chris sets his hand on Abbot's shoulder and grins over at Ned. "Can't have you two carrying on without a disclosure form."

Ned blinks. "Disclosure form?"

"Of your relationship." Chris slings his arm around Abbot's shoulder, smiling and cheerful next to Abbot's stiffness. "Have I told you lately how happy I am for you two?"

"You have." Abbot's eyes are wide behind his glasses. "Repeatedly."

Disclosure form. Of their relationship. Ned stares at Abbot. No. This isn't how this was supposed to go.

Chris hugs Abbot into his side, jostling the arm he has a grip on. "Gotta make this official and above board." Chris looks between Ned and Abbot and his smile slips. "What's the problem?"

There are so many problems. Just so, so many of them. *Say something,* he wants to bark at Abbot. This was his damn idea, so he can be the one to get them out of this. But Abbot looks like a deer in headlights, a tall slim deer with an expensive haircut. Abbot's mouth hangs open slightly as he stares at Chris, and Chris's expression only grows more concerned.

One afternoon, Abbot had promised.

"What's wrong?" Chris asks more slowly.

"Um." Ned gestures with his mug at Abbot. Cold coffee sloshes in the bottom and next to him, the coffee maker drips its fresh hot brew into the carafe. Four cups, now, only eight left. Ned wants to *go.* "Abbot and I . . ." *Henry,* Ned reminds himself. *We're done with this shit,* he wants to say. Chris is standing right there, eyebrows raised and waiting for him to speak. "We don't have that form."

"No problem at all." Chris reaches into his briefcase. "I've got a copy right here. You know, Henry, I'm so glad you asked for the VPN, we want you and Ned to work out, don't we?"

"Of course," Abbot says. It comes out sounding like a question. Abbot licks at his lips and rubs his thumb over his fingertips.

"Gotta start fresh. Ned, you're so understanding, of course you are," Chris says. "But it's only a couple weeks until the conference, that's not that bad, right? To have to share Henry's time?"

"Not at all," Ned echoes. *What?* he mouths at Abbot, who looks away from him.

"Drop this back off with the department." Chris puts the paper on the counter and reaches for the coffee. It's only half-brewed, but he pours a mug for himself anyway and puts the carafe back. "Can't wait for Friday, gentlemen!"

Ned walks over and shuts the door after Chris. He can think they're making out in here, for all Ned cares.

The form stares up at him, *Consensual Relationship Agreement* printed across the top next to Callahan's seal. At the bottom, there's a spot for two signatures.

Ned steps away from it. "What the fuck did you tell him to get the VPN?"

"Ned—"

"Did you know about the form?"

Abbot's head shakes. "I didn't."

"What the hell is this about your conference?" Ned puts his hands up. "You know what, I don't actually care. We did it, you got your VPN, and we can find a time to meet at some point. Beyond that, we're done here."

Abbot presses both hands to the counter, his weight on them and his head down. It pushes his shoulder blades into two hard bony peaks, his shirt pulled tight across his lower back. "Chris has apparently jumped to several conclusions," he says as if Ned hadn't spoken.

"One of which is that this is still going on between us," Ned hisses, waving the form back and forth, even though Abbot's not facing him.

Abbot tips his head back and stares up at the ceiling, his fingers gripping the flat surface of the counter until the skin around his nails turns white. He swallows, his throat working behind the perfect knot of his tie. "I'm sorry. I didn't think this would go so far."

"What the hell did you think would happen, then?"

Abbot closes his eyes and the overhead light reflects off his glasses until he shifts and Ned can see him blinking.

"I only have the network access if Chris thinks we're still together," Abbot says. "Hence the form for HR."

Ned sucks a breath in through his teeth. Who the hell says *hence*? "Yeah, I got that. Didn't we do enough?" Ned kissed the guy. He went to that damn game with him, held his hand, let Lee ogle them. And he's probably facing a good long while of Lee needling him now that they're back on campus. Ned squeezes his eyes shut hard enough he sees stars. "Abbot, you can't want to keep this up."

"I don't."

"Then why the hell would we?"

"I want to finish this paper even more."

"I thought we were done with this. That we'd be working on my project and that would be it," Ned says. "And now what's this about your conference? What the hell does Chris think you're doing?"

Abbot takes a breath, and to Ned's surprise, rubs at his eyes behind his glasses, which are bumped askew for a moment before he rights them and smooths down his tie. "I have a grant with my ex. This paper and conference are the final projects we need to complete."

"Oh," Ned says. He opens his mouth. A laugh comes out. "Oh, holy shit, really?"

Abbot sniffs. "It was a good idea at the time."

"You started a grant with your boyfriend and then you two broke up? Shit. You come up with the absolute worst plans."

Abbot's eyes close. "I'm becoming aware of that."

Ned has to laugh again. *Absurd.* All of this.

Share Henry's time, he hears again in Chris's voice. "What the—does he think I'm going to be jealous of this guy? That you're still working with him?"

"That, and"—Abbot squeezes his eyes shut tighter —"and, from what he said, it would seem that Chris is expecting you to join us this weekend."

"No, the *and* is that we have to sign a goddamn official form for the university. The fact that Chris thinks we're going to spend a weekend at his house with the rest of the department is just a fucking bonus."

"To be fair, I don't think everyone's coming."

"To be fairer, this is a batshit idea," Ned says. "Do you really want our pretending to date each other on record? Everyone will think it's still going on between us."

Abbot inhales deeply, his chest rising. "I very much want to finish this paper."

"Because you thought it was a grand idea to get a grant with a boyfriend." Ned holds up his hands. "Not my problem, man."

"I can't help you until I'm done with this paper," Abbot says softly. "And it'll take longer if Chris thinks we're not together and takes away the VPN. I can help you after the conference, which is the first weekend of October, but not until then."

Which is goddamn great. The first weekend of October is right when Ned needs to be scheduling his dissertation defense, so if they don't work on it now, it'll be next semester when Ned graduates.

Fucking Abbot. Fucking Chris. And fucking Jeff, too, while Ned's making a list of everyone who's ruined his life. Jeff's probably going to see Peggy tonight. Pick her up from school, maybe. Ned's own daughter, tucking her hand into Jeff's as she crosses the street and tells him about her day.

Ned will do anything for her, but this . . . this is a lot.

"You can't be serious," Ned says. Already, he can feel his image of the rest of the semester unravelling, the one where he doesn't have to speak to Abbot ever again besides one last professional meeting. "You'd really consider signing that? Spending a weekend together?"

"We can do your work while we're there," Abbot says, like it's just that simple. "We can probably finish most of it, if not all."

Ned lets out a hard laugh. "Dude, I'm just going to remind you that you don't like me."

"I don't?" Abbot asks like it's another damn question.

"You think I'm dumber than a rock, and you can barely stand to be in the same room as me. Why in all hell would you declare to HR that we're in an ongoing, steady relationship? Let alone spend two days trapped together with our coworkers?"

Abbot's head tips. "I don't dislike you."

Ned snorts. "Sure."

"Of course I don't dislike you at all, and I think you're incredibly smart, I just—"

"I'm sorry, what?"

"I don't dislike you," Abbot says, more slowly. He blinks behind his glasses. "I'm not sure why you think that."

"You think I'm smart?" Ned asks. He wants to scrub a finger into his ear. "Don't just stand there and lie to me. What the hell, man?"

"To be fair, I don't think you're particularly skilled at statistics."

"I thought you wanted to boot me out of your class."

"I wanted you to find help, either from myself or a class-mate." Abbot's forehead pinches. "Though your preferred method of just obstinately trying over and over again until you finally succeeded was effective, I suppose."

"You barely bother to talk to me," Ned says. "You act like I'm something you've scraped off your shoe."

Abbot presses his lips together. "I never know what to say."

"What the hell does that mean?"

"I just . . . I'm not good with people."

Ned's staring. He knows he is, and he can't stop, even as Abbot's eyes shift toward him. "I didn't think you gave a crap what anyone thinks," Ned says.

Abbot lets out a breath. "That would certainly be easier."

"You really, really act like you can't stand me."

"You get along with everyone as soon as you meet them. I'm not like you."

"I didn't get along with you," Ned mutters.

He can hear what Abbot's not saying—the guy's shy. And feels awkward more often than not. He's just apparently managed to turn that into a constant stream of being a complete asshole, instead of coming across as simply quiet and withdrawn.

Ned stares up at the ceiling. He wanted to be done with the absurdity of pretending to date. Already, the easy jog down the stairs to get a simple cup of coffee feels so long ago.

"Think we can really get my analysis done this weekend?" he asks.

"I don't see why not."

No, Ned doesn't want to have to spend any more time with Abbot, let alone spend it as his ostensible boyfriend. But he wants to graduate this semester even more. Pretending that he's dating Abbot is a way out, and Ned's grasped at enough straws to know when to just grab them and hold on tight.

"Fine." He tosses up his hands. "All right. Let's go to Chris's."

"You're sure?"

"No. But I gotta get done with my dissertation so I can get back home. So, okay."

Abbot's so stern. The exact same expression today as when Ned had shown up with his midterm and his tail between his legs. This is a bad plan. An absolutely terrible plan. The single last thing Ned wants to do.

No. The very last thing Ned wants to do is miss any more of Peggy's life. He presses his palm to his stomach. His hands are clammy. "We need to talk about some—some parameters," Ned says. "If we're really going to do this."

"I want to talk about the game, first," Abbot says.

Ned clears his throat. "Right. Pretending to date is just a public thing. For the show of it."

"That's fine, but Ned, at the game—"

"And you'll help me get my analysis done."

"I will. But, Ned, listen, I—"

"Okay," Ned says. He rubs his palm over his face. "And you're going to be nice to me, none of this grumpy-professor-of-a-dumb-student thing that you've got going on."

Abbot's eyebrow twitches. "You keep calling yourself that; I didn't."

"Whatever." Ned grips at his mouth with his palm and then drops his hand. "One more thing."

Not even a gesture for him to continue, nothing, no response at all except for that steady, even stare. What the hell is he getting himself into with this guy?

"No seeing anyone else," Ned says. "You end up meeting someone and our entire arrangement is off."

"Fine."

"And you tell me. Right away," Ned adds. "Even if it's just something—" *that's just sex*, Ned means to say, but can't get the words out with Abbot sitting there, as prim and proper as they come. "Casual."

"Whatever you want. Anything else?"

"You really went in on a grant with your boyfriend?"

Abbot blows out a breath. "It didn't turn out how I thought it would."

Ned wants to laugh again. Instead, he rubs at his face. He'll really be gone come next term. With or without a job, he'll be back in Boston, working out a new custody schedule, getting his feet back under him, moving home. A chance to restart his life again, after this hellacious, dragged-out pause it's been in for so long now.

Energy runs through him. Or maybe that's just nerves.

"All right." Ned pours himself a cup of coffee, adding a dash of milk to it. He shakes his head to himself. "This is a really, really bad idea, but all right."

"Ned, I do want to discuss—"

"I've got a class to teach." Ned doesn't, but it gets Abbot's mouth to shut.

"I'll email you an outline to work from for your analysis by the end of the day," Abbot says.

"A detailed outline."

"A detailed one."

"You're driving on Friday." Ned grabs a pen from the counter and signs the form quickly, his signature more of a scrawl than any real attempt at his name. "I can be ready after my last class."

"I'll see you then," Abbot says. "Bring your laptop and we can work in the car."

Ned nods. Good Lord, but this had better work. Ned pulls open the door and Aliyah's there in the hall.

"What were you two doing in here?" Aliyah asks. "Is that coffee?"

"Chris took a cup while it was brewing and the entire pot is super weak," Ned says.

Lee pokes her head in. "What're you two up to?"

This is it. In it to win it. Oh goddamn, this really sucks. Ned puts on a smile. "What do you think we were doing?"

"Ugh," Lee says. "The break room? Really?"

Ned winks at her. "I'll let you decide that." He turns and flashes Abbot a grin. The smile comes easier than he expects it to, though the thought of going home will do that. "See you soon."

"Lovebirds," Lee mutters and picks up the coffeepot, examining the color of the coffee. "Chris Hausman, you ruin everything."

"That he certainly does," Ned says and heads for the stairs.

Peggy, he thinks and takes them two at a time.

CHAPTER EIGHT

"Let me get this right," Pat says. "Abbot. Charles Henry Abbot. That's who we're talking about."

Ned adds another T-shirt to his backpack. "Yep."

"The Charles Henry Abbot whose textbook you threw darts at, until the darts had to be taken away because of peripheral damage to the wall?"

"The same."

"Your aim sucks, dude." He punches Ned on the arm. "You're really going on a goddamn weekend vacation with him? And your boss man Chris believes that you two are falling deep, madly in love?"

Ned pushes his fingers into his hair and then tries to straighten it. Abbot would not date a guy with a bird's nest for a hairstyle. Abbot would also probably date someone without a hole worn in the knee of his jeans, but Ned can only do so much. "He thinks we're dating, and that's more than enough."

Pat bounces on the foot of Ned's bed, where the red plaid comforter's kicked down and Ned's sheets are twisted. He probably should've made at least a try at straightening it this morning, after a night of tossing and turning this way and that as he tried to fall asleep.

"It's going to be so damn romantic," Pat says. "Are you guys going to walk on the beach at night?"

"Pat."

"Count shooting stars together?"

"Patrick."

"Collect fallen leaves?" Pat flops back on Ned's mattress, his hands clutched to his chest. "Press them between pages of novels and keep them forever?"

"Get your feet off my bed." Ned shoves a pair of socks into his bag.

"I can't believe you're really going for this." Pat rolls onto his side and props his head on his hand, grinning up at Ned. "A weekend away with a new squeeze. You know, that's when my parents always told me relationships got serious, planning a trip together. The rubber meets the road and all that."

"We're not planning a trip together." Ned shoves Pat's feet aside and drops his backpack next to them. "We're being forced into the world's worst two days."

"Three." Pat counts on his fingers. "Friday, Saturday, Sunday."

Ned sighs and pushes his bag away. He bends down and takes Baxter by the head where he's sprawled at Ned's feet, a hand behind each of his ears. His tail wags back and forth against the floor. "You're my only true friend."

"Don't listen to him, Bax." Pat flops over on his stomach and reaches out to ruffle the fur on Baxter's back. "He's full of lies. He's beside himself about this weekend but can't actually admit that he might be experiencing a positive feeling."

"Don't corrupt my damn dog while I'm gone," Ned says. "I don't want you filling his head with those sorts of ideas."

"Baxter," Pat whispers loudly. "We have to be careful. If Ned doesn't watch out for himself, he might even have a good time."

"Feed him," Ned says. "And I told him that if you don't remember to take him out for a walk, to feel free to use your room as his personal fire hydrant."

"You're such a grump. I don't know why your professor likes you."

"He doesn't. He and I are in total agreement, for once."

Phone cord, shaving cream, comb—he needs his toothpaste too, and the list of notes Abbot made him. Though knowing his luck, Chris is going to be doing bag checks at the door.

"What?" Ned asks, catching Pat staring at him, eyebrows raised. "What's that look for?"

"Abbot's always watching you."

"So?" Ned pulls another flannel shirt out of his closet. He doesn't trust Maine's weather most of the time, and certainly not in the fall.

Pat shrugs. "Just saying."

"Abbot's not exactly the most socially gregarious person in the world," Ned says. If he spends any time staring at Ned, it's probably because he's still trying to work out how someone with such a low IQ made it so far in their education. *Incredibly smart*, Abbot had said. Well, he'll probably nail this fake dating thing, if he's willing to say what Ned wants to hear to get him to agree to this damn plan.

"No, I just mean . . ." Another shrug. "I don't think he exactly hates you."

"He thinks I'm the dumbest doctoral candidate to walk Callahan's halls."

Pat rolls onto his back, his eyes narrowed. Ned turns away and shoves the shirt into his bag.

"You don't hate him either," Pat says.

"Of course I don't hate him, never said I did." Ned tugs the zipper closed. "He's annoying and irritating and not the type of guy I want to spend my time with, but I don't *hate* him."

Ned doesn't hate anyone. Not even Jeff, no matter the months Pat had spent telling him that he should. Mostly, he's just tired. Anger requires a certain type of energy that long ago left him numb in its wake.

"Hmm."

"What's that?" Ned asks. "What the hell does that mean?"

"Nothing." Pat snaps his fingers at Baxter, who heaves himself to his feet and ambles closer.

"Patrick Connor."

"I'm just saying." Pat scratches at the top of Baxter's head. He looks entirely too thoughtful. "Your main man, Charles Henry, kind of gets under your skin."

"Sure, he does," Ned says. "You spend time with the guy, see how you do."

"Yeah, but . . ."

Again, Pat falls silent. Baxter nudges his nose into his hand when Pat stops petting him.

Ned shifts his weight. He needs to go. Pat chews at his lip, clearly still thinking.

"What are you getting at?" Ned finally asks.

"Nothing." Pat rolls to his feet. "You've just spent the last year or so ignoring everyone you meet is all."

"Most people aren't as absolutely infuriating as he is. What of it?"

"Nothing." Pat backs out of the room, hands spread wide. "Absolutely nothing."

"I'm sorry you have to deal with him all weekend," Ned says to Baxter. His tail flops against the side of the bed. "And I know, you're sorry for me too."

The sidewalk's empty of sternly quiet statisticians, and Ned frowns, looking up and down the street, past an old junker of a pickup truck, a sleek jet-black sedan, and a Jeep. It's not like Abbot to be late. Ned had texted him and gotten a reply back that Abbot would be there—a punctuated, correctly capitalized reply, even. Wherever Abbot is, he's definitely not waiting outside the café for Ned like he said he would be, unless he drives a dusty, shitty truck or a . . .

Ned looks again. The sedan's door opens.

"That's your car?" Ned asks.

Abbot looks down at it, then back up again. "Yes?"

"Shit, man, how much does Callahan pay?"

Abbot ignores him and opens the trunk, which slides up so smoothly that Ned wants to grab the lid and close it again, just to watch it reopen. The small duffle already sitting in there is nice, none of the beat-up scuff of Ned's backpack. The dark blue sweater Abbot's wearing is nice too, and of course the cuffs aren't frayed like Ned's own flannel shirt, and the face of Abbot's watch probably isn't scratched. Everything about Abbot is that same sort of neat delicateness. His car, his shoes, even his phone when he pulls it out.

"I'll turn my VPN and hotspot on so you can use the network as we drive," Abbot says.

Ned glances over his car again. "Maybe I wanna drive," he says.

"No."

"Maybe I was joking," Ned mutters and pulls his laptop out of his bag.

Peggy could do a number in Abbot's car. Hell, Baxter could, and he doesn't have a five-year-old's eye for clean, pristine surfaces, just a fur coat and entirely too much enthusiasm for car trips. Ned can see it now: peanut butter and jelly smeared into the black leather seats, crayons mashed into the canvas of the seatbelt, dog hair matting the carpets, and stuffed dinosaurs filling every nook and cranny, like some sort of prehistoric airbag system. And still, Abbot's car would be nicer than what Ned drives.

Ned can't help but glance over as Abbot starts the engine. Even Abbot's glasses are nice. Not fancy, not really —nothing about him is—but that kind of understated, careful craftsmanship that speaks to him dropping some serious change. Ned's got sunglasses with him that he bought at the pharmacy by campus and his wallet's held together with a strip of duct tape.

He sighs. This is going to be a hell of a long weekend, stuck together like this.

Ned scratches his eyebrow with his thumbnail as they pull away from the curb. Maybe Abbot would go for an audiobook or even a dry, informative podcast lecture series since it's not like the radio's on. Ned folds his arms over his chest and scoots down in his seat, drawing his knees up, then shifts again and pushes his legs out in front of him as far as he can manage. Outside his window, trees rush past, their branches tipped with leaves changing to a bright, vivid red and orange.

Music? he'd ask if it were anyone else. Probably scoot his seat back too, but it'd likely make Abbot's eye twitch to have the interior of his car so altered.

"It's pretty." Ned unfolds his laptop as they merge onto the highway and leave behind the winding streets of the city.

He gets a silent glance in return. With one hand, he gestures to the trees and their riot of colors, like Abbot can't see them for himself.

Abbot nods. Ned'll take that as a victory.

"You been up to Chris's place before?" Ned taps at his keyboard to wake his computer up.

"I have."

"Know any good car games?"

"No."

"Right." Ned closes his eyes. When he opens them, the clock on the dashboard has edged forward by one minute. This is already painful, and they're still technically in the city limits.

"Password?" he asks when he clicks on the single available network, *Henry's Phone*.

Abbot's mouth tightens.

"Don't know it?" Ned prompts. He reaches for Abbot's phone in the console between them. "I can look it up."

Abbot snatches the phone and turns it facedown.

"Sorry," Ned says. "You were driving, I just thought—"

"It's fine."

The black slim case on Abbot's phone stares back at Ned. He lifts an eyebrow. "What's on it?"

"On what?"

"Your phone?" Ned kicks his legs out again. "Something good?"

"It's just my phone."

Ned pokes his tongue into his cheek. Stuck together all weekend . . . yeah, he might as well have some fun, even if he's long since learned that Abbot's apparently allergic to anything of the sort. "What kinda apps you got on there?"

Abbot blinks behind his glasses. "It's a long drive; will you need to stop at any point?"

"Oh, *those* kind of apps," Ned says. "Trust me, buddy, I've seen 'em."

Used them too, for a short while at least, back when Ned had taken various pictures in front of Pat's bathroom mirror, shirtless with his thumb hooked in the waistband of his boxers. He'd been pretty damn motivated by Jen not exactly hesitating to move on with her own life. Up until he just . . . wasn't.

Fucking Jeff. Ned sucks in his cheek, chewing on it hard enough to hurt.

Abbot grips the wheel. "It's not that."

"Sure."

Abbot sighs. Loudly. Louder than Ned's ever heard him and reaches over to grab his phone and toss it in Ned's lap.

"I told you I wouldn't be seeing anyone else and I'm not," Abbot says.

He sounds so pissed. But on his lock screen picture, he's not. Abbot's grinning and his kid sister is too, their heads tipped together with a shimmering, shining blue lake behind them, snow-capped mountains in the background. *The Alps*, Ned's brain supplies. Abbot's eyes shine bright, a breeze lifts his hair, turning it a lighter shade of brown, and he hasn't shaved in a day or two. He's taking the picture, Ned realizes seeing the small slice of Abbot's arm holding his phone out, his other curved behind his sister's shoulders.

"The password is 'Liesl is awesome,'" Abbot says, and his hand twitches from the wheel to the gearshift to the wipers. "One of the *i*'s is a number one, but I don't remember which."

Ned closes his mouth. His teeth click. "Right," he says.

"The passcode is 5-5-5-5."

"That's an awful passcode."

"Thanks for your feedback." Abbot clicks his wipers to spray the windshield. It's not dirty. "Do you have questions about what I emailed you?"

"Plenty. Where were you in this picture?"

"I think digging deeper into some of your findings would best position your analysis."

"Is that where you guys are from?" Ned asks.

"Especially your research on graduation versus dropout rates."

"Who came up with the password? I'm going to go ahead and assume it was you, so this is your chance to tell the real story."

"Your findings have implications for policy initiatives in terms of how universities support first-generation students."

"Were the sprinkles on that hot chocolate your idea or Liesl's special request?" Ned grins at him. "Yours? I knew it, I'm two for two over here."

Abbot's hands shift on the wheel. "Switzerland. We're from Switzerland."

"Ah, 'Do-Re-Mi'?" Ned asks. "It's gorgeous."

"That's Austria."

"*Sound of Music*'s from Austria?"

"Do you know where Switzerland is?" Abbot asks.

"Sure," Ned says. "Right in the middle."

"More specifically?"

"Absolutely. You tell me how many outs are in each inning, and I'll point to it on a map."

"I went to the game." Abbot glances over at him. *Oh no*, Ned has time to think as Abbot's mouth opens. His eyebrows pinch and Ned's stomach drops. "And about the game, Ned, I really think we should discuss—"

"Yeah, my research findings." Ned turns back to the phone and copies the Wi-Fi password into his computer. *Don't bring up Jeff*, he thinks. Of course, Abbot would be curious. Pat had tried to make him talk about it, and Ned had spent enough energy dodging that discussion that he doesn't exactly want to go for another round. He doesn't need Abbot to know that about him. He doesn't need Abbot to know anything about him. "All right, so yeah, I interviewed a lot of freshmen who weren't sure if they'd return for their sophomore year."

"So retention rates," Abbot says. He glances over again, and Ned can feel it on the side of his face. "All you need to do is graph first-generation students against the general population. But, Ned, the other day—"

"Against the general population. I'm on it."

He types quickly as Abbot puts on his blinker and changes lanes. *Focus*, he tells himself. With a couple taps at his mouse, he highlights a column of data. Retention rates. He sat and listened to a dozen different first-generation students talk about the choice to continue pursuing college, despite how different it was from their lives at home, the alienation from other students, and often even their families. Plenty chose an associate degree over four years to get their bachelor's, or trade school, or returning home to work. Hell, he knew that choice well enough himself, and with a tape recorder between them and a notebook on his lap, Ned heard those memories repeated back to him, over and over again, of that foreign feeling on a campus where everyone else belonged so seamlessly.

"The rate goes on the y-axis," Ned says.

"No, you're comparing two averages."

"Right, that's what I meant." He pokes his tongue into the corner of his mouth. He can do this. It's just statistics. *Don't think about Jeff, don't think about Jeff.*

Abbot drops his hand to the gearshift. "And then, all you have to do is run a p-value test to determine if the difference in the rates is statistically significant."

"Righto," Ned says. He flexes his fingers above his keyboard. Doing this in the car was a mistake. He's nauseous, though, given the car's smooth ride, it's unfair to blame the motion.

"Which involves opening the statistics program in order to do so," Abbot says.

Ned frowns. "I knew that."

"Okay."

"I did."

"I'm just trying to be helpful."

For once, Ned could mutter. Just the sight of the application loading sinks his stomach. P values. Null hypothesis. Standard distribution. The car's too hot.

"To import the data, you need to—"

"I know how to do it." Ned stabs at his keyboard to import the column of data. It's the correct column. It's probably the correct column. He's done this dozens of times over the semester he spent in Abbot's course, and he should be able to do it now.

He enters in each piece of painstaking parameters the program wants. In class, the other students around him flew through this stage, hitting tab with their pinky finger, hands dancing over their keyboards. Ned would be slumped in the back row, poking at the mouse on his laptop and trying to not meet Abbot's eyes.

Ned taps *Enter.* His computer beeps at him. He closes his eyes so he doesn't have to see the error message staring back at him.

"At the bottom of the screen, the option to—"

"I know, I just—"

"If you select that box, it should work."

It does work. Ned blows out a breath. "Great," he says.

Abbot clears his throat. "Ned, at the game—"

"I don't want to talk about it."

"I think we have to."

Ned shakes his head harder than he needs to. "No, we don't."

"Given the weekend ahead of us—"

"It's not up for discussion."

"I think it'd be more comfortable for us both—"

"We're not doing this."

"Ned, that afternoon—"

"Can't we just work on this?"

"Ned," Abbot says, sharper this time.

"I don't want to talk about the damn game."

"Then we shouldn't be doing this," Abbot says and waves his hand toward the road in front of them. "If we could just be on the same page—"

"It's none of your damn business!"

Abbot's mouth opens. Closes. "What?"

"It's not." Ned turns back to his laptop.

Abbot looks at him, then back at the road. Ned slumps farther down into his seat and feels Abbot's eyes on him again.

"What, exactly, is none of my business?" Abbot asks slowly.

Ned feels his own mouth work. He wants to get out of this damn car. "Jeff," he gets out.

"Oh."

Ned clears his throat, then clears it again. "I don't want to talk about it."

Abbot nods slowly, his chin tipping down. His eyes dart toward Ned. "I was referring to kissing each other."

"Oh," Ned says. "That."

Abbot's hands shift on the wheel. "We don't have to talk about your friend."

"He's not my friend."

"Former friend."

Ned huffs out a breath. Jeff wasn't that either, or he wouldn't be with Jen. Jeff's an asshole. Ned rubs at his eyes. Jeff's an asshole who's living in the house Ned bought, spending time with Ned's kid, and even driving Ned's old car, slotting perfectly into the life that Ned apparently never fit well enough to be able to keep it.

"What do you want to talk about?" Ned asks from behind his hand.

Anything's better than discussing the myriad of Ned's failures. And all he has to do to see yet another one is open his eyes and look at his computer screen.

Abbot takes a deep breath. "Given our professional positions, I wanted to apologize."

Ned presses backward into the headrest and drops his hand. "What?"

"For what happened at the game." Abbot adjusts his grip on the wheel again.

"You want to apologize?"

"Of course." Abbot darts a look at Ned. "You were my student. And now I'm working with you on your dissertation."

"Oh."

"So, if you were uncomfortable with what happened, you have every right to feel—"

"It's okay." Ned blinks. Abbot's words sound rehearsed. He must've been thinking about this all week. Or maybe he's just covering his own ass. This would be a hell of a case to bring to the university's HR department—Ned can only imagine the look on the face of whichever rep would be assigned to him, trying to explain the ins and outs and convoluted mire of what he and Abbot have gotten themselves into.

Ned shifts in his seat. "No, it's—it was fine."

"I understand if it wasn't." Abbot adjusts his grip again. For as still as he's sitting, he looks downright twitchy. "And now this weekend is happening too, which only complicates things."

"Oh," Ned says again. "Well, to be fair, I told you this was a bad idea."

"And you also told me you wanted to graduate." Abbot

casts another look across the car. "But I certainly don't want to coerce you into anything you're not comfortable with, nor would I expect you to compromise—"

"Dude," Ned says. "It's fine."

Ned's probably the first person to ever call Abbot dude in his entire life. And he doesn't look even halfway convinced.

Ned clears his throat. "I'm, whatever, comfortable with you, if that's what you're trying to get at."

"If that kiss was too far past what we agreed on, then I understand—"

"Yeah, I get it, you understand."

"As I said, I didn't think this would go this far."

"And as I said, you're shitty at coming up with plans."

"We're likely to be expected to share a room."

Ned breathes in through his nose. He's been trying not to think about it. "Yeah, I figured."

"But if you'd rather—"

"Oh, stop," Ned says. "What are you going to do, sleep on the couch? Convincing, really."

"I'd thought about it."

"Are you even listening to me? I told you it was fine."

"I am listening; that's the point. I'm trying to talk about—"

"Then are you hearing what I'm saying? You're fine, man," Ned says. "I don't think you're doing this entire thing to like, hit on me, okay? So I told you, it's fine, and I mean that it's fine. If that changes, I'll tell you."

"I really can find somewhere else to sleep."

"Oh, for fuck's sake, I don't care." Ned scratches his fingers through his hair. He cares about Peggy and this damn statistical analysis and whether Pat's really going to remember to feed Baxter—sharing a bed with a guy is very,

very low on that list. "And taking the couch isn't going to do much to convince Chris, now is it?"

"Not all couples share a room," Abbot says.

Ned opens his mouth. He shuts it again before he can say anything. No, not all couples do. Maybe Abbot's prim-and-proper schtick he's got going on extends that far.

"Are you uncomfortable?" Ned asks. "Is that what this is?"

"I'm fine."

"Well, if you aren't, you can say so, and we can—"

"I told you, I'm fine."

"Okay." Ned puts his hands back on his keyboard. Then, he folds his computer closed. "I'm carsick, let's just do this when we get there."

Ned tries not to look over at him. If they were really dating, Ned would sure as hell be planning to share a room with Abbot. They'd have spent last night together, and Ned would probably be whiling away this drive with his hand on Abbot's thigh, thinking up all sorts of ways to deface his boss's guestroom if he's going to be stuck on a work trip for the weekend.

Ned coughs into his fist, staring out the window. He doesn't need to think about Abbot like that. He doesn't want to think about Abbot like that. Still, he rubs his hands down his thighs and makes himself say, "I can find a couch too, if that's what you'd prefer."

Abbot exhales through his nose. "And you accuse me of not listening."

"No, I just, if you, if when you're dating, if sharing a room isn't okay with you, then—"

"I lived with my ex; it's fine."

"Okay." Ned sits back in his seat. That was more information than he was expecting. Lived together. He glances over at Abbot. Lived together when? The guy must've been here in Portland at some point in that case, since Abbot's been at the university for a while. It was serious between them, then.

Shit. Chris and Susan must've known the guy. So they've seen Abbot in a real, genuine relationship. Abbot's jaw works, a muscle flexing in his cheek. Ned shifts in his seat. However this weekend goes, it has to stack up to that level of convincing. No wonder Chris had been needling him and Abbot at the end of the Sox game to give each other a proper goodbye—he'd seen Abbot with a guy he loved and knew the difference when he saw it.

Ned shoots a look toward Abbot. "How long's it been? Since—what's his name?"

"Louis."

Louis. Ned tries to picture him, but only can come up with someone as equally buttoned-up and austere as Abbot is. They were probably two peas in a pod, spent their free time ironing their pillowcases and sorting their bookshelf by the Dewey Decimal System.

"How long?" Ned prompts again.

"A year." Abbot's cheek twitches again.

"Where's he live now?"

"He moved back to Paris."

"Oh." Paris. And Ned moved back in with his parents, when he's not at Pat's. *Killing it,* he thinks. "Were you married?"

"No."

Ned smooths his palms down his thighs. "You know I had a wife, right?"

"I do." Abbot rubs his thumb over the steering wheel. "And you have a daughter."

"Yeah."

"Peggy?"

"Yeah." How odd to hear her name out of Abbot's mouth.

"Chris asked if I met her."

"Chris can find somewhere else to stick his nose other than our business," Ned mutters, shifting to look out the window.

"I told him I hadn't."

"Good."

"And he asked about your—about Jeff, about what happened at the game."

"Fuck him," Ned says. He slips lower in his seat.

"Chris or Jeff?"

"Both of them." Ned sighs and rubs at his forehead. "We were friends. Jeff and I. That's how he and Jen know each other."

Abbot looks over at him. "I can understand why you wouldn't want to discuss it, then."

"I don't want to do any of this. Date again, even like this." *That's right, isn't it?* he thinks. A resolution he'd made long ago at the bottom of a bottle of whiskey with Pat, the world slowly spinning around him.

"Me neither."

So that's two of them, then, who've sworn dating off. Great. And look at them now.

"Not exactly trying to get back out there yet?" Ned asks.

"No," Abbot says. "I'm not."

"Well, we're on the same page about that, at least," Ned says, and Abbot gives a short, small nod.

By the time they exit the highway, Ned's got a crick in his neck from staring out the window. Chris's house rises up against the water, stately at the end of the winding road Abbot steers them down. There are already other cars in the crushed-stone driveway, and Chris opens the door to the house, a hand raised in greeting.

"Ready?" Ned unbuckles his seatbelt.

"Are you?"

"Nope."

When Ned opens the door, charcoal and the scent of burgers mixes in with the salt of the sea breeze. He glances over the car at Abbot. "Right after dinner, we're going to bail on all of them so we can get more work done, okay?"

Abbot nods. Chris is halfway to him and Abbot, already smiling. He looks so damn pleased with himself. Ned's stomach turns over. The wind picks up again, and when he looks back at Abbot, the breeze stirs through his hair, like in that picture on his phone. How starkly different, that smile with his sister to the bloodless line of his mouth now.

Ned shuts his door so he can't just dive back into the car and makes himself start walking toward Chris.

CHAPTER NINE

THE CLOUDS ARE ONLY TURNING pink around the edges, the sky still a bright blue over the ocean. Dinner's coming, but not soon enough. Ned pops open his beer and takes a long drink.

"Give it here," he says, holding his hand out for Abbot's bottle, instead of checking his watch like he really wants to do.

Abbot doesn't hand it to him, so Ned takes the beer from him. He sets the lip of the cap against the edge of the railing and gives it a smart smack with the flat of his hand. "It's not a twist-off."

"That's certainly one method to open it." Abbot takes his beer back carefully. He looks awkward holding the bottle, not the easy dangle from his fingers that it could be.

"Veggie burger or a salad?" Chris taps the butt of his spatula against Abbot's arm. "Which is it? Both?"

"Salad's fine," Abbot says.

"I'll make you both."

Ned taps Abbot's other arm with the bottom of his own bottle. "Grilling on the deck isn't the time for a salad."

Abbot's lips press together. That was maybe one comment too much. In Ned's book, idling around the porch with everyone while the grill heats up, drinking beer, and loosening up with gentle ribbing is actually not a bad way to spend a Friday evening. In Abbot's, he's sure it's something else entirely.

I'm not good with people, Abbot had said, and no matter what else Abbot has tried to convince Ned of, he sure as shit hadn't been lying about that.

Abbot's not one to rest a hip against the railing, but apparently, he does throw in for watching the waves crash up on the rocks beneath them. No sandy beaches of Cape Cod up here, just rough, jagged shoreline that's often covered in a thick heap of fog. At least tonight the water's clear out to the horizon, the clouds lit up with reds and golds, holding off on rain to let the sunset slip through. Ned sidles closer, his elbows on the railing.

"You don't eat meat?" he asks quietly.

"No."

"Were you gonna mention that?" Ned tilts his head closer. "What'd have happened if I handed you a burger?"

"I wouldn't have eaten it." Abbot arches an eyebrow, one that Ned can only see in profile.

"Any other astoundingly obvious things about you I should ostensibly know by now?" Ned asks.

"I don't drink beer."

"Great." Ned downs a healthy swallow of his own. "Next time, throw that out there before I grab a bottle for you."

"It's not like I expected you to get me a drink."

"'Thank you,' I think you mean."

Chris putters around the grill, and Lee reaches to grab another beer for herself. They're all crammed too close together. Ned shifts his weight. What would standing happily next to a guy like Abbot look like? Ned'd be smiling, he's pretty sure.

He squints at the sunset. "Do you drink at all?"

"Occasionally."

"What's occasionally?"

"Not often."

Ned blinks. Abbot could be joking, just so wryly as to be hardly recognizable.

"Right," he finally says.

No use trying to make sense of it, picking apart what Abbot could mean. He's stiff and awkward, and if the car ride's still wearing on Ned, the same must be true for Abbot.

Ned turns around, leaning the small of his back against the railing. On the other side of the deck, Lee has her arm around Minori, the two of them laughing at something Aliyah said. Ned picks at the label on his bottle with his thumbnail, careful to not let his arm brush against Abbot's. He's even more careful to not look at Lee and Minori. He sure as hell hasn't wanted to look for something serious with anyone. Getting through each damn day has been enough to focus on, dragging himself through the hours until he could fall into his bed. But sometimes . . . very *occasionally*, he looks at Lee and Minori or how Aliyah smiles at Tom. He had that once.

"What can I help with?" Ned asks Susan as she comes out with a handful of plates. He's had more than enough of standing here, watching Lee holding Minori, her hand moving up and down her wife's arm. "Let me get those for you."

"Oh, how sweet of you," Susan says. "Just set them there on the table, and there's some rolls inside to bring out, let me show you."

Abbot's still staring out at the water, his full beer resting on the railing. Ned gives him one last glance before he ducks inside after Susan.

The kitchen is just as gorgeous as the rest of the house, open and airy and with a hell of a view of the ocean through the sliding glass door. Ned runs his hand over the edge of the counter. The entire house is nice, even the stairs where Ned's bag sits, scuffed and sagging, his laptop hidden inside of it. Ned and Abbot had been ushered straight through to the drinks and appetizers. Ned still wants to go back and tuck his bag behind Abbot's to better hide his things, like a gentle nudge and their gambit will be up, Ned's tired zipper parting for Chris to see the laptop they've snuck in.

Either that, or Ned would be happy just bringing both bags upstairs, where his would no longer have to sit next to the nice leather and canvas of Abbot's. Maybe he'd just stay in their room, bent over his computer as it beeped error messages at him, a respite from standing stiffly at Abbot's side.

But no dice. Dinner, drinks—hopefully, that will be all. Everyone worked today; Ned can't be the only one who's tired and more than done with his coworkers, no matter the backdrop of the ocean and the setting sun.

"These?" Ned asks Susan, grabbing a bag of rolls.

"Yes, thank you." Susan pulls a bowl out of the refrigerator. Salad, by the looks of it. No wonder Abbot's so damn skinny.

"Anything else?"

"Ketchup, mustard." Susan opens the refrigerator and holds the mustard toward him. "I wasn't sure you two were coming, you know."

Ned puts on a smile and takes the bottle. "Happy to be here. Thanks for having us."

"With Henry's father and all." Susan smiles back. "It's so good that Henry was able to make it this weekend."

"Yeah," Ned says, but the same itch of discomfort starts up in his gut as it did when he first held the beer out to Abbot and just got stared at. Ned searches his memory, but no, he's sure that Abbot hasn't mentioned anything about his father. He edges toward the door to the porch. "Anything else to grab?"

"I'm just so glad Henry brought you." Susan's still holding the ketchup. Ned casts a look toward the door. "After everything last year, I wasn't sure when we'd see him back on his feet again."

"Absolutely." Ned nods, the motion probably too quick. "I can take that out for you, if you'd like."

"Oh sure, sure," she says, and he shuffles the ketchup on top of the buns. "It's wonderful he's found you."

Ned's cheek wants to twitch under his smile. "I'm glad you think so."

He hates lying. This whole weekend . . . Ned sighs and opens the door with his elbow. This is really a hell of a lot deeper than he ever thought this damn pretend relationship would get. Susan standing there with her soft smile, a fondness to her that Ned isn't all that comfortable with. Lee and Minori outside with likely more good-natured teasing to come. Chris in his conviction that Ned and Abbot are really dating. Ned's going to get a stress ulcer from pretending, he's sure. And if not that, then a guilt complex that sure as hell isn't going to be easy to shake.

Carefully, Ned sets down the ketchup and buns on the table outside. Abbot's still standing at the railing, his attention on the horizon and a good margin of space between him and everyone else. *Probably just how he likes it*, Ned figures. He walks over there anyway and sidles up close enough that he can drop his voice and be sure no one else can hear them.

"What the hell is Susan saying about your father?"

Abbot doesn't even look at him.

Ned takes a long drink of his beer. "Give me something here. I didn't know what to say, don't leave me out in the cold like that."

Abbot squints at the ocean. "He's visiting."

"Again?" Ned waits. Silence, still. "When?"

"Sunday evening."

"Great." Ned stares at Abbot over the top of his beer. "Great, that's great. When were you planning on mentioning that?"

"It'll be after we're back."

Ned takes a deep breath through his nose. "What else? Vegetarian, don't like beer, family visiting. Susan said you had a shitty year last year, was it just 'cause of your ex? What happened last fall? Is that when you two broke up?"

Abbot pulls away. Okay, clearly that was the wrong thing to ask. There's a solid foot between Ned and Abbot now.

Ned sighs again. Shifts his beer to his other hand and presses his palm to the small of Abbot's back.

Abbot jerks.

"Chill out," Ned whispers. "What the hell am I supposed to say when Susan says stuff like that?"

Abbot won't even look up at him. Ned taps a finger against Abbot's back. His shirt's warm. And his body beneath it is firm, though Ned could've guessed that. The guy doesn't have a wasted ounce on him, so it's no surprise that the knob of Abbot's spine pushes through the fine weave of his sweater.

"Hey, Abbot. We're in this together, bud. Throw me a goddamn bone."

But Abbot's still staring out at the water. Ned blows out a breath. Dinner and then work. That was their deal, and so far dinner's a real treat. Ned doesn't want Abbot digging into his own life, and he can certainly return the favor, though hell if it wouldn't be easier if Abbot weren't tossing him to the wolves.

With a long swallow, Ned finishes his beer and heads back inside to find the recycling. He pulls open the fridge and stops, staring at the bottles lined up there. No. He should just drink Abbot's beer, though it's likely gone warm from his grip on it. Ned turns to glance through the sliding glass door at Abbot. The guy's slim back is still to the crowd. He'll probably stand there all night if everyone lets him. *And they probably will*, Ned figures. Nobody's all that inclined to strike up a conversation with Abbot than when they're at work, Susan and Chris aside, and they're busy with their cooking and hosting.

Ned scratches at the back of his head, watching the silent scene out there on the porch. He could bring a glass of water out there for Abbot, though already he can hear Lee's ribbing over it. Well-intentioned and not deliberately heartless, but only sure to draw Abbot's shoulders in even tighter.

Ned crosses the kitchen in a couple steps, pulls his bottle out of the recycling bin and searches the glass for breaks. Then, he rinses the bottle until the scent of beer is gone and fills it up with water.

"Here," Ned says, nudging the bottle into Abbot's elbow. The sun's sinking down and the breeze isn't quite chilly, but it's certainly on the other side of warm.

"I told you I don't like—"

"Take it," Ned says and when Abbot still doesn't move, Ned swaps their bottles.

Abbot's beer is warm. Ned takes a sip and rests it back on the railing. He clears his throat. "I heard you, you don't like beer."

Abbot looks at the bottle in his hand. "It's the taste."

"Well, there're better brands out there than these, I'll show you sometime." Ned tips his head. "You all right?"

Abbot lifts the bottle and takes a careful sip. His eyes open and he hesitates before he swallows.

"Thank you," Abbot says.

Ned clicks the neck of his bottle against Abbot's. Tonight will be over at some point soon enough. The entire arrangement between them, too. He and Pat will laugh about it someday, and Ned will remain quietly horrified that he ever pretended he was dating Abbot. And hell, maybe there'll be a day that he and Abbot can do the same. See each other at some talk, run into each other at some function, they'll trade a memory or two and what passes as a smile for Abbot.

"One veggie burger," Chris says and presents a plate to Abbot.

There's a handful of chips on it and Ned snags one. Abbot glances at him. Well, Abbot never was going to eat them. Ned settles against the railing. Their arms are so close that with a slight shift, they could be brushing. He takes a second chip, and then a third, his warm beer cradled in his other hand.

"This is just an adorable sight," Lee says when she wanders over, handing Ned a plate. "Look at you two, you're so damn cute."

Ned squirts a healthy dollop of ketchup onto his burger. "Just trying to keep up with you and the wife."

"Speaking of, what room do you guys have?"

"Haven't been upstairs yet," Ned says.

He doesn't want to think about it, more like. A weekend crammed into the same room as Abbot—no thanks.

"The end of the hall," Abbot says.

Ketchup oozes out the side of Ned's burger. Of course, Abbot's been here before, yet another thing Ned has to try to remember. Too many damn balls in the air for a Friday evening.

He picks up his burger and takes a bite, wiping his mouth with the back of his wrist. Next to him, Abbot spears a piece of lettuce with his fork.

"Nice." Lee gives them a wink. "We'll try to keep it down."

"Aw, c'mon," Ned says around his mouthful.

"An entire weekend stuck in this place?" She punches him lightly on the arm. "Chris doesn't even have Wi-Fi, what else is there to do here?"

Work, Ned thinks. He doesn't need the internet, if Abbot's phone gets a signal. Though now, with that grin on Lee's face, the idea of heading upstairs together is entirely more awkward.

"I don't want to think about it, thanks," Ned says. "You were, after all, my professor."

"Well." Her grin is entirely too wide. "I'd apologize, but turns out, you're kind of into that, aren't you?"

Ned feels himself blush all the way down his neck. And Lee must be able to see it in the gathering dusk because she just laughs and pokes a finger into his shoulder.

"I'm collecting her, I'm sorry." Minori hooks her arm around Lee's waist and pulls her away. "Hon, what'd you do to poor Ned?"

"Hmm, hi, babe." Lee covers Minori's hand on her stomach with her own and turns to give her a kiss. "You done eating yet?"

"I might be," Ned says.

Lee just laughs and snags the ketchup from the table. When they're gone, Ned still doesn't look over at Abbot, just chews his way through his cooling burger. Hell if he knows what he was expecting if not Lee and her teasing. Enticed by the chance to get a rise out of Ned, of course she wouldn't be scared off by Abbot's reserve.

"You have interesting friends," Abbot says.

Ned clears his throat and drags his burger through the puddle of ketchup forming on his plate. "Sorry."

"It's the room at the end of the hall." Abbot sets his fork on his plate. "You still want to try to finish your work tonight?"

No, Ned thinks. He makes himself nod.

"Then I'll meet you up there whenever you're ready," Abbot says.

Ned eats slowly as Abbot heads inside. He watches him in the kitchen talking to Susan, finishing his food with his plate set on the counter. Maybe Abbot hates standing and eating, as awkward as it is to balance a plate and fork. Or maybe he just wants to get away from Ned. Maybe between the car ride and the evening out here on the porch, Abbot has reached his maximum quota for how much he can stomach Ned.

I don't dislike you, he'd said. Well, if Ned can lie his way through this weekend, Abbot can also fudge the truth and say anything to get Ned to agree to this whole schtick.

Ned swallows another bite as Abbot puts his plate in the dishwasher and then heads for the stairs. Then, Ned turns to where Tom is and helps himself to a spoonful of the potato salad Susan sets out. Abbot can go sit by himself upstairs. Ned's not exactly going to rush to join him.

Though when he's done eating and finished his beer, there's nothing left for it. He stands, waving off the bottle Tom holds out to him. Ned needs his wits about him if he's going to suffer through statistics tonight. Not that another beer wouldn't dull the grin Lee tosses his way as he slips inside. Ned sighs. The sad truth is Ned hasn't gotten laid in so long he's not entirely sure the condoms he has aren't expired.

At the end of the hallway, there's one door and it's shut tight. Ned blows out a breath and reaches for the handle.

Abbot's in a chair by the window, his phone set on the arm of the chair, and his laptop on his thighs. Ned knows that pose, keeping his computer steady as he video chats with Peggy, who bounces in and out of the screen, grabbing a stuffed dinosaur or holding up a picture she drew, his parents' living room in the background, and the battery wearing down on his laptop as he sits there and grins.

Of course, Abbot isn't a grinner. He just holds up a finger to Ned and keeps right on talking in German, like Ned hasn't even walked in. Which is fine, because if they're going to be stuck in a room together, it's all the easier to hear what must be Liesl's voice drifting up from the speaker, rather than have to actually talk to each other. Ned rifles his fingers through his hair, straightening it from the wind blowing off the ocean and trying not to look at his backpack set against one side of the bed and Abbot's bag by the other.

It's fine. All of this is fine. The voices drifting up from the deck below them, the double bed—not even a queen that would give them more room to spread out—the bathroom that they'll apparently be sharing, the edge of a sink visible through the half-open door and a shower beyond. Ned unzips his backpack and pulls out his laptop, plugging the cord into the socket behind the nightstand next to what Abbot has apparently decided is Ned's side of the bed. Ned sighs as he straightens. He's long since adapted to sleeping right in the middle, but back when he was used to sharing a bed, he always liked the other side better.

It doesn't matter. It's not permanent. It's two nights, at the end of which they can part ways again.

"Ready?" Ned asks when Abbot says goodbye. "Isn't it late for her with the time change?"

"It is," Abbot says.

"She's coming with your dad, I assume? Or staying home with Mom?"

154

Abbot smacks his computer closed. "What's the p-value that you found this afternoon?" He doesn't move from the chair, leaving Ned with no place to sit but on the bed.

Ned sinks down onto the corner of his appointed side, opens his laptop, and squints at his screen. "Point oh four."

"Which means . . ."

Even after avoiding that last beer, Ned still can't understand goddamn statistics. He scratches at his cheek. "That means, uh."

Abbot waits. Ned shifts, trying to get comfortable on the mattress. It feels hard as a brick. No wonder Abbot likes this room; he probably loves sleeping on a concrete slab.

"The null hypothesis," Abbot finally says.

"Right, that."

"Which is . . ."

"A hypothesis," Ned says slowly.

"That states . . ."

Ned blows out a breath. "Fuck it man, I don't know."

"If you remember class, then you'd recall our discussion of statistical significance."

"And if I don't remember class?" Ned rubs his hand over the back of his neck. It's too warm in here. Abbot's just sitting there watching him, probably enjoying this. Ned makes himself drop his hand and sit straighter. *Screw you*, he thinks. "I told you, I'm not good at this stuff."

"I know it's been a couple years since you took my course," Abbot says. "It's understandable."

"I thought I was done with this crap." Ned rubs his hand over his face and then rolls his eyes. "Sorry. It's not crap, it's your career."

"At least you're honest with what you think."

Abbot stands and Ned hopes he'll reach for the window, but Abbot doesn't let in the freshness of the evening breeze, just crosses the room and takes Ned's computer off his lap. It leaves Ned's hand too empty, and he rubs his palms down his thighs, working at the thin worn denim of his jeans. Abbot must not be as warm as he is, despite the sweater he's still wearing. Maybe he just runs cold, and when Ned's kicking off the blankets tonight and wishing it was at all appropriate to sleep in just boxers next to a professor, Abbot'll be curled up, the quilt tucked under his chin.

"This"—Abbot spins the computer around so Ned can see the graph he's created—"is a normal distribution curve. Given the standard deviation—"

"I think I do need another drink," Ned mutters. He scoots forward a couple inches, squinting at the screen. "Right, your favorite bell curve."

Maybe Abbot has that same graph tattooed somewhere. Right on his ass, if Ned had to guess. Ned points a finger at the screen. "What does this have to do with your special value again?"

"The p-value."

"Yeah, that."

"The p-value is used to evaluate the likelihood of rejecting the null hypothesis."

"You're just talking in circles now."

"And if you recall, we're comparing two averages in this test. Those two averages being . . ."

Ned hates the look Abbot levels at him as his words trail off. It's the same one Abbot used on him in class, a combination of silence and expectation that Ned knows he's supposed to fill in with an answer.

"Um. Rates."

"Rates of?"

Fuck. "First-generation college students?"

"And what, specifically, is the variable you're measuring?"

"If they . . ." Ned licks at his lips. "If they come back for sophomore year?"

"Exactly."

Warmth flares through Ned. He wants to wipe his forehead on his sleeve. He's going to start sweating soon.

"And you're comparing them to whom?" Abbot prompts and gestures to the screen.

Ned leans forward again, trying to search out where Abbot pointed. He can smell Abbot's laundry detergent. "I don't know." Ned pulls back. "I can't do this."

"The general populace. If you don't do this, you won't finish your dissertation."

"Don't fucking remind me."

"At least try," Abbot says, like it's at all that simple. It probably is for him. Ned's head hurts.

"I hate trying, I suck at this."

"You passed my course."

"Barely."

"No, not barely," Abbot says.

"I basically failed. I was last in the class."

"Which is still not failing."

"You made me redo my first midterm."

"And you did," Abbot says. "With quite a bit of improvement."

"Still had to live through reading your stellar comments the first damn time," Ned mutters.

Abbot straightens slightly. "Is that the problem?"

"The problem is that statistics is an absolute nightmare and only you would freely choose to do it every single damn day of your life."

"I assure you, I'm not the world's only statistician." Abbot's head tips to the side, and he lowers Ned's laptop. "What's your GPA at Callahan?"

"Worse off for your class."

"It must be high."

"Was higher."

"For you to be offered classes to teach, I mean. Chris doesn't award that, nor fellowships, to just anyone."

"Well, I'm a lucky guy, sitting here," Ned says. "Dissertation not done and dragged off on this weekend."

"Was my course the only one you struggled with?"

"Looking to corroborate your assessment of my intelligence?" Ned spreads out his hands. Screw it, but he really does want another beer. "Fine. I'd have a four point oh if it weren't for you, so thanks for that, really."

"And your undergraduate GPA?"

Ned glares at him. "I got a full ride to Callahan, a stipend, and a pretty sweet health insurance policy for the kiddo. I did well in undergrad, all right?"

"And high school?" Abbot asks. He folds Ned's laptop closed. "And your master's program?"

"Does this end with you patting yourself on the back for singlehandedly ruining my academic career?" Ned throws his hands up. "Yes, okay, I did well everywhere else except in the hallowed halls of your goddamn lecture room."

"Was my exam the first assignment you ever failed?"

Ned turns and looks out the window. It's so goddamn hot in here. "I studied for it, all right?"

"I'm sure you did. Ned, you're just not used to coming from behind. To struggling, academically at least."

"You know what, I don't remember asking."

"You've got a crisis of confidence, not a lack of intelligence." Abbot hands the computer back. "Write up a couple paragraphs on what we just did, and I'll look at it."

"Thanks for the input. You run a two-factor mean analysis on that?" Ned asks. The nonsense Ned'll end up scribbling down will be a good show for Abbot, probably finally get a smile out of the guy as he laughs.

"See?" Abbot says. "You do know what you're talking about."

Ned doesn't follow him out of the door, just listens to it close and then flops back on the bed, the heels of his hands pressed to his eyes. Fuck Abbot. Fuck statistics and doctorates and Callahan University and Chris Hausman.

Laughter rises up from the deck, and Ned's glad the window's shut tight against it. He blows a sigh into his wrists and tries to pretend that when he opens his eyes again, he'll be back at Pat's, the TV on too loud, and Baxter whining to go out. Or hell, that Peggy will be there with a book for them to read, one of her games to play, or a movie she wants to watch, curled up together on the couch, her warm small weight on his lap.

He groans. And he rolls up to sitting. Ned's computer cycles through its screen saver, and he taps the keyboard before another picture of a grinning Peggy pops up, all bright brown eyes and pink cheeks.

Abbot's an ass, going on about Ned like that. If he could teach the damn subject he's supposedly an expert in, Ned wouldn't be having these issues. *Crisis of confidence*—he sounds like Pat, droning on about that goddamn horse. What else has Ned been doing with his time than trying over and over again, banging his head against the wall?

His phone says it's too early to go to bed when he's done with Abbot's damn paragraphs, but he heads for the bathroom all the same. Ned doesn't have it in him to go back downstairs and listen to Lee's needling or watch Chris and his smile. Ned sighs and squirts too much toothpaste on his toothbrush. He stares at himself, his toothbrush working back and forth in his mouth.

He's confident. He hasn't thrown in the towel on this damn program yet, and he even halfheartedly tried to date again when he found himself suddenly, unexpectedly single.

Ned plucks at the hem of his shirt, then lifts it, looking down at his stomach. He pokes his abs, still flat and even fairly defined. Maybe when he and Abbot are finally done with this farce, he should get back out there once more, instead of giving the entire sex situation a rest. Do some more sit-ups, take running more seriously, and drag himself through the misery of actually having to talk to someone with the hope it'll end in bed.

He drops his shirt, leans over the sink, and spits. Whatever, no use thinking about it now. Sounds like a hell of a lot of effort anyway. He slips into bed and clicks off the lamp, plunging the room into darkness.

Then he sighs. It really has been too long since he's shared a room—he should leave a light on. He groans, sets his feet on the floor, and makes himself walk back to the bathroom, turn on the light in the shower, and shut the door most of the way. That should be enough so Abbot won't break something trying to find his way to bed, or worse, wake Ned up, stumbling around.

Ned has a chance to sleep well tonight, no dog launching himself on Ned's feet in the middle of the night, no Peggy dashing in at three in the morning with a nightmare—or even better, a fact she's burning to share about an acrocanthosaurus. Ned pulls the blankets up over himself. Though to be fair, it's a pretty awesome dinosaur.

Peggy's the best damn kid in the world, and worth this sham. Ned lets himself relax. No matter how utterly absurd pretending to date Abbot is becoming, she's worth it.

CHAPTER TEN

NED WAKES to the beeping of an alarm and turns his face into his pillow. It's really, really early for that. He flops backward, his palms pressed to his face. Still the beeping. No, ringing. That's a phone ringing.

Ned yawns into his wrist. The sheet on the other side of the bed is pulled taut and the pillow set against the headboard. Abbot couldn't have made the bed any neater without waking Ned.

Ned glares at the damn phone from beneath the arm he drapes over his eyes, but all that accomplishes is the bathroom door swinging open.

"Your phone," Ned says.

Abbot steps out of the bathroom in a puff of steam and a towel. Ned jerks his eyes up to the ceiling.

Wet hair, wet skin—he gives Abbot another glance, his arm crooked over his forehead. He's got his back to Ned, thumbing his phone on. Muscles shift in his shoulders as he raises it to his ear. And that towel fits him . . . Ned looks away again. That towel fits him well. Really well. Wrapped tight at the flat plane of his lower back, beneath the slant of muscles and the dip of his spine, above the round, tight curve of his ass. That isn't what Ned was expecting under those dress shirts or slacks. Not at all.

Ned rubs his hand over his mouth. Water drips down the back of Abbot's neck, and a drop rolls down the slope of trim muscles that lead into the fabric of his towel. Which is a lot to spring on Ned first thing in the morning. He rolls away and pats at the nightstand for his own phone, though there's no notifications on the screen, and when he swipes it open, there's nothing in particular to look at, but he stares at it anyway.

The bathroom door closes behind Abbot again. Ned lets out a breath. That just happened.

Okay. Well, whatever. Abbot can walk around in a towel all he likes. Ned doesn't care. All he particularly wants to do is brush his teeth and find his way toward a cup of coffee.

Though Abbot reemerges before he can. Ned scratches at his stomach and Abbot adjusts his T-shirt. Ned's never seen Abbot's arms before. He tries not to look at the veins running down the insides of his forearms. The guy clearly has done a push-up or two in his day. Or yoga, maybe. He's got that type of frame. Ned swallows.

"Sorry," Abbot says. He's wearing pants this time, at least. Must've brought clothes with him in the bathroom to change into after he showered. Thank God. There's only so much Ned can take.

"S'fine." Ned scrubs his palm over his face. "The sister?"

"Yes."

"Cool." Ned pulls his legs up, bending his knees. If he gives himself the chance, he's going to end up looking at the neat line of the cuff of Abbot's sleeve against his arm and he just woke up—he doesn't need to encourage the tent threatening at his boxers. But his eyes creep over to Abbot all the same. The guy's got a bicep on him. Where the hell was Abbot hiding that body of his under what he wears to work? Not that Ned thought to look exactly. He tugs the sheets up and stares at the quilt.

"Done?" Ned asks, pointing an elbow toward the bathroom, and even though Abbot nods, Ned waits for him to leave before he tosses the covers off his lap.

The bathroom smells like shaving cream. He splashes cold water on his face and grips the sides of the sink, only then making himself look at his reflection. His hair is all sorts of sticking up. So that's cool; Abbot was clean, showered, and put together while Ned was lying there with his hair in a rat's nest and probably drool on his chin. Abbot doubtlessly wakes up with creases still ironed into his pajamas and his hair as neat as if he just combed it.

Downstairs, the house is empty and quiet except for Abbot perched on a stool at the island counter. Ned glances at the clock on the stove, tucks his hands into the cuffs of his sweatshirt and uses the fabric to rub at his eyes. Trust Abbot to have woken him up before anything that could be considered a decent hour on a Saturday morning.

"I'm sorry about that," Abbot says. He's got a steaming mug in front of him, and there's a kettle on the stove. No coffee maker, though.

Ned opens a cupboard. There's a stack of plates inside, and bowls next to them. He frowns. "Better than a five-year-old jumping on my stomach." Or a dog licking his face and making that high-pitched whine that means Ned's shoes are in high danger of getting peed on. "You got the sports section there?"

Abbot pulls it from the stack of newspaper beside him that he hasn't read. Probably isn't going to read, either. Ned unfolds it and scans the first page. "You go out this morning for it?" he asks, raising an eyebrow at the date.

"Clearly."

Ned checks the Sox score and sets the paper aside. There's no coffee maker anywhere as far as he can tell. There's coffee, though, in a tin can. He holds it up, like the dark beans will explain how to brew themselves. "What time did you get up?"

"Earlier than you did."

That's got to be tea he's drinking, though Ned wouldn't put it past Abbot to be happily sipping on the austerity of plain hot water first thing on a Saturday.

Ned rolls his eyes. "Clearly," he parrots back.

And Abbot obviously went to bed later, too. Maybe that's why he's always in such a mood—chronically sleep-deprived and cranky as all hell.

"You read the paper every day?" Ned opens the tin of coffee. It's ground already. Slowly, he turns in a circle, like the kitchen will cough up a coffee pot.

"Yes."

"Huh."

"Do you need help?" Abbot asks.

Ned stops his spinning. "No."

"You're sure?"

"Absolutely."

"A percolator," Abbot says and points a finger.

"Right." Ned looks at the stove where Abbot's pointing.

"For coffee."

"Of course for coffee." Ned picks up the only thing sitting on the stove, a tall shiny pot that's a far cry from the coffee maker he really wants to materialize. "Anything interesting happening in the world today?"

"You fill the bottom with water, and the filter in the top with coffee."

"Yeah, yeah." Ned tries to pry it apart. The most he gets is the lid flipping up. "You don't even drink coffee."

"It's European."

Of course the damn thing is. Ned considers giving it a solid whack against the counter. Or maybe Abbot's head.

"Unscrew it," Abbot says.

"Thought you were reading the news." Ned twists at the perca-whatever. They should put instructions on the damn thing. "How's that going for you?"

"Quite a bit more successfully than your morning."

"Funny," Ned mutters.

He splashes milk into his hard-earned cup of coffee when it's finally ready, wrapping his hands around the mug. The morning's still cool, and Ned wipes dew off of one of the Adirondack chairs on the deck with the cuff of his sweatshirt. He settles himself down, one hand tucked into the pocket of his hoodie. It's quiet out here except for the crash of the ocean below. He can almost pretend he's alone.

The door to the house slides open. Abbot settles himself in the chair next to Ned with none of Ned's own sprawl.

"I want to enjoy my coffee in peace," Ned says. "No statistics."

"That's fine." Abbot flicks his paper open.

The clouds haven't quite blown away, despite the breeze that's cropping up as the sun hovers just over the horizon. It'll be warm again today. Not hot, not like the summer fading around them, but one of those autumn days that puts Ned in mind of warm cider and football games. Beside him, Abbot sets his mug on the arm of his chair. Ned sips from his own, watching the swell of the waves as they roll toward the shore, unending in their slow repetitious pattern. When Ned finally shifts, tucking himself deeper into his sweatshirt, he lets out a contented sigh and opens the sports section.

By the time he's done, the house is stirring and his stomach grumbles. Inside the house, the floor creaks and doors open and shut, and the smell of fresh coffee wafts onto the porch. Ned glances at his mug. A single cup is hardly his usual amount.

"Bacon?" Chris asks from the stove when Ned walks inside. "Morning, Ned. You sleep all right?"

"Yes please to anything you're cooking."

"Eggs too?" Chris asks. "I thought we could go hiking, so fuel up."

"Hiking," Ned repeats. Not exactly a day working on analysis.

"Get some fresh air, after a week in the office."

"The Sox are playing today," Ned says. "I was going to watch it."

"You turning Henry into a fan?"

"Um, trying to." Ned catches Abbot's eye as he comes into the kitchen, gently shutting the porch door behind himself. "Hey, we were going to watch the game, right? Today?" *Go with it*, Ned tries to convey with a hard look. "Chris wants to go hiking, but we were going to watch the Sox," Ned says more slowly.

"We'll be back to catch the end of it," Chris says.

Ned pushes his mouth to the side and looks down into his mug. He makes himself nod. Less than ideal. Though what the hell is he going to do, other than fake-cough and insist that he and Abbot can't possibly go outside and enjoy the day?

"Eggs?" Chris asks Abbot brightly, but Abbot pulls a container of plain yogurt out of the refrigerator.

Ned's mouth pulls into a grimace. Abbot doesn't put granola or fruit on it, or even honey or maple syrup, just spoons yogurt into a bowl and eats it plain. Ned drags a strip of bacon through a pool of egg yolk and tries to ignore the clink of Abbot's spoon against the side of his bowl.

Upstairs, after Chris has shooed them along to get

ready, Ned slowly pulls a pair of shorts out of his backpack while Abbot clicks through Ned's laptop. They've only got so long that they can stall, and Abbot's never been light-handed on editing Ned's work. He's not now either, deleting half of what Ned wrote and adding a long comment, typing faster than Ned had all of last night.

"You're close," Abbot says when he straightens.

"Are any of my original words still there?"

Abbot looks at the screen. It shouldn't be weird to change in the same room as Abbot, no more so than a locker room or changing in front of Pat. But there's a lot of space between "shouldn't" and "isn't," and Ned hesitates, his fingers on the button of his jeans.

"Some." Abbot manages to look up the very moment Ned pushes his pants down.

Abbot turns quickly back toward the computer. Ned kicks his jeans off and yanks his shorts up to his waist. It really, really shouldn't be weird.

"I'll be downstairs." Ned backs quickly toward the door.

Chris's idea of a hike is unfairly gorgeous and entirely a pain in the ass. Ned tips his wrist so he can see his watch—he could be working right now, not following along behind Abbot up the hill Chris chose, the ocean rolling beneath them, and a quaint, adorable town spread out along the curve of the coast.

It's all the worse that the hike's actually almost fun with the warm sun, crisp air, and the trees showing off their striking reds and oranges and golds. Ned shoots a look at Abbot in front of him. Abbot's got nice legs, slim calves that flex with each step, annoyingly brightening Ned's day that much more.

"This is certainly one way to spend a Saturday," Lee says when they come to a viewpoint and pause there, the breeze playing past them.

"Amazing, right?" Chris asks.

"Do we get extra points for being here this weekend and a quicker return to our normal work lives?" Aliyah asks.

"I can't believe you're thinking about the office," Chris says.

"I can't believe we want to pay our mortgages." Lee tips her head toward Ned. "Except for this one, who just wants to graduate. Hey, since we have a grad student here with us, can we send him on a coffee run? I bet there's a cute little coffee shop down there."

Ned grins at her. "Sure, I bet they have Wi-Fi too."

"No, not fair," Lee says. "Never mind, you're staying here with us. Plus, you peaced out last night—rude, by the way—so here's your comeuppance, get ready."

"I was tired," Ned says.

"How did this start?" Lee asks, her chin pointing between Ned and Abbot and her hands on her hips. "Make this forced-climb up this mountain worth it."

"How did what start?" Ned asks. "And this is barely a mountain."

"You two," Lee says. "Dating. Details, all of them, please."

Ned opens his mouth and closes it again. "It's not tall enough to be a mountain."

"We want the story."

"Doesn't a mountain have to be two thousand feet?"

"With the entire story, nothing left out," Lee says.

"Give it up, Ned," Aliyah says. "You can't just sit on this forever, and here we've trapped you in the wilderness."

Ned points to the town below them. "Let me go get you those coffees."

"I'm desperate to hear." Susan's kind, warm smile is so much worse than the good-natured pestering of his colleagues. "Henry won't say anything about it."

Ned turns to Abbot. Good, Abbot can tell her no, sounds like he's done it before. Hell, Abbot can tell the lot of them no, turn some of that good old attitude on the group and get them to shut up.

"There's not much to tell," Ned says and catches Abbot's eye. "Right?"

"C'mon, that can't be true at all," Lee says. "Ned, you bellyached about Abbot's class for months. Something has to have changed."

Ned licks at his lips. "It wasn't that big a deal." He pins Abbot with another look. "Was it?"

"It wasn't," Abbot echoes.

"We just, ah—" Ned catches his eye again. "Decided to give it a try."

"Exactly," Abbot says.

Lee crosses her arms. "Whose idea was it?"

"And when did it start?" Aliyah asks.

"First date?" Lee asks.

"Did you guys end up matching on an app?" Aliyah asks. "'Cause I've got ten bucks that says yes."

"Don't tell him that," Lee says.

"You bet on us?" Ned asks.

"Lee bet twenty bucks that you made the first move, Ned," Aliyah says.

"I didn't bet on you," Tom says.

Minori lets out a breath. "I did, but I was forced into it, okay?"

Ned huffs out a laugh. How awkwardly horrible. "Well, now I'm definitely not saying."

"Which is why we weren't supposed to tell him," Lee says to Aliyah. "He's never going to say if we're making money off of it."

"It's not the money, it's the thrill of the win," Aliyah says. "Ned, I'll give you thirty bucks to tell us."

Ned puffs his cheeks up on a breath. He likes these people. Might want to push them off a steep cliff if this hill were tall enough for it, but they're his friends. He gives them a grin.

"Done." Ned holds his hand out.

"Ned," Abbot says.

"Ooh, someone doesn't want the beans spilled." Lee claps her hands together as Aliyah pulls out a twenty and two fives.

"Ready?" Ned thumbs through the cash, making a show of counting it.

Lee actually leans forward a bit. "I have literally thought about nothing else since the Sox game."

Minori sighs. "That's so unfortunately true."

"Well, at the beginning of the semester, Henry and I—" Ned casts one more glance at Abbot. How odd to say that name out loud. Ned slots the bills into his wallet, folds it closed, and tucks it back into his pocket. "Decided to start dating, the end."

"Ned!"

"I'll give you half when I get change," Ned says to Abbot.

Even Chris shakes his head. "Those are not details."

"No matter how you two got together, I'm glad you did," Susan says.

"Were you pulling for them?" Lee asks. "'Cause I gotta be honest, this really came out of left field, if you ask me."

Ned shifts his weight. Even Abbot looks a little squirrely. Lee's only too right that Ned didn't exactly make a secret of his loathing of Abbot's course. He forces his smile wider.

"We're happy about it." Ned grabs Abbot's hand and tugs him close enough to give him a soft, hopefully convincingly affectionate look. "Right?"

"Well, it's about time, I'd say," Susan says. "We've all known Henry's had quite the thing for you for years."

Ned's smile drops. "What?"

"Susan," Abbot says quickly.

"What, can't we tell Ned about it now?" she asks.

Abbot tries to pull his hand away. Ned's shock is nearly enough to let him, but he tightens his fingers, even as Abbot twists at his grip.

"You what?" Ned asks.

"Susan," Abbot says again, "please."

"Oh, it was just harmless." Susan pats Abbot's arm.

But the look on Abbot's face is anything but, a pink tinge to his cheeks and eyes that won't meet Ned's.

Lee's mouth drops open, a smile at the corner of her lips. "Charles Henry Abbot, did you have a crush on your student?"

"No." Abbot yanks his hand out of Ned's.

"Oh my God, you did," she says.

"Well, you know how everyone was talking when Ned first started at Callahan," Susan says. "I hope you don't mind me saying, Ned, but you're really quite handsome."

Tom turns back toward the trail. "I'm going to keep going."

Minori snorts a laugh. "I think if Ned hasn't dragged Lee to HR for all of the crap she's spewed, you're probably good, Susan."

"I really did hear quite a bit about Ned," Chris says.

"Good we're immune to his manly charms," Lee says, setting her elbow on Minori's shoulder. She shoots a grin at Abbot. "Course, you're apparently not."

"Anyway, just a bit of gossip over a glass of wine." Susan pats Abbot on the shoulder. "But funny how it's worked out, isn't it, all these years later?"

Lee laughs as they head up the trail. Abbot slips away

from Ned's side to walk in front of him, as silent as he ever is. The back of Abbot's neck is red beneath his perfectly precise haircut. *The sun*, Ned would like to believe. Ned's own face feels warm. Abbot, talking to Susan about him. It's an itchy feeling, to know he was being discussed, no matter how long ago. And itchier that the discussion wasn't what Ned would've expected: a long-winded complaint to a university dean about Ned's performance.

Or maybe he was complaining and Susan misunderstood. Ned glances at her, chatting with Aliyah now. Maybe Susan brought the whole thing up, and Abbot, in his quiet, reserved way, just didn't correct her. That makes a hell of a lot more sense than what Susan was going on about. Abbot, having a thing for him—that's just absurd.

Back at the house, Ned checks the Red Sox score on his phone before tossing it on the bed. He wipes his forehead on his sleeve. He should probably shower. He kicks off his shoes and bends down, hooking a thumb under the top of his sock.

The door swings open and Ned straightens. "Hey, there you are."

Abbot's mouth presses tight, and he looks past Ned. "Sorry, I didn't realize you were up here."

"I was going to shower and then look over the edits you made." Ned lifts the hem of his T-shirt and wipes his forehead. "But if you need the bathroom, I can wait."

Abbot backs up, nearly out the door. "I'm going to go running."

"We just went hiking."

But Abbot takes another step back. "I'll be back later."

And he's gone. Ned frowns as the door swings shut. Why the hell did he come up here, then?

The sun slips lower in the sky as Ned sits against the

headboard, his laptop on his thighs and his hair drying from his shower. Abbot wasn't joking around with these edits. By the time Ned gives up, a headache threatens. He finally blows out a breath and sets his laptop next to Abbot's computer so Abbot can check his work whenever he gets back.

"Henry still out?" Chris asks when Ned wanders downstairs.

"Running, yeah, I guess so."

Ned should probably know if Abbot's some sort of ultra-marathoner and an entire afternoon pounding the pavement is normal for him, though Chris doesn't seem overly concerned. Ned opens the refrigerator and pulls out a beer for himself and another one for Chris.

You break an ankle? he texts Abbot, only to remember that Abbot left his phone upstairs in their room so Ned could use his VPN. He glances out the window, trying to figure out how long Abbot's been running.

Though there he is, a dark figure perched on a rock at the edge of the driveway, his hands by his thighs and his elbows locked, leaning forward to watch the ocean. Ned slips out the door. Abbot's face is red from the wind and what must be the run he just finished, his shirt sticking damply to his shoulders, darkened with sweat along the spine.

"I rewrote those paragraphs," Ned says when he's close enough he doesn't have to shout.

Abbot jumps, clearly startled.

"Sorry," Ned says.

Abbot stands. "I'll go look at it."

"You okay? You were gone for a while."

"I'll leave any other edits for you."

"Dude, if this is about what happened on the hike—"

"As well as a list of next steps to take."

"Everyone was just giving us a hard time. Though we may want to get our story straight."

Abbot takes a step away from him. "This is over between us after this weekend. I hardly think it matters."

Ned shrugs. Abbot's probably right about that—and it's a hell of a nice thought, this ploy being over between them. Freeing, certainly. Ned eyes Abbot, a bead of sweat rolling down his cheek. Though irritating and annoying and awful to spend his time with, there's something fun about teasing Abbot. Far more so than Ned would've ever guessed.

Ned tips his head to the side and cocks his eyebrow. "Susan was just joking anyway, right?"

But Abbot doesn't rise to the bait with a cutting remark designed to take Ned out at the knee. He just walks away, gravel crunching under his feet.

"I'll be down for dinner," he says as he passes Ned.

"Hey," Ned calls after him, but Abbot's disappearing into the house, and by the time Ned makes it back inside, Abbot's upstairs and Chris is pressing a knife and cutting board into Ned's hands, pointing him toward tomatoes that need to be chopped.

"You're so good for him," Chris says, like Abbot didn't just walk in here and head silently upstairs.

Ned pauses, a hand on the tomato, and looks over at Chris. If that's what being good for Abbot's like, Chris has low standards. Ned slices the tomato in half. Or maybe Abbot does, what with that ex of his—Chris and Susan don't seem too beat up about him not being in Abbot's life anymore. Ned pokes his tongue into his cheek. There's a story there, he's sure, not that he'll likely ever hear it.

By the time Ned wanders up to bed after a drawn-out dinner and too many drinks, Abbot's off by himself somewhere in the house. Even Lee's done foisting beer on everyone, yawning into her fist and trailing Ned down the hall. Ned flops onto the bed and shoves his face into his pillow. It'd be better if the other side of the bed wasn't going to dip under Abbot's slim weight, whenever he comes up here. Ned blinks, staring at his nightstand. He misses his bed at Pat's. Misses the ease he feels there, none of the charged sing of the air between him and Abbot, the two of them always picking at each other like they do, especially with Abbot more prickly tonight than normal.

Baxter still alive? he texts Pat.

He gets a picture back of Bax rolled onto his back, paws in the air, and Pat's socked feet in the corner of the frame. Ned flicks to search for the baseball scores from the day, and from there to idly scroll through news headlines. He props his head on his wrist, his arm bent backward against the pillow.

When the door creaks open, he rubs at his eyes with a knuckle and drops his phone onto the nightstand. "Hey."

Abbot looks like he's going to turn around again and dash into the hallway. "I didn't mean to disturb you."

"No problem." Ned flicks off the light next to him, and finally, Abbot steps in and closes the door. It's so uncomfortably odd, stuffed together in this room. As Abbot moves softly around in the bathroom, the sink running and water splashing, Ned pictures Abbot behind his lectern, pointing out this and that on his slides, his shirt tucked into his slacks and the light from the projector reflecting in his glasses.

The blankets shift when Abbot lifts them. He's in a T-shirt again. A black one. It hugs his torso nicely. Ned looks up at the ceiling.

"Do you mind if I leave the light on for a minute to read?" Abbot asks.

Ned shakes his head against the pillow. "No."

Sleep is a long way away. It'd be easy to blame it on Abbot's lamp on his nightstand, or the regular, metronomic rustle as he turns pages. It's been a long damn time since Ned's needed to keep his feet on his own side of the bed. And this was easier last night, Ned asleep when Abbot came to bed and not waking when he got up.

Maybe the guy really doesn't sleep. Abbot might be up for another round of regression analysis by the light of the burning midnight oil. Staying up with his treasured p-values would really be something; anyone walking by in the hallway would hear their quiet conversation and assume something else entirely. Ned rubs the heel of his hand into his eyes.

No, Abbot probably just doesn't want to have to lie here in silence after what Susan said. Ned can hardly blame him.

"Hey," he says into the quiet.

Abbot turns to him. He's taken his glasses off. When, Ned didn't notice. It's odd to see Abbot like that, those black frames folded neatly on the nightstand beside him. His face looks more open like this. Younger, even though, like Ned, he already has the suggestion of crow's feet in the corners of his eyes.

"Um, Susan really was joking, right?"

Abbot turns back to his book. "I'd rather not discuss it."

Ned lets out a soft laugh. "C'mon, was she serious?"

Abbot turns a page, silent.

"Did you really have a thing for me?"

"No."

"No?" Ned rolls onto his side and props his head on his hand. "Is that what gave you the idea for a fake relationship between us?"

"Chris gave me the idea; you were there."

"Just wondering." It's flattering that maybe Abbot had an idle thought or two about Ned so long ago. Funny, too. Ned grins over at him. "Is that why you're so weird about this sharing-a-room thing? And at the game?"

"You were my student." Abbot flips a page in his book. "These aren't normal circumstances."

Ned has to laugh at that. "No, they're certainly not. But —that's not exactly a no, man."

"I really don't want to talk about it."

Ned has half a mind to kick Abbot's ankle, but the way Abbot's drawn up tight, he'd probably crawl out of his own skin at the contact. Abbot looks like he might anyway, his shoulders hunched and his eyes fixed on his book.

"I've, you know, had students who are objectively attractive," Ned says slowly. "I mean, I don't go talking about it with a dean, but it's happened."

"I told you; it's not up for discussion."

"I'm just giving you a hard time." Ned flops onto his back. Teasing Abbot's no use—he's not the type of fun that Pat is, or even Lee. The very mention that Abbot might feel something, and he shuts up tighter than a clam. Ned rubs his palms over his face. Besides, anything Abbot might have idly thought is all water under the bridge anyway. Ned was married back then and wasn't exactly one to step out on his wife, no matter how things turned out in the end. And Abbot was probably with his ex at the time—nothing was ever going to happen, then or now.

Though Ned will hand it to Susan, it's funny how things turn out all these years later, him and Abbot now here together. Abbot might've brought that guy—Louis— here once or twice and had this same weekend away that Ned's now sharing with him. Hell, they probably got it on in this bed. Ned looks down at his toes and then over at the twin lines of Abbot's long legs beneath the quilt. He really can't picture that—Abbot rolling around with someone. Enjoying it, even. Lost in it, the way good sex can carry you away from yourself into a hot haze of pleasure.

The memory of Abbot in his towel rises in Ned's mind.

And after Abbot's run, the dampness of sweat at his temples and the nape of his neck. How the cling of his shirt pressed to his shoulders, outlining the thin, lean shape of his frame.

A throb of blood pulses in Ned's groin.

Whoops. He closes his eyes. Null hypothesis. Standard deviations. Not those hands holding that book with long fingers and broad palms. He tries to remember Abbot behind his lectern, a stern tilt to his mouth, and Ned's midterm in front of him.

You're kind of into that, Lee had said, and Ned draws his legs up.

"If it's a problem, I can still find somewhere else to sleep," Abbot says.

Ned jerks his head up to look at him. He didn't—there's no way Abbot could tell what Ned was just thinking. He can't possibly. . . "If what's a problem?" Ned asks.

"What Susan said." Abbot turns another page of his book. Ned slowly relaxes into the pillow.

"Oh, no, it's fine."

"It was inappropriate."

"I mean, it's not like she knew not to bring it up," Ned says.

"And it's not true," Abbot says.

Ned pushes his face into his pillow. "Yeah, I figured."

The soap bubble of amusement that's risen through him pops, settles into a slow beat of what he only belatedly recognizes as disappointment. Hollowness drops softly into where interest and the slightest press of expectancy had sat. He's surprised enough that the shock nearly carries away the entirety of the letdown, but he can still recognize the dullness of disappointment. Moving toward each other . . . no, that wouldn't have been the worst idea to let coalesce, the ocean crashing against the rocks outside, the crispness of the autumn breeze in the air, and the stick of naked sweaty skin beneath the blankets.

Ned blinks at the ceiling. It's been a hell of a long time for him if Abbot's starting to sound appealing. He looks at Abbot again and finds him looking back. His dark shirt, the fall of his hair over his forehead, how different he looks without his glasses. *Oh*, Ned thinks. The moment seesaws. Ned waits for something, for some noise to jar them, some indication of what Abbot's thinking.

Maybe he's going to apologize again.

Maybe he'll lean over here, Ned thinks.

Heat rises tight and full through his chest. But on the verge of motion, paused together in the place between thinking and action, the long moments of silence and their shared inaction drift by them, and the time to have done anything passes by, easing out of the room as steadily as it came.

Abbot looks away again and Ned rolls over, keeping his back to him. It's a long time until he falls asleep.

CHAPTER ELEVEN

NED OPENS his eyes to the dimness of a gray morning, watery light filtering through the curtains and his head heavy. He drags himself up slowly, glad for the neatly made mattress next to him and the empty bathroom. When he makes it downstairs, he's all the happier that there's already coffee in the pot, and he pours himself a mug, cupping it in both hands.

Milk. He wants milk. And to have slept better than he did. Maybe Abbot won't mind if he naps in the car on their drive south. That'll at least prevent any further conversation between them, which sounds to Ned like a hell of a good idea.

"Where's—" Ned stops, the jug of milk in his hand. *Henry*, Susan calls him, when he was about to blurt out *Abbot*.

"Your professor?" Lee asks. She's perched on a chair at the table.

It's too damn early for this. His professor. God. Ned unscrews the lid of the milk and pours too much into his mug. Finds a spoon too and stirs it quickly.

"He's on the phone," Lee says.

Abbot should be looking through Ned's work, but sure enough, when Ned glances onto the porch, Abbot's there, his phone raised to his ear, and the wind whipping through his hair. It looks cold out there. Ned draws his mug closer to himself. All the pleasantness of yesterday has melted into low steely clouds that hang close above the gray of the ocean, and if it's not raining yet, it will be soon.

"We're going to go jump in the water before we go," Lee says. "Wanna come?"

"Um, no."

"Where's the fun in that?" Lee tips her head toward the door to the porch. "Two boring peas in a pod. What're you guys going to do, discuss philosophy?"

That what the kids are calling it these days? Ned would ask if it were any—any—other situation. Last night still burns too bright in his mind. What the hell had he been thinking, letting his mind wander, picturing Abbot like that?

You could've gotten laid, he thinks. He maybe could've gotten laid. Or Abbot might've turned away, and instead of lying there with an unfamiliar wanting, Ned would've fallen asleep utterly mortified for having tried.

Ned wanted to get laid is the real truth, and he swallows against it, coffee burning down his throat. It's been a while since he's even seriously thought about actually having sex. It's been even longer since the option was at all close to being immediately at hand.

He rubs at his eyes, gritty and heavy with poor sleep. He's glad that nothing happened. Abbot was clear enough that he didn't want anything, and really, Ned doesn't either. A messy complication to an already tangled, overly complicated situation they've found themselves in. Better to think nothing of it and move on.

Soon enough they'll be done with this whole ruse and Ned can go get his itches scratched if he still feels like it.

Abbot can too. *Matched on an app*, Aliyah had said, and for the first time that morning, Ned lets himself smile a bit. That would be funny in its own way, flicking through his phone and swiping on various pictures and profiles, only to find one he recognizes. Portland's a small city, it's not impossible that they'd stumble upon each other like that.

Though really, he hates using his phone to meet men or women. The awkwardness of someone he doesn't know well, the baldness of what they're doing, and what they're there for. Ned's always preferred dinner and drinks to just jumping right into bed. *Like last night,* he thinks.

Hooking up with Abbot would've been all too convenient, a closed door and a quiet room, plenty of privacy as long as they kept the noise down. He's gone to a hell of a lot more trouble for less. And he could've, really. Leaned right on over there and kissed Abbot, if the guy wasn't going to do it himself. Nothing at all what Ned might've expected to happen this weekend, but opportunity staring him in the face—it wouldn't have been the worst. No, far from it. Which is an uncomfortable thought in and of itself. Ned might well have actually enjoyed himself. Another body against his, after what has been entirely too long. Hands on him, someone to touch in return . . .

"You with us?" Lee asks. "Earth to Ned."

"Huh?" Ned jerks around to look at her. "Yeah. What?"

"Tell me honestly, is there any amount of money I could offer you to get you to jump in the water?" She nods toward the window at the ocean beyond. Abbot's out there with his back to them, still on his phone. Ned smooths his shirt with his palm.

"No way," he says.

He knows it comes a beat too late. Quickly, he picks up the section of the paper that's sitting on the counter. It's the sports section. Today's even. *I'm tired,* he decides. That's the fogginess gripping him this morning, making his eyes bounce over the page instead of catching on any of the articles. He tries to blink that fatigue away and chases it with a long drink of coffee, though it lingers with a stubbornness that has him staring blankly at an article about the Sox's pitching rotation.

The door to the porch pushes open in a rush of cool air and the scent of rain. Ned frowns. "You okay?"

"Yes," Abbot says, already halfway to the stairs.

"Right." Ned jogs up the stairs after him and catches him outside of their room. He taps the newspaper against the doorframe. "What's going on?"

Abbot looks like he's about to close the door in Ned's face, leaving him there in the hallway. Ned pushes in before it can turn into any sort of reality.

"Hey," he says.

"I have to drive to Boston." Abbot zips up his bag, his phone still folded into his palm. His fingers are tight on it, white around the edges of his nails. "I apologize."

"Okay?" Ned smacks the paper against his thigh. "Why?"

"I'm sorry," Abbot says again. He shrugs into his coat. Ned raises his eyebrows and doesn't move from between him and the door.

"Wanna give me a clue here?"

"I'm already late."

"For?"

Abbot huffs out a breath through his nose. Behind his glasses, the corners of his eyes are drawn tight. Ned doesn't have to fish all that far to ask, "Your dad?"

"It's not any of your business."

"By Boston, do you mean Logan Airport?" Ned's right, he can already tell from the annoyed set of Abbot's shoulders. The guy's going to zip on down to the city's airport on a moment's notice. That's a hell of a way to spend a Sunday. "What's the deal, he says run, you ask where and how fast?"

"I don't do that."

"Huh, sure," Ned says. There's a light knock on the door and Ned reaches for the knob, Abbot already turning away from him again.

"Didn't mean to bother you," Chris says, his hands held up. "Henry, you all right?"

"He's fine," Ned says. "Can I hitch a ride back with you?"

"Henry taking off? Susan can drive you back to Portland if you need, she's heading home just after lunch," Chris says. He drops his voice as if Abbot can't still clearly hear him. "He's really okay?"

Ned casts a look back over his shoulder. Abbot has his coat on, zipping it up a short, sharp jerk. "Says he is."

Chris eases the door shut with a quiet squeak of hinges. Abbot yanks the hem of his jacket to straighten it.

"I'm sorry," Abbot says and then he's gone, his steps creaking down the stairs and the front door shutting behind him.

"Later," Ned says, though it's not like Abbot can hear him.

The front door shuts. This weekend over all the sooner, what with Abbot gone. He should be happy. Slowly, he tosses a shirt toward his backpack and picks up a pair of his socks. He straightens and—oh. There are two laptops on the small table.

"Wait," Ned says, but from outside the window, Ned can hear the low purr of Abbot's car and the crunch of gravel.

Ned picks up Abbot's computer, shiny and unblemished, next to the scratches that mar Ned's own. He'll text Abbot. Or drop it by his office. It's not like he needs his computer right now, hours of driving ahead of him and dear old Dad to hang out with.

By the time Susan's ready to leave, the wind whipping off the water has lost its warmth. Ned tucks his hands into his pockets as he follows her to her car. From the light, midafternoon looks like early evening, and he's sure the gloom will only darken as they drive south, a storm kicked up over the ocean and settling in for the rest of the day and probably into tomorrow. Maybe Abbot's father didn't want to drive in this type of weather and that's why Abbot's giving him a ride. Maybe Ned was right that he's got Abbot trained to respond to every damn whim.

Susan would probably know, he figures as he pulls open the car door. That and more. Ned sits gingerly in the passenger seat. *Were you being serious about Abbot yesterday?* he so wants to ask.

"Thanks for having us this weekend," he says instead.

"You're welcome anytime." Susan shifts the car into gear. "Even if we're not using the house, if you two just want a weekend away. I keep telling Henry, but he's got his work."

"Right." The idea of a weekend up here, just the two of them—Ned presses his lips together and studies the trees gliding past his window, the sky a steely gray behind them.

"You know, he was the real impetus behind Chris's grand plan for this semester."

Ned turns away from his window. "He was?"

"Always working, every hour of the day. The rest of the faculty too, of course, but Henry's been stuck in such a rut these last few months, and nothing Chris said to him made a lick of difference."

"So, we can blame this on Henry," Ned says. The name doesn't fit right in his mouth, but the idea of laying the fault for Chris's absurd initiative at Abbot's feet feels pretty good.

"Not that a culture of overworking isn't rampant across the university," Susan says. "I have half a mind to institute something like this in the rest of the departments. Time with family is so important, as you know."

"Sure."

"Though Henry just needed that push to get his head out of his work and take care of himself. What with his mother."

Ned glances across the car. Whatever Susan means, Ned should probably know by now, though if Ned hadn't run into Abbot's father, he'd probably believe the stork dropped Abbot off, for all that he discusses his family.

Ned clears his throat. "Of course."

"At least that damn Louis is gone now."

Ned shoots another glance at her. That was surprisingly vehement. As casually as he can, he asks, "You weren't a fan?"

"Oh my goodness, no."

Don't ask, Ned tells himself. It's none of his business. Abbot's his former professor and the statistician helping him complete his dissertation. Their ruse of a relationship has already gone further than either of them intended, and he tries to firmly tamp down on that flare of curiosity that sparks through him.

"Of course, we all thought maybe Louis would be like Henry's dad had been," Susan starts.

Stop her, Ned instructs himself. She's clearly just as much of a talker as Chris is, and if he lets her, she's going to spill all sorts of details Abbot wouldn't want Ned knowing. Ned nods for her to go on.

"You've met Charles, Chris said? He was just so lovely when he started dating Cathy."

Cathy, Ned thinks. Abbot's mother, apparently, though that's not exactly the name Ned would've picked out for her. He tries to replace the image he has of her in his mind, as tightly buttoned-up as the rest of the family, with a *Cathy*. That's a Catherine, then, or Cathleen. Caitlin, maybe. *American*, he thinks, not some austere, refined European woman wrapped in fur coats and wearing lipstick.

"Charles was just so distant, but of course around her, he'd just melt," Susan says.

Ned's eyes widen. "Of course," he echoes. Abbot's father, melting. Impossible, all of this.

"But that wasn't Henry and Louis," Susan says. "And Henry deserves better, especially taking so much after his father like he does."

"Absolutely," Ned hears himself say.

"Now Liesl, she's the little troublemaker of the family, got that right from her mother, she did. The only toe Charles ever put out of line was marrying Cathy, while Cathy up and ran away to Switzerland with him."

"She did," Ned echoes.

"Oh, I'm sure Henry's told you this, fresh out of college, no job, no money, and off Cathy goes on her great adventure. I thought her parents would just die. And Liesl, she's just cut from that same cloth. I'm sure she's a handful for Charles to have on his own these days, but he just loves her so much. Of course, he does—she and Henry are all that he has left."

Ned pulls in a breath. Questions flood through him. *What happened, when did it happen, how did it happen?* Cathy's not around anymore, Ned can fill that in for himself, and if he couldn't, Susan's soft, sad smile is enough to color in the edges of those lines. *How did you know her?* he so wants to know. *Why are you and Chris so close with Abbot?*

Don't, Ned tells himself. Move on, change the subject,

bring up about absolutely anything else. "Henry never talks about it."

"He never did," Susan says. "Cathy was sick for so long, and he never said a word."

"Oh," Ned says. *Oh.*

He settles back into his seat. *Sick with what?* he doesn't let himself ask. He looks out the window. *Awful,* he thinks, and something soft settles into his stomach.

"And poor Liesl still doesn't sleep well, from what Charles has said." Susan shakes her head. "Though it's not something you get over, just have to learn a new way of living with it."

"Of course." Ned's mouth is dry. Oh God, how horrible. Liesl's so young. And *Abbot.* His throat hurts a little. "No, yeah, of course."

Susan smiles at him. "Which is why we're so glad Henry's found you. We've been so worried about him for so long now, and then he turns around and is dating again. And dating you, of all people. You're just what he needs." Susan pats at Ned's forearm, warm and gentle, her smile soft with delight.

Ned swallows. Well, shit, now he feels bad. Feels terrible, really. For Abbot, for his family, and now—*shit*—for lying to Chris and Susan about what he and Abbot are really doing. He pushes his palms down his thighs. It's wrong to keep this up, though it feels even more wrong to imagine Liesl awake at night, missing her mom, and Abbot too.

Abbot, who apparently doesn't sleep well either. Ned rubs his hand over his mouth. Maybe he should've been a bit nicer to him.

"I'm just sad Cathy won't ever meet you, and get to see you two together." Susan sighs. "You'd have liked her. You remind me a bit of her, I said that to Chris. She got along with everyone she met—real good with people, she was, just like you."

"Thanks." Ned clears his throat. "Uh, yeah, thanks."

"As long as Henry's happy, that's what matters, I'm sure you'd agree," she says and he forces his head into a nod. God, he's such an utter heel. "And he is, with you. We can both tell."

"Yeah, good," Ned mutters. He shuts his mouth and presses his lips together.

"Chris couldn't believe it when Henry told him. Called me right away, and I was in a meeting. I had six missed calls from him, I thought someone had died." She laughs lightly. Ned tips his chin toward the window and stares blindly at the trees.

"Well," he pushes himself to say, though what the hell comes next, he's not exactly sure. "It was, uh, a surprise to us as well."

She's going to ask about them again. He can feel it in the air between them, wanting to know the details about how the two of them found their way toward each other. She's probably spun a pretty picture in her mind, something cute and light and sweet between them.

He doesn't need to hear more of this—he and Abbot had an agreement, and hell if it ever included the personal details Susan seems so happy to share. Though of course she's happy to chat—she's talking to Abbot's boyfriend, as far as she knows. Ned rubs his fingertips along his eyebrow and clears his throat before she can continue.

"I have Henry's laptop, he left it behind," Ned says for lack of anything better. "Are you going to see him before work?"

"I can just drop you by his place," she says. "I'm meeting Charles for dinner tonight. Are you coming as well?"

"Oh, that's—" Ned shakes his head. "No, I—I can give it to him at the office."

"I'm sure you're right that he'd want it. You have a key?"

Ned nearly cringes before he can catch himself and gives her a quick shake of his head. To his surprise, she reaches over and gives his knee a pat. "Sorry. You're not there yet, are you?"

"No." Good God, no. Not at all.

"Henry's a tough cookie, isn't he?" She shakes her head. "But you're good for him, I'd think. Get him to open up a bit, no?"

Ned forces a smile and turns back to the trees rushing past outside his window, wishing they would move by a little bit quicker.

The low clouds have turned black by the time they reach Portland, and as Susan takes the exit from the highway, they open up in a heavy splatter of rain.

"Glad we got as nice a weekend in as we did." Susan turns the windshield wipers on high.

"Yeah," Ned says. Nice. Ned wants to be back at Pat's with Baxter and a beer.

It's normally so cozy to be in a car with rain thundering down. Now, he just feels trapped as Susan steers them through a part of the city Ned hardly ever goes to. The houses are bigger out here, up on the hill with a view of the water and trees lining the streets. They're a sight for sure, all of their red and orange and yellow glory. Once, he walked up here with Baxter and Peggy in the spring, marveling at the blossoms on the trees and how pretty they were, scattered over the huge lawns.

The block Susan stops at is more demure, but still a far cry from Ned's own street, with its rows of apartments and Pat's bar mixed in among the restaurants and noise of downtown. Here, each row house has a neat front garden, and the doors are painted charming blues and greens against the brick facades of the old New England architecture. Ned unbuckles his seatbelt, sure that he should know which door to head toward.

The house to the right of where Susan stops already has carved pumpkins on its stoop, and the one to the left has a pile of gourds artfully arranged to look like they're tumbling down the steps. Between them sits a house with the lawn raked free of leaves and the walkway swept clean. Ned ducks out of the car, rain plastering his hair to his head before he's taken two steps, and, clutching at his bag and trying to keep it sheltered, he dashes across the sidewalk. Ned raises his fist to knock and hopes Susan isn't watching.

The door opens before Ned's quite ready for it.

"I have your computer," he says. Abbot's feet are bare. Rain drops in a sheet from Abbot's roof and courses over Ned's arms. Ned shoves his backpack forward. "Susan drove me, here, it's getting wet."

And—crap, she's driving off. Apparently intending to leave him here. Which is . . . Ned shakes rain from his face. Perfect is what it is. Well, he can find his own way home. Pat'll pick him up if he asks, and there's always walking. He's soaked through, anyway, water dripping from his hair into his eyes.

Abbot just blinks at him, one hand on the doorframe and the other holding the door.

I'm sorry about your mom, Ned wants to blurt out.

Abbot takes a slow step backward. "Come in," he says.

Ned's got a dog waiting for him at home, a dry change of clean clothes, and a football game to watch with a beer bottle balanced on his knee. He's got work to do. Reading for his classes tomorrow, the notes from the weekend to go over. Curiosity flares through him, same as in the car, and makes him crane his neck to see the slice of Abbot's home behind the slim span of his shoulders.

Don't, he tells himself sternly.

"All right," he says and moves forward into the space that Abbot makes for him.

CHAPTER TWELVE

Ned kind of expected Abbot just slept under his desk in his office, so he certainly never pictured such a delightfully charming home with a brick fireplace, old wood beams, and polished wide pine floors.

Ned has half a mind to ask for ID, just to make sure Abbot didn't break in here at random and get Susan in on the scheme. But there's a framed picture of his sister on the mantel over the fireplace, and nobody except Abbot would read a statistics textbook in their spare time, set on the coffee table like he just put it down.

Water rolls down Ned's face and puddles on the floor where it drips from his clothes. Outside, the rain keeps drumming down. Even his socks are wet.

"Here," Ned says, working his backpack open with cold, stiff hands. He pulls Abbot's laptop out and gives it to him, his fingers leaving clammy, damp prints on the metal. "I didn't see your cord lying around."

"I have it."

"Good."

Ned's not entirely sure what to do with his hands when Abbot takes the laptop. Even with the rain pounding at the closed front door, Abbot's place is quiet. Most of the lights are off and the house has a certain early evening dimness to its rooms, as if whatever Abbot was doing, night began to fall around him before he quite noticed.

"Sorry if it got wet," Ned finally says. *What a warm welcome*, he can't help but think. *What happened to your mom?* he still wants to ask.

"It didn't."

"Great."

Ned wants to poke through Abbot's house. See whatever room sits beyond the living room and what lies up those narrow stairs. The kitchen's in the back of the house, by the look of it, the edge of a counter visible down the hallway. Ned would put money on it being unfairly gorgeous.

He slings his bag over his shoulder, creasing his wet shirt against his skin. He tries not to grimace, a shiver wanting to crawl up his spine. "Anyway. Susan completely abandoned me here, but I'll get out of your hair."

"Thanks for bringing this back," Abbot says.

Ned pats at his pocket for his phone and shrugs. "Sure."

Then he pats at his other thigh. And sticks his hands into his back pockets, too. Quickly, he drops his bag back at his feet and shoves his hand into the front pouch, and then the main one, sorting through the weekend's socks and shirts.

"Oh, goddamn it." His own computer, his toothbrush, his shaving kit—the rest is just underwear, and Ned's not exactly going to pull that out and dump it on Abbot's floor. "Do you have Susan's number? I left my phone in her car."

Abbot nods, pulling his out. He leaves Ned standing there shivering, shifting his weight in shoes that squish damply around his feet as Abbot calls. And hangs up. And then calls again, only to finally just shake his head. "She didn't answer."

"Yeah, I got that." Ned holds his hand out. "Can I borrow it? I'll call Pat." Quickly, he Googles the bar's number, 'cause hell if he knows Pat's cell off the top of his head. "Hey, is Pat there?"

"How can I help you?" someone asks. A kid's voice, younger than Pat, and Ned sighs.

"Pat," he says again. "I need to talk to him. It's Ned."

"Pat's not in."

"Who's this?" Ned asks.

"I can take a message."

Ned shakes his head. "Pat, I need him. Where is he?"

"He's not here."

"Can you look upstairs?"

"He said not to bother him."

"Bother him. It's fine."

"I think he's out."

"You think or you know?" Ned asks.

"I'll have him give you a call."

"No, I don't have my—dammit." The phone beeps at him as the kid ends the call. Ned flicks back to the screen of apps. "Any chance you could give me a lift?"

"I don't have my car right now," Abbot says.

Ned tips his head. He wants to ask, but no, he's not pushing for details; he's leaving. "I'll walk."

"You're not going to walk," Abbot says.

"Sure, I am." Outside, the wind whips water at the windowpane hard enough to sound like it's pinging off the glass.

Abbot cocks an eyebrow at him. Ned sighs, loudly.

"Well, I'll wait at least a couple minutes."

Abbot nods and just keeps standing there. And so Ned does too, rocking onto his heels and then his toes, his feet squishing in his shoes, and a drop of rainwater rolling down the back of his neck to soak into his already damp shirt.

"My father has it," Abbot says.

"Has what?"

"My car."

"Oh." Ned nods. That makes no sense, but whatever—he's standing here in his statistics professor's house because the dean of the university dropped him off because they're supposed to be dating. Nothing makes sense and his feet are getting cold. "Okay."

"Or I would drive you."

"Yeah, thanks."

Ned works his tongue around his mouth. If he tried to, he's sure he could hear Abbot's watch ticking.

"We can do some work," Abbot says.

Ned nods, reaching down for his bag. "Yeah, let's do that," he says quickly.

Ned's shoes squeak as Abbot leads him into the house, past the living room and into the dining room that separates them from the kitchen. It's nice. *Formal*, Ned can't help but think. And kind of odd, for a guy who lives alone to have a table with this many chairs. What does he do, eat by himself at one end of the table? Maybe he has company sometimes. Chris and Susan at the very least.

Ned pauses with his backpack midair, then sets it on the floor. It wouldn't do to get one of the nice chairs wet. Maybe he'll just stand so his jeans won't soak any of the furniture. Or maybe he really will just leave and not have to stand here, all of Susan's words ringing in his ears. *I'm so sorry about your mom*, he wants to say again and bites at the inside of his cheek.

"Um," Ned starts. Eloquent, isn't he? He pokes his tongue against his teeth. But it's not fair that Ned knows, and Abbot doesn't know that he knows. And moreover, that Ned knows that Abbot doesn't know that he knows, and—

dammit. He rakes wet hair off his forehead. "Look, I have to tell you, Susan really thinks we're seeing each other."

Abbot draws out a chair across the table and sets his laptop down. "Good."

"Yeah, good." Ned puts his computer on the table and then lingers before sitting, his hand on the back of the chair. "Except that she—she went into some details. About you, I mean."

Abbot's eyes come up slowly. "Okay," he says as he sits.

"And, I'm—" Ned shifts his weight.

Ned could stop there, and if Abbot wants to know the particulars, he could ask. He probably won't, and Ned doesn't have to offer, and they can move on. But that doesn't feel right. Talking about it doesn't feel right either, but keeping quiet is even worse.

Ned tightens his hand around the chair and softly, he says, "She mentioned, your mom? I'm so sorry, Abbot."

Abbot doesn't blink, doesn't move. He doesn't even look like he's breathing. Outside, rain drums against the window and pounds down on the roof. A siren warbles a few streets away.

"I am," Ned says.

Blinking too fast, Abbot looks away.

Ah, hell. Ned shifts his weight, floundering for something to smooth this over. Or jolt Abbot from wherever he's gone, some private, hidden place behind the blankness in his eyes.

"I didn't know," Ned says, like that will help. Of course, he didn't know. Nobody knew, or Ned would've heard about it from the rest of the department. A card would've gone around at the very least. Abbot might not be friends with any of them, but he's still one of theirs. "Um, I won't say anything to anyone."

Very slowly, Abbot opens his laptop and stares at it, the blue light reflecting off his glasses.

Shut up, Ned tells himself.

"Susan said you were trying to put your life back together," Ned says. "So, I'm sorry if I was—I don't know, hard on you, I guess. I didn't realize you were going through all of that."

Abbot doesn't even nod, just sits there as frozen as a computer that needs to be rebooted. Ned apparently just gave whatever thread Abbot's hanging by a good, solid yank, fraying something that was already worn thin.

How long has he managed to live like this? Ned would so like to know. A year at least, like Susan had mentioned. Before that too, Ned's sure, if his mom was sick, if Louis was really such an ass. Ned studies Abbot, trying to not see his former professor but just a guy handed the shortest straw of the bunch. The thought renders Abbot in a softer image than the one Ned normally carries of him, blurring the edges of that austere expression from haughtiness into too familiar self-defensiveness.

Ned knows that thousand-yard stare all too well. Pat used to wave his hand in front of Ned's face, and he never had the energy to do much more than turn away, wanting to be left to the mire of thoughts he'd wrapped himself in. Ned adjusts his grip on the back of the chair. Maybe this is what Pat felt all those times, poking at Ned's shoulder until Pat would huff and just start shaking him.

But Ned's not going to prod at Abbot until annoyance gets the better of him. Ned can't exactly bounce around the house and wrestle Abbot, either, beating him with a couch cushion until Abbot feels marginally better—or at least feels something. Pat certainly does have his own special touch. A small piece of the ache in Ned's chest loosens.

In the kitchen, Ned finds a kettle sitting on the stove.

He lights the burner and sorts through perfectly organized cupboards. Boxes of granola, labeled containers of flour and sugar, plain white dinner plates, salad plates, bowls—he finds a mug and pulls it down, and opens tins on the counter until he finds one full of teabags.

And then he waits, his mouth pushed to the side, sure that Abbot's going to come in here any moment and just bodily shove him out the door and back into the rain. Ned's back crawls, his shirt's still wet and a chill growing through him. Abbot's kitchen is entirely too pretty, granite counter-tops and hardwood floors, and Ned's here, dripping all over it.

The guy's got a damn yard too, though he's probably never had the good sense to stick a grill out there and kick back with a couple beers. Ned peers out the window, and no, there's nothing other than some flowerbeds, a tree, and a tidy square of fenced-in grass.

Milk or no milk, Ned debates as he pours boiling water into the mug. He bobs the tea bag by the little string, and then just grabs the quart of milk from the refrigerator, a spoon, and the mug, and brings it with him. Gently, he sets the tea in front of Abbot.

Abbot doesn't react. Just drags his finger across his trackpad, rows of numbers filling his screen. "Did you look at the notes I left you?" Abbot asks.

"Not yet." Ned should go back around to the other side of the table. *How can you focus on work right now?* he wants to ask Abbot. Ned hovers over him, and his mouth works, empty and unsure of what words might make Abbot feel better.

Abbot would probably feel better if Ned just left. Gave him his space, got out of his hair, and never brought any of this up again. Abbot could go back to his austere wall of silence and Ned could bumble along the next few weeks pretending Susan didn't say anything.

But how raw can that grief be, to be working at the corners of Abbot's mouth like that as he furiously studies his screen? Gently, Ned reaches out, slow enough that if Abbot looks at him, he'll see Ned's hand before it settles on his shoulder.

Abbot's slim. And warm. And Ned's hands are probably cold through Abbot's shirt. Ned waits, but Abbot doesn't twitch away, just turns to eye Ned's fingers. Ned lets his thumb move back and forth over the bony knob of Abbot's shoulder.

Silently, quickly, Abbot stands. He was sitting and now he's up and his chair's between them and he got there faster than should be possible. Ned's hand falls back to his side.

"Would you like dry clothes?" Abbot straightens his chair. And his laptop, moving it so it's perfectly aligned with the edge of the table.

"Abbot," Ned starts. Abbot's cheek twitches. Ned clears his throat. He can say yes or not, but it looks like Abbot's going to walk out of here anyway, so he nods.

Upstairs Ned probably shouldn't peer around, but he does anyway. There's a small bedroom, books in neat piles on the bed and a desk set against the wall. Abbot's home office, apparently. It's not a huge house, not like some in the city are, but sure as hell nice. The larger bedroom Abbot walks into looks over the street, with a view of the trees and probably on a sunnier day, plenty of natural light. It's got those gorgeous old windows Ned's always loved, warped glass and layers of paint on the sills, from years and years of different colors, one after the next. He rubs his hand over the pitted wood.

Ned eyes Abbot's back as he sorts through his dresser. It looks old too, all worn oiled wood. The bedroom's nice, even if the gray duvet is pulled achingly tight across the bed and the pillows are too precisely set against the headboard. They're down, he's sure, and the sheets are likely softer than should be legal. Maybe Ned should've stayed downstairs. That set to Abbot's shoulders could be from having someone else up here—Ned in his life, in his house, and now in his bedroom.

Abbot pulls out a plain white T-shirt. It looks a size smaller than what Ned typically wears, but goosebumps are working their way over him, and he's not going to complain. *Tea*, he thinks again. He can get changed, and they can go back downstairs, and he'll make himself a mug. He shucks his shirt off and lays it over the footboard of the bed, rather than get the gray comforter wet.

"Thanks," Ned says as Abbot sets out a pair of sweatpants too, Callahan's seal on the left leg in red against the gray fabric. Ned doesn't hesitate unbuckling his belt and trying to unstick his jeans from his legs, happy to be out of them.

"Of course," Abbot says and finally looks at Ned. At his face, first, then Ned's bare chest, and then down, as Ned steps out of his pants.

Ned looks down too, where his boxers cling to his thighs. He looks up again and Abbot's cheeks flush pink, his eyes darting from the bed to the dresser to the closet door.

Ah. Well. Ned knows that look. *We all knew Henry had quite the thing for you for years*, Susan had said. Apparently, she might've been right. Ned licks at his lips and Abbot turns, sorting through a drawer Ned's sure doesn't need to be fussed with.

Abbot's rubbed raw, no matter how tightly he draws up his shoulders, trying to fight that fact. Picking up his father today, Ned finding out so much about his past—hell, probably just a weekend with so many people. Abbot might as well have "introvert" stamped across his forehead, and here he is, stuck with Ned in his house when he probably was so looking forward to the drone of silence and an evening to himself.

Ned's chest softens all the more, the thawing that started in the car easing through him now. For once, the itch doesn't rise through him to butt heads with Abbot. The two of them are just trying to find their way through a bad streak, sort out days into weeks and form them into months. Rebuilding a life sucks, very differently for them, but it sucks all the same. And maybe it could suck a little less, if Abbot wants it to.

If Ned does too. Ned holds his wet pants in front of him. Carefully, he folds them in half, and then in half again, and sets them next to his shoes. Abbot's neck flexes as Ned walks across the room. Abbot shifts two pairs of dark socks to the side in the drawer he's playing with and a tendon tightens at the base of his jaw.

This is a safe enough chance to take. It's just Abbot—if he pushes Ned away, a hand on the center of his chest and a firm, sharp shake to his head, it's only Abbot, of all people. Embarrassing, sure, but at least they're not trapped at Chris's house. Ned can slink off across the city if this goes south. Getting back on that horse, like Pat's always going on about. Though this is a pony, more like. Or a very large dog.

Ned should've figured this out last night. Just kissed Abbot, and if he had, it'd be all the simpler now. He flexes his fingers and Abbot's gaze shifts toward him, peering from the corner of his eyes, away again, and back. They were already in bed and warm and it would've been so easy— easier than now, at least, as Ned touches two fingers to the inside of Abbot's elbow, drawing his hand away from his dresser, his stomach fluttering with nerves.

A crisis of confidence, he hears in Abbot's voice.

Ned frowns, leans forward, and kisses him.

The inside of Abbot's lip slips wet against Ned's, and his glasses bump Ned's cheek. Ned can smell Abbot's skin, up this close. Abbot kisses back softly, more gently than the hard line of his mouth would suggest. Ned pulls back for a breath, waits to see if he's going to get a shove or a look or just the silence of Abbot walking out of the room.

Their noses brush, and Ned kisses him again, surer this time. That's more like it, Abbot's lower lip between Ned's, Abbot's head tipping to the side, and the line of his neck beneath Ned's palm. Abbot steps forward and fits his hand to Ned's side.

And that's—that's good, Abbot's fingers pressing into his skin, the taste of him in Ned's mouth, the press of his cheek against Ned's nose. Ned remembers this, the spark in his stomach as their tongues brush, the suspense of where Abbot's hand will slide when he slips his palm around to Ned's back.

Ned brings his hands up to Abbot's chest. His sweater is really soft. The hand on Ned's back tightens, and Abbot pulls at Ned's lower lip with his own. Ned steps into Abbot's body, his slacks brushing Ned's bare knees and his sweater warm against Ned's stomach.

It's been so long since Ned's kissed another guy. The scratch of it, the height that matches his own, the strength in Abbot's grip on him—yeah, he likes this. There's a firm collarbone to run his palm over, the flatness of a stomach to press his hand to, and Ned does. Opens his mouth, ducks his fingers under the hem of Abbot's shirt, and holds onto him too tight, his other hand gripping the side of Abbot's neck and keeping him there as Ned kisses him, draws back to change angles, and kisses him again.

A noise catches in the back of Ned's throat when Abbot lets him swipe his tongue into his mouth. It's good. He tastes good. Feels good too, all slim taut muscles in Ned's hands. A power in Abbot's body, locked up in the tightness of his back, the play of muscle over his ribs. Abbot's fingertips push under Ned's waistband, grazing the skin beneath the elastic of his boxers, reminding Ned all over again that he's mostly naked and Abbot's clothed, and they should work on fixing that.

He rubs his palm over the line of Abbot's spine instead, fingers working into the dip of the muscles and his other thumb stroking over the bristle of his jaw. Ned's lips are wet. And he needs to breathe, he's sure, but the wet smack of their mouths isn't something he wants to stop. Opened eyes, air pulled in, the need to look at each other—no, Ned doesn't want to have to find his way through awkwardness and hesitancy. The bed is just behind Abbot, and when Ned pushes, Abbot takes a step backward.

That's so much better. Horizontal, Abbot spread out below him for Ned to crawl over—it's real damn good, a long body pinned beneath Ned's, and a large hand warm on Ned's ass. Abbot squeezes and Ned's boxers are in his way. Both of their ways. Abbot's pants too, and the sweater that Ned works up to his ribs.

Ned kisses him harder and lets his hands explore. Abbot's got a nice, defined stomach and Ned rubs his thumb across the line of hair leading down from Abbot's navel. Abbot's knee knocks into the outside of Ned's thigh, pins him there as Ned's thumb slips lower on that flat plane of muscle above the line of Abbot's leather belt.

Ned unbuckles it and blood beats in his cock. Abbot must be able to feel how hard he is, and Ned lets himself press to the firm line of his thigh, relief singing through him and a sound climbing from his throat.

"Jesus," Ned breathes when Abbot slips his hand between them and palms him.

Ned squeezes his eyes tight. Abbot's sure of himself, no soft sort of fumbling, just a firmness to how he works his fingers over the outside of Ned's boxers. Thin cotton and that warm touch—Ned lets his hips flex into it and pleasure sings hot across his skin. He remembers this. Being touched by someone else. He likes it, too. The unpredictability of someone else's hand on him, when he's so damn used to his own. He likes touching too. And kissing. And the warm, solid length of another body pressed beneath his own.

"Like that," he says when Abbot's hand hesitates. That's a long, thick ridge under Abbot's slacks and Ned slides his hand toward it, but Abbot's chin tips to the side when Ned leans down to kiss him again. Ned's stomach sinks. "What?"

Abbot's eyes are wide. "The door," he says.

"The door?"

Abbot's hand on the front of Ned's boxers shifts to shove at his hip. "Move. Please."

"Abbot?"

"Be quiet." Abbot sits up, pushing Ned off him. Quickly, Abbot pulls his belt closed. "Did we lock the door when you came in?"

The timbre of the fall of rain changes. That's from the front door being open, isn't it?

"Oh," Ned says. "No, I don't think so."

"Henry?" someone calls and Abbot pats at his hair, smoothing it down.

"Susan?" Abbot calls back.

"I've got Ned's phone," she yells.

"Great," Ned mutters.

He plucks at the soaked fabric over his crotch and stares up at the ceiling. His blood sings beneath his skin. He wants to grab his cock and stroke it. He wants Abbot to touch him again, start up a rhythm that Ned can rock into. He squeezes his eyes shut.

Chill, he wants to shout at himself. Think of something —anything else—that damn bell curve of Abbot's, whatever he calls it—a normal distribution. But all Ned can remember is Abbot's silhouette against the projector screen, his shirt hugging his bicep as he gestures, the long lines of his legs. Ned puffs up his cheeks and holds his breath.

"And your dad has your car here," Susan calls with a cheer in her voice that sends cold through Ned's stomach. Abbot's too, by the widening of his eyes. "Thought we'd drop it off and take mine. Is this a bad time?"

"No," Abbot says. Ned gestures frantically to himself. Not a bad time, his ass. The stairs creak, weight on them. "Not at all."

"What the actual hell?" Ned whispers, but Abbot's already grabbing the shirt from the floor and shoving it at him.

"Have you met Ned?" Susan asks, her voice lower. She's talking to someone. "Henry's boyfriend? Oh, he's lovely, Charles."

A pause. Abbot's eyes close.

"I've met Louis," a voice says. Deep and accented. Abbot doesn't look like he's breathing. "Who, as I last heard it, is his current boyfriend."

Slowly, Ned stands. There's the hysteria of a too-loud laugh lodged in his throat. *What the fuck?* he wants to ask of Abbot, of Susan downstairs. Himself, too. Behind him, the bedspread is wrinkled, no longer the pristine state Abbot clearly prefers. And Ned's blood is still beating too fast. He can smell Abbot on him, a touch of his soap clinging to Ned's skin. Abbot's stock-still, a hand on the doorknob. The stairs creak again.

"It's okay," Ned says. He's lying, he knows. His chest is flushed. He steps closer to Abbot and carefully, gently, like approaching Baxter when there's thunder clapping outside or a vacuum running in the next room, and lays his fingers on Abbot's shoulder. Ned still wants to laugh. Or maybe pop a window open and shimmy down the brick facade. Hell, Abbot can come with him, if he wants. "Hey, it'll be okay."

CHAPTER THIRTEEN

ABBOT'S MOUTH presses into a bloodless line.

"You didn't tell your dad?" Ned whispers loudly. He shoves his arms into the T-shirt. Backward. "Shit." He spins it around. "About your ex? That you broke up?"

Abbot's eyes close. "Clearly."

"Henry?" Susan calls.

"Coming," Abbot says more loudly.

"Jesus, man." Ned tries to peer past Abbot, yanking the shirt down around his stomach. "He's going to think you're cheating on him."

"Yes."

"It's been a year, hasn't it?" Ned jams his legs into Abbot's sweatpants.

"To be fair, it hasn't come up." Abbot's chest rises on a long inhale. Ned's still too warm. And standing too close to Abbot. He backs up a step and trips over too-long pant legs. Quickly, he yanks the sweatpants up higher.

"How convenient," Ned says, and Abbot ignores him, smoothing his sweater once more like it isn't already perfectly, painfully neat.

"Hey," Susan says as Abbot walks down the stairs. Ned

makes himself follow, a hand on the banister. Susan's smiling, her raincoat dripping on the floor and her hair damp. And beside her Abbot's father—even if Ned hadn't met him before, the resemblance is still unmistakable. Same height, same build, and eye to eye when Abbot steps off the last stair. Ned stays behind, as if he could blend into the staircase, shrink into the risers and be left out of this.

"What's this?" Charles asks, and hell no, Ned's getting the fuck out of here.

"Well," Ned says brightly and puts on a smile. "I should go. Thanks for bringing my phone back."

"Oh, of course, of course," Susan says. "But really, we're just swinging by; we didn't mean to interrupt."

"No problem," Ned says. He's wearing a different shirt than she dropped him off in. And pants. And he's barefoot. An oversight, for his grand escape. And probably a very clear indicator of what they were just doing. He keeps his smile pasted on his face.

Susan's still smiling too, like the standoff between father and son is just par for the course. They look as if they're about to start circling each other any moment like giant irritated cats. It's like a slow-motion car crash. If this was Ned's father, he'd be having a laugh over the two of them caught upstairs, and Ned'd have gotten a slug on the arm and a gentle whack on the head for leaving his phone lying around.

Ned clears his throat. Nothing for it but to soldier through. With a deep breath, he steps forward. "Ned," he says, holding his hand out. "Nice to meet you."

Abbot drops his stare to his feet. A long horrible beat hangs in the air.

"Charles," Abbot's father says, and only slowly lifts his hand to shake Ned's. That cool stare must be some sort of genetic predisposition. The back of Ned's neck itches.

And then he's ignored all over again as Charles turns that look back to Abbot with a shoulder angled toward Ned. Well, that, Ned finds all sorts of ordinary, though the head turned away from him normally doesn't have dark hair peppered with white.

"Explain," Charles says, and then launches into a litany of quick, coldly soft German. Abbot's chin tips away, his eyes a blank stare toward the back of his house.

The door blows open, rain splattering onto the floorboards and the wind whipping in, damp and chilled. Liesl shoves the door closed again, the cuffs of her raincoat tugged over her hands and water sliding from her hood as she pushes it back. Ned shifts his weight. He wants to go.

"Liesl," Susan says. "Come here, darling. This is your brother's friend, Ned. Come say hello to him."

"I don't want to go to dinner," Liesl says. "I want to stay here."

"Henry," Charles says.

"Hey there," Ned says to her, trying for the friendliest smile he can manage. He wants to go, go, *go*.

Liesl pushes loose hair from her face with her palm and says, "I'm not going to dinner."

"You are." Charles turns back to Abbot and starts talking again.

"No," Liesl says. She's mostly raincoat, the shadow from her hood over her face. Still, brown hair peeks out and when her mouth pinches in a frown . . . yep, Ned's seen that frustrated, stubborn expression a time or ten before.

"She can stay," Abbot says.

"You said you were busy." Charles tips his head toward the dining room where their laptops sit, the light on against the gloom of the house, and the chairs pushed back. Abbot's lips press together again, hard enough to turn white.

"It won't be a long dinner," Susan says, rubbing Liesl's shoulder. "And I want to hear all about how school is."

"We will discuss this tomorrow," Charles says to Abbot. He says something to Liesl that Ned can't understand and she crosses her arms.

Abbot shakes his head. "We won't."

"We will," Charles says firmly. With one last look at his son, he crosses to the door and holds it open for Liesl, shepherding her through with a hand on her back.

"Enjoy your evening," Susan says, and finally hands Ned's phone over. He watches her, that smile she has and the wave she gives Abbot. How commonplace this type of family scene must be, to not even faze her.

And then the door shuts behind Susan, and it's just the two of them. Ned rubs his thumb over his phone. Rain thunders down outside, obscuring the rumble of the car pulling away from the curb.

"Well," Ned says into the silence. He's not entirely sure that Abbot's actually breathing. "Your dad seems nice."

Ned gets a look. One that was just on Charles's face.

Abbot lets out a long breath. Slowly, he crosses from the bottom of the stairs, sinking down onto the edge of the couch. His hands dangle between his knees as he stares at the coffee table.

"You okay?" Ned asks. He should be back on his couch with Baxter whining to go out, and Pat prattling on as Ned tries to watch the Patriots game. He could be there. Now. Or in a few minutes, if he gets going. He can still smell Abbot on his skin.

He sits beside him and leans forward, trying to catch his eye. Abbot's hands hang limp and lifeless between his thighs. Ned looks away. That palm was on the front of his pants. Would've gotten a lot further too, had Susan not come a-knocking. Ned rubs his fingers over his mouth.

"I apologize for my father," Abbot says quietly.

Ned holds his hands out in a wide shrug. His elbow comes too close to Abbot's arm. "How is that your fault?"

"He's . . . difficult."

"Well, you come by it honestly, at least." Ned shrugs again. "What exactly happened? You didn't bother to share with him that you and the good Mr. Louis parted ways?"

"It's none of your business."

"Might not be," Ned says. "You going to tell him that you and I aren't actually . . ." Ned waves between them.

From behind his glasses, Abbot tracks the movement. "He would tell Susan."

"Who would tell Chris," Ned finishes for him. He leans back on the couch. Abbot's hair is messed up. Just slightly, there on the back of his head. Anyone else and Ned'd probably smooth it down for him. "Listen. That clearly wasn't . . . whatever's up with your dad, we don't have to do this. Keep this up. I get it."

His dad apparently cares who Abbot dates. Cares a lot, by the looks of it. Apparently not about gender, but whether that person is good enough for his son. He must've known Louis and liked him, probably thought he was a much better match than Ned. Of course, Louis probably never had the audacity to be barefoot in sweatpants and T-shirt, with rumpled wet hair. Ned runs his fingers through it, trying to straighten it.

Abbot's head tips just far enough to show Ned his cheek and the shadow of stubble over his jaw.

"If it's too much," Ned says again.

"You say that like we have a choice."

"Well, look, abandoning my work this close to finishing isn't my favorite option but . . . well, it looks like you've got a handful to deal with already. I'm not here to make your day any worse."

"I don't talk about my personal life with my father."

"Yeah, I got that," Ned says.

"And I'm not going to start. Our . . . arrangement is immaterial to my relationship with him."

"He's always been like that?" Ned laces his fingers over his stomach. Abbot does indeed come by his whole schtick as honestly as anything, if that's how he was raised. Though what did Susan say? Charles would melt around his wife? Impossible. "Don't you and Liesl ever want to give him the old 'So Long, Farewell'?"

"Again, that movie is set in Austria."

Ned hums a few bars under his breath. It only makes Abbot stand up. With an entirely too hard flick, he turns on the lamp next to the couch. Ned blinks against the glare, though the room does look nice like this. Cozy. He wonders if that fireplace actually works.

And then Abbot's gone, leaving Ned on the couch as he walks toward the back of the house. Ned waits, wondering if he's just pacing, but there's no footsteps back across the floors, just the sound of the refrigerator opening and then a cork popping out of a bottle.

"Oh." Ned lets a grin spread across his face as he pops up off the couch and makes for the kitchen. "Is this occasionally?"

Abbot ignores him, pouring white wine into a glass.

"That for me?" Ned asks. "'Cause I can sort of imagine you just going straight for the bottle."

"Funny."

"Cheers." Ned snags the glass from Abbot's hand. "Thanks for offering, so kind of you."

It's good wine, a hell of a lot nicer than Ned's had in a long time. There're probably worse ways to spend an evening. Ned stops himself from even glancing toward the stairs that lead to Abbot's bedroom. Better ways too, though. Slowly, he swirls his wine around his glass.

"He's different with Liesl," Abbot says. His glass is far fuller than the one Ned holds. With the heel of his hand, he works the cork back into the bottle.

"Who is?"

"My father."

"Huh." Ned sips at his wine again. Abbot just stares at his. "Well, who doesn't want a do-over kid?"

"Chris once told me that you're emotionally intelligent." Abbot eyes him. "I remain unconvinced."

"I'm serious." Ned waves his glass around in emphasis. "You think it isn't appealing as all hell? A blank slate to start over with, after you learn so much from the first go-round?"

"Is that what you want?"

"Me?" Ned asks. "Look, I get it, is all."

Abbot picks up his wine but doesn't drink it. "What would you have changed?"

"I wouldn't have started a goddamn doctorate program."

Though that's not right, is it? He applied well before they'd known Peggy was on her way. Ned takes a long sip.

"That's all?"

"You want a what's what of my terrible parenting? Will it make you feel better? I live two hours away from my daughter, and I'm lucky to see her more than a handful of times a month." The list of things he'd have done different-ly . . . he sips at his glass again. "It never ends up how you plan is all that I meant. Everything's a good idea in theory, but in practice turns into some sort of upside down funhouse mirror of a mess."

Abbot's quiet again, his eyes on Ned. Well, he can chew that over for as long as he wants. Ned crosses his arms over his chest, his wineglass bumping against his side. Outside, the rain keeps drumming down. A hell of a night, isn't it?

Ned sips at his wine until Abbot's special brand of waiting around in interminable silence grates at him, and he gestures with his glass again.

"Jen was unhappy here in Portland," he says. "I didn't notice as well as I should've."

"Jen?"

"My ex." New baby, new city, their friends and family back in Boston. Ned buried in books more often than not. He stares down into his glass. His anger over all of it is so much duller now, a hard sort of ache at what might've been if he'd gotten his head out of the sand any sooner, if Jen'd bothered to tell him what was really going on with her, instead of a litany of exasperation and annoyance.

There's a long damn list of things he'd have done differently. Jen seems happier now, at least. And he's fine, or some version of it. With his forefinger and thumb, he rubs at his eyes.

From behind his palm, he adds, "She was sleeping with Jeff."

"Your friend Jeff?"

Ned rubs harder. "We're not friends."

"Former friend."

Ned pushes at his eyes again and drops his hand. "While we were still married. He was my best friend and they were . . . yeah. I found out later. A lot later. So no, I wouldn't have minded if that had gone differently."

"I'm sorry," Abbot says.

Ned drains half of his glass. "Yeah, me too."

For too long, he stares down at his wine, slowly rolling the stem of the glass back and forth in his fingers. *Fucking Jeff*, Pat had taken to calling him, until he'd stopped bringing him up altogether. Pat had stayed angry for longer than Ned, since Ned'd skipped forward onto a deep, long series of morose months. Years, nearly, by this point. With a breath, Ned pulls himself upward again, propping himself more firmly against the counter and unbending from his slouch.

"So, that's the story," he says. "More or less. Just in case you wanted some commiseration on this really fantastic day you're having."

The two of them here, with their wine and the messy, painful pasts. However Abbot ended things with Louis, it probably wasn't pretty. Never is. Just different types of clusterfucks, the type of goodbyes nobody wants to anticipate in those heady early days at the beginning of a relationship.

"Anyway. I hear you about wanting to finish up your grant. Try sharing a kid with someone. You don't get a final presentation and paper out of it, and then can just walk away."

Abbot nods, his eyes on the dark panes of glass of his kitchen windows. Their own reflections stare back at them, wavy and watery with night beyond them. Ned can watch twofold as Abbot turns toward him, takes a sip of his wine, and asks, "Would you like to come back upstairs?"

Ned jerks his head up. Abbot looks back with an entirely too benign expression.

"Is that a good idea?"

"That's not an answer."

Ned ruins everything he touches. Surely Abbot knows that by now.

"That was just my kind of luck that your family showed up," Ned says. "Your house is probably going to be struck by lightning."

"Is that a no?"

"No." Ned licks at his lips. "It's not."

Ned trails up the stairs after Abbot with a churn in his stomach. What a terrible idea. Though, isn't this entire fake relationship they're embroiled in? Everything they're doing together—it's all been a bad plan from the get-go. Maybe this is some modicum of payoff.

Abbot's bedroom is silent except for the rain. He takes his watch off and Ned swallows. While he'd far prefer to be with someone he's actually seeing, as much as he dislikes sex with strangers, there's something simple about it. Being caught here in the middle of that spectrum is the most awkward. A horrible beat of quiet stretches. Ned curls his toes against the floor. Abbot's got a nice rug beneath his bed. Soft, and matches the quilt.

Ready? Ned nearly wants to ask. Surely there should be some sort of more natural lead-in to hopping into bed together, though this is apparently the way they're going to do it instead: Abbot just standing there and Ned shifting his weight.

Well, nothing else for it. Ned closes his eyes and kisses Abbot.

And Abbot kisses him right back. Which is a hell of a lot better than just staring at each other, their mouths working against each other's and Abbot's hand settling on Ned's shoulder. A lot, a lot better. Ned moves closer and angles his head to the side. Slowly, he kisses Abbot again. Abbot's mouth is soft and he's responsive, his fingers drifting around the back of Ned's neck, his body pressing close.

Yeah, Abbot feels good. Kissing feels good too, Ned remembers all over again. Putting his hands on someone else and being touched in return. Foreign after all this time, like a nearly forgotten memory rising through him as he fits his hands to Abbot's sides and kisses him more firmly.

Abbot's hand drifts from Ned's neck down his back, and then he's lifting Ned's shirt. Oh hell yeah, Ned can get behind that decision. He skims it off and drops it on top of his wet clothes, still slung over the footboard. Then he stops.

It's Abbot's shirt, not his own. He folds it and sets it on Abbot's dresser.

When he turns back around, Abbot's sifting through the nightstand drawer. He pulls out a bottle of lube and a condom and sets them next to the lamp.

Ned's skin heats, despite the chill of no shoes and now no shirt.

Abbot skims his sweater off over his head. Ned watches as he unbuttons the shirt beneath, the fabric parting with each loose button. He's . . . Jesus.

He wants to touch Abbot's abs. The sharp, fine lines of his pecs, peeking out between the open sides of his shirt, the points of his hipbones behind the strap of his belt.

"Anything you don't like?" Ned asks. His voice sounds too loud, shattering through the quiet drum of rain.

"Idle chatter," Abbot says.

"Probably coulda guessed that."

"What did I just say?"

Abbot's stomach is warm. And his skin jumps when Ned brushes his fingers over it. "I heard you."

Abbot's hands fall to his own belt buckle. Ned stares the entire time it takes Abbot to work it open, and then his pants too. Zipper and button gaping open over boxer briefs, now that's a hell of a look.

This is—they're really doing this. Ned's about to have sex for the first time in—he blinks. He slips his hand down Abbot's side. It's all warm skin and the harder bump of ribs that give way to the soft dip of his waist. Gently, Ned tugs Abbot's shirt off those long arms. His pulse skitters through him in a hot race of anticipation.

Abbot takes his shirt before Ned can toss it aside and lays it neatly on his dresser. Of course he does. Muscles play over his torso under thin skin. He's not shy as he drops his pants, his thumbs hooked into the waistband. Businesslike, almost. Ned draws his finger along the black elastic of Abbot's boxers. There's interest there, pushing at the fabric. Ned touches his thumb to the tip of that bulge. Not even an inhale of breath, but behind Abbot's glasses, his eyes flicker. Ned does it again.

Slowly, Ned fits his hand between warm fabric and warmer skin, palming over the firm swell of Abbot's ass. Fits his mouth to Abbot's collarbone too, and then his neck. Ned's always loved that thin skin over the stretch of tendons and the slight roughness of stubble on men, and he loves it now as he mouths under Abbot's jaw.

Ned pushes and Abbot's boxers drop to the floor. Ned kicks them aside with his foot before they can get folded too.

And then Abbot's hands are on him and it's hard to think. Abbot's mouth, tipping to catch Ned's in a searing kiss, warm, long fingers shucking Ned's sweatpants and boxers off his hips. Oh fuck yeah, that's a lot of naked skin and Ned grabs Abbot's waist, hauls him in closer, pressing against him and kissing him until his chest burns for want of air.

He doesn't give a shit if he can't breathe. He's got Abbot naked in his hands, his tongue in Abbot's mouth, and the firm, wet drag of their lips working at each other's. It's good. It's so fucking good and it's been so long, and when Abbot takes a step backward toward the bed, Ned follows so eagerly he's amazed he doesn't trip in his fumble to follow Abbot down onto the mattress.

Abbot, who turns onto his stomach and with one long arm, grabs the condom and lube and presses them into Ned's hand.

Ned sucks in a breath. It shakes, anticipation skating through him and lighting up his stomach.

They're doing this and they're doing it right now and—

Calm the hell down, he tells himself. Deep breath in and then another one.

Be cool, he thinks loudly, the words banging around in his head.

"Never fucked anyone who gave me a C, you know," he says.

He can actually see Abbot's sigh in the flare of his ribs. "Was I not clear about the talking?"

"Just saying." Ned sets the condom aside and smears a bead of lube over his first two fingers with the pad of his thumb. "Zero data points, as of yet."

Another sigh and Ned grins at the back of Abbot's head.

Gently, he kneels on the edge of the bed, and when he touches the back of Abbot's thigh, Abbot spreads his legs so willingly that Ned's stomach sings with a burst of excitement. Oh hell yeah, this is happening. And Abbot's gorgeous and eager, what with how he rocks his hips a little as Ned squeezes his ass. This is . . . wow. A lot. And also really, really fucking awesome.

"Okay?" Ned asks as he presses a finger into Abbot. Abbot nods, his forehead against the mattress. Ned would try to flip him over, wanting to see the play of expression across his face, but for as much as Abbot rocks into his touch, Ned's sure he much prefers not having to face each other.

Hell, maybe Ned does too.

Still, all Ned has to go on is the soft sigh Abbot lets out as Ned crooks his finger inside him. He does it again, watching the shift of muscles in Abbot's back. He's not unresponsive, but he's certainly quiet, even when Ned reaches around his thigh, urges Abbot up onto his knees, and wraps his fingers around Abbot's cock. There's a bead of moisture at the tip that Ned slides his thumb through and Abbot catches his breath.

"Is that good?" he asks. "I think it was a C minus, actually. Might have to actually use some words."

"No—ah—thank you."

Ned shakes his head at Abbot's back and presses his finger in deeper. Abbot's shoulders flex. Ned props a knee on the edge of the mattress and shifts his weight onto his shin, watching his finger move inside Abbot. Ned loves that sound of slick fingers, and at least he can hear it in all of this wonderful silence. He has half a mind to say exactly that.

But moreover, he wants to answer that dull beat of pressure in his own cock. Sex is so damn fun. He knew that once and forgot it and knows it again now. And it's going to complicate his relationship with Abbot even more, but Ned can't bring himself to care over the sight of Abbot kneeling on the bed or the sing of his own blood as he watches his finger disappear into Abbot.

With each slow pump of Ned's fist on his cock, Abbot's back ripples and his breath comes a little faster. It looks like it feels good, even if Abbot doesn't want to voice that, and there's a keenness building in Ned too, an eagerness that he hasn't felt in so long. He squeezes Abbot's cock and lets go, sliding his finger out of him too. *You're fucking your professor*, a voice in his head keeps repeating. Ned rips open the condom with his teeth, his fingers too slippery to grip it. He rolls the condom on and strokes himself through the barrier, thankful for the thin layer of rubber as he spreads lube over himself.

He's even more thankful as he kneels behind Abbot and carefully, slowly, presses into him. He can't look down at where his cock is disappearing into Abbot, he decides quickly. He'll lose what little composure he has, his cheeks heating and his hands gripping and releasing and squeezing up Abbot's waist and sides, leaving red marks on that thin, pale skin.

Ned leans forward and sets his teeth against the bump of Abbot's spine at the base of his neck, slowly pushing all the way inside him. *Relax*, he'd say, though he'd probably just get an elbow in the gut for it. Ned smooths his palm up the ladder of Abbot's ribs and feels the clench and release of Abbot's breathing until it evens out. And oh God, that's good. *Like that*, Ned thinks and thrusts shallowly.

"All right?" Ned asks. He's breathless already. Fucking each other was a really, really good idea.

Nothing. Abbot's head dips down and his shoulders flex as he adjusts his weight on his hands and knees.

"Abbot?" Ned asks.

Abbot nods once, the motion jerky.

"Okay?" Ned asks again and sets one hand on Abbot's waist. With the other, he reaches around the front of Abbot's body and finds his cock. "Yeah?"

Another nod. When Ned thumbs the tip of Abbot's cock, it turns into a shiver that races down the muscles in Abbot's back, and Ned grins.

He bends forward and noses into the dip of muscle at the base of Abbot's shoulder. Kisses him there, and then starts to move. Slowly at first, trying to pace it out with the rhythm of his hand on Abbot's cock. But it's been so long and Abbot feels amazing. Slick and warm and he lifts his ass into Ned's thrusts with an eagerness that belies his silence. He smells good too, a hint of clean sweat and the headier, deeper notes of sex.

"Oh God," Ned gets out in a puff of breath. A spark of pleasure lights his stomach with each drag of his cock inside of Abbot.

Slow, he repeats to himself, *slow, slow, slow*, but his hips speed up. Abbot's head arches back and Ned grabs his shoulder, hauling him back onto his own cock. So fucking good. Heat builds in time with how they move and Ned strokes Abbot quicker, harder, until Abbot's hand lifts from the bed and covers Ned's.

That's even better, the slide of their fingers tangling together, the pressure of Abbot's grip as he guides Ned's hand. Abbot's pace quickens and Ned rocks his hips into Abbot faster, chasing after that hook of heat flaring through the base of his spine.

When Abbot comes, it's with a silent shiver, his neck tensing and his shoulders drawing up. He spills hot and slick over their hands and Ned bites his lower lip hard, desperate for a bit of that grace. Instead, he hears himself grunt, yanking Abbot's hips back against him as he thrusts again and again, messy and quick until heat flares outward and he comes with a groan.

Pleasure ebbs back out again, leaving Ned heavy. His hands are shaking and he can hear the gasp of his own breath. Abbot straightens his glasses.

Ned takes two tries to get the condom off, and when he does, he tosses it in the trash can next to the nightstand. He flops backward, panting lightly. Worth it. Completely so, no matter what the hell is going to come of this. With a contented sigh, Ned folds his arm across his face. He'll have to pry himself upright soon enough, but for now he just wants to lie right here, enjoying the fact that he feels absolutely fucking amazing.

"It was a seventy-one percent." The mattress shifts. Abbot must be standing up, though Ned doesn't move his arm to find out. "It's lucky you didn't fail the exam."

"Are you kidding?" Ned mumbles. His skin is still buzzing. "You'd have gotten another semester of me in your class. You should be so lucky."

"The thought did occur to me."

In the bathroom, the sink runs. Ned's getting up in a second. In a minute. Another one. His jaw hinges in a yawn and he flexes his feet. He feels so damn good. A hell of a weekend, this was.

When he blinks his eyes open, it's fully dark outside the window, none of the lingering gray of evening. The bed's empty beside him, though that can't be right because he blinks again and the sheet's pulled to his waist and Abbot's there next to him, his mouth parted in sleep and his face lax.

He really does look younger like that, without his glasses. Ned rubs at his eyes. He's getting up, though instead, he turns into the pillow and doesn't quite manage to move before he drifts off again.

CHAPTER FOURTEEN

NED SITS UP. This is very much not his bedroom.

"Shit," he mutters and swings his feet to the floor.

His jeans are fucking folded, set neatly on the dresser. Who the hell even does that? Dry too, when he shakes them out.

Abbot's bathroom is free of any clutter whatsoever. Just a bare countertop around the sink and a precisely hung towel outside the shower. It's wet. The shower. And the towel, too.

Ned avoids his reflection, rubbing a hand over his jaw and bending over the sink to splash water on his face. Toothbrush, hairbrush—his backpack's sitting against the foot of the bed. For a long moment, he stands with his fingers gripped in his hair under the bright lights of Abbot's unfairly nice bathroom, with its glass shower and double sink, and stupidly appealing coordinated towels. His eyes squeeze shut. He should be home. Not . . . here. Not here and not feeling really great in a way he wants to poke at himself for, betrayed by his own sex-starved body.

Ned glares at his feet, annoyed at himself all over again.

Then, he drops his hands and works his shirt smooth, the one he'd grabbed and pulled on. Abbot's shirt. Dammit.

Downstairs, the lights are on in the kitchen against the gloom of the morning rain, and at the table, Abbot is completely hidden behind his opened newspaper, only his hands visible. Ned clears his throat.

"Morning." He sticks his hands in his pockets, only to pull them back out again. The paper twitches and Ned hooks his thumb over his shoulder. "I gotta head out."

Abbot stands, folding the paper neatly in half. "You're awake."

Ned takes a beat too long to say, "Obviously." He doesn't let himself scratch at his neck.

Abbot's got his shoes on already. Ned squints at the clock on the stove. Traitorously, his stomach growls.

"Oh," he says when Abbot picks up his keys. Ned shakes his head. "I can—I was just going to walk."

"I'm driving to campus anyway."

"Right." What a damn morning this is, and it's not even seven. "Well, then."

In Abbot's car, Ned shoves his backpack between his feet. His eyes are still gritty. "Sorry," he says as Abbot pulls away from the curb.

"For?"

Ned tips his head against the window. He doesn't want to actually have to say it. "Didn't mean to, you know, crash." *Last night*, he could add.

Abbot's the type to like specificity. Ned stares at the parked cars they're driving past, unwilling to let his mind drift back to the sight of Abbot's pale slender back.

"It's fine."

"Still." Ned rubs his fingers over his chin. He really needs to shave. Abbot clearly has. Probably had breakfast too, and a cup of that tea he loves so much.

When Abbot drops Ned off in front of his apartment, Ned musters up a tight grin.

"See ya," he says and pushes out of the car and into the rain. He tosses the car door shut before he has to find out if Abbot's bothered with a farewell of his own.

Gingerly, Ned turns his key in the door. "Pat?" he calls as he edges up the stairs.

Please, if he's only out this morning, or at the café already, or dead to the world after a night of drinking, and he isn't going to be awake until well after Ned's showered and made his way to his first class—

A clatter of nails, a gleeful bark, and eighty pounds of dog barrels out of Pat's room and straight into Ned's knees.

"Hey there," Ned says. He rubs at Baxter's side, trying to shush him. "Keep it down, you mongrel."

Though, there's Pat right behind him, his hair sticking straight up and his arms crossed. He grins, a slow wide smile that twists Ned's already knotted stomach.

"Well, well, well," Pat says. "Good to know you weren't murdered and your body dropped in the harbor."

"I don't want to hear it."

"Hello to you too. It's only early ass o'clock and pouring buckets, and I've been up all night worried sick."

"No, you haven't."

"No, you're right, I haven't." Pat comes closer and Ned would turn and bolt back downstairs, but given his luck, Abbot's still out there waiting to pull into traffic. "Where were you?"

"Out. Bax, do you need your breakfast?"

"Out," Pat repeats, the word drawn out slow. "Huh."

"It was raining," Ned says. "Yeah, you hungry, boy? Time for food?"

"Have a good weekend?" Pat leans his hip against the arm of the couch.

"It was all right."

"How was Charles Henry?"

Ned ducks down to grab Baxter's bowl. "Fine."

"Hmm, good."

"Yeah." Ned lets the drop of kibble into the bowl fill the quiet. "I gotta get to work, so I'm gonna jump in the shower."

"Cool, cool," Pat says. "Coffee? I was going to make some."

"Sure," Ned says slowly. That's too kind of an offer, and Pat's still smiling at him.

"Hey," Pat calls after him, just as Ned reaches the door to his room. "You get a new shirt?"

Ned closes his eyes. When he opens them again, Pat's still grinning and Ned shuts the door as hard as he can without just slamming it.

———

BY THE TIME Ned's last class lets out, the sun peeks through the clouds and there are patches of dry pavement between puddles. He slips out of the department building by the back staircase, where he won't have to run into Chris or Lee or Aliyah and face them asking about the rest of his Sunday and his ride back to the city. He won't have to run into Abbot either, which he chalks up to a necessary sort of cowardliness. He'll figure out what he's going to say next time they do have to see each other, but right now he just feels too damn *good* to trust himself that it'll be anything other than *wanna do that again?*

Because: no. They're not. Once was a mistake, and Ned's good at mistakes. Twice would be digging himself deeper into a hole, and he's spent the last year trying to climb back to his feet. He doesn't need to mess up his own progress now.

In the evening sunlight, Baxter spends his walk sniffing each streetlight, tail wagging, and Ned follows, hands tucked into his pockets. He's more than ready to get away from campus. Even now, his back itches like any moment he'll turn around and find folks staring at him.

Cool it, he tells himself. It's not anyone's business. It's not even a big deal. Everyone already thinks they—that he and Abbot—that for weeks now, Ned and he have been doing . . . that. Matching up fact to speculation doesn't matter, when all sorts of conclusions have already been drawn. He rubs his hand over his face.

His phone buzzes in his pocket when they reach the edge of the park, the one up high on the hill with a view of the harbor, where there's already other dogs running back and forth. Ned slips off Baxter's leash and lets him go, a black-and-white streak across the grass, barking his head off without a care in the world.

"Dad," Ned says when he finds a bench and answers his phone. "Hey."

"Your mother says not to ask you how your dissertation is going," his father says. "I think she's worried for your delicate constitution. But I know you're made of sterner stuff. Tell me, are you or aren't you currently whacking your head against your laptop as we speak?"

"I'm at the park with Baxter. But thanks for the vote of confidence."

"That's my boy."

"It's going fine." It's going to hell in a handbasket, but Dad doesn't need to know that. *To get you started this semester*, his dad had said in late August as Ned packed his car, folding a handful of bills into his palm. Ned tried to give them back and had just gotten a pat on the arm for his troubles and then a long hard hug.

"You know you're welcome back here, when you're all done up there."

"Oh. Yeah." Ned scratches his fingers through his hair. "Thanks."

"We don't want you to worry about where you'll land. I think your mom's angling for you to move home, frankly. And listen, for as long as you need, Ned."

What a goddamn catch he is, moving back in with his parents. This is why he doesn't try to date—anyone in their right mind would run for the hills the moment they learned anything about him. Maybe last night will be as good as it gets—maybe this whole fall will be, stumbling through playing at a relationship, when a real one is far more than he'll ever be able to manage again.

"Thanks," he says again. "Yeah, I'm still waiting to hear back from some jobs."

"You okay?"

"What? No, yeah, I'm fine."

"You sound out of it, sport."

"No, I'm . . ." Ned picks at the leg of his jeans. Across the park, Baxter splays out on the ground, letting a golden retriever wrestle with him. "I don't know."

"Look, I know it's not the glamorous life, moving back in with your parents, but—"

"No, no, I appreciate it." Ned squints against the sunlight. His throat feels funny. Hurts, maybe. "I just . . . I have this weird thing going on. With this guy."

"Aha," his dad says.

Ned rubs his thumb and forefinger into his eyes. He didn't mean to say that.

"What sort of weird thing?"

"Just . . . weird."

"You should consider getting a doctorate with that vocabulary."

"Dad," Ned sighs.

"You like him? You don't like him? He likes you, he doesn't like you—no, that can't be right, you're you, he'd be frankly an idiot to not like you."

"Dad."

"Need me to come up there and have a word with him? I'll do it. Throw down, you know. Give him a lesson on how to treat my kid."

"Oh my God, Dad. You don't even know what throwing down is."

"I do! Cheryl—Cheryl! Come tell Ned that I know what's what."

"You don't," Ned hears his mom call. "Hi, sweetie."

"I do, too. Your mom says hi."

"Hi, Mom," Ned says.

"Listen. Ned. It can be hard to meet someone when you're about to move. It's okay to feel conflicted."

"No, that's not—" Ned shakes his head. "That's not it."

"You've got one foot out the door up there, and now if there's someone you're seeing . . . well."

Ned stands. Baxter's too far across the park, having dropped his new best friend for the chance to sniff circles around a maple tree.

"Look, I gotta go."

"All right, kiddo. But call me if you want to talk, okay? I love you."

"Love you too," Ned mumbles and taps at the screen to end the call.

Baxter abandons the tree to get his ears scratched by some kid and he's absolutely loving it, tail waving back and forth. Ned shoves his phone into his pocket. He shouldn't have said anything to his dad. Didn't mean to and didn't want to and now it's out there.

Well, Dad won't bug him about it, not if he knows Ned doesn't want him to push. Pat will, though. Ned shoves his hands into his pockets, his knuckles bumping into his phone as he makes his way across the park. It was dumb to stay at Abbot's last night. To sleep with him. Even kiss him. Ned should've put the brakes on. Not just fallen into it like he had.

"Bax," he calls when he's close enough. Then, he stops walking. "Oh. Hi."

The girl standing over Baxter looks up. It's Liesl, with her long hair in a braid that falls down her back, and her hand freezing on Baxter's head.

Awkwardly, Ned points to himself. Liesl's just staring at him. She looks like Abbot. So much younger though, and without glasses in front of her brown eyes. Baxter noses into her wrist, trying to get her to start petting him again. "I'm— we met. Last night. I'm Ned."

Baxter whines at her and shoves his nose into her palm. Ned waves toward him.

"That's Baxter," he says. "He's friendly if you want to . . . yeah." If she wants to pet him. Which she's already doing. Clearly.

"You, uh, is your brother here with you?" Ned looks around. Wouldn't that be the icing on the cake, Abbot coming out of the woodwork? For all Ned knows, he was within earshot while Ned was on the phone with his dad. That'd be typical. Ned so wrapped up in his thoughts he'd completely missed their subject standing nearby.

But no. Walking toward them is another treat altogether.

"Hey," Ned says to Charles. *Hello* would've been

better, he's suddenly sure. Abbot's father just looks him over. Ned clears his throat. "Nice to see you again."

Or, well, something like it at least. Ned ducks forward and loops his fingers into Baxter's collar, pulling him against his knees.

"C'mere," Ned says. He's talking a lot, it feels like. He spins Baxter's collar around his neck, working to find the ring. When he straightens, looping the leash over his wrist, Charles and Liesl are still watching him. "Well. Good to run into you."

Before Ned manages to take the step backward that he's damn intent on, Charles catches his eye.

"That's your dog," Charles says.

"Yeah." Obviously. Ned tightens his grip on the leash and gives it a gentle tug to bring Baxter closer to him. "It's an off-leash park, so."

And Baxter was cooped up all day. Most of the weekend too, Ned's sure. Pat's given over to lying on the couch watching movies on afternoons he's not working, and he probably let Baxter share half his popcorn. Ned doubts there was exactly an outdoor adventure involved for either of them. He shuts his mouth tight before all of that can come spilling out.

Charles's even, stern gaze doesn't shift from Ned. He must've given his kids lessons. Maybe lined them up and critiqued their ability to stare others into submission. Ned can feel a lecture coming, what with letting his dog rampage his way across the park, tongue lolling and tail wagging, with all the benign enthusiasm of hoping someone will toss a stick for him.

It's not a stretch to imagine Charles hardly approves of such frivolity, and that he has all sorts of standards about the ways owners should and shouldn't handle their dogs. A typed list, for all Ned knows, about to be handed to him as

Charles arches a disapproving eyebrow behind those glasses.

Baxter's tail starts its happy wag back and forth. *Don't*, Ned would tell him, but he's not going to talk to his dog in front of this guy.

"Sit," Ned says, giving him a light tug on the leash.

But Baxter's tail just starts going harder, and when Ned looks up from him again, Chris is there.

"Baxter," Chris says, already bending down to ruffle the dog's ears. "And Ned!"

"Bax, no," Ned says and tugs at the leash when Baxter makes like he wants to jump. Chris would let him too. Always does whenever Ned brings Baxter by the department, letting muddy paws plant themselves on his thighs and happily getting his chin licked. "Chris, you're back in town."

Relief pumps through Ned, settling in the pit where his stomach had dropped out. Chris is here with Charles, then. And Ned can slip away gracefully with a much easier goodbye to all three of them, tempered by Chris's good cheer.

"Henry told you?" Chris asks.

Quickly, Ned shakes his head. "No, I just . . . Baxter, c'mon man, don't do that, don't jump."

"He's a good boy, yes, you are," Chris says, scratching his ears. Baxter turns in a happy, frantic circle, his legs tangling with his leash. "You're coming?"

"What?" Ned asks. "Baxter, c'mere."

"Dinner." Chris looks between Ned and Charles. "Ready to go?"

"Oh." Ned's blinking too much, he's sure. Slowly, he sorts out Chris's words. Oh God, *no*. "No, I'm just—I was walking Baxter, I'm not . . . we should get back."

"You can't be working tonight," Chris says and damn

him and his cheerful grin. "C'mon, family dinner at Henry's."

"I've got Baxter, and I wasn't—I'm actually headed home," Ned says.

He's got laundry to do and all of Pat's asinine innuendos about Ned's weekend to avoid, which is suddenly more appealing than standing here watching Chris tip his head in the direction of the houses lining the park. Because . . . damn. Now, Ned recognizes this neighborhood. He's been here a hundred times with Baxter before, apparently gloriously ignorant to the fact that only a handful of blocks away is Abbot's street.

"Who doesn't love Baxter?" Chris asks and gives the dog one last scratch on his head. Before Ned can stop him, he snags the leash out of his hand. "Charles, when are you going to let Liesl get a dog?"

"We travel too often," Charles says.

Chris hands the loop of the leash to Liesl, who hesitates and then takes it. Baxter eyes her with the same adoration he has in spades for anyone willing to scratch that spot just behind his ears. *Traitor*, Ned thinks at him. It's all the more horribly awkward to consider grabbing the leash back from a kid who's now patting the top of Baxter's head.

"I should really get him back," Ned tries.

Chris claps a hand to Ned's shoulder. "We've got all evening," he says. "And Susan's bringing her apple pie. It'll be so great to have you there, too."

I'm not actually invited to this, Ned wants say, but Charles is already walking. *We're not seeing each other*, he would add. Baxter trots after Liesl, his nose poking into her thigh in his unending quest for even more attention. Chris smacks Ned on the arm again.

"Charles isn't out here a lot," he says, dropping his voice. "Good to get to know him while you can, right?"

"Look." Ned licks at his lips. "I'm not sure that it's really appropriate if I—"

"Oh Ned, don't worry about that," Chris says. "Henry needs someone to push him along sometimes. You and I both know that. Hell, he knows that too. It's what he likes about you."

Henry. The name is still so jarring.

"I'm sure it's not," Ned says, but Chris only grins.

"Come on." Chris steers Ned around toward the edge of the park that Charles, Liesl and Baxter are already halfway to. "Henry'll be glad to see you."

Ned grimaces at his shoes and slowly follows Chris.

CHAPTER FIFTEEN

NOSE TO THE FLOOR, Baxter jogs through Abbot's living room. His tags jangling, he trots down the hall, into the kitchen, and circles back again, his tail whacking into a chair.

"Sorry," Ned says to Abbot as soon as Chris and Liesl start toward the kitchen. "I didn't—I'm sorry. I can go."

"This is unexpected."

Ned spreads his hands. "You think?"

"You can ask him," Chris says to Liesl from the doorway, a hand on her shoulder, turning her back toward Ned. She won't quite meet his eye, and he's seen that look before on Abbot's face, such similar brown eyes angled away from his. *Shy*, Ned thinks, like how Peggy clings to him, her face mashed into his thigh whenever he tries to introduce her to someone new.

Of course, he's also seen Liesl dash out of Abbot's office after being told not to, and clearly slip away from her father at the park. Ned'd put money on a good deal of spunk hiding behind her familial tendency toward a stonewall of stoicism. Maybe that's genetic too.

Ned bends down a little. "Yeah?" he asks. "What's up?"

"May I take your dog into the yard?" she mumbles to the floor. Liesl's got a cute sweater on, a pattern of trees on it. It looks like something his mom would get for Peggy.

"Oh. Sure," Ned says. Then thinks, *No*. This is just going to keep him here longer. He should be backing his way out the door, but Liesl is already halfway to the kitchen and instead of following her, Baxter's still sniffing around the room, untrained mongrel that he is.

"C'mere, Bax," Ned says. There's a door in the kitchen, leading into the yard. Ned wishes he didn't know that. He opens it and pushes Baxter through. "Be good, y'hear?"

Golden evening sunlight streams through the windows that were inky black last night, lighting up the granite counters. Abbot's got something cooking on the stove, steam escaping from under the lid. It smells good. Ned really, really should go.

"I ran into them," he says to Abbot as softly as he can as Chris sorts through the refrigerator and Charles studies the screen of his phone. The rest of that bottle of white wine is stuck in the door of the fridge. Ned can see it over Chris's shoulder, the cork neatly pressed into it. "I'm sorry."

Outside, Baxter dodges back and forth in Abbot's small yard, a stick hanging out the side of his mouth and Liesl grabbing for it, her braid swinging. It's Baxter's favorite game, second only to tearing around the house with a shoe Ned needs to put on. Ned pushes out of the door and smacks his palm against his thigh.

"Baxter," he calls. "Drop it."

Baxter sinks into a bow, tail wagging so hard it shakes his entire butt.

"Baxter," Ned says, slower this time. Gingerly, Baxter lays the stick down, though his mouth hovers over it.

"He's awful," Ned says to Liesl. He feels too tall next to her and he crouches down, patting at his knee. "Bax, I'm taking you to the pound. Drop it, would you?"

Baxter grabs up the stick as soon as Ned leans closer and starts running in circles again, his paws tearing up tufts of grass, but Ned snags it on one of Baxter's dashes past him. It's not their first round of this game.

"Here," he says, holding the stick out to Liesl.

It's gross, covered in slobber and splintered at one end, a clear mark of Baxter's handiwork. That something so untidy could be found in Abbot's lawn—Ned wouldn't put it past him to have a predawn checklist of tasks, one of which is sweeping the lawn for any sorts of detritus. He probably did it while Ned slept this morning, naked in the sheets they'd tangled.

He clears his throat. He'd feel better if that image of Abbot sitting at his table with the paper didn't rise to mind. What a domestic tableau, steam curling up from his mug and the rain-wet windows casting the room into a cozy little bubble of warmth. Ned wasn't ever supposed to see that. Nor was he ever meant to stand here, wiping his fingers on his pants and watching Abbot's kid sister toss a stick across his yard to Baxter.

"Nice throw," Ned says. Baxter trots back with the stick, shaking it furiously. To Ned's surprise, Liesl smiles and she's cute as a damn button. Maybe Ned can just hide outside with her and Baxter all night, let the rest of the adults have their dinner and Ned can find out if twelve is too old for dinosaur facts.

"He knows tricks," Ned says. "Even does them sometimes."

"Sit," she says. Baxter wags his tail at her.

"Sit," Ned tries. Baxter's tongue lolls out of his mouth

and he takes a step toward the stick. "Think your brother's got any hot dogs we could cut up?" Ned asks. Liesl just looks up at him. *Not sure if I'm joking,* he figures. He gives her a wink. "Carrot sticks? String beans? Vegan quinoa bites?"

"What are quinoa bites?" Abbot asks. Ned spins around. Abbot's just there, a step outside of the door to the kitchen. He must've just come out. Or maybe not. Maybe he was standing there this whole time.

"My mom makes them, they're actually not bad," Ned says. Abbot's pants fit him nicely. Hug the outside of his thighs. Ned points toward the kitchen and tries to ignore how he wishes Abbot would spin around and give Ned the view from behind. "You have any of those fake-meat things? Burgers?"

"No."

"Good. Baxter's got a discriminating palate," Ned says.

"I find that highly unlikely."

"Run the numbers, you're the statistician."

"We need carrots," Liesl says.

Abbot opens the door for her. "In the refrigerator." He eyes Ned. "I would encourage you to do it yourself, considering your burgeoning prowess."

Ned snorts out a laugh. "Well now, that's the nicest thing you've ever said to me."

Chris and Charles follow Liesl back outside, a bag of carrots clutched in her hand. Susan too, bringing glasses and a bottle of red wine. She waves at Ned and he gives her a smile in return. Baxter turns in tight, excited circles as Liesl pulls out a carrot.

"You should see what he does for bacon," Ned says. He snags the carrot from her and breaks it into pieces. He wants to get the hell out of here. To be gone already. To have never come. But horribly, he wants even more to get a better look at Abbot's slim runner's thighs in those pants.

Get your shit together, he snaps at himself. Baxter's ears prick with each snap of carrot, and Liesl holds her tiny thin hand out before Ned's done. "Here, tell him to shake."

Baxter's paw misses her outstretched hand, but apparently Liesl doesn't throw in for perfectionism the same way her brother does, because she lets Baxter swallow up a chunk of carrot, and then do it all over again, his paw batting at the air. She smiles and gives him another carrot. A real smile, one that stretches on her face and dimples her cheek.

"He can roll over too," Ned says and hands her another fistful of carrots.

"What's the point?"

Ned turns. Charles might have his eyes on Baxter, but there's no pretending the question isn't aimed at Ned. "The point?" Ned asks.

"The point of training him to do this." Charles gestures with his wineglass to where Baxter's flopped on his side in the grass. Baxter won't bother to roll the whole way over if he thinks he'll get a treat just for going through the motions. And sure enough, Liesl's already got a carrot held out that he gobbles down.

Ned raises his eyebrows. He's staring at Charles, he knows. It's probably rude. Well, it must've rubbed off on him, all that time with Abbot. Ned's going to have nailed the familial silent stare before they're done with this sham of a relationship.

"There's no point," Ned says. "It's just for fun."

Charles arches an eyebrow. "I see."

Ned turns back around. *Be polite*, he tells himself, but he angles his shoulder toward Charles all the same. *The point of it*. What a trip this guy is.

"Bax, roll all the way," Ned says.

"He won't do it," Liesl says, her voice soft. That smile on her face fades, and she tries to push the carrots back at Ned.

Ned doesn't take them, just kneels down next to her. "Let's see if we can convince him to, huh?"

There'll be grass stains on his pants for this. Probably a first-rate offense in the Abbot household, dirtying clothes for the audacity of having fun.

"Hold it up like that and move it in a circle," Ned says and shows her how. "Baxter, roll over."

Baxter's got Liesl's number because he only bothers to begin to lie down before coaxing the treat out of her fingers with a lick of his tongue.

"Try again," Ned says, but Liesl shakes her head. Again, she pushes the carrots toward him, her fingers tight around them and her head ducked down.

Gently, Ned pries up her pinky finger and plucks a carrot. "We'll let an expert try. Look alive," he says and tosses the carrot underhand to Abbot. He catches it and just holds it. Ned tips his head toward Baxter. "C'mon."

"He's not an expert," Liesl says. She's almost whispering. "We don't have a dog."

"Wanna hear something?" Ned whispers back. "He can get a class of undergrads to settle down, and this is just one dog."

Ned gets a blink from her. Not a smile, just a long, even look. He grins back all the same.

"He can balance it on his nose," he tells Abbot. "Give it a try."

No, he can so clearly hear on the tip of Abbot's tongue. But he doesn't return the carrot and wipe his hands off. Instead, he walks toward them, and Charles's lips press together. He turns, walking back inside, and when the door shuts, Abbot crouches down next to Ned, his knees carefully clear of the dewy, wet grass.

"Baxter," Abbot says. His inflection is all wrong, like Baxter's a colleague at some professional function. Abbot probably doesn't like dogs to begin with. Probably doesn't like cats, either. If he had one, it'd lie right on his paper every morning and throw his routine off.

Only slowly, Abbot holds out the carrot between two fingers as if it's some sort of ticking bomb he doesn't want too close to himself. Baxter wags his tail.

"Roll over," Ned says and instead, Baxter jumps to his feet, grabs the carrot from Abbot, and rushes toward him, licking at his chin.

Next to him, Liesl lets out a loud, startled laugh. Ned grabs for his damn dog, but not before Abbot's glasses get bumped and a paw lands on his shoulder. Ned's laughing too, and Liesl claps her hand over her mouth, giggling.

"Whoops," Ned says, hooking his arm around his squirming, wagging, excited dog.

Abbot blinks, righting his glasses.

"Whoops," he echoes, his voice so flat and dry that another laugh sputters out of Ned.

Ned sits back on the grass, tugs Baxter into his lap, and holds him there so he can't maul Abbot again. Over the top of Baxter's head, Ned can see Charles through the kitchen window, watching them, his eyes moving back and forth between Abbot and Liesl.

During dinner, Baxter lies under the table while Abbot dishes them plates of something Ned can't pronounce. There're potatoes in it, and cheese too. He swallows down a crack about fondue. At least there's only one fork next to his plate, and he doesn't have to sort through a plethora of silverware. With Charles eyeing him like he is, Ned's only too sure he'd manage to use the wrong fork.

"So nice you're here tonight, Ned," Susan says.

"Oh." Ned pushes his palms down his thighs. His arm brushes too close to Abbot's, sitting there next to him. *Napkin on your lap,* he tells himself in his mother's voice. "Of course."

"Salad, Sue?" Chris asks. "Ned?"

No thanks, he nearly says, sure he'll manage to drop one of the wood tongs, or that Baxter will get a whiff of canine-approved produce and beg to be fed from the table. Ned takes the bowl and peeks into it. And smiles.

"Spinach?" he asks softly. "All right, Popeye."

Ned gets a look from behind Abbot's glasses. A glance from Charles too. Maybe Abbot's glare doesn't itch up and down Ned's neck anymore, but his father's sure does.

"Henry, how's the work on the grant coming?" Chris asks. "You finishing up?"

"Nearly," Abbot says as Ned drops a pile of greenery onto his plate.

"Good, good. You'll send me the paper?" Chris asks.

"I'd love to read it too," Susan says. "We won't be able to make your talk down in Boston."

"Boston?" Charles asks. "You aren't presenting in Paris?"

"No." Liesl has her fork in her hand, already eating her dinner.

"Henry," Charles says.

"Want some salad?" Ned sets the bowl on the table. Abbot stares at his spoon. Ned nudges his knee into Abbot's. Nothing.

"He's not going to Paris," Liesl says and puts a potato in her mouth.

Charles sets his fork down. "Why?"

"I'll get you some," Ned says and dumps a heap of spinach onto Abbot's plate. "Liesl, you want some too?"

"No," she says and eats another potato.

"We had such a lovely weekend with Ned and Henry," Susan says, cutting in as Charles opens his mouth again. "So nice to spend some time together away from the office, isn't it?"

"Though we're still waiting on the rest of the story," Chris says, pointing his fork between Ned and Abbot.

"Story?" Ned asks. He wants to swallow the word back down as soon as it's out there, because Chris only grins.

"How this happened," he says and points between them again.

Abbot pulls his knee away from Ned's.

"It was about time," Susan adds.

And there goes Abbot shifting in his chair, like he can lean away from Ned and this conversation both. Heat crawls up Ned's neck at a memory of last night, fingers dipped beneath clothing and hot, panting breath.

"It really wasn't that interesting," Ned says quickly. "How did you two meet?"

"Oh, Cathy introduced us, of course," Susan says. "Back in our own grad school days, while Cathy and I were post-docs and Chris was in his first year of teaching."

"Oh," Ned says. No wonder Abbot knows them so well. He glances at Abbot, who's slicing a potato into perfectly neat cubes.

"Not so different than you two, really." Susan smiles at them again.

"You're a postdoc?" Charles asks.

Charles is staring right at him. Ned knows that look; he used to see it aimed at him from the front of the lecture hall. And great, now he's right back to sweating, sure he's going to get the answer wrong, no matter that it's not about multivariate regression and just a question about his life.

Oh God, Ned thinks. Next to him, Abbot neatly cuts another potato in half.

"No," Ned says.

"You're an assistant professor?"

"Doctoral candidate." Ned waves his fork toward Chris and Abbot before he can think better of it. "In the sociology department."

Charles spears a piece of onion. "I see."

Ned's sure he does. He lets out a breath. Beneath the table, Baxter scratches at his neck, the tags on his collar jingling.

"And you'll be finished when, exactly?" Charles asks.

"Soon." Ned nudges Baxter with his toe. With Charles staring him down, Ned's never believed that less in his life.

"And your plans for afterward?" Charles asks and adjusts his grip on his fork. Ned hasn't ever felt worse for a vegetable than he feels for that onion. "Graduating in December is less than ideal."

Ass, Ned thinks. "A job down in Boston," he says.

"You have a position already?"

"My family's there. So no, just . . ." Ned says. Still, the jingling. "Bax, hey, cool it buddy."

Charles eyes him. Ned's neck flushes. He takes a deep breath. This is what Abbot apparently has to deal with all the damn time. Ned doesn't blame him for having a chip on his shoulder the size of the Alps.

"I'll figure it out," Ned says as easily as he can. And yep, that does it, a blink in that stern gaze.

"Will you look elsewhere if a position in Boston isn't available?" Charles asks.

"Nope." Ned offers up a shrug, like he feels even half that casual stuck in Charles's crosshairs. "It'll work out."

"Will it," Charles says flatly.

Ned sips at his wine. Abbot's looking at him now, probably entirely certain that Ned's spewing a load of bullshit, but at least Abbot'll have the fun of correcting him later. "Sure it will."

"Ned's quite the teacher, you know," Chris says. "His students love him. Highest evals in the department, and by quite a bit, too."

Charles's forehead creases. "If you can't find a position in academia, you'll remain in Boston regardless?"

"Yes," Ned says. "Of course."

"A doctorate is a considerable investment to not take advantage of."

Ned shrugs again, and it comes easier this time. "I'll be in Boston next year. A postdoc or tenure-track position is ideal. And if not, like I said, I'll figure it out."

"And what'll you two do then?" Susan asks. "Chris, I will have some salad."

"What'll we do?" Ned asks.

"You and Henry." She smiles fondly at Abbot. "That's a long drive down to Boston."

He and Abbot . . . next year. Ned sticks a piece of potato in his mouth so he doesn't have to answer. It's good. Abbot apparently can cook, and cook well. He swallows and takes another bite, like he can just ignore Susan's question if he focuses on chewing.

"It'll work out," Abbot says. He's got his eyes on his plate, his surgical precision turned loose on yet another potato. Ned glances at him, surprised. Surely Abbot was just going to eat this dinner in silence, weathering his way through until it was over.

"It will," Ned says and tries to not let it sound like a question.

"Well, we're looking forward to seeing your finished

work," Chris says. "And I'm sure it's going great with Henry here giving you a hand."

"You're helping him?" Charles asks.

"Ned's nearly finished," Abbot says. "His work has been really good."

"What?" Ned asks.

"It is good," Abbot says.

"No, the—nearly finished?"

"By the end of the week, I imagine," Abbot says.

Ned blinks. That's . . . that's so soon. Excitement bubbles through him, tempered immediately by a thick sludge of dread. Chris is going to read over everything Ned's worked on, and chances are, Ned will be back where he was already this semester, Chris shaking his head over his work. Ned knows how this goes, trying and failing and trying again. He's getting good at it, like Sisyphus rolling his damn dissertation up one of Portland's hills.

Next to him, Abbot finally puts his knife down and digs his fork into his spinach. Ned drops his voice and leans closer.

"The end of this week?" he asks softly.

Abbot lifts a shoulder. Ned nudges him with his elbow.

"Really good?" he asks even quieter.

"Relatively speaking," Abbot says.

Across the table, Susan smiles at them, gentle and kind. Ned shakes his head and turns back to his plate, elbowing Abbot once more, harder this time.

"Nice to have met you," Ned forces himself to say to Charles after the meal. He gives Liesl a grin and would give her a high five too, but Charles is already steering her toward the door as Chris and Susan shrug on their coats. Ned lingers, his hands in his pockets. There's no way in hell he's going to get stuck walking in the same direction as Abbot's old man.

"Well, that was fun," Ned says when the door finally shuts. Baxter snuffles at the base of each chair. *Peggy's not here*, Ned should tell him. Liesl's probably not one to dump food on the rug for a hopeful dog. Ned fits his hands deeper into his pockets and wanders after Abbot when he retreats toward the kitchen.

"I'm sure it wasn't," Abbot says, his back to Ned, his shoulders stiff beneath the fabric of his dress shirt. He's still in his work clothes, unlike Ned—or maybe that's what he wears normally in the evening.

"S'fine," Ned says. He runs his palm over the counter, coming closer to where Abbot scrapes food from plates. "Like I said, I didn't mean to end up here. But hey, thanks for the meal. It was good. Family recipe?"

Abbot rests the plates on the counter. There's still a bit of spinach from the salad stuck to the top one and he grips a fork too tight. "My mother's."

"Oh."

Abbot shifts his weight to his other foot. His shirt moves across his back, catching on the ridges of his shoulder blades.

"You might need another drink." Ned tugs the plates away. "Give me those, I'll do that."

"I've got it."

He frees the fork from Abbot's grip and pops open the dishwasher. It's unloaded and empty, of course. Probably perfectly, intentionally prepared for having guests over. Ned can picture Abbot in here this afternoon, running a cloth over the counters and straightening knives and spoons in their drawer, the house silent and empty around him.

"I'm sorry," Ned says gently. "About your mom. I really am."

"Please don't," Abbot says. Softly, too.

Ned turns, a hand still on the top rack of the dishwasher. "Okay." He lets a handful of forks and knives drop into the silverware holder. Carefully, he sets the plates on the bottom rack. "I like Liesl."

"She's quite enamored with Baxter."

Ned turns around and smiles down at Baxter, sprawled on his side against the base of the counter. "Who wouldn't be?" He adds the wineglasses to the dishwasher too. Abbot plucks them back out and sets them in the sink. "Stop it. I'll wash those."

"I'm going to do it."

"Jesus, fine." Ned holds up Liesl's water glass. "This okay or does it need a special brand of TLC?"

"Stemware should not be washed in—"

"Oh, it was a joke," Ned says and sticks the glass in the top rack. "Want me to write you up a research protocol to recognize them?"

"Please."

Ned snorts. "Fine, I will."

Outside the window, the sun is setting. It's going to be a gorgeous night, a crisp breeze blowing in after all that rain. Baxter yawns and then stretches, his toes flexing. Ned should take him home. He adjusts Liesl's glass to sit neater.

"What was that about Paris?" Ned asks.

"Nothing."

"Didn't sound like nothing. Liesl seemed to know what's what."

"I was going to present there." Abbot turns on the sink and runs the water until steam curls up. "We were."

"With the ex? You nixed that plan?"

"Clearly."

"Good for you," Ned says. "The good old Louis still presenting?"

"I haven't asked."

"I went to one of your talks a couple years ago." He

leans back against the counter. Abbot's going to burn his hands with that water. "Back on, I don't even know, changing urbanization trends? Thrilling stuff, it was."

"Suburban zoning and its effects on population density." Abbot runs a sponge under the tap.

"Right. It was good."

"You enjoyed it?"

"I didn't say that." Ned leans over and turns the handle of the sink a bit cooler. "No, I didn't enjoy it. I think Peggy was up the entire night before, and I wanted to sleep in the back row. You were good, I meant. At speaking."

"Is that supposed to be a compliment?"

"I just meant that I never got the sense you really like teaching all that much, but all of that research . . . you seemed to be into talking about it."

Abbot looks over at him.

Ned raises both eyebrows and shrugs. "Frankly, I got the sense you hated your class as much as I did, and then I saw you give that talk and you were totally different."

Different like he is with Liesl, letting Baxter bounce over him, playing at getting him to roll over if it'll make his sister smile. Ned knows that switch to his personal life well enough, shaking off the weight of professionalism to toss Peggy up in the air, catch her, and toss her again as she shrieks and laughs.

Watching Abbot wipe away the harshness of how he is in front of a classroom is odd, though he clearly does so under the right circumstances. *Henry*, Ned thinks and wants to shake his head at the name. No, Abbot fits him better, as if *Henry* is Charles's son and the man Ned's come to know, carving out a life for himself, is someone else entirely. That picture on his phone, Ned remembers again, eyeing the outline of the case in Abbot's pocket. And last night, too. The thoroughness and eagerness in his kisses. Ned clears his throat and turns back to the dishwasher.

"I don't mind talking about my research," Abbot says.

"But did you like it?" Ned asks.

Abbot squirts a bead of soap onto the sponge, silent and not looking at Ned.

"Right."

"I didn't say anything."

"Right," Ned says again.

Abbot can tell himself whatever he wants to, but Ned's spent enough of his life in classrooms to be able to spot the difference. Abbot went over his syllabus like he wanted to be anywhere else.

Abbot pauses, his hands under the water, his mouth pursed, and then starts quickly soaping up a wineglass when he realizes Ned's watching him.

It's fine, Ned could say. It's not some great secret to the universe, something that can't be spoken aloud—Abbot doesn't love teaching. Big deal, Ned doesn't exactly love doing research. If he did, he might not still be slogging through his dissertation.

Which is what he should be doing right now, not standing here in Abbot's kitchen. Ned rubs his hand over the back of his neck. He's going. Now, as soon as he can collect his things. He might not be able to do his work tonight, but he can at least get to bed and hit his desk early tomorrow.

Get to his own bed, that is.

Don't offer, he wants to tell Abbot, 'cause Ned's not all that sure that he wouldn't say a hearty *yes* to another trip up that narrow staircase.

"Can we meet up again to finish the analysis?" Ned asks. "Or I can just send it to you to look at."

That'd be better. Less need for them to see each other

outside of work. Ned doesn't need another quiet evening to stretch between the two of them, night falling and with it the idle hours between dinner and sleep that could be filled with a myriad of poor choices.

"It's mostly done," Abbot says.

"It is?"

"I told you, it's not overly complicated."

"Funny."

"But I'll still take another look at it sometime this week, if you want me to."

Good. That's easy, casual. They can figure it out.

Ned pushes the top rack of the dishwasher in and starts dumping silverware into the rack. He pauses, reconsiders, and sorts them by knives and forks and spoons. He and Abbot can see each other again, finish up the work for Ned's project, and go back to how this was supposed to be. No more dinners with family, no more weekends away, none of it, just their work and their colleagues' assumptions and gossip.

Ned straightens and rolls his shoulders, trying to get them to loosen. That should be a relaxing thought, though his stomach tightens. *Nerves about actually being done with the work*, he figures. Abbot must also be feeling better that they're getting close to ending this fake relationship. Hell, any kind of a relationship between them.

Though when Ned looks at Abbot, he's just staring down at the floor. And then Abbot frowns and Ned looks down too and—

"Baxter, hey!" Ned grabs for his collar. "No!"

Tail wagging, Baxter licks off another plate, oblivious until Ned drags him back from the dishwasher. "We don't let him do that, you know. At Pat's, I mean."

"Does he do so anyway?"

"No," Ned says quickly.

Behind Abbot's glasses, his eyebrow lifts. His hands are soapy, the stem of a wineglass held between his long fingers.

"Right," Abbot says and his mouth quirks at the corner.

Ned shuffles Baxter a step backward and closes the dishwasher, trying to see if that's really a smile that pulls across Abbot's face.

CHAPTER SIXTEEN

NED TAPS his finger against the whiteboard. "Do we have any questions about any of this?"

Blank stares back at him. Ned claps his hands together.

"Right," he says. Nodding is good. Note taking is better. Those empty, panicked stares mean he's not doing his job as well as he should be. "Okay, let's back up to last week's reading."

He clicks backward through his slides, and then picks up a marker and pulls the cap off. "Bourdieu's theory of habitus," he says, raising the marker to write on the board. It leaves a weak streak of color and then nothing. Ned sighs, pitches it toward the trashcan, and grabs another one. "Breaking it down, we're really just talking about individual perceptions of our social world. Let's get some examples out there—yeah, throw one out."

"Food," says one of the girls in the front row, her fingers on her laptop keys and her legs crossed, a sandal dangling from her toes.

Ned gestures for her to go on. "Food, yes, but more specifically?"

She doesn't need to be here, and neither do either of her

friends. The three of them have always been good students, sitting in the front row of each of his courses they've taken.

"Phil," Ned calls toward the back of the room. "What aspects of food?"

Nothing, just Phil slouching lower in his seat. Ned writes *food* on the board and then hovers his marker a couple inches above it.

"Food . . ." he prompts.

The girl in the front brushes her hair back and smiles at him. "Favorite foods, how you cook, what you do and don't tend to eat."

"Right." Ned turns to write those down too.

She and her friends really shouldn't be here. This review session is for students like Phil who need the help, but he appreciates not having to drag out the silence or fill the room with his own voice.

The door at the back of the room opens and Abbot's there, though he quickly backs up.

"Sorry," he says, loud enough for the students to turn toward him. "Lee said you were in here, but I didn't realize you were teaching right now."

"Just a quick review," Ned says. "We're almost done, just going over a few things there were some questions about." He points toward his students. "Which you all understand now, right?"

The three girls nod. Phil slumps farther down behind his computer.

"Great." Ned tips his chin toward Abbot. "What's up?"

Abbot shakes his head and takes a step backward. "I'll find you later."

"'Kay. Or I can swing by your office after this."

"That'd be fine."

Abbot looks really good standing there, the light from the hall outlining his long legs and the fitted cut of his shirt.

Ned wishes he hadn't noticed. He wishes more that he could stand here and take in the sight, but two of the girls turn to look at Abbot again, then glance at Ned, and lean toward each other and start whispering.

"Okay, so individual experiences of the world around us," Ned says, loudly, in hopes they'll stop their chatter.

He glances up again to where Abbot hasn't moved, though at Ned's look he does, finally stepping out of the classroom and letting the door fall closed. "And what we're really getting at is the way that past experiences tend to inform and shape our interactions."

Silence again, except for the three girls still whispering. One of them giggles and claps her hand over her mouth. Phil rests his cheek in his palm.

"All right," Ned says. "Backing up even further, let's remember our conversation about how we form habits and work our way more slowly toward our good friend Bourdieu."

By the time the bell rings, Ned lets himself grow slightly more optimistic that the bottom third of his class won't fail the semester—or at least their exam. It doesn't exactly look good to have them bringing in low scores, though had they bothered to do the reading . . . Ned sighs and starts putting the caps back on the markers. He'd take the kids even reading the Wikipedia article, if it helped with the bored, glazed stares he gets. The problem of teaching introductory courses that so many students have to take to fulfill requirements—there's a reason he's stuck with this class, and all the tenured professors get sociology majors in their seminars. Someday, he'll get that too. If he ever gets a job.

The three girls linger behind the rest of the students, and Ned waits too, sure they have questions. They don't, just finally bend their heads together, whispering their way up the steps and out. Ned follows them down the hall to

Abbot's office, where he gently taps his knuckles against the door. One of them glances back again, and he gives her a small friendly smile before just opening the door. Now is not when he wants to start answering questions if she's just thought of them. He wants to get this damn analysis done.

And he wants to get another look at how that shirt fits Abbot. He presses his lips together against the thought, trying to fight it from his mind as he steps into the office.

"Hey," Ned says and then stops, halfway inside the door.

Abbot holds up his index finger before Ned can say anything else, his phone pressed to his ear. He looks tired. He looks pissy too, a sharpness to his features Ned's so familiar with.

Your dad? Ned mouths.

Abbot shakes his head, his phone still held against his ear. And then he says something in . . . Ned stares. French. That's definitely French. That's . . . kind of hot.

Stop, Ned instructs himself. They slept together once and look what it's turning him into. They're not doing that again—they never were supposed to in the first place, and it was a brief and incredibly satisfying slip up of an arrangement they're both incredibly clear on.

"Now's not a good time," Abbot says in English.

"Sorry," Ned says quickly. He shouldn't just be standing here, listening in. "I'll catch you later."

Or maybe he'll email first, set up a time to meet. That fits Abbot's style far better than just dropping by unannounced. Abbot'll have a chance to slot Ned into the rest of his work schedule. Ned already showed up at his house twice with no warning; he doesn't need to be making a habit of it here in the department building too.

"No, Ned," Abbot says, tipping the phone away from his mouth.

"Sorry, I, it's a bad time, I know, I—"

"Wait, Ned, just—"

"I'll email you." Ned steps backward. "Text, whatever, sorry to interrupt."

"No, it's—Louis, *stop.*"

Ned stares. He knows he's staring. And he knows he should leave. But Abbot sets his phone aside, faceup, and the screen clearly shows he hasn't ended the call. A jumble of tinny words come through the speaker.

"That conference is next weekend," Abbot says. He's clearly just going to ignore the call. Louis. He's ignoring Louis. Ned sort of wants to walk over there and give him a high five. "We're just discussing the paper for it."

"Sounds like it's going well."

Abbot closes his eyes. Then, he takes his glasses off, sets them by his phone, and rubs his fingers against the bridge of his nose. He really does look tired. "As well as ever," he says into his hand.

Ned grimaces. "That sucks."

Abbot just shakes his head. On the phone, Louis is still going strong.

"Let me know if you're free later," Ned says, patting a hand at the doorframe and backing out of the room. "And uh, good luck."

Abbot slips his glasses back on, his mouth a flat line. "Thanks."

Ned gently shuts the door. He's had those conversations with Jen and knows full well the throb of the headache that accompanies them. Pat used to come over, mess up Ned's hair, and hand him an ice-cold beer from the fridge. Ned looks at the door, Abbot's nameplate right there. He could do something like that, now. Should, maybe. They're not friends, not really, not like Ned and Pat are, but they're . . . something.

Though, no. They're nothing. Abbot's helping him with a project, and Ned just walked in on a private conversation. He sticks his hands in his pockets and goes to collect his computer from his office. He's got to stop this, ogling Abbot every time he sees him and interrupting his life.

Except that, slumped in his stool at the bar as the happy hour crowd thins out and Pat starts making dinners, Ned can't stop thinking about it. Abbot looked so exhausted, and he's probably still at work right now, trying to finish that paper. Ned taps at his computer, letting the statistics program beep at him, and he doesn't even bother to frown at it.

"Hey there, look, it's my favorite grad student," he hears, and hands fall to his shoulders.

He knows that voice. Ned bends over his laptop. "I'm working."

"Go to the library," Lee singsongs in his ear. She jostles his shoulders again, and his barstool moves with the motion. He steadies himself on the bar and again shakes his head.

"I gotta finish this," Ned says. And he's got minutes to do it before his VPN shuts down. He pushes his tongue into his cheek and keeps typing.

"Hey Pat, can you get our boy here a drink?" Her thumbs dig into the muscles at the base of Ned's neck. He frowns, hating that it feels so good. "Shots? Tequila? The good stuff."

Ned quickly shakes his head. "No—Jesus, Pat, no tequila, what's wrong with you? I have work tomorrow."

"We're supposed to be enjoying our time away from the office." Lee swings herself onto the barstool next to Ned. She grabs his computer and spins it toward her.

Ned yanks his laptop back. "I told you, I'm working. Grad school, you might've heard of it, dissertation, doctoral studies—"

"Spending your evenings with your computer instead of with us humans," Lee says and before he can grab her hand, smacks his computer closed. "Live a little, Ned. Wasn't that the point of this grand experiment?"

"Don't you have your own bar to go to?" Ned asks. Pat hands over two full glasses of beer, foam spilling down the sides. Ned nudges his computer away. The last thing he needs is a beer poured all over his dissertation. "No, Pat, I've gotta—I'm going to go upstairs."

"No." Lee hooks her hand through his elbow. "C'mon. Minori's on her way too."

He pulls his laptop toward him. "Lee, no, I've gotta finish this. Abbot told Chris I'd send him a draft this week, and I have three classes to teach."

"Abbot," Lee echoes back to him. Ned wants to wince, though when he turns to her, she's got a grin on her face, not a question written across her expression of why Ned's not fondly calling him *Henry*. She holds a finger up and taps at her phone, waggling her eyebrows at him as she holds it up to her ear. "Geez, he doesn't even have a recording. 'You've reached two oh seven,'" she repeats and rolls her eyes.

Ned frowns. "Who're you calling?"

"Tell your man to put a greeting on his voicemail." Lee taps the call off without leaving a message. Ned licks at his lips. Abbot's going to have a missed call from her. And he's busy. And shouldn't be subjected to Lee, just 'cause she likes to rib Ned.

"What are you doing?" Ned asks.

"Incentivizing your evening." She presses the glass of beer into his hand. "Drink, would you? You're going to give yourself a stress aneurysm. I'm getting flashbacks to my own dissertation writing just looking at you."

Ned opens his mouth. *He's not "my man,"* he wants to

say. Instead, he clears his throat. "Which you finished, exactly what I'm trying to do, as it so happens."

"I'm sorry for her." Minori pushes toward them in a rush of cold air from outside. "Hi, sweetie. What are you doing to poor Ned?"

"Reminding him that all work and no play makes for an ulcer." Lee smacks a kiss on Minori's cheek. "That's my jacket."

"And you can have it back the day you manage to remember to put it on your own damn hook," Minori says. Lee kisses her again on the same spot. "Ned, cheer up. You'll be out of here and away from the horror of this woman soon."

Ned props his elbow on the bar and rubs at his forehead. "Hopefully."

He meant it as a joke. It just comes out sounding depressed. He should've gone to the library. At least there he could be surrounded by other students also wallowing in fall semester ennui.

"Geez, it's just a dissertation," Lee says and Ned blinks his eyes open again. "You look like you're going to cry."

"I'm fine," Ned says, but he lets her push his glass into his hand again. His laptop is still right there. He needs to go upstairs and get this done. He needs to not be thinking about Abbot on the phone as Lee's call probably beeped in his ear over that rapid patter of French. Instead, he takes a drink and wipes the foam off his lips with the back of his hand. Lee steps away from Minori and hugs him, wrapping her arms tight around his waist.

Gently, Ned pats at her back. "Um, thanks." Then, he frowns and jerks backward, grabbing at her wrist as she fishes his phone from his pocket. "Hey!"

"I'm not even looking at your pictures." Lee swipes to the lock screen.

"Seven four six seven," Pat says.

"Pat!" Ned says.

"You probably don't even have anything good, is it all just your dog and kid?" Lee unlocks his phone and taps at his contacts. "Boring."

"Stop." Ned makes a grab for his phone. "Lee, stop."

"I'm sorry for her," Minori says. "She's the worst. Terrible, really."

Lee holds his phone out of his reach, unless he's going to lunge for it. Behind the bar, Pat's grinning. Ned folds a hand over his laptop. He's going is what he's doing. They can have their fun. Ned's got his work to finish. And anyway, even though Lee taps at Abbot's name, he doesn't answer again, and she just sighs when it goes to his voicemail once more.

"Enjoy your evening." Ned grabs his phone from her. He tucks it deep into his pocket. He picks up his laptop too, shoving it into his backpack.

"Live life." Lee tips her glass toward him.

"Dissertation," Ned says. "I'd like to be done this century."

Lee rolls her eyes and takes a long swallow of her beer. Ned's phone buzzes against his thigh. He puts his hand on it through his jeans without thinking, and Lee's eyes travel there above the rim of her glass. Her mouth quirks on a grin and Ned sighs and pulls his phone back out.

"Hey," he says, turning away from her as he answers it. "Lee called you."

"I know," Abbot says into Ned's ear.

"No, I mean—" Ned closes his eyes. "She's here. At Pat's, I mean. I was just working."

"I see," Abbot says. Ned grimaces at the bar. There're too many coats of varnish on it. He works his thumbnail into the worn and chipped wood. Abbot told him now wasn't a good time, and here's Ned, calling. It's overbearing, is what it is. Embarrassing, too.

"So, that's why . . ." Ned trails off. "I know you're busy right now."

"We're done."

"Oh. Good."

"Finally," Abbot adds with that dry tannic note to his voice.

"What're you up to, then?"

"Speaking with you."

"Ha ha," Ned says. *Didn't mean to bother you*, Ned should say, though Lee's not so subtly listening to his half of the conversation. At least Pat's at the other end of the bar, pouring wine into glasses and not rolling his eyes at Ned. "Well, Lee wants me to drag you out here for a drink."

It can't be an accident that Abbot lives across the city from campus. He can shut his door against all of the chatter of colleagues after work, probably exactly how he likes it.

"I have a book for you," Abbot says. "I can bring it by if you're there now."

Ned glances at the clock above the bar. It's so close to Chris's witching hour, all the more reason Ned should tuck himself away upstairs with his work, rather than let any more time slip by down here.

"Okay," Ned says. "If you want. Though you don't have to."

"If I show up, are you going to try to convince me that beer tastes good?"

Ned lets out a laugh. "I dunno. I might."

"Well, I'll consider myself forewarned. See you soon." Abbot hangs up.

Which leaves Ned there on his bar stool, pocketing his phone again and dodging the smile Lee aims toward him.

He spins slowly back and forth, turning his beer glass this way and that, watching bubbles rise through it.

"Another?" Pat asks when his beer gets low.

"Nah." Ned shakes his head. There's something sticky on the bar. And it's on the elbow of his shirt now.

"Want the game on?" Pat asks.

"What?" Ned pulls his head up. "Yeah."

"Look alive." Pat tosses over the remote. Fishing, golf, the news—there it is, the Sox playing out in Oakland, even though it's just the pregame chatter being shown. Ned picks at his shirtsleeve, idly rubbing at the patch left on the fabric.

"Good evening," he hears and quickly spins his stool around. "For you."

Abbot presses a book into Ned's hands. He's got a jacket on, unzipped at the collar.

Ned ducks his head over the cover of the book, holding it at an angle toward the light Abbot's blocking. He's standing close. Ned licks at his lips. Well, the bar's crowded; of course Abbot's standing close to him. "*A Beginner's Guide to Statistics*?" Ned asks, reading aloud.

"Liesl's finished with it."

Ned smacks the book against Abbot's arm. "Thanks."

"I thought it might be helpful."

"I do need another drink," Ned says. He's really supposed to be working. Instead, he points to the tap at the end of the bar and then to the small tumblers sitting near the shelf of liquor. "Hey Pat, a sip of that one too, and the pale ale."

"I'm not your short-order cook," Pat says but pours a splash of each beer into the glasses anyway. Throws in a wink too and a glance toward Abbot that Ned ignores.

"Here," Ned says, holding out one of the glasses. Abbot's close enough to touch. The skin of Abbot's neck above the collar of his shirt is just right there. Ned had sucked on that spot. Bit at it too, so lightly that it's not like there's a mark. He tries to look away.

"It's fine," Abbot pronounces.

Ned pulls a face. "Fine?" That should be enough to render the guy something less than attractive, despite how Abbot's long fingers loosely hold the glass. "That's a damn good beer, so if you think it's 'fine,' then you're beyond all hope."

"How unfortunate."

"You came," Lee says to Abbot. "You never come."

Abbot's mouth settles back into its normal stern line. Ned pats at Lee's arm, moving her to the side. "Don't scare him off, you hear? Be nice."

"I am nice," Lee says.

Ned pushes the other glass toward Abbot. "Let's call Chris and tell him his grand plan is working."

"This one isn't fine." Abbot sets the glass back down, pushing it away from himself.

"You have absolutely the worst taste." Ned opens his mouth again to make a crack about Louis, but stops himself —it's none of his business.

"Yes?" Abbot asks when Ned just sits there, poised to talk.

"How's your presentation coming?" He pulls the glass toward him. There's enough left for a good-sized swig and the rim is fogged from the press of Abbot's mouth. "You guys ready for the conference?"

"Nearly." Abbot's eyes flick to Lee and then back to Ned. "Which I appreciate."

"Yeah." Ned gives a nod. This whole pretending to be together thing worked. Is working. It should be a relief. He licks at his lips. "What do you have left to do?"

"Finishing that paper." Abbot shifts his weight slightly, then rests his elbow on the back of Ned's chair.

Move even closer, Ned thinks and then tries to stamp out the image of Abbot's arm brushing against his shoulder. His hand too, resting on Ned's own. God, it would feel so good.

Ned clears his throat. "You're not done with it?"

"I had certainly thought so."

"Dissension in the ranks?"

"Differing assessments of quality." Abbot too opens his mouth like he's going to speak. Instead, he picks up the first beer Ned handed him and examines it.

"Want one?" Ned offers.

"I wasn't going to stay." And no, he isn't, is he? His coat is still on, and he's got a bag slung over his shoulder with what has to be his laptop in it, and a manilla folder stuck in the side.

Ned nods. "Sure." He can watch the game with Pat. Or do what he meant to do and retreat upstairs with his work. Maybe he can text Abbot the questions he has, now that they have each other's numbers. It'd save them from having to spend the evening together, lingering here over another drink.

Abbot looks down into the beer again, then holds the glass up to the light. "Perhaps if you can find one slightly more tolerable."

"I've got a better pilsner than that upstairs," Ned says and then presses his lips together. He hadn't mean to say that, such a bald-sounding invitation. And Abbot's looking at him now, instead of his drink. Ned hears himself add, "Isn't that German?"

"I'm Swiss."

"Still."

"And pilsners originated in the Czech Republic."

"Well, whad'ya know. We've got a beer expert on our hands here."

Pat leans over the bar and thumps him on the arm. "Are you watching this?"

"Yeah." Ned has to twist around to see the screen where an umpire is yelling at a coach. Pat's not the only one waving at the TV. Across the bar someone shouts, "That's bullshit!"

Minori wraps her arm over Lee's shoulder. She whispers something and Lee laughs. Watching another couple settle in for an evening together hurts like it always does. Seeing them so comfortable together. Ned slips off his stool, careful to not brush too close to Abbot.

"You're leaving?" Minori asks when he picks up his jacket.

"Yeah, I'm gonna run," Ned slings his backpack over his shoulder.

"I thought you were here to watch the game," Abbot says. His voice is softer like this, Ned standing right next to him.

"I've got Baxter. Gotta feed him. Look, come up if you want." Ned's stomach swoops. Well, at least he sounds casual.

He tugs the open sides of his coat more firmly around himself and works his way through the crowd. Abbot can follow if he wants to. Ned doesn't care. No, he doesn't want to care. Because he's got a warm thick bloom in his stomach when Abbot waits on the sidewalk while Ned coaxes his key into the sticky lock.

The stairs creak beneath them. He hasn't noticed that in a long time, the way they sound off with each press of their feet to the treads. At the top of the stairs, the door bounces against its frame with a click of nails.

"Hey, hey now," Ned says as he eases open the door to a squirming, panting Baxter. "Back up, no back, Baxter, c'mon."

Abbot stares around himself. Well, there's plenty to look at. Ned might've straightened up if he'd known he was going to have company. Then again, maybe not. There's something satisfying about Abbot, so primly put together, standing next to Ned's running shoes where they're tossed by the door, and the socks Pat left on the arm of the couch. He takes in the empty pizza box from last night, the books on the coffee table, and the blanket thrown over the back of the couch. It's been folded exactly one time since Ned moved in, just before Pat's mom came over for dinner.

"Just put it wherever," he says as Abbot hovers, slowly pulling his jacket off, and then just holding it, an eye on the overfull coat rack. "Here, give it."

Ned drapes the jacket over the back of one of the kitchen chairs where it'll at least stay mostly clean of dog hair and tosses the pizza box toward the pantry. Baxter gives Ned's hand a snuffle, and then in a click of nails, jogs over to sniff Abbot's ankles.

"Hello," Abbot says to him.

"I think he might be wanting Liesl to turn up behind you."

"You live here."

Ned shakes his head. What a genius this guy is. "Sure do."

"For how long?"

"A year, year and a half."

Or so. He knows the months down to the day. Has ever since Jen drove away with Peggy in the backseat and Pat poured him a shot of whiskey at this very table, Ned's clothes sitting in bags in what had been the guest room.

"Do you like it?"

Ned glances back over his shoulder. "I don't know," he says. "It's all right."

"Is this you?" Abbot has a framed photo in his hand, plucked from the top of the bookshelf.

"Me and Pat." Neither of them have front teeth in that picture, and their cheeks are pink from the sun. Ned remembers that summer if not that photo, racing their bikes down their street, forts made out of couch cushions, and the sprinkler going in Ned's yard for them to jump through.

"You've known each other that long?"

"Since we were toddlers. I apparently threw a Lego at Pat and made him cry, and the rest is history." Ned grabs a bag of dog food set above Baxter's bowls and opens it. "Hey Bax, here, eat. It's dinnertime, buddy."

Really, it's early to feed him, but still, Baxter sticks his head gamely into his bowl. Ned ruffles his ears. When he straightens, his hands feel empty. Quickly, he turns the TV on, clicking through to the game. "So, you're going back over your paper with a fine-toothed comb?"

"Apparently," Abbot says, still studying the picture.

"What's the deal? Louis didn't work on it?"

"Not that I can tell." Abbot tips the photo toward the light. "Why did you throw the Lego?"

"I can only assume it was a premonition of dealing with him for the rest of my life. Thought I'd get a shot in early while I could."

"I don't understand," Abbot says slowly. "You live with him, and you always complain about him."

"Pat?" Ned laughs. "I love him. My best friend."

Abbot shakes his head. "It's hard to tell with you; you're so . . ."

Ned waits, but that was apparently it. "I'm so what?"

"Irritable," Abbot finally says.

"Pot, kettle."

"What?"

"I'm just saying."

"Irritable and confusing."

Ned licks at his lips. Behind him, Baxter's crunching through his dinner, the bowl skittering across the floor as he pushes it in his excitement. "Yeah," Ned says. "Uh, sorry?"

What the hell do you mean? he wants to ask, but Abbot just replaces the photo and sets his bag on a chair. It looks odd there, against the scratch and scuff of the kitchen, no granite countertops and white pristine cupboards. The single window set high in the wall overlooks the alley behind the bar, not a neatly maintained backyard.

Abbot sits down at the table. "How's your analysis coming?"

"Yeah, good." Ned unroots himself. *Irritable and confusing.* It's not the worst thing he's ever heard said about himself. Probably the truest, too, at least that first part, even if he can't parse the second. "I only got five error messages this time, which is a record low."

Ned sets his laptop in front of Abbot, standing behind his chair and reaching past him to open up the right document. He really shouldn't be this close to him because it makes him want to study the back of Abbot's neat haircut and the length of his neck above his collar. Ned had kissed right there, that soft skin just beneath his ear.

"You're nearly done, it looks like," Abbot says, two long fingers dragging across the mouse. His lips purse. Ned tries not to look. "Though this is wrong." He highlights a couple sentences, deletes them, and then keeps scrolling.

"Well, it wouldn't be me if I didn't mess up every single attempt." Ned forces himself to take a step backward.

"That's hardly true." Abbot deletes another couple sentences, then quickly retypes them, changes the font color, and points to the screen. "Rewrite that in your own words."

"Is that the comment you left for Louis, too?"

"If I thought he'd bother doing it, I would've."

"Is that going to be your weekend, then, sorting through edits?" Ned asks. It doesn't matter. Abbot's weekend plans aren't anything to Ned—he has Peggy to go see and he could use a breather from all of this, as far from campus and Abbot and his coworkers as he can manage.

Abbot blows out a soft breath. "Apparently."

"Did you have other plans?" *Don't*, Ned tells himself even as he says it.

"My family's still in town. I was going to spend the weekend with Liesl, but Louis is submitting the paper on Monday regardless," Abbot says. "I would prefer it to be actually finished."

"Bullshit," Ned says.

Abbot glances up at him, clearly surprised. Maybe Ned is too, at least a bit. Slightly taken aback by how pissed this makes him. Surely he never meant this, to be standing here wanting to go to bat for Abbot of all people. But . . . no, it's bullshit. "Go see your sister and tell Louis to pull his damn weight."

"I'm not going to do that."

"I'll do it."

"Don't."

Ned tosses his hands up. "Fine." He stalks over to the refrigerator. There's probably too much beer in there for two guys who live above a bar where they spend most of their time. Ned fishes out a bottle from the back and pops the top off. "You want a glass?"

"What does it matter?"

"Some people prefer it. We might have one in the freezer."

"The edits," Abbot says.

"You can't want to spend your weekend working on that instead of kicking it with Liesl," Ned says. "Is this why finishing up your grant is taking so long?" Ned bumps his fists together, knuckle to knuckle, awkwardly holding the neck of the bottle. "Butting heads this whole time and him giving you the runaround?"

Ned turns back toward the cupboard. Abbot's clearly a glass guy, even if he doesn't know it. Ned pours out half of the beer, the foam rising to the top rim before it begins to settle back down again. Maybe . . . maybe the crux of their incomplete paper is that Abbot and Louis aren't really over each other. Not quite ready to cut ties and they're stringing it out for a reason to keep in touch. Ned rubs his palm over the back of his neck.

"Look," Ned says, watching the fizz and pop of the foam recede. "It doesn't matter. Whatever, live your life."

"What would you do?"

"What would I do?"

"Isn't that what I just asked?"

"Well, do you . . ." Ned feels his mouth work. He takes a sip from the bottle. Belatedly, he holds out the glass. *It's not your business*, he tells himself. "Is this still a—a thing with him? The two of you?"

"A what?" Abbot echoes. "A 'thing?'"

The word sounds odd coming out of Abbot's mouth. Laughable, even. Ned's cheeks heat, embarrassed for wanting to know. He shouldn't have invited Abbot up. Or to the bar in the first place, or let Lee grab his phone like that.

"Like, do you still—are you not over him?" Ned asks anyway.

"He told me I was, at best, unfit to—" Abbot's lips press together, tight enough the color blanches. Quickly he takes a sip of beer.

"Unfit to what?" This was never in their plan, these details between them. Still, Ned steps closer.

Abbot's chest rises on a deep breath. "I wanted children." His voice is tight. Ned stares. Abbot's throat works in a swallow. "He didn't. At least not with me. There's no 'thing' between us."

"Oh." Ned's mouth is open. He shuts it. "Okay."

Baxter pushes his bowl across the floor as he licks at the bottom. Ned watches him, that familiar routine of every dinner he's ever fed him. Kids. Abbot, with kids. Abbot wanting kids. And the esteemed Louis deeming him . . . Jesus, the guy's an ass. Unfit. What the fuck kind of thing is that to say to someone? To Abbot. Heat rises through Ned's stomach.

"That's—" Ned shakes his head. "You didn't listen to him, did you?"

"No." The word comes too quickly.

Ned presses his teeth together. "Is this it?" He plucks the folder from the side of Abbot's bag.

Abbot takes a step toward him. "Don't."

Ned scans the first page. "Jesus Christ, is he your professor? This is what he sent you?" Ned flips a couple more pages into the paper, nearly every paragraph high-lighted with another set of comments. "Well, I can see where you get your style, at least." He drops it onto the table. "He thinks this is fine? Done? Finished?"

"I think we're having difficulty reaching a consensus."

"Who's the first author on this?" Ned waits and nothing comes, but Abbot's silence is enough. "He's heading up this grant and yanking you around to do all the work?"

"You don't understand."

"Seems pretty clear to me."

"It's different for you," Abbot says. "You're able to—I can't do what you do, argue over this with him."

"Well that's just bullshit. You're the most stubborn son of a bitch I know. You—you, Jesus, Abbot, you don't want to change up your schedule to meet with me." Ned starts ticking off on his fingers. "Don't want anyone else to touch your fancy ass wineglasses, don't eat meat, don't like beer—hell, man, look at us." Ned waves back and forth between them. "This entire fake dating shit was your idea."

Abbot's unblinking. Unmoving too. Ned's got another item he could add to the list of Abbot saying *fuck it* and doing what he wants: inviting Ned upstairs the other night. Ned closes his mouth over the words before he can say them. Talking about the other evening is the last thing they need. He can already feel it hanging in the room between them, the two of them alone like this. Ned picks at the paper again. It's not even creased at the staple from Abbot reading through it, though he clearly has since there are neat notes in his tidy handwriting.

"Sorry," Ned says.

"Are you upset?"

"What?" Ned looks up.

Abbot's got his eyes on his beer, the glass held loosely in his fingers. "That we're—" Abbot waves the glass between them. "Doing . . . this."

"What?" Ned straightens. "No, that's not—that's not what I meant. At all."

"It is easier. With you." Abbot's fingers tighten on his beer. "To say those things."

Ned swallows. "Oh."

"I like this beer." Abbot's cheeks are brushed with the faintest stain of red, up high on his cheekbones. "And I would stay here, tonight. If you invited me to."

Ned points at Abbot's glass with his own bottle. He's buzzing. His skin, his head, the fingers gripping the neck of his beer. "You didn't even drink it."

"I did."

"Barely."

Ned has no clue what he's doing. He tips his bottle up

and takes a long swallow. Another night together is as bad an idea as it was the first time. Ned rubs his palm over his chest, right where that burn is. But maybe it shouldn't be a big deal. It's just sex. It's nothing serious. "Yeah. Stay."

His bottle of beer bumps into Abbot's hip when Ned wraps his arm around him. Abbot's a good kisser. Really good. Methodical, how he goes about it, that soft tug at Ned's lips and the hand that settles on the back of his neck.

The solid and warm press of Abbot's body is what Ned remembered. Thought about too much, really. With a hum into his mouth, Ned hauls him closer, walking them toward his door.

The overhead light in his bedroom shines garishly bright. Ned turns on the lamp next to his bed and hits the switch to turn off the bulb above them.

"No," he says and pushes Baxter back into the living room with his knee.

He shuts the door on those pleading brown eyes. Still, paws and nails scratch against the floor. Ned wipes his hands on his pants. His own cheeks feel flushed now, too.

"Nice decorating." Abbot turns in a circle as if to fully take in the bare white walls of Ned's room. The door rattles against its frame.

"Thanks." Ned's got a dresser, a bed, a nightstand, and he doesn't own any of them. Even the sheets are borrowed from Pat. "Did it myself."

"Clearly."

Outside the door, Baxter heaves out a huff. Again, the door shakes. He sounds like he's trying to dig his way in. "Um," Ned says. His face is burning. "Hold on a sec."

Baxter jumps against Ned's thighs and Ned shoves his head down. "Cool it," he mutters. He wants to jog to the kitchen. He makes himself walk to the freezer. Ice cream, an empty ice cube tray, an ice pack . . . the bones are wedged behind a frozen pizza. He yanks one out and drops it into Baxter's waiting, open mouth. "Knock yourself out, and for fuck's sake, keep it down."

Ned eases his bedroom door shut again. In the kitchen, the bone scrapes against the tile floor. Ned's too hot. He wants to strip his shirt off. He wants to take Abbot's off even more.

"Bedtime reading?" Abbot holds up a book. He's already got a second one in his other hand too, *Conceptual Practices in Contemporary Sociology.*

Ned grabs it and tosses it onto his dresser. "Want a selected reading?"

"Perhaps."

"Hmm." Ned dips a finger into Abbot's collar. Crooks it, and runs the back of his knuckles along Abbot's skin. "Later."

"I'll look forward to it."

"I'm already horrified by the fact that you probably will."

Ned shuffles a step forward. Moves his hand around to the back of Abbot's neck and presses a dry kiss just there, above the collar of his dress shirt. Abbot tips his head to the side and softly, Ned kisses his neck again, wetter this time. Oh fuck yeah, he's wanted his mouth on Abbot's skin for days now and it's even better than he remembered.

With both hands, Ned pulls Abbot's shirt from its neat tuck into his waist band. He shoves his hands up under it and traces over the trim muscles at the small of Abbot's back. Another kiss, to the tendon that stands out on Abbot's throat. He smells good. Like the aftershave he uses and the clean scent of himself beneath it. Blood sings through Ned's cock.

Slow down, he tells himself. Gently, he bites at that

tendon. Hands fit to Ned's shoulders and squeeze. Ned squeezes back, his fingers curled around Abbot's slim waist.

There's a soft hollow between the muscle of Abbot's shoulder and the hard roll of his collarbone. Ned kisses it through warm fabric and then pushes his nose into the dip of Abbot's throat, palming up Abbot's ribs. He squeezes again, and then once more, higher at the sides of his pecs, Abbot's shirt draped over his forearms.

Abbot flicks at the buttons on Ned's shirt and lifts an eyebrow. Ned can take a hint. He unbuttons it and drops his shirt to the floor, and Abbot quickly unbuttons his own cuffs. Ned pulls in a breath through his nose and shoves Abbot's shirt off his shoulders so he can rub his palms over Abbot's chest, those tight high pecs, the hard nubs of his nipples, and around to the points of his shoulder blades. He's . . . Abbot's so . . .

"C'mere." Ned's got a type, and right now he's got his hands completely full of it.

With a push, he turns Abbot toward the bed. A knee on the mattress, Ned shoves him down onto his back. Abbot's hands catch on Ned's sides, and Ned crawls over him, licks up the long line of his neck and into Abbot's mouth that opens eagerly for him.

Abbot's hand fits between them, pressing into the front of Ned's pants. He groans and grinds down into Abbot's palm. *Slow*, he tries to tell himself again, like he isn't a hot second away from humping those fingers.

Ned's slacks loosen with the pop of the button, and then Abbot's working his zipper down over the bulge in Ned's boxers. Ned licks at Abbot's tongue, groans again, and sucks at his lips. He needs to breathe. Needs to kick his damn pants off.

Shoes, he thinks dimly and rocks into Abbot's touch.

"Fuck," he gasps. "Wait."

"I would prefer not to."

"Oh, shut up." Ned props himself on his palms, locking his elbows. Abbot's cheeks are flushed. Slowly, he pumps his hand up Ned's cock and drags back down. "Stop, stop."

"Are you sure?" Abbot's tongue touches his bottom lip.

"No," Ned groans. He tilts his hips into the pull of Abbot's hand on him. Moves with it and lets his eyes close. He feels his lips part. How is this so damn good?

"Very well." Abbot lets go.

"Oh, dammit." Ned tucks his chin to his chest and gasps into his own shoulder. Keeps his eyes squeezed shut and just breathes. He's about to fish around for Abbot's hand, put it right back where it was, and so fucking what if he embarrasses himself.

But Abbot pushes him gently off. Ned goes, flopping onto his back. Yes, shoes. Abbot has the right idea, bending down to take his own off. Abbot stands and slips his pants and boxers down his hips and *oh*. Yes, that's better. Abbot naked. Naked and kneeling on the bed again so he can strip Ned's pants off too. At least one of them is thinking. *Socks*, Ned realizes belatedly. He's not fucking Abbot with his socks still on.

And condoms. In his nightstand. Ned's hand is shaking as he grabs them and the bottle of lube. "Lie down," he says and his damn voice nearly cracks. He can't actually look at Abbot there, lazily palming himself. He's got a nice cock. Ned didn't really look last time, not like he wanted to. He licks at his lips, fumbling to squirt lube onto his fingers as Abbot lies there, eyes hooded and stroking himself with those long slim fingers of his.

"Stop," Ned says.

"I'm not doing anything."

"You are." Breathing. Lying there. Fucking touching

himself. Ned smacks Abbot's hand away and kneels between his thighs.

Abbot lets out a breath as Ned pushes a finger into him. His palm slides down his stomach, all long fingers and trim nails.

"Don't," Ned warns, but Abbot takes himself in his hand again. "M'serious."

Abbot's jaw works. "Apparently," he says, the head of his cock disappearing into his fist.

"I am." Ned crooks his finger inside Abbot.

Ah, there it is, Abbot's mouth dropping open. Ned does it again and Abbot turns his face to the side, like he could bury it in the mattress. It's a hell of a sight, Abbot spread out before him, a blush tinging his cheeks and down his neck. Ned yanks the condom out of its wrapper and fumbles to get it on himself.

Ned grabs both of Abbot's wrists, pinning them to the mattress next to his shoulders. He awkwardly scoots his knees in closer, trying to line himself up without a hand to help him. Though—yeah, like that. Ned feels his breath catch. Abbot's hands flex in Ned's grip, and slowly, Ned pushes into him.

"Okay?" Ned gasps. He's not. He can't breathe. He thrusts shallowly, his lips pressed together over his teeth. He'll never breathe again, but this is so worth it. Tight and warm and wet and Abbot's thighs tip outward and Ned groans as he sinks in fully. "Oh, fuck."

"Your commentary is—ah—is as colorful as ever."

"Shut the fuck up," Ned gasps.

His ribs are too tight when he tries to breathe. He flexes his hips, pulling out, and then pushing in again. He does it again, faster. This is too much. Abbot's too much. Ned drops his head down to kiss him, breathless and messy. Gives up on holding his wrists too, to better brace himself, and lets himself keep thrusting, pushing into Abbot again and again, noise building in the back of Ned's throat with each dip of his cock.

Abbot's fingers press into Ned's back. His breath hitches as Ned adjusts his angle. *Fuck yes*, Ned thinks and focuses on pounding into Abbot right there, that spot that makes Abbot's head arc back.

He's got his eyes shut behind his glasses, his head dropped to the side. Ned presses his mouth to the corner of Abbot's own in something less than a kiss. With a push, Ned sits back on his heels. That's better, more air to breathe, and a gorgeous view of Abbot's body, stomach flexing and chest moving on his breath.

Ned's rhythm breaks for a moment, but he gets it back again, finding that same angle that makes Abbot's chin lift, tendons tightening like cords in his neck and his eyes squeezed shut. Ned can touch him like this. He takes Abbot's long cock in his hand and squeezes, stroking, and watching each flick of his thumb tighten Abbot's stomach, the corner of his mouth.

Look at me, Ned would tell him if he thought it'd make any difference.

Might be better like this, though. Ned might just shatter if Abbot turned those eyes on him. It'd go straight to the pit of heat building in Ned's stomach if he got that cool, assessing stare right now. Ned presses his lips together on a whimper, stroking Abbot faster. His hips don't slow and Abbot moves with him, a foot planted against the bed. Blotchy ruddy-red stains Abbot's neck, stretches down to his chest, and Ned quickens his hand until Abbot's tongue peeks out, licking over his lower lip.

"Yeah," Ned says and Abbot's body tightens as he comes, his stomach rigid and his shoulders curled in.

He doesn't open his eyes. Ned works him through it,

milking out those last splatters against Abbot's stomach. Gently, Ned kisses at his chin. Props his hand on the bed, tucks his face into Abbot's neck, and pushes into him over and over.

Too much? he means to ask.

He can slow down. Give Abbot a breather. Change positions. See if Abbot's up for another. He can—oh *fuck*. Ned hears himself whine. From the base of his stomach, heat blooms.

"Oh," he says and his breath catches on the burst of pleasure, his hips pumping as orgasm races through him.

He's shaking. Or Abbot is. No, it's Ned. His entire body is trembling and Abbot's quiet beneath him, eyes shut. He's got long eyelashes, fanned against his cheek. Clumsily, Ned straightens his glasses.

"Okay?" Ned swallows. His mouth is dry.

Abbot's eyes blink open. "Yes."

"Okay." Ned's arms don't feel strong enough to hold him up. Again, he says, "Okay." He shifts to the side, just far enough to pull out. His hands are too heavy. His whole body is.

That was fucking amazing. Still is amazing. Ned pushes his face into Abbot's shoulder. He doesn't want to move. Abbot feels so good, lying under Ned. Warm. And he smells nice. *Thank you,* he suddenly wants to say. He clears his throat. "Did you really like the beer?"

"The beer?" Abbot blinks behind his glasses. "It wasn't that bad."

"Okay." Ned needs to find a new word. Abbot's palm settles on the small of Ned's back. Ned wonders if he wants him to move. "I'll read your paper."

"You will?"

"Go to Boston this weekend, and I'll read it for you." Ned really should move. Let Abbot breathe. Abbot blinks at him again. "Hell, go on Friday and make a couple days of it."

That might be a nod in how Abbot's head shifts. Maybe Ned's just suffocating him into compliance.

"I'll think about it." Abbot draws his finger through the sweat on Ned's back. He probably wants Ned to clean himself up, not drip sweat all over him.

Ned shifts gracelessly to the side and fumbles for the condom. The sheets are too warm on Ned's skin. He wants to toss open a window, let the night's breeze in. He's flushed too, down to his stomach. "Need anything?"

"No, thank you."

"Okay." Ned wads the condom into a handful of tissues. He's still too shaky. Water, at least. In the bathroom, he splashes water onto his face and then drinks from his cupped palms. He wets a washcloth and hands it to Abbot. "Here you go."

"I have office hours on Friday." Abbot neatly wipes at his stomach. His neck is still flushed pink.

Ned sits on the edge of the bed. Abbot's not getting up. Maybe he really meant that he'd stay all night.

"Is anyone going to go?" Ned asks.

"It's always a possibility."

"Says the statistician." Ned takes the washcloth back when Abbot's done and chucks it toward the bathroom. "Cancel it."

"I'll think about it."

Ned stretches out on his back. He doesn't want to be sitting up. This is much better. His body is entirely too loose and heavy to bother with anything other than horizontal.

"There's a new exhibit at the aquarium right now. Of course, I've never been because my spawn of a child won't go anywhere that doesn't have dinosaurs, but I've heard it's good. Liesl might like it."

Abbot shifts slightly, turning toward him. "Why the interest in dinosaurs?"

Ned snorts a laugh. Their shoulders are close enough to nearly brush. "I have no clue."

"I liked them as a child."

Ned rolls his head against the pillow to look at Abbot. "You did?"

"Apparently. I don't really remember." Abbot takes his glasses off, folds them, and sets them on the nightstand where Ned normally tosses his phone. "Though at least I wasn't throwing Legos."

"Your dad still tells you?" Ned can all too clearly picture teasing Peggy about it someday. Though who knows, maybe he'll be watching her go through her own doctorate, the world's leading expert on paleontology.

Abbot shifts to look up at the ceiling. "Not my father."

"Oh." Abbot moves like he's going to sit up. Ned lays a palm over his stomach. *Stay*, he nearly says. "I'm sorry."

"Please stop saying that."

"What happened?"

Abbot tenses. He's trying to sit up, from the feel of it. Ned keeps his hand where it is and beneath his palm, Abbot pulls in a breath. "She was sick."

"That's hard," Ned says.

Abbot's still so stiff. "It's fine."

"It's not."

"It happens."

"Doesn't make it any easier," Ned says. "Or any more fair."

Abbot presses his fingers to his forehead. "Don't. Please."

Ned shifts closer. "I really liked what you cooked the other night. It was good."

"Do you not know how to stop?"

"'Fraid not." *Take another breath*, Ned wants to tell him. "That exhibit has octopuses." Abbot's eyes shift toward Ned. That's something at least, rather than the steely staring at the ceiling. "Just saying. They're no megalodon, but they're all right."

Abbot's cheeks are still pink. Ned wonders how long that color will stay there, staining his skin above the shadow of evening stubble. With a finger, he touches Abbot's chin.

"Go to Boston," Ned says. "No offense, but literally nobody's going to show up for your office hours."

"Why Americans use 'literally' as a means of exaggeration remains beyond me." Abbot could tip his chin away from Ned's touch. He doesn't. "And I don't believe you meant no offense."

"Fine." Ned traces his knuckles down to Abbot's jaw. "I did, but only a little bit."

Later, Ned stares into the dark of his bedroom while Abbot sleeps. He wants to touch Abbot's glasses, folded neatly on the nightstand. Wants to touch Abbot too. Roll right over into the warm line of his body. The door edges open with a slice of light from the living room and Baxter shuffles in. It fades again as the door swings closed on creaky hinges.

"Quiet," Ned whispers as Baxter sniffs up the length of Abbot, curled beneath the blankets. "Sorry bud, find somewhere else to sleep."

Baxter whines and chuffs out a breath, his chin propped on the edge of the mattress and his eyes raised hopefully at Ned. Slowly, he lifts a paw onto the edge of the bed.

"No," Ned whispers and leans over Abbot to push Baxter away. "Go sleep in Pat's room."

But Baxter huffs again and circles in a click of paws to flop onto the floor. Ned lies back against his pillow, listening to the familiar sounds of Baxter scratching at his neck, and under it, Abbot's soft, even breathing. Ned's bed feels small like this, with someone beside him.

He rolls onto his side, his feet brushing against Abbot's. He won't even know if Ned scoots closer to him. Ned might as well get his kicks in now while he can, with that long stretch of a gorgeous body to nestle near and one night to sleep pressed up against someone, after all the ones he's spent alone.

CHAPTER SEVENTEEN

NED RUNS his finger beneath the sentence. "You know that word. Starts with an *f*."

"Ffff," Peggy tries.

Ned's leg is going numb with her sitting on his lap. He smooths back her hair before her wriggling can get it stuck into his mouth. To think she was once so little he could balance her weight in one hand.

"An *f* and then an *o*," he coaxes and then reads back the part she's already gotten. "The Montana plains have many . . ."

"Fossils," she says. Ned kisses the top of her head. Slowly, she fumbles through. "A lot of—"

"Archeologists."

His dad sticks his head into the living room. "Lunch is ready."

"We're not done," Peggy says.

"Yeah. We're not done."

"And no books at the table," Peggy says.

"No books?" Ned echoes, cocking his head at his dad from behind Peggy. "What kind of rule is that, Pop?"

"No books or Baxter and I are going to eat your lunch. We're having Jurassic era swamp stew," his dad says, bending over Baxter, who's sprawled in the doorway to the kitchen. "Aren't we, Baxter? Yes, you're a good boy, aren't you? Yes, you are."

"Up," Ned says, tapping his fingers into Peggy's leg, and when she doesn't move, into the bottom of her feet until she squirms, giggling. He stands and slings Peggy over his shoulder, her feet drumming against his stomach and her hands pattering soft fists on his back.

"M'not hungry," she says, wriggling.

"That's not your stomach growling?" Ned picks her up from his shoulder to hold her stomach against his ear. "That must be a velociraptor in there, then. Don't worry, mister, we're feeding her soon."

"S'not a velociraptor." She laughs, her feet thumping against his chest. "I wanna read."

"Eat first." Ned drops her into her chair at the table.

Afterward, he sends her back to the living room with a stain of chili on her shirt and the book in her hand. He's got to pack up her things. He knows well enough what'll happen if Jen shows up to get her and Ned and Peggy are embroiled in a gripping tale of a slowly extracted vertebrae. He's been there before, Peg whining and begging to finish what they've started and Jen eyeing her watch. Best to let Peggy study the pictures. He sighs, collecting her clothes from the floor of her room. Soon enough, she'll be reading it by herself, no need for him there at all.

"Ned," he hears and straightens. His dad pokes his head inside the room.

"Yeah?"

Dad sits on the edge of Peggy's bed. It was a guest room once, back when Ned was growing up. Now, it's covered in stuffed dinosaurs, and it's long since been repainted a cheerful bright yellow. Home away from home for Peggy, or something of the like. And will be for a while to come, until Ned can find his own place again.

"You all right, kid?"

"M'fine." Ned picks up a stray sock. "Is Peggy's coat downstairs?"

"You got a lot on your mind?" Dad leans forward, his forearms on his thighs. "You don't seem fine."

"Busy. Work, school, the usual."

"Okay."

Ned fishes a stuffed dinosaur out from beneath Peggy's desk turned dino-hospital. The stegosaurus has a cold, Peggy had told him when he'd picked her up Friday night. It'd been immediately admitted for scans and nursed by a triceratops. Ned's pretty sure his knees still hurt from kneeling on the carpet for diagnostic procedures carried out with an old calculator long out of batteries and a single knitting needle.

"Come here," his dad says.

Ned shakes his head. "Jen's on her way."

"Name the last time that Jennifer was on time." His dad pats the mattress. "Sit for a second. Tell me what's going on."

"I'm fine," Ned tries again, but sinks onto the bed next to his dad.

"You said at dinner that your work is going well."

"It is."

"And your classes, except for the esteemed Phil."

"Yeah."

"How's your gentleman friend?"

"What?" Ned pulls back, which is useless on a kid's bed, with his dad right there next to him. "He's not—we're not like that."

"What're you like, then?"

Lonely, Ned thinks.

Go back to sleep, Abbot had whispered, easing out of bed at the crack-ass of dawn. Ned had been barely half awake and too out of it to tell him to stay. When he'd woken up again later, Baxter had been on Abbot's side of the mattress, and that wasn't a fair trade at all.

Ned smooths his palms over his thighs. Being back at Mom and Dad's is what it always is: a reminder in how very far he hasn't come over the last few years. And to be moving back in once the semester's over . . . he drops his head down, staring at his feet. Moving back in if he graduates, that is. Which involves actually submitting his dissertation, not just poking at the document over and over again, wondering which paragraphs Abbot would delete and which variables might make Chris sigh, smile, and tell Ned to try again.

"I need a job," Ned says to the carpet. And a life. A real one, not this liminal mess he's been living in for too damn long now.

He doesn't even know anyone in Boston anymore. Last night, he flicked through his parents' TV after they and Peggy went to bed, slouched on the couch with Baxter's head on his thigh. It'll become normal as soon as he moves back, no Pat around with his mess and noise, and no bar so conveniently downstairs to spend his evenings at. Just this, the quiet of a house he's long since outgrown, and his mom delicately picking dog hair off the carpet before Ned can jump up and do it himself.

"You'll find one," his dad says.

"Nobody's emailed me back. I've applied to a bunch."

Abbot's father was probably right about Ned floundering through his career. And Boston's a hell of a city to be competing in for a job. There's plenty of folks coming off of a postdoc, fellowships, and more prestigious programs than

Ned's . . . he shoves his face into his palms, rubbing at his eyes.

"Easy there," Dad says.

"Grad school was the worst choice I could've ever made," Ned mumbles into the heels of his hands.

"It's hard. But you'll see it through. You're nearly there."

"I keep messing up. First everything with Jen, and then trying to finish this research, and I told Peggy I'd be back this fall and I'm not, and—" *Abbot*, which he won't say. Not out loud, and not to his dad. To try to explain this ridiculous mess . . . no.

"You're going to miss your friend?"

"Don't call him that."

"I meant Pat."

Ned rubs at his eyes. "No, you didn't."

"No, I didn't." Dad bounces his shoulder into Ned's. "I want to meet him. Your mom does too, but she's far too nice to pry."

"I told you, it's not like that with us. I'm not . . . I don't want to date anyone." Ever. *Forever ever*, like Peggy would say. Isn't that one of the first things he and Abbot ever agreed on? Having his life go up in flames once was entirely more than enough, no matter how Ned's stuck on the warm drowsy memory of dozing next to Abbot the other night.

"Maybe you should," his dad says. "Might cheer you up a bit, you know."

"I'd just mess it up."

"You?" Dad picks up a stuffed T. rex and playfully closes its soft mouth over Ned's arm. "Not you. I know what Pat's been telling you, getting back on that horse. Or T. rex as it were. Did you know there's a theory they had feathers?"

"Dad."

A knock sounds at the door downstairs and Baxter starts barking. Jen used to have her own key to this house. Ned peers out the window and sure enough, that's her car pulled up to the curb. Ned's car, it once was.

"Pegasaurus," Ned calls, jogging down the stairs with her backpack. He tucks the T. rex into the top of it, zipping it closed. "Time to bounce." He pulls the front door open. "Hey."

His stomach twists. It always does when he has to be face-to-face with Jen. *You not over her?* Pat had asked once when Ned tried to explain it. The answer to that had been —and will forever be—a strong *really fucking over her*, but still, seeing Jen is uncomfortable as all hell.

Though today, he tips his head when he sees her, frowning. "You okay?"

Jen looks exhausted, circles under her eyes and not a trace of makeup that Ned can see. He can't remember the last time he saw her like that, not done up like she always is to leave the house.

From behind him, Baxter crashes down the hall, his entire body wiggling with the force of his tail smacking back and forth. Ned looks away, past Jen bending down to scratch his head.

"Hi, yeah, good." She tucks her hair back behind her ear and pulls Baxter toward her. She'd picked him out all those years ago, plucked him from the squirming pile of his brothers and sisters. "You?"

"Good, fine." He lets go of the door and steps back for Peggy who joins the fray. Jen's in sneakers. Not heels. And jeans, he realizes. Old ones.

"You not feeling well?" he asks as she kisses Peggy's forehead.

"Oh, I'm fine." Her hair, normally carefully straightened, is tied up in a messy knot. He remembers running his hands through it, pushing it out of her face, but it's like a story someone told him once, or something that happened to a friend, a memory he can't quite grasp.

"You sure?" he asks as she sets Peggy back down.

"Yep." She tugs her jacket straight. Bloodshot lines smudge her eyes. "Peg, get your things."

"Here's this." Ned holds out her backpack. He cups Peggy's tiny shoulder in his hand, steering her back toward the living room. "Your book, and your shoes too, kid. Say goodbye to Grandma and Grandpa."

"Is this everything?" Jen unzips the bag. The T. rex peers up at her, mouth gaping wide open.

"I think so. What happened?"

Jen crosses her arms over her chest, her jacket bunching up. She looks horrible standing there like that, curled in on herself.

"You sick?"

"No, I'm . . ." She breathes out a laugh, staring down at her feet and rocking back on her heels. "I don't think I want to tell you."

"I'm not going to . . ." Whatever. Fight with her. Ned takes a couple steps toward the living room. "Peggy, let's go, you can look at that in the car."

"M'reading," she calls back, half-draped over the couch, her book open again.

"Mom and you gotta go." Ned glances back at Jen. God, pregnant maybe. He doesn't let himself grimace. "Come say goodbye."

But Peggy just turns the page. Once, he would've grinned. *She gets this from you*, he would've said to Jen with a smile, and she would've rolled her eyes at him. He sticks his hands in his pockets.

Jen kneels down, Baxter licking all over her face. *Gross*,

she'd said more than once, pushing him away. Today she lets him, going as far as leaning her cheek on top of his head when he settles down.

"Jen?" he asks.

"Can you take Peggy on Saturday night? Around five?" she asks.

Ned purses his lips. *I'm not here to babysit so you can go on a date*, he wants to snap. But it's Peggy and he's not going to do anything other than give a nod and say, "Sure."

"I'm going out with a friend." She sniffs.

"Okay."

"Girls' night." Her voice sounds like it's going to crack.

"Yeah?"

"Jeff and I broke up," she says into the top of Baxter's head. She strokes Baxter's back, gently scratching at his fur.

"Oh."

She stands up and Baxter leans against her legs. She keeps petting him, bent over so she's not looking at Ned. "I'm sure you're glad."

"Well." He runs his fingers back through his hair. "Uh, sorry, I guess."

"I—" She sniffs hard. With one knuckle, she wipes beneath her eye. "I was cheating on him."

With his best friend? Ned could ask. "Oh," he says again.

"Yeah." She wipes her cheek on her shoulder. "So um, I guess I'm going to think about seeing someone. A therapist, I mean. I think I've got a—a problem."

A couple of them, Ned could tell her. He works his hands deeper into his pockets. "That'd probably be good. I mean, not—" He shakes his head. "That came out wrong. Just . . . helpful, maybe."

She laughs again, no humor in that huff of breath. "I hope so. Peg?"

"I'll get her," Ned says, backing away.

Jesus. He wipes his hand over his face. Jen and Jeff, over and done. For good, it sounds like. That's . . . something. He bends down and scoops Peggy up, book and all.

"Come on, Miss Margaret." Ned kisses her round cheek, the book squished between them. She's so utterly, impossibly perfect. He kisses her again, loud and smacking until she giggles. "I love you, missy. You gonna have a good week? I'll be thinking about you."

"Don't wanna go."

"I know, sweetie." He kisses her again. In the front hall, Jen's wiped her eyes dry. Ned deposits Peggy at her feet. "You be good, okay?"

The rumble of the car starting is familiar as anything and Ned waves as Jen backs out of the driveway. He waits for the taillights to fade and only then steps back inside, trying to swallow down that routine ache that starts up whenever he has to watch Peggy be driven away.

Broke up with Jeff. Cheated on Jeff. Wow.

"Was that Jen?" his mom asks when he wanders into the kitchen, his hands still stuffed in his pockets and his chin tucked down as his mind works. "Are you driving back up tonight? You can stay here, you know, miss all the traffic."

"I have an early class." There's a numbness to how he feels. Slowly, Ned sinks into a chair. *A problem.* Jen had once told him he had enough of his own problems to fill one of the damn books he was always buried in. Her voice had been so hot then, none of the smallness that it had today.

"Your dad's worried about you." Mom rests a hand on his forearm. "You okay, sweetie? I know it's tough seeing Jen and saying goodbye to Peggy after a weekend together."

"No, I'm . . ." Ned frowns. The breath he takes comes easier than he would've thought it might. He tries again, waiting for his slow inhale to catch on the sharp edges of pain he's so used to. Jen, cheating on Jeff. Damn. "I think I'm okay."

And he is. An odd sort of feeling courses through him. He rubs at his forehead, staring down at the dinged and dented wood countertop. Slowly, he exhales.

"You sure?" Mom asks.

"Yeah." Ned nods. "I think so, anyway."

His phone buzzes in his pocket. Slowly, he pulls it out. There's a text from Jen that she's running a few minutes behind, and another from Pat asking when he'll be back. He swipes both of them away and then stands. The picture shows the blueish glow of a giant fish tank. And there's Liesl silhouetted against it, her hands on the glass, her back to the camera.

You actually in Boston? he'd texted Abbot on Friday afternoon. You better be, Ned had typed out, and then deleted it. He hadn't wanted to bug Abbot, and anyway, he hadn't seen him around the building all day, and his office door had been shut when Ned left after his last class.

Ned sinks onto the couch. He hovers his thumb over the keypad, pushing his mouth to the side. Octopuses are probably smart enough to run multiple regression, he types. He takes a breath and hits send.

I might let them edit my paper, Abbot writes back.

Ned grins. He fishes into his backpack, past a book and his laptop charger, to pull out Abbot's paper. He can read it before he drives to Portland. It'll give him something to mull over on the way instead of just two hours of missing Peggy.

Can they help with my analysis afterward? Ned texts him.

I'll ask them.

Ned grabs a pen from his bag and swings his feet around to sit sideways on the couch, folding back the title page of Abbot's paper.

Let me know what they say. I've got a great book on statistics for dummies if they need a refresher.

"Who's that?" Mom asks.

"No one." Ned quickly drops his phone. He'll feel it buzz against his thigh if Abbot texts him again.

"Nice to see you smile." She presses a kiss to the top of his head. "Did you write that?"

"No." Ned angles the paper toward her. "Just looking it over for a friend."

"Can't wait to read your work. Your dad wants to read it, too. Soon, right?"

"Soon."

As soon as he sends it in to Chris. He gives his mom a small smile as she heads upstairs. Maybe he'll get Abbot to look over his dissertation once more, before he emails it to Chris. It'd settle his nerves at least, one more set of eyes on his work before submitting it. *And an excuse to see Abbot again,* he thinks and then shoves the thought away. He reaches for his phone, unlocking the screen and rereading their texts.

Can we meet up tomorrow? he types and sends it before he can stop himself.

They could meet tonight, nearly. They're both in Boston. Though Abbot has his sister with him right now, and they've both got a drive back to campus ahead of them. Still, it's a nice thought.

I'll come by your office.

Ned had meant after work. Dinner maybe. Though his office works too. That's far more appropriate.

He sends back a thumbs up, then considers, and sends an octopus emoji as well.

Maybe that'll make Abbot smile, though maybe he already is, a day away from the office with his kid sister.

Ned picks up the paper on his lap and tries to focus on the words, not the memory of Abbot's grin in the photo on his lock screen Ned had accidentally seen, his eyes bright and an easier expression on his face than Ned could've ever imagined.

CHAPTER EIGHTEEN

"Nedster," Sameer says, clapping him on the shoulder. "What's good?"

"Check this out." Ned tips his laptop towards him.

"'The Socioeconomic Trends in First-Generation College Matriculation,' oh wow, I just fell asleep." Sameer holds his hand up for a high five. "Nice job, my dude. Look at you, already ordering up new business cards?"

Ned drops into his chair and rolls toward his desk. "I think my mom is."

"Let me know when to pop the champagne." Sameer turns his chair toward Ned. "So you definitely gone then, after this semester? 'Cause I gotta start throwing in for a good office mate if that's the case. I don't want just anyone up here."

"Still gotta defend." Ned saves the file again, scraping his teeth over his lip.

"Do you know when you're doing that?"

After Chris reads this, which means after Ned submits it, which means after Ned's really, truly certain it's ready. His stomach jumps. "A week or two."

Oh God, Ned just wants to crawl under a rock. Not

have to face down his committee as he sweats his way through thinking he can talk about statistics.

But on the other side . . . Ned stares down at his desk. He'll have to clean it out. And let the department know not to assign him any classes to teach next semester. Fill out the forms to graduate, get things sorted out at Pat's . . . Ned's been here for a long time, working out of this room. A long, long damn time, and there's a bedroom waiting for him at his parents' place, and Peggy.

He'll find a job. And a place to live on his own. No matter that his email inbox remains empty, no response from a single university he's applied to. He takes a breath. There'll be more jobs posted eventually, even if he has to wait until the semester's over. He'll find something. Probably. And either way, he'll be done here.

He lets out a breath, tension knotting his stomach beneath a high-strung wheel of giddiness.

"Hey, Mr. C.," a voice says from the doorway. *Doctor*, Ned might get to say soon. He spins around.

"Phil. What's going on?"

"Is it, like, your office hours now?"

Ned glances at the clock. "No."

"Well, you're here." Sameer points to himself, his coffee mug, and then the door, slipping out of it. Ned sighs. He'd go too given the chance.

"Get me a cup," he calls after Sameer. "What can I do for you?"

"The reading," Phil says. "I can't get the book."

"The book? It's due the end of this week."

"Well yeah, but the library doesn't have it."

Ned raises both eyebrows. "The library doesn't carry a copy. Like I told you. In the beginning of the semester."

"Right, so."

"So?"

"Can I read it next week? I ordered it but, like, it isn't here yet."

"It's not here yet."

"Yeah, so, if I read the book when it comes . . ." Phil shrugs. "It's just a week."

"I'm teaching it next class," Ned says slowly. "That's the point. To have read it beforehand. You have a response paper due."

"We do?"

"You do." Ned sighs and leans over to his bookshelf. The annoyance Phil typically sparks in him is largely absent today. Has been all day really. Ned's in a far better mood than he's been in all semester. It's a treat, Pat had said just that morning, and Ned had tossed a pencil at him and his big mouth. "Here." Ned hands Phil a copy of the book in question.

"Thanks. But I ordered it, like I said."

"Right, but I'm lending you a copy. Which you're going to read. On time." Ned holds up a finger. "Bring it back to class."

"I probably don't have time to read it between now and then, anyway."

Ned shoves the book into Phil's hand. "Try."

Phil shuffles to the doorway. "I guess."

"The paper, too," Ned calls after him.

But all he hears is footsteps leading away in the hallway, until they're joined by Sameer walking back to the office.

"Did you put milk in it?" Ned asks before he turns around, but it's Abbot. Ned grins. "Hey there."

"I don't have any milk," Abbot says.

"Or my coffee." Ned leans back in his chair. "What's up?"

"You're sending undergraduates to bring you coffees? I thought only full professors did that."

"No, just putting in requests with other grad students." With his heel, Ned spins his chair back and forth. "We're used to it, you know. Pretty good at it, even."

"A marketable skill."

"Knew I learned something here in all this time." Ned bends and reaches into his backpack. Abbot's paper is now creased, the corner bent. "This was good."

"I'm assuming you didn't actually enjoy reading it."

"Took a nice nap halfway through." Ned hadn't, but he'd eaten dinner, then read the rest of it before driving back to Maine. "I even understood part of it. Not all of it, mind you, but at least half. Less than half. The introduction. And the conclusion. It got real shady in the middle."

Abbot takes it from him. "You're better at statistics than you give yourself credit for."

"I have a grade on my transcript that would argue otherwise. Also a midterm, a final exam, and an email from this professor I know asking to see me, out of 'concern for my future in the program'—or something of the sort."

"Which you never answered."

"Self-preservation," Ned says. "Listen, I know I'm no expert, but I don't see what other edits it could need. I think you're good."

Abbot flips through the paper. "I really don't want this returned by the journal with more work to be done."

"Make Louis do it if that's their answer. Put your foot down."

"That's not exactly my strength."

"Tell him what's what," Ned says. "How you really feel."

Abbot's lips press together. "I'm not going to do that."

"Fake it till you make it."

"Excellent career advice," Abbot says, his voice as dry as

ever. "And here I thought you struggled with such shows of confidence."

"Me?" Ned asks as innocently as he knows how. "I'm moments away from submitting my dissertation, and definitely, in no way, about to throw up on your shoes."

Abbot looks down, then back up, and there's a spark in his eye, a little shine of laughter that lights his face. "Thanks for the warning."

"Can you take one more look at it?" Ned asks and holds out his laptop. "Please? 'Cause I'm going to die on the spot if Chris says I need to start over again."

Abbot rolls Sameer's chair across the short width of the office until he's next to Ned, crowded there at his small desk. Ned sets the computer down between them, his arm brushing against Abbot's.

"I read it already." Abbot scrolls through the document. His knee nudges Ned's thigh. "It looks good."

"But is it right?"

"I'm not going to let you submit something that Chris is going to return again."

"Yeah, but—"

"Did he have comments on the rest of your work?"

"No." Ned fidgets. He wants to lean against the warmth of Abbot's arm just there on the armrest of Sameer's chair. "No, he said all of that was fine, he just wanted me to add all the dumb statistics."

"All the relevant and helpful statistics," Abbot says, his eyes on Ned's computer and his voice dry.

Ned elbows him, catching him in the forearm, and to his surprise, Abbot elbows him right back.

"Ned, you did it." Abbot scrolls through the document once more, and then sits back in his chair. "I don't know what you want me to look at."

"The writeup."

"Which is fine."

"But it could be better."

"Are you just looking for reasons to put off submitting it?"

"Yes. No." Ned scratches at the back of his head. "I thought it was finished when I submitted it this summer and that bit me in the ass."

"Scared to try again?"

"No," Ned mutters and scratches at his hair again. "Okay, yes. It's terrifying."

"One failure isn't a reason to never take another risk."

"I certainly think it is." Ned lets out a laugh. "One disaster and I'm done, thank you. In all walks of life, not just this damn dissertation. I thought you'd know that about me by now."

He means it as a joke, but Abbot's face shutters.

"Well," Abbot says. The dry humor's gone from his voice. "I suppose that's up to you."

Ned doesn't like that fading spark in Abbot's eyes, how his tone has slipped from teasing to something else.

"No, I just meant . . ." *That fucking horse*, he thinks, Pat's words rising through him. And what had Abbot said? A crisis of confidence? Ned blows out a breath. "No, okay, I'll email Chris."

Ned sets his hands on his keyboard and types quickly. Abbot stands, pushing in Sameer's chair and taking a step toward the door.

"Wait. I just mean—give me a sec, I'll send it right now."

He's sure Abbot's going to walk away any moment. Though Abbot doesn't, just hovers as Ned types Chris's email address in, then attaches the file. Doing this would be easier with Abbot still sitting next to him. Ned could press into the nudge of Abbot's knee against his leg, maybe let him tease him again about his hesitancy. Though, that humor seems to have flown out of the room so suddenly that Ned doesn't know how to catch it and reel it back in.

"Okay," he says. His stomach twists uncomfortably. *Sit back down*, he wants to say. He clicks send. "Okay, that's that."

Well done, he'd expect to hear in Abbot's dry tone, but when he looks up, Abbot's just watching him, his fingers rubbing against his thumb.

"That's that," Abbot says.

He wants to go, Ned's sure. Abbot has something to get to. Probably touching base with Louis, sorting out the end of their grant. Or maybe he just has his own life to get to. Of course, he doesn't want to linger here in the cramped space of Ned's office, no matter that Ned would be happy to have him stay.

Because . . . Ned blinks. Because submitting his dissertation and Abbot being done with his paper is the last of what they had originally arranged.

It's like a stone dropping into his chest and his smile fades. Chris might come back with edits for him to do, Ned might have to track Abbot down for a question, or to check what he's done, but the bulk of their ruse . . . pretending to date is behind them, *message sent* shining on Ned's laptop screen and the paper in Abbot's hand.

Don't go, Ned suddenly wants to blurt, but Abbot's already in the doorway, and Ned's not sure enough of how Abbot'd respond to get those words out, so instead he only spins his chair toward Abbot, sucking in a breath.

There's only one place their agreement ever was going to end, and it's apparently right here, their work complete and their lives parting ways.

Ned clears his throat. "So look, I don't think we need to, you know, make a big deal about this."

"This?"

"That we're not—" Ned waves between them. This was the plan, wasn't it? Dissertation, Abbot's grant, done and done. His hand feels heavy. "That we don't have to keep this up. Letting people think that we're . . . um, dating."

Abbot nods. The gesture's stiff. "I see."

"I just think, everyone's going to be nosy, want reasons we broke it off, right? Better to keep the—the end of this low key."

"I hadn't thought about it."

Bullshit, Ned nearly says. He's sure Abbot's thought about nothing else since they first started to pretend to date. Isn't that what they agreed on? That neither of them wanted to actually be in a relationship? *Never again*, Ned had thought to himself so often, and relief should be coursing through him. But it's swamped with the anxiety of sending in his dissertation, and the confusion of how Abbot just hovers there, zinging through Ned with a coursing uncertainty.

And a deeper, heavy hollow in his stomach.

Ned's disappointed, he realizes. Keeping up this scheme with Abbot wasn't as bad as he initially figured. Playing at pretending was fun in its own way. And now it's over and Abbot's going to walk out of here and *that's that*, Ned hears again. Over and done with and finished and any reason to keep seeing each other . . . no, they'll go back to how they once were, professor and grad student.

And then even less than that, once Ned moves back home.

Which is—that's what he wanted, right?

"Okay." Ned nods. "Well, if you want to tell everyone, that's . . ." He has to clear his throat. He doesn't like talking about this. "That's fine, if you want to go that route, let everyone know we—we broke up."

"Not particularly."

"No, me—yeah, me neither."

"One coffee, milk in it—gross, man—and—oh, hey." Sameer draws up short in the doorway. Then, he flashes them a grin. "Am I interrupting?"

"No." Abbot straightens. "I was just leaving."

"I'll see you around," Ned says quickly, and Abbot's gone.

"For you, Ned Coppola, almost PhD." Sameer sets the mug on Ned's desk. He claps both hands on Ned's shoulders. "I'm happy for you, man. Getting on out of here."

"Yeah." Ned gets himself to nod.

He slips out from Sameer's hands. The coffee's all right. Not all that hot. Sameer put way too much milk in it. With two fingers, Ned rubs at his stomach. He doesn't feel great. And he'd doesn't like the thought of Abbot walking away down the hall. When once he couldn't wait to see the back of that guy.

Wait, Ned nearly calls out. He turns to his desk. He's got work to do. That was the whole point of this: finishing his work, so he can get home to Peggy. *It still is*, he tells himself firmly.

And he doesn't need the type of distraction Abbot would lend, anything drawn out between them. Ned opens his laptop again and bends over it, checking his inbox to see if Chris might have responded already.

CHAPTER NINETEEN

SLUMPED on the couch with his laptop balanced on his thighs, Ned flicks back to his email again. Refreshes it once more. Stares at the screen, refreshes it yet again, and sighs.

"You're killing me," Pat says. He leans across the couch and shoves the remote into Ned's ribs. "Watch the game."

"I am watching the game." Ned clicks back to his presentation for his dissertation defense. He highlights the bullet points under his research findings, deletes them, and then clicks undo to make them appear once again. With a tap, he switches back to his email.

Pat smacks Ned's laptop closed. "Stop."

"Hey." Ned opens it again. "I'm working."

"You're not, you're just twitching slightly. Drink your beer."

"I am." The bottle resting on the coffee table by his foot is probably warm by now. Still no new emails. Nothing from Chris, not today, and not yesterday either. *I'll read it soon*, Chris had written back, and Ned's stomach had leaped. Since then, it's hovered somewhere in his throat, heavy and thick every time he tries to swallow.

"You said you were going to actually relax for once," Pat

says. "I know it's been a while, so let me lay it out: football game. Drinks. Want some chips? I'll get some chips. Baxter, go get a bag of chips, yes, that's a good boy."

Ned crosses his arms, frowning at his laptop. Maybe his dissertation really was that bad. Maybe Chris is trying to figure out how to gently tell Ned that he's going to be here at least another year. Maybe Abbot's spent his week across town in that house of his, rolling his eyes at Ned's attempt. Maybe he told Ned his work was finished just to be free of him, now that his own paper's done. He's probably enjoying his VPN access, getting ready for his conference presentation, and hoping Ned doesn't notice that his analysis couldn't possibly have been worse.

Stop, Ned tells himself. Those thoughts aren't helpful. Abbot's not that much of a dick to throw Ned to the wolves. And imagining him in his house isn't going to lead anywhere good, the thought of him in his beautiful living room, or at the table in his kitchen, a mug of tea in front of him.

How's your week going? Ned nearly texted more than once. They're not . . . friends. Not really. They're not anything, and he can all too well imagine Abbot sliding his phone back into his pocket, Ned's message unanswered.

"Hi, Earth to Ned, watch the damn game."

"Yeah." Ned rubs at his thighs again. "Sorry. Just . . ."

Pat leans across Ned, grabs the bottle, and fits it into Ned's hand. "Sit back, drink up, watch the game like you're supposed to. You like this, I'll remind you. All that time with your Chuckie H., you might've forgotten."

Ned frowns. "Don't."

"What? I'm just saying, buried in statistics all hours of the day. What's the average distance run tonight?" Pat waves his bottle toward the football game. "Oh, that's right, you aren't watching, so you'd have no idea."

"I'm watching," Ned mutters, refreshes his email again, and sighs.

His email is at least something to ruminate over, rather than the mess with Abbot. No, the lack of mess with Abbot. The clean, crisp break they've made, which niggles at Ned far more than he was ready for. He picks at the corner of the label on his beer. What they were doing was ridiculous, but it was a good distraction. Something to think about, at the very least. Ned . . . misses it. Misses him.

Which is absurd. He can see Abbot whenever he wants. He can knock on Abbot's office door, let himself in, and listen to pedantic, overly involved explanations of statistics to his heart's content. Could do it now even, get there as Abbot's class lets out and he'd have Abbot to himself, since God knows his students have the sense to give him a wide berth.

"Heard something funny," Pat says. Ned grunts in answer. "Jen and Jeff called it quits."

"Oh." Ned waits for his stomach to jolt at the mention of their names. It doesn't, and he rubs at his forehead. "Yeah, she mentioned."

"Heard something even funnier about how it happened." Pat taps Ned's leg with his bottle. "A little extracurricular activity from the good Jennifer."

"Yeah, she . . . yeah."

"That's two for two. Lather, rinse, repeat."

"Guess so." Ned works his nail under the edge of the label. It's wet with condensation, tearing the more he fusses.

"I think you dodged a bullet there, man."

Ned stands and heads for the kitchen. "You and your metaphors."

He sets his beer bottle next to the sink and stares down at it. Then he turns and paces across the apartment. Pat watches him, tracking him like it's a tennis match and Ned's the ball flying back and forth.

"How long you gonna be mad for?" Pat asks.

"I'm fine."

"How long until you move on?"

"I've moved on. I'm moving on."

"Hmm."

"You know what? I hate when you do that."

"There's this thing called a horse, see—"

"Oh for the love of—"

"And when you fall off, your best friend steals your dog and drags you out for some fresh air." Pat pushes to his feet. "You've got that 'I'm going to crawl in bed for the next six months' air about you. Breakups don't look good on you, so c'mon."

"We're watching the game."

"No, we're stretching our legs, because you're in a mood," Pat says, and to Baxter's panting, wagging delight, clips his leash onto his collar.

Ned gets a shoe thrown at him. It catches him in the chest. The second follows, sailing past his leg.

"C'mon," Pat says again.

"I already took him out."

Pat picks up Ned's phone and slips it into his pocket. Grabs Ned's computer too and pushes it into Ned's backpack, then puts it on his own back.

"What the hell are you doing?" Ned asks.

"Nothing." Pat reaches behind the TV and pulls the plug out.

"The fuck?"

"We're going," Pat says cheerfully, grabs the back of Ned's shirt, and drags him out the door.

It's nice outside. Ned straightens his clothes and scowls. Baxter's thrilled as anything, dragging Pat along behind him, nose pressed to each streetlight and parking meter before he huffs out all his inhaled breath and moves to the next.

Ned trails along after them. He should tell Pat not to let Baxter tug on the leash like that, it's a bad habit Ned's been trying to break him of. And really, he should just turn around and slip back home when Pat rounds the corner ahead of him. Though . . . Ned pats at the pockets of his sweatpants. He doesn't have his keys, and he's entirely sure that's not a mistake on Pat's part.

"Pat," he calls out, jogging to catch up. Baxter lets out a bark and Ned hurries faster, dodging a woman with a stroller. "Pat, wait—"

Baxter's got all four feet digging into the concrete side-walk, head down as he drags Pat. Who's laughing, because of course he is, and Baxter's going to spring himself on some poor, unsuspecting child, and leap up like he's doing now—

On Abbot. Pristine running shoes, a fleece jacket, and Baxter's paws on his thighs.

"Hello, there," Abbot says as Baxter's entire body wiggles, his tongue lolling out and his head pushing again and again into Abbot's hand, desperate to be scratched.

Well, shit. This isn't how Ned meant to run into Abbot again, in sweatpants frayed at the cuffs, his hair unwashed, his face unshaven, and bleary-eyed from so many hours in front of his computer today.

"Hey," he says. He clears his throat. "Hi."

"Howdy," Pat says, and Ned's cheeks heat. *Shut up*, he wants to say. *Be cool*.

Pat finally tugs Baxter away from Abbot, where wet smudges mar Abbot's shorts. Ned's mouth is too dry.

"Out for a run?" Pat asks.

Obviously, Ned could say. He works his tongue through his mouth, like he'll find some words there.

"I was just heading home." Abbot's cheeks bear the pink, ruddy flush of exercise in cold weather. It looks good on him. Healthy. Ned's had more beer than can possibly be good for someone and ate cold stale pizza for lunch. He was going to have the same for dinner, too.

"You run down by the harbor?" Pat asks.

"I did," Abbot says.

"Nice route," Pat says, like he's ever run a day in his life. He smacks his hand into Ned's shoulder. "Ned runs too, you know."

"Only sometimes," Ned gets out, and Abbot glances at him and away again.

"All the time. Gotta stay in shape, right?" Pat smacks Ned's stomach this time.

Again, Abbot looks at Ned, but by the time he can glance back, his focus is on Pat.

"That's probably a nice loop, all the way across town and down by the water," Pat says into the silence. "You do that one a lot, right? I feel like this isn't the first time I've seen you this time of day."

Abbot looks good. Really, really good. That flush on his face, the slight shine of sweat and dampness of his hair. He's got long, toned legs, and on Abbot those shorts are something else, the way they hug the lean lines of his hips and outline that ass. Abbot's calves flex as Baxter butts his head against one slim thigh. Abbot bends to lightly stroke Bax's ears.

Ned pulls his eyes away, pressing his lips together. "How's your week been?" he asks.

Abbot nods quickly. "Good."

"That's good." Ned's has been complete shit. He tries for a smile, and it's probably the twisted ghost of a happy expression. "Yeah, great."

"I'm surprised you're not watching the game," Abbot says.

How do you even know it's on? Ned wants to ask. His heart hammers in his throat, and he fits his hands into the pockets of his sweatpants. "Yeah, well."

"I wanted to head out for some air and Ned came with, such a good dude, right?" Pat asks.

"I don't mean to keep you," Abbot says and takes a step back.

Ned makes himself nod. No, of course, Abbot's going to get cold, standing there in the autumn chill with sweat clinging to his temples. Ned wants to lean forward and push his face into Abbot's neck. He squints up the street where a car's stopped at an intersection.

"Not at all," Pat says. "Hey, come by sometime, yeah? I ordered some new teas, I could use an expert."

Abbot's tongue peeks over his lips. "I could do that."

He doesn't want to, Ned could say to Pat. Of course, he doesn't. He wants to be with his laptop and in the silence of his own house, not at Pat's bar of all places.

"Anytime." Pat hooks his thumb at Ned. "Gotta keep this one and his caffeine addiction company, right?"

Abbot shifts his weight to his other foot. He works his fingers across his thumb and glances at Ned. "It's pretty extreme."

"This weekend?" Pat asks. "Saturday? It's some good stuff, I got it from this fancy-ass tea place online."

"I can't this weekend."

"Another time, then, soon, okay?" Pat claps Abbot on the shoulder like they're old friends and grins at him.

"I don't have a caffeine addiction," Ned gets out, but it's too late because Abbot's started jogging down the block and only Pat's there to hear him.

"Abbot's cool. I like him."

"No, you don't."

"I do, he's fun. When you move back to Boston, I'm totally going to try to get him to hang out with me. I need a new bro."

"He's not fun."

"He is fun. I love me a tea enthusiast. He's like, super cool, you just can't admit it because you always see what you want to see."

"No one asked you."

"Which is too bad because I'm always right." Pat tugs Baxter along up the street. Ned glances back where Abbot disappeared, and then makes himself follow, hands in his pockets and his feet scuffing the sidewalk after the excited patter of Baxter's paws.

By Friday, Ned figures he's going to end up spraining his thumb given how many times he's refreshed his email on his phone. He checks one last time before driving south, his car's heater blowing over him as he sits in the driver's seat, rain splattering against his windshield.

Abbot's glasses would fog, Ned thinks. He frowns and drops his phone into the cupholder. Abbot's busy this weekend. Probably running a marathon to keep in shape, unlike Ned, who's going to watch his parents' cable channels. He sighs and turns the key in the ignition. His car echoes a groan back at him, spluttering and then finally starting.

Maybe Abbot's got a date. Maybe that's what he's doing, and Abbot decided it was too awkward to mention that, when he said he couldn't swing by Pat's. Ned's been worrying at that thought all week, and it just sinks heavier in his gut. Ned's probably right that Abbot's out with someone right now. Abbot's probably driving that slick black car to pick someone up, and here Ned is, coaxing his sticky gearshift into reverse. He tugs. The gearstick doesn't want to move.

The transmission, he thinks. He leans his forehead on the old, worn steering wheel. Maybe it's a sign he should stay here in Portland for the night. He's not going to see Peggy until tomorrow anyway. He could go out to a bar—one that's not Pat's and filled with people he knows, but across the city, maybe. Find someone and see if he can muster up the charm to manage to go home with them.

Ned gently taps his forehead on the wheel. He'd end up lonelier than he is now, he knows, and feel all the worse for it. He straightens and reaches for the gearshift again. At least his parents'll be home, and he can have dinner with them. Better start getting used to it, 'cause that'll be his entire social life when he moves back—Mom, Dad, and Peggy's cache of stuffed dinosaurs.

That is, if Chris ever returns his email.

Ned sighs and tugs at the gearshift again, and this time the car eases more willingly into reverse. Rain batters the windshield as Ned heads toward Boston. He clicks his windshield wipers up to a higher speed, letting them whip water away. The drum of the rain is loud, even over the rumble of the road and the radio channels Ned clicks through as Maine's stations fade into New Hampshire's and then Massachusetts's. He glances in his mirror and flicks on his turn signal, wanting to get around a lumbering, slow-moving truck, though his car protests, refusing to speed up.

He tries again, pressing on the accelerator. The pedal literally hitting the metal and Ned's practically at a standstill. He tries again, presses hard on the gas, and his engine whines, but his car just won't go any faster. Abbot's would—it'd zip right through the clogged streets and move easy and smooth.

"Shit," Ned says. What a metaphor for Pat to chew on—his own damn car won't even go in the direction he points it.

Outside his window, traffic whizzes by on the highway.

Ned edges his car toward the shoulder. A light blinks on the dashboard, on and off again, before it starts glowing solidly, staring right up at him. He flicks on his turn signal and coasts toward the first exit he sees.

"Shit," he mutters again when he parks outside a Dunkin' Donuts. He wraps his hands around the wheel, leans forward against his seatbelt to rest his forehead on his wrists. "Shit, shit, shit."

"I'll be there in a jiffy," his dad says when he answers Ned's call. "You're on 93 all already? That's not far."

"I'm sorry." Ned wraps his arm over his stomach.

"Nothing to worry about, kiddo."

Ned waits with his head tipped back, watching head-lights cut through the gloom. This fucking figures. He squeezes his eyes shut. He can't afford a new car. And he doesn't have a job lined up. And he still doesn't know if he'll even graduate this semester. Of course breaking down in a rainstorm on a busy highway in Friday-evening rush hour would happen too.

Ned only rouses himself at the deep rumble of his dad's tow truck.

"Jump in!" his dad shouts over the rain.

"I'll give you a hand," Ned calls back.

"No, don't,, you'll get soaked." And there Dad is, jumping out of the cab with no raincoat, jogging around the truck, and opening Ned's door for him. "C'mon, get in. That's all you have, the one bag?"

The heater's going in the truck. Ned rubs his hands in front of it as his dad winches Ned's car onto the bed. It's a sorry sight, dinged and rusted along the wheel wells. Amazing that the rust bucket brought him this far, really. Though Ned can't muster up much more than a weak sort of gratitude.

"I'm sorry," Ned says again when his dad jumps back in

and fastens his seatbelt. Ned's wet from the dash to his dad's truck, the sleeves of his dress shirt dappled with rain, but it's nothing next to the drip of water off his dad. "I know it's your day off."

Ned gets his hair ruffled. "Mom packed you a cookie. It's buckwheat and raisin. I'm not going to tell if you just chuck it out the window."

"Gross." Ned takes a bite. Abbot would like it. Ned sighs and shoves the rest of the cookie into his mouth, chewing slowly against the dryness.

"I'll get you a real one."

"M'fine." There's a cup of coffee in the cupholder. Ned sips at it. It's cold.

"Well, I want one. Last week, it was chia-seed oatmeal cranberry bars. Don't ever retire, Ned, this'll be what's in store for you."

Ned tips his head against the window. Can't retire if he can't get a job, now can he?

"I think we should stage an intervention and demand our chocolate chip rights," Dad continues on. "Or just make them ourselves? We could figure out cookies, right, kid?"

Ned closes his eyes. "Probably," he mumbles.

"That's the spirit." Dad smacks Ned's knee. "We could do it. You, me, Pegster showing the world what it means to enjoy a good cookie."

The truck smells familiar, like engine oil and diesel. Ned stares at the road. There's no real need to get on the highway, not this close to his dad's shop. Still, the drive will be slow, the streets clogged with the rain and Friday-evening traffic. His breath fogs up the window when he slumps against it.

Gently, Dad touches Ned's knee again. The truck bumps along, stopping at a red light. Ned stares at the rain streaking down, falling with a splash onto the pavement and forming deep puddles. A little girl and her father walk past holding hands. She jumps over a puddle, and he lifts her high over the next one. Peggy loves that, doesn't she? Any chance for sending a splash up around her tiny rubber boots, soaked-through socks aside. She's got a raincoat with dinosaur spikes all down the hood and back. Last time Ned had put her into it, the sleeves had been short, her little wrists showing beneath the cuffs.

"Ned," his dad says.

"What? Yeah." Ned sits up straighter. They're stopped again, not at a traffic light but in a small parking lot of a bakery, and his dad's turning off the truck.

"This is between you and me." Dad unfastens his seatbelt. When Ned was younger, his dad used to say *just us boys* during their bike trips to the park to get ice cream. Pat would always careen out of his driveway to pedal after them. Ned's chest loosens, just slightly.

"You going to get Mom something anyway?" Ned asks.

"Of course I am."

One time, they'd biked back home, a cup of ice cream thawing in his dad's palm, his other hand steering. Ned'd thought it a miracle that his dad could ride like that. Now he thinks of the front door opening and his mom there, how she'd smiled and fed his dad a spoonful of ice cream, chocolate chips falling and melting onto the stoop.

That's what Ned had so wanted from a relationship. What he so briefly thought he'd found.

"Two coffees with milk," his dad says at the counter. "And that one there, what flavor is it?"

"Chocolate chunk," says the guy behind the counter.

"Now we're talking. Three of those, please." Ned gets a wallet pressed into his hands. "I'm gonna take a whizz. Old age is coming for you too, Ned. Enjoy what you've got while you can."

"Thanks for that."

He takes the bag with the cookies, the paper crinkling in his fingers. Ned doesn't think he's hungry. He sips at the coffee before fitting a lid on the cup. It's all right, strong and still piping hot despite the milk.

Cheer up, he tries to tell himself. His dad'll fix what's wrong with his car. And there's going to be a home-cooked meal tonight, no matter what new culinary experiments Mom plans on conducting.

Ned shuffles away from the next folks in line, leaning against the wall near the door. Most of the tables are full, the late afternoon pack of a Friday. Ned sips at his coffee again. Students, most of them, by the look of the books and laptops. Well, Boston's chock-full of colleges and universities, just none that want to hire Ned.

"Sorry," a guy says, his phone to his ear.

Ned steps to the side as best he can, letting the other man push his way out.

"Ned?"

Ned lowers his coffee cup from his mouth and looks around at the sound of his name. And there, his computer open and a cup of tea next to it, is Abbot.

Ned blinks and Abbot's still there.

"What are you doing here?" Abbot stands up, a hand pressed to his table.

"Um. Hey."

Abbot eyes are glued to the two coffee cups Ned's holding. "You're here with someone?"

"I'm on my way home. Why are you here?"

"The conference."

Ned looks around, like a projector and a presenter are going to crop up out of the crowd. "It's here?"

"This is a coffeeshop."

"No, I know." Ned shakes his head. "I thought it was in, like, Newton. Or Waltham."

"It's not."

Ned pushes his tongue into his cheek. "Obviously."

"It's at the hotel."

Ned nods, like he knows which one Abbot's talking about. Close by, apparently. No rain dots Abbot's shoulders or hair, nor the jacket neatly laid over the back of his chair. Though maybe he's been here a while. There's more than just his tea on the table. A plate, too, with crumbs on it, and a mug, empty except for the dredges of coffee and foamy milk.

Abbot's here with someone. Ned takes a step back. "I don't mean to interrupt."

"No, it's fine," Abbot says quickly and nods at someone past Ned. That someone gives Abbot a small wave back and a grimace, pointing at his cell that he's still talking on. He's . . . not hard on the eyes. Tall, nice curly hair, a suit jacket that fits him well. Ned swallows.

"I'm sorry," the guy says, tipping his phone away from his mouth. "Steve, hi, nice to meet you."

"Ned." He'd hold out his hand, but he's got the coffees. Or maybe he wouldn't. He wants to get the hell out of here, not stand here and meet Abbot's . . . friend. He glances toward the bathrooms, but there's a crowd of people in the way. His dad has the keys to the truck.

"My kid," Steve says with a sigh, pointing to his phone. "My wife's—what, honey? No, the address was on the invitation."

Wife. Ned blinks. Right.

"Steven's presenting this weekend as well," Abbot says. He's still standing, his fingers pressed to the table.

"Oh," Ned says. Okay. That's right. Makes sense.

"He's at Adams. Adams University." Abbot adjusts his

laptop slightly, lining it up with the edge of the table. "I wanted to talk to him."

"Oh," Ned says again and nods.

"On the party invitation," Steve says again into his phone. "I don't know, hon, sixteen Everett Street, is it not there? Did you call?"

Ned glances over. "The bouncy—" Ned gestures with his coffee. Whatever the hell it's called. "Palace? Castle?"

"Yes." Steve tips the phone from his mouth again. "You know it? Bouncetacular? That place."

"It's behind the grocery store. You can't see it from Everett, , you have to turn into the parking lot and then go around the back."

"Oh my God. Sweetie, did you hear that? Drive around the back of the grocery store. Thank you, thank you."

"Yeah, no problem." Ned shrugs as Steve hangs up his phone.

"This is Ned," Abbot says. "Edward Coppola." He clears his throat and looks at Ned. "Are you waiting for someone?"

"You're . . ." Steve stares for a long moment. Then, he reaches forward to shake Ned's hand again. "Oh, my—okay, Henry was just telling me about you. You're—you applied. To our department. Sociology."

"I did," Ned says slowly. Abbot's watching him too closely. Ned gestures toward the bathrooms. "I am, I'm just—"

"You're researching first-generation college students," Steve says.

Ned straightens. "Yeah, I am."

"I'm on the search committee, we've gotten a million applications, it's, oh my God, think twice about going for tenure, honestly, it's a pain. But, you're here, hi. I want to talk to you about your work."

"You do?" Ned asks.

"Ready to go, kid?" A hand falls onto Ned's shoulder.

Abbot's eyes flick past Ned and then back again. Ned clears his throat.

"This is, um, this is Dan, my dad," Ned says.

Steve shakes Dad's hand, introduces himself again, then says, "I was just talking to Ned here, he applied for an opening we have. We're going out for a drink, some of the others in my department who're also at this conference. You want to come with? Meet them?"

Ned does. Holy hell, he does. Dad catches his eye, glancing at Abbot and then back at Ned again.

"And Dad, this is uh—Henry. Doctor Abbot. We—he works at Callahan with me."

"Doctor Abbot." Dad shakes Abbot's hand too. His eyes narrow. "I think I heard about you."

"Dad."

"No, I did. Statistics, right?"

"Dad. Stop."

"Come with us," Steve says. "Henry, you're not coming? No, you're not, you never do, but, Ned, you got time? And do you have a résumé with you, by any chance?"

"Go," his dad says. "Go out and relax for a change. I'll take care of your car."

"You've got a kid to get home to?" Steve asks. "I get it, trust me, if you can't make it, we'll find another time."

"She's at her mom's." Ned wants to wipe his palms off on his pants. Adams University. Jesus. He doesn't want to talk to Steve some other time, he wants to talk to him right the fuck now. And he does have his résumé with him, stuck in his backpack where he's taken to carrying a copy so he can stare at it, like a typo will appear out of the ether and explain to him why he hasn't gotten a damn job yet.

"You have kids?" Ned's dad asks, whipping out his

phone. "Here, Ned's far too polite to make everyone look, but that's my granddaughter."

Ned rubs at his forehead. He should never have taught his dad how to set his phone's wallpaper.

"Cute," Steve says. "What'd you say, Ned?"

"Sure." Ned swallows. Abbot's looking at the screen too, Ned's dad tipping it toward him. "If, Dad, if that's okay."

"Of course, it's okay. Just—yep, those two cookies are mine, here you go. You need your bag, Ned? And which one's my coffee? Call me for a ride later if you need one." Dad holds a finger up and pushes a cookie into Ned's hand. "No drinking and driving, any of you."

"Dad," Ned says. "Please."

"If you do it right, they never outgrow being embarrassed," Dad says to Steve. He slings his arm around Ned's shoulders. "Come get your stuff, kid."

"You could try to be less mortifying," Ned says over the roar of the rain. He hooks his backpack over his shoulder.

"I love you." Dad ruffles Ned's hair. "Have fun with your friends."

Steve grins and points his thumb at Abbot as Ned jogs back. "This one's in for a drink too, wonder of wonders. Meet you at the hotel bar, yeah? My car's full of squished animal crackers. I'll spare you two."

Ned loops his thumbs through the straps on his bag as Steven jogs across the parking lot with a hand clapped to the top of his hood. Next to him, Abbot watches Ned's dad pull out.

"Funny coincidence." Ned scrapes his foot backward on the pavement. "Um."

"I didn't realize you were in Boston this weekend," Abbot says.

"Yeah." Ned squints out at the rain. "Wasn't supposed to be, but I have Peggy tomorrow night."

"Is your car okay?"

Ned sighs. "Been better."

"I can imagine."

"You really coming to get a drink? I can't believe you know that guy. Really?"

"They had the position filled, so I never thought to tell you." Abbot takes his keys out of his pocket. "Their candidate backed out."

"Wow." Ned shakes his head, water dripping into his eyes.

"I thought your work would be plenty to draw Steven's attention. I had no idea that directions to the Bouncetacular were so necessary. Perhaps I should inform other students."

Ned laughs. "Well, kids' birthday parties. We parents have to stick together, you know." He bites at his cheek. "That's why I was late."

"When?"

"To the game." Ned straightens his shirt. He should've put his raincoat on. "That Red Sox game. I was dropping Peggy off there and it's impossible to find. I wasn't trying to be a jerk."

"I—" Abbot stops. Tilts his head. "That's good to know."

"Here." Ned breaks his cookie in half and holds it out. "I'm sorry I stuck you with Chris and all of them."

"Oatmeal raisin?"

"No, Jesus." Ned elbows him. He probably shouldn't. "Take it, it actually tastes good."

Slowly, Abbot reaches out for the cookie. "Thank you."

The bar in the hotel lobby is crowded. From the far end of the room, leaning against a high-top table, Steve waves them over to where he sits with two women.

One of whom Ned realizes he knows. *Julie*, he remembers and she smiles at him. Ned's seen her before. From the back of a lecture hall, at one of the first conferences he went to, so many years ago back when he was still doing his coursework and the idea of graduation was a far-off, hazy image.

He wishes his shirt was ironed nicer. That he hadn't just shrugged it on that morning, taught two classes, sat in his less-than-pristine car, and walked through the rain. Maybe he could've looked in a mirror too, to make sure his hair isn't sticking straight up.

"You made it," Steve says. "That's some traffic out there, isn't it? Ned's working on first-gen student retention, you remember his application? Ned, a drink? Abbot, you want something?"

"I'll get it," Abbot says.

"I do remember your application." Julie holds out her hand. "You're down for the conference?"

"Just in the neighborhood." Ned introduces himself to their other colleague, *Lisa* printed on her conference lanyard. *Yes*, he so wishes he could say. Presenting something with stunning, never-before-seen results, guaranteed to blow their socks off.

"Sit." Julie pushes out a chair for him. "You're finishing your doctorate soon, is that right?"

"I'm about to defend." Maybe. Hopefully. In his pocket, his phone burns against his thigh with its lack of emails from Chris.

A glass of beer appears in front of him. "I got you what looked most unappetizing," Abbot says softly. In his long fingers, he cradles a glass of white wine.

"Thank you." Ned lets out a breath. He can do this. *Relax*, he tells himself. He pushes another chair away from the table. "Want to sit?"

Abbot slips into it, setting his glass next to Ned's. "Ned published a paper last year on trends in high school graduation, stratified by familial income levels."

Ned turns to him. "You read that?"

Abbot sips at his wine. "It didn't take long."

He lets his knee knock into Abbot's. The beer's good. *Thank you*, he tries to think loudly, with that touch of their knees. And maybe Abbot hears him because he doesn't move his leg and eventually Ned relaxes, leaving his knee there, brushing against Abbot's thigh.

CHAPTER TWENTY

STEVE SPREADS his hands on the table, palms down. "And then," he says. "And then, Henry raises his hand again, and of course our professor won't call on him, so Henry just emails the entire class afterward."

"You didn't," Ned says.

"He did," Steve says. "All two hundred and twenty of us."

Ned cups his hands around his beer, his mouth open. "Of course, you did."

"He wasn't teaching us the right method," Abbot says.

"Which," Steve says, drawing a finger down the table, "came back to bite Henry right in the ass 'cause, come time for him to select committee members for his dissertation, he was reduced to begging to get a statistician to work with him."

"I didn't beg," Abbot says.

"I'm telling it like it is." Steve sits back in his chair and pushes his empty glass away. "Henry, tell him about what happened over your exams."

"Don't you have to get home to your kids?" Abbot asks.

"He finished his exams so fast, his entire committee had to meet about whether they were difficult enough."

"Have a good evening," Abbot says. "Bye."

"Work with us down at Adams." Steve jostles Abbot's arm. "Like old times, come on."

Abbot primly pulls his arm away. "I'll see you tomorrow."

"Have fun with him, Ned," Steve says and claps Ned on the shoulder. "And don't let him dodge the rest of the story, okay?"

"Night," Ned says. Steve pushes out of the empty bar, and Ned leans across the table. "What else happened?"

"Nothing."

"Abbot."

"I completed my qualifying exams and continued with the rest of my doctoral program."

"C'mon."

"Steven's been known to exaggerate."

"Steve's awesome." Ned takes the last swallow of his beer. "I should've pegged you for a total troublemaker in class. Does Chris know about that? Are you giving him hell most days at faculty meetings?"

"Would another drink be enough to bribe you onto another topic?"

"No," Ned says.

"Pity."

Ned tips his chair up on two legs, then rights it again. He's probably already had one too many drinks on an empty stomach to balance like that. "What'd Steve mean about coming down to Adams? You thinking about it?"

Applying for that same job, maybe. Ned licks at his lips. He doesn't have an inch on Abbot's résumé. Not a damn chance if Abbot decided to send in an application.

"No." Abbot flicks open the billfold and starts counting

the cash that Steve, Julie, and Lisa left behind.

"Here," Ned says, holding out a twenty.

"It's fine; there's enough."

Ned sticks the bill under the receipt. "Are you applying too?" He pulls his cheek between his teeth. "For that professorship?"

"I said I wasn't." Abbot sorts through the rest of the bills, turning them so they all face the same way. All right side up, too. With a tap, he straightens them, adds Ned's twenty to the mix, and gives him eighteen dollars back. "There's a research institute."

"Oh yeah?" Ned leans forward and braces his forearms on the table. "At Adams?"

"It's only in the planning stages."

"That's something you'd be interested in?"

"It's not even fully funded yet."

"But could be good, no? It's not like you love teaching."

"I don't dislike teaching."

Ned grins. "If I argue with you, are you going to email me and the entire department to outline the ways in which I'm wrong?"

Abbot's eyebrow rises. "I may seriously consider it."

"I think I'd want to read that." Ned grins again. "I could see you focusing on your research. Like I said, your paper was great."

Abbot glances up at him. "You think so?"

On the table, Ned's phone buzzes. He covers it with his hand and shrugs. "Of course, it was good. Boring, I'm not going to lie, but good."

"Do you need to go?" Abbot asks, nodding toward his phone.

"No. Why, do you?"

"No." Abbot pushes the billfold to sit neatly parallel with the edge of the table. "Don't you have your daughter?"

"Tomorrow."

Abbot pushes three empty glasses together in a neat line. "She looks like you."

I'm taking your mother out to the movies, his dad has texted him. Ned glances up at Abbot. "Yeah. She does."

Abbot clears his throat. "Are you hungry?"

"Oh, um. Yeah."

"There's a restaurant across the street."

Need a ride now or is later fine? Dad's message shines past Ned's fingers over the screen.

"Unless you have plans," Abbot says.

"No, I'm—" Ned shakes his head. "Watching bad TV by myself. My parents are out at the movies, apparently, so that's my fun Friday night."

"I don't mean to keep you."

"Not at all." Later, Ned texts back. "Let's—yeah, dinner would be way more fun."

Ned hasn't eaten out in . . . a while. Not in a real restaurant, at least. One that isn't a bar, or just the counter at Pat's, where the most recently messed up meal is dropped in front of Ned to polish off.

The last time Ned'd done the whole dinner thing had been a real sorry attempt at a date, so long ago it's mostly—thankfully—faded from memory, though Ned certainly recalls apologizing at the end of the evening. *I'm not ready*, he'd said, and he'd crawled into bed that night, his pillow over his head, ignoring Pat's questions of how it went.

His stomach growls. Lunch was back on campus and hours ago besides.

They jog across the parking lot and Abbot opens up the door. He waves Ned through as he holds it.

"You didn't want to find a fondue place?" Ned asks, looking around. This is nicer than Ned would've chosen, certainly.

"Too bad your sense of humor hasn't improved in concert with your abilities in statistical analysis."

"You don't have to admit it, I know it's true."

The corner of Abbot's mouth twitches and Ned grins at that hint of a smile.

Their table's in the back and Ned eyes the other diners as he follows Abbot toward it. Ned's not exactly dressed for this. Or he was, before he got rained on all day. He tugs his shirt straighter.

"Your menus," the host says. "And the wine list. I'll bring you some water."

It's a hell of a menu. Ned glances around the room. The restaurant is full, too. Must be good. He glances through the list of food. Yeah, he is hungry. And he wants steak. A giant, expensive, delicious steak.

Abbot picks up the wine list. "Would you want some?"

"Um, sure."

Abbot's got such nice hands. Ned closes his eyes and when he opens them again, he stares down at his menu. And finds out exactly how much a steak here costs. Jesus. He and Pat can get steaks for half the price at the store.

"Any preferences?"

"I don't know the first thing about wine." Ned lays his menu down. "We used to get it in a box in college."

Abbot inhales through his nose. "Of course, you did."

"And, inside there's a bag, you can pull it right out." Ned grins at him. His phone buzzes against his thigh, and he pushes at the button on the side to quiet its alerts. "Pat used to just carry the bag around."

"Also during college?"

"Visiting me. He never went to college. And if you're going to ask red or white, the answer is just: yes."

Abbot's eyebrow twitches. "What are you going to get to eat?"

"Food." Ned's phone buzzes again, and again he thumbs through his pants to dismiss the alert. But his phone just vibrates once more, and he sighs. "Sorry."

"Do you need to take that?"

"Nah." His dad's probably calling again, or maybe Pat. Though knowing his luck, it's Jen saying she can take Peggy tomorrow, he doesn't need to be in town, and he'll find out he drove down here and ruined his car for nothing.

Abbot flicks through the menu, the soft light from the restaurant playing over his face. Well, maybe not for entirely nothing.

His phone buzzes again and Ned yanks it from his pocket, trying to hold it beneath the table. He'll just shut it off. Though he glances down and—

"Oh," he says.

"Everything all right?"

"It's Chris." Ned's mouth goes dry. "Oh, shit, it's Chris."

"Go on." Abbot nods toward the front of the restaurant. "Good luck."

Ned's palm sweats on his phone case, and he presses his finger into his other ear, answering his phone before it can go to voicemail.

"Yeah," he says quickly, slipping into the restaurant's lobby. "Chris? Hey."

"Ned, my man," Chris says. "I got a couple things for you, if you have a minute."

Ned swallows. He can see the edge of the table and Abbot's shoulder as he flicks through his menu. "Yeah, sure."

"Good, good, just trying to get some things wrapped up before the weekend." Chris sounds distracted. "I looked for you in your office earlier, but you must've left."

"I'm down in Boston. I'm sorry, I would've stuck around."

"Oh, with Henry, of course, I should've thought of that." Ned opens his mouth, then closes it again. Across the restaurant, Abbot points to the wine list and the waiter nods. "Listen, I just finished reading your work."

"Oh, the draft, yeah," Ned says, trying like hell to sound casual. "Isn't it Friday? Aren't we not supposed to be working?"

"Lots to catch up on. Listen, Ned, this looks great."

"It does?"

"It definitely does, I can tell how much work you put in."

Ned nods, like Chris is there to see him. "So you think there's much more to do?"

"No, no, not at all, you're pretty much there."

"Wow. Okay. What does . . . what does that mean, exactly?"

"It means you should see about reserving a conference room for your defense is what it means. Well done, Ned."

"Really?" Ned switches his phone to his other hand. "Isn't there more I need to fix?"

"I think you're good. Get an email out to your committee members, and we'll schedule your defense for next week, okay?"

"Okay." Ned's hand gripping the phone is numb, and his stomach flips over once and then again. "Really? You're sure?"

"I'm sure. Hey—have a good weekend, all right?"

"I will," Ned says softly, and Chris's call ends in a quiet beep in his ear. He lowers his phone, letting it dangle from his fingers. The draft of his dissertation is done. He just has to defend it. Nerves grip through his chest, crawling up his throat. No, that's excitement. Unrestrained, eager glee mixed with a strong shot of worry that his committee will reject his work.

They won't, he thinks. They might think he's finally turned in an acceptable draft. He might be done, actually, entirely, and wonderfully done.

Ned's legs carry him unsteadily across the restaurant. He wants to tell Abbot. He wants to tell Pat, and his parents, and Peggy. *Wait,* he thinks, *wait until it's really for certain,* but still elation bubbles through him.

Back at the table, Abbot's talking to some guy who isn't the waiter. Blond, clean shaven, and cheekbones that could cut glass. There's something steely about Abbot's face.

Ned pauses, the glee high in his chest slightly fading. "Ah, sorry, I'm interrupting?"

"No." Abbot stands up. "He's leaving."

"We need to talk," the guy says.

"We don't. And especially not now."

"Oh, now you don't want to?"

"No."

The guy scoffs and turns toward Ned. "Who are you?"

"Ned," he says slowly, holding out his hand.

"Goodnight, Louis," Abbot says.

Louis. Ned looks him over again. Tailored suit jacket, fancy-ass looking shirt, and all long legs and a trim, fit figure —Abbot can get it, can't he? Though now Abbot's just staring down at the table, his throat working. Ned puts on a smile and drops his hand. "Hi, nice to meet you. If you'll excuse us, Abbot and I were having dinner."

"And we were talking." Louis moves a finger between himself and Abbot. "And I'm sorry, 'Abbot'?"

How the two of them must've been, with those attitudes of theirs. Ned lets his eyebrows rise. "We were having dinner," Ned says, more slowly. And having a nice evening besides. All the better for Chris's call. Ned shifts to stand between Louis and the table. He's not in the mood for this, not when he wants to let spill what Chris just told him. "So not a great time for a chat. Have a nice night, bye."

Ned pulls out his chair and sits. Neatly, he arranges his napkin on his lap. Beneath the table, Ned knocks his foot into Abbot's ankle.

"Always on your schedule," Louis says.

"A bottle of the pinot noir?" the waiter asks.

"Thank you." Ned glances up at Louis. "If you don't mind."

"Christ," Louis mutters, walking off.

Abbot sits slowly, propping an elbow on the table and his face in his hand. Ned taps the wineglass in front of him. "Pour him extra, please."

"What can I get you two for dinner?" their waiter asks.

Abbot just rubs at his forehead and doesn't look up.

"Um, the, whatever, the fish for me," Ned says. He scans the menu. "He'll have the risotto."

"Wonderful choices," their waiter says. When he's gone again, Ned leans over and gently grasps Abbot's wrist.

"Hey," he says.

"I'm sorry."

"Don't be." Abbot's skin is warm. Ned maybe shouldn't be holding his wrist like that. He squeezes and lets go. "I have to see my ex-wife all the time and it always sucks. Maybe we can introduce them, conveniently strand them on a desert island, something of the sort."

"Tempting." Abbot takes a long sip of his wine. "I don't believe I like risotto."

"Everyone likes risotto." Ned wants to grab Abbot's wrist again. Wants to lean right over there and grin and wipe the look off Abbot's face that Louis put there, that pinch between his brows. "Have you even ever had risotto? It's fancy rice."

Abbot just sighs and Ned nudges Abbot's foot again with his own.

"Hey." He leans across the table, pats his hand on it, and ducks to catch Abbot's eye. "So, good news from Chris."

Abbot blinks like he's rousing himself. "He read your draft?"

"He did."

Abbot sits up straighter. "And?"

"And he said I should go ahead and defend it."

"You'll do great."

"I don't know about that." Ned smooths his napkin in his lap. He's nervous. He's going to be nervous all damn weekend and this coming week, too.

"You will," Abbot says. "Chris wouldn't let you defend if he didn't think you'd pass."

Ned exhales slowly. "I hope so."

"You'll be done. Like you wanted."

"Like I wanted." Ned'll be here in Boston for good. *Peggy*, he thinks. "Hey, um, well, thanks. For all the help."

"I should be thanking you." Abbot gestures with his chin toward the bar. Ned turns, but Louis must've left because there's no striking tall blond sitting there, eyeing them across the restaurant.

"Was he over there? Eating alone, I hope." Ned sips at his own wine. It's good. "I know a thing or two about wanting to win a breakup. And he's a real treat. Everything on your schedule, huh? Not the most flexible?"

There's something soft around Abbot's mouth. Tired maybe. Ned always was, after running into Jen. Still is. "I wanted to move to Boston. He didn't."

"You did?" Ned asks. "You'd leave Callahan?"

Abbot turns his wineglass in a slow circle. "I thought . . ." He spins his wineglass in another neat circle. His eyes cut over to Ned's, and then he's back to studying his wine. "If I were in Boston, it's that much easier to fly to Switzerland. I'd see Liesl more often. She could come on her own, not just when our father travels."

How sweet of Abbot. Wanting his little sister in his life, wanting to be in hers. Once, Ned wouldn't have pegged him for the type, but now . . . it fits. Slots right into who Abbot is. "That's something, you know, to want to do that for her."

Abbot shakes his head. "It's nothing."

"I don't know about that." Ned can imagine all too clearly the future Abbot was likely envisioning. His sister in the house now and again, a kid or two, happily married in a gorgeous, unfairly tidy, and put-together Boston brownstone. "How long were you and Louis together?"

"Three years."

"That's a while."

Abbot, in that type of relationship. Planning a future with someone. Odd, almost, to think about.

"He's who I thought I should want," Abbot says, his eyes still on his wine.

"Well, be glad you get to be done with him after tomorrow. Good thing you guys didn't get around to the whole kid thing."

"In retrospect . . ." Abbot lets out a breath. He takes a sip of wine too, glancing across the room.

"Yeah? Change your mind about that?"

"No, I haven't." Abbot, with kids. All of the mess and the noise and the constant, unending interruptions. He's still staring at some hapless spot on the wall. He clears his throat. "In retrospect, I don't think he would've been the right partner for that."

"No? You run a statistical regression? Analyze all relevant data points?"

"Something of the sort."

"You're still, ah, looking for someone?"

"Now?" Abbot looks up from his glass. "Not currently."

Ned nods. Of course. Abbot had said that, hadn't he, that he didn't want anything? *Doesn't* want anything. Ned feels his forehead pinch as he looks down at his knife. The two of them agreed on that—he doesn't want anything either. He lets out a breath and takes a sip of his wine.

Well, it'll give him plenty of time for Peggy when he moves back. Maybe Ned can continue on with his lackluster social calendar and get Peggy more often on weekends. Round after round of hospital calls for triceratops, and Ned's personal life can continue to languish. It'd be a fair trade for getting to watch Peggy wrap an imaginary wound with an entire box of Band-Aids. Ned rubs his fingers through his hair. Abruptly, he stops. He's in a restaurant and here with a guy who looks as handsome and put-together as he ever does. Ned tries to smooth it back down.

"Are you looking for someone?" Abbot asks.

Ned lets out a soft laugh. "Um, no."

"No?" Abbot leans back in his chair as the waiter approaches with two plates. "Thank you."

"Thanks," Ned says. "No. Oh my God, no, I just . . ." He shakes his head and pulls his plate another inch toward himself. His dinner looks good. A hell of a lot nicer than anything Ned's eaten in a while, that's for sure. "I would just ruin it."

Abbot takes a bite. His forehead furrows.

"Oh, don't be annoyed that you like it." Ned helps himself to a forkful from Abbot's plate. "Mmm, it's good."

Abbot's forehead is still creased. "Do you think you ruined things with your ex?"

"Well, I don't know. Yeah. She—that's what she told me."

"And you believed her?"

"Yes?" Ned frowns down at his fish. He hates that it

sounds like a question. "I don't know, she—she was cheating on Jeff, too. But . . . I mean, I was half of that problem."

"You wouldn't mess it up."

Ned looks up. "What?"

"You wouldn't. May I try some?"

"Fish?" Ned blinks. "Aren't you a vegetarian?"

"Pescatarian."

"Well, that's news."

"I didn't want to give you more ammunition, as you would say."

"Pescatarian," Ned echoes. "Is that even a thing?"

"Ned, I very much doubt you are as at fault as you might assume."

Ned frowns. "How can you even know that?"

"And whatever mistakes you might've made, you wouldn't repeat them." Abbot delicately pierces a piece of fish. "Were you to try again."

"Well, glad one of us is sure." Ned tugs his plate back toward himself. "Eat your rice."

It's the sort of restaurant Ned's parents would go to once a year, for an anniversary, or his mom's birthday. Abbot probably grew up with this as commonplace. Maybe he and Louis ate like this all the time—cloth napkins, a waiter that comes by and fills up their wineglasses for them. There's more than one fork at each place setting and bussers that circle the tables, placing lighted candles in the middle as night gathers outside. *An entire new sort of life for you,* Ned's dad had said when he'd gotten into college, and again when he'd chosen to get a master's over simply finding a job to settle in at.

Ned's happily full by the time he finishes. Warm too, the wine and the chatter of tables around him enough to drive away the memory of the rain soaking outside. His phone buzzes against his thigh and Ned sighs. "Jesus," he mutters. It's Chris, with a text that he went ahead and scheduled the conference room for Ned's defense.

"Everything okay?" Abbot asks.

"He's the world's worst boss. I mean, he's not, but he totally is. First thing Monday morning, I'm telling Aliyah that Chris is texting me on Friday night."

He holds his phone beneath the edge of the table and types back Thanks. He's pretty sure he did this same thing in Abbot's class, all that time ago, texting beneath his textbook. Ned glances over at him, then back at his phone. That's just wild, that Abbot could be that same person from all those years ago, so severe at the front of the room, Ned's hands sweating as he tried to keep up with his notes.

"Be right back with that," the waiter says and Ned pushes his phone under his thigh. The waiter takes Abbot's credit card and tucks it into the billfold.

"Hey," Ned says, but he's already turning away.

Abbot shakes his head. "It's fine."

"I have some cash." Ned reaches for his own wallet.

"I've got it." Abbot clears his throat. "Please, let me."

"Okay." Ned wants to clear his own throat. "Um, thanks."

"Of course."

There's no "of course" about it. Ned settles his hands in his lap. He flicks his thumb at his phone case, then quickly stills his fingers.

"I'm going to be a wreck waiting for this defense to happen," Ned finally says.

"Part of the experience."

"Yeah." Ned takes a last sip of his wine. He knows he'll barely sleep tonight and probably the next few nights too. Tomorrow will probably be even worse, no Peggy to distract him until the evening and empty hours to fill. At least this evening has been a break from fretting by his lonesome, here with Abbot instead of bumming around by himself.

"It's uh—I don't know, good to have run into you."

That didn't come out right, he doesn't think. He opens his mouth, sure he wants to try again, but the waiter comes back and hands the billfold to Abbot.

"Yes, it was." Abbot has a nice signature. Neat writing too. And Ned can't see the total of the bill, but it sure as hell looks like it's got an entire third digit on it.

"Do you two have a midnight study session planned to get ready for tomorrow?" Ned asks.

"Absolutely not."

"What're you up to, then? Trying to make Louis practice?"

"I don't particularly care what he does with his evening. As long as he shows up tomorrow."

"Do you have your presentation memorized? Oh, you totally have it memorized, don't you?" Ned grins. "Go on, how does it start?"

"I've given this same talk numerous times."

"Hi, I'm Doctor Abbot; please ignore this jerk beside me. Today I'm going to fry your brains in the most painful and dry way possible."

"Sounds like you could give the talk yourself."

"I can't even pronounce half the words you're going to use," Ned says. "Though I might pay to see you talk over Louis. Are you going to just interrupt him every time he tries to speak?"

"We've divided it into sections."

"Nice." Ned grins. "Who's going to take the questions? I might just come up with a whammy."

"You're going to come?"

"Oh." Ned picks up his napkin from his lap, folds it, and places it where his plate had been. "I don't know. Maybe."

"You're welcome to."

Ned laces his hands together over his napkin. He'll have to trek all the way back over here, and he doesn't exactly have a car.

"It would be nice," Abbot says. "To have you there."

"Well, then." Spending a free Saturday in a lecture on statistics? Who the hell is he turning into? "Yeah, I'll come."

Outside, the rain's slackened enough that Ned's more dry than less when he and Abbot reach the hotel lobby. Still, drops fleck Abbot's glasses. Abbot pulls them off, rubbing them on a fold in his shirt over his stomach.

Ned snags his glasses. "You're blind," he says, holding them up.

"I didn't know you'd added an ophthalmology degree to your work in sociology."

"Just saying." Ned hands them back. Abbot looks nice as he puts them back on. They suit him. Nice with them off, too. Ned scratches the side of his mouth with one finger. "So, I should probably call my folks."

It's like high school again, or something close, needing a ride home from his parents on a Friday evening. And after dinner too. Well, whatever. It wasn't . . . wasn't a date. Ned digs his hands into his pockets.

"I can give you a ride," Abbot says.

"It's fine, my dad doesn't mind the drive."

"Is their movie done?"

"Probably not." Still, Ned calls anyway. His shoes are wet enough to squeak on the tile floor of the lobby as he listens to the ring in his ear, and then the start of his dad's voicemail message. "No, it's not."

"You're welcome to come up," Abbot says. "While you wait."

Oh, that's a hell of a bad idea. Or a really, really good one. Abbot looks at him evenly. That's . . . they've done this.

And Ned knows exactly where it leads. Where it's led. Twice.

"Um." Ned works his heel into the tile beneath him, a squeak at each turn of his shoe.

"If you want."

Which Ned does. Ah, hell, does he ever. But going upstairs to hotel rooms wasn't part of their deal. Ned's dissertation, Abbot's paper—no invitations laden with the certainty of jumping into bed if Ned accepts, Abbot looking at him with a heat in his eyes.

Ned could just go back to his folks' house. Lie on the couch, remote in his hand, and a beer warming on the coffee table.

"Yeah," Ned says. It's a different sort of evening than what he's grown used to. And maybe . . . maybe that's a good thing. "Yeah, I'd like that."

In the elevator, Ned can feel his shirt where it brushes his skin. He studies the light flashing with each floor that ticks by. Ned reaches out to touch Abbot's arm, running his fingers down the buttons at the cuff of his sleeve. Abbot's skin is warm beneath the fabric, and his hand turns so Ned can push his fingertips into that broad, strong palm.

The moment they step inside Abbot's room, Abbot backs Ned up against the wall, kicks the door closed, and the latch snicks shut. Abbot kisses him, his mouth tugging at Ned's bottom lip. Ned folds his hands around Abbot's sides and pulls him in tight.

A soft grunt rises from the back of Ned's throat. It's just so damn good between them. Abbot's body, muscles wrapped over a slim frame, his fingers finding Ned's neck, the skin beneath his collar, the hollow behind his ear.

Abbot turns Ned's head to kiss him at a different angle, his mouth retreating and coming back again. Ned pulls in air when Abbot dips away once more, and it burns in his lungs when Abbot kisses him all over again, Ned's shoulder blades pinned to the wall, and Abbot's sides filling his hands.

Ned drags Abbot's shirt out of his waistband, grinning against his mouth when the perfectly pressed fabric wrinkles and creases. He shoves his fingers under the strap of Abbot's belt, under the band of his pants, down into the elastic of tight boxers, and digs his nails into the soft, firm swell of Abbot's ass.

"Oh," Abbot says.

"Yeah?" Ned whispers and squeezes again. He fumbles for Abbot's belt buckle with his other hand. Ned knows exactly what's under those pants, what pushes at Abbot's fly. He palms Abbot's cock, already hardening, and Abbot's eyes flutter closed.

"I—" Abbot braces his palms on the wall, trapping Ned's shoulders. Ned rubs again, finds the tip of Abbot's cock through his pants, and circles there with his thumb. Abbot's hips jerk.

"Do you have any condoms?" Ned feathers his fingers over the tent in Abbot's slacks.

Abbot pulls away and turns on the light in the bathroom. Ned watches Abbot's long legs, the way he walks, all full of grace. A knot burns in Ned's chest, a niggle of smoldering jealousy as Abbot grabs a condom and lube from his shaving kit. *What the hell did Abbot bring condoms for?* Ned wants to wonder. He's just the kind of guy to be prepared. But still.

Ned pushes him toward the bed. Sits and drags Abbot down over him, onto his lap. He's fucking gorgeous. And feels so damn nice, his weight on Ned like that. Ned's cock sits up and takes all sorts of interest with Abbot perched on his thighs, Abbot pressing his thumbs beneath Ned's ears and tipping his head back to kiss him again. Ned grabs his ass, pulls him down and grinds up, sighing through his nose against Abbot's cheek. It feels so good, getting some pressure on that stab of hot, painful pleasure.

"Lie back." Abbot slips Ned's belt free from its clasp. A tug at Ned's waist and his pants loosen.

Ned does, and at the touch of Abbot's fingers through his boxers, his mouth parts. And then Abbot's sliding off his lap and cool air hits Ned's thighs as Abbot pulls Ned's boxers down and—

"Shit!"

Ned arcs upright, hands going to Abbot's hair. "Fuck," he whines.

Pleasure sings through Ned's belly. Abbot's mouth is warm. Warm and slick and fucking moving all over Ned's cock with the lick of his tongue, the soft wet inside of his cheek. Ned's heel drums against the floor. A hand circles his ankle, holds with a firm, strong grip, and Abbot hums, the vibration shooting straight through Ned's cock.

"Oh my God," he gasps. Ned grabs for a fistful of the bed covers. With his other hand, he clutches at the back of Abbot's head, fighting to not knot his fingers in his hair and yank.

Abbot's tongue circles the top of Ned's cock and Ned groans. He's going to die. This is going to be how he goes, that mouth driving him masterfully, expertly mad. Absolutely fucking worth it. Ned lets his hips flex with the urge to move. It's so good. It's so fucking good and it's been so goddamn long and Abbot's just so—

Abbot pulls off, wiping his mouth with the back of his hand.

"No." Ned looks down his own body, his stomach heaving, his cock wet and flushed dark with blood. "No, don't stop."

"Seems prudent." Abbot shifts forward and scrapes his

teeth over Ned's hipbone. Long fingers brush Ned's shirt up his torso and Abbot bites at the skin just beneath Ned's navel.

"Fuck you," Ned groans. "Please."

"That being the general idea."

Oh hell *yes.*

Ned sits up and grabs a handful of Abbot's shirt in his fist. Kisses him and his glasses bump against Ned's cheekbone. Ned folds his fingers into Abbot's soft hair and holds him there to explore with a rough, slick sweep of his tongue.

"I am going to fuck you," Ned whispers when he pulls back. Abbot licks at his lips and nods, eyes dark.

Ned strips off his pants and boxers and grabs the condom. His skin is too sensitive. His cock too, wet where it brushes his shirt. He skims it off without unbuttoning it and drops it on the floor inside out.

When Abbot pulls his pants off and starts to fold them, Ned says, "Don't." He takes them from Abbot, tosses them on the floor. "Boxers and shirt too, let's go."

"Thanks for the specificity." Abbot pulls his boxers down his long legs. Ned touches himself, hissing at the grip of his own fist, and watches. Ned's a damn idiot, to not have jumped at tonight all the quicker. For hesitating, even a moment.

Abbot's neck is flushed, his eyes bright. Ned reaches for his glasses with both hands, slipping them off. Those, he doesn't toss. He folds them and sets them on the nightstand as neatly and precisely as Abbot would.

"Get on the bed," Ned says, and Abbot sits. Gently, he reaches out to touch Ned's thigh, fingers circling over his skin. Ned's skin flares with that light, sure touch. Ned covers Abbot's hand and stills it, then sets his knee on the edge of the mattress between Abbot's.

Abbot shifts backward, making room for Ned between

his thighs. It's nice, that soft, silent invitation. Ned kisses him once, quickly, and presses their foreheads together. Abbot slips the condom from Ned's hand and that's the goddamn hottest thing Ned's ever seen, Abbot rolling the condom onto Ned's cock. He sucks in a breath, his stomach tightening.

"Oh God," he whispers as Abbot strokes him once, slowly. "Oh my fucking God."

"Do you really need to talk so much?"

"You're as—*oh*—as pedantic as you are blind." Ned licks at his lips and watches as Abbot keeps stroking slowly, those long fingers wrapped around Ned's cock. He's suddenly glad for the barrier of the condom, Abbot looking up at him like that with a messiness to his hair he'd never otherwise allow and his thighs gently spread open.

"Pedantic," Abbot repeats. He touches his tongue to his bottom lip. "A false equivalency."

"Shut up," Ned groans and palms Abbot's shoulders, shoves him back onto the bed. He's good, Abbot is—the foot he drags up Ned's calf, the hands that settle on Ned's ass. Feels good too as Ned slips a finger into him and then slower, hissing against the pleasure, his cock.

Abbot tips his head back and Ned kisses over his neck, the scratch of stubble at the hollow of his jaw, the jut of his collarbone, and the thin skin over his breastbone. Gorgeous. He's so fucking gorgeous and naked and Ned's inside of him and this is the absolute best day ever.

"S'nice," Ned mumbles, his weight on his elbows, letting his hips rock with how Abbot moves under him in tandem. Abbot's fingers dig into Ned's ass in a hard squeeze.

"Adequate," Abbot says. He sounds breathy.

"Adequate," Ned murmurs back.

He can barely think. He tucks his face into Abbot's

neck, nosing into where he can feel Abbot swallow, the place in his throat that air catches, releases, and catches again. Ned should do this more often. All the time. Every damn day, so he can feel the spark over his skin, have hands sweep over his back, into his hair, down to his thigh and up along his ribs. That tight, warm, wet around his cock. He thinks of Abbot's mouth sucking at him and moans, his hips thrusting faster.

"Oh." Abbot's chest flexes, his arms tightening around Ned. His head tips back into the mattress and Ned loses the crook of warmth to bury his nose in and the clean scent of sweat on Abbot's skin.

"Okay?" Ned asks. He kisses the base of Abbot's throat and feels Abbot's hum beneath his lips.

"Fine." Abbot's voice cracks.

"Good." Ned adjusts his elbows, shifts his weight forward, and thrusts harder. Puts his back into it and pushes into Abbot again and again. "Wanted to get beyond—ah—beyond adequate, though."

Abbot's hand snakes down between them. Ned watches to watch, wants to drink in the sight of Abbot touching himself. Doesn't want to move either. Doesn't want to sit up, sit back on his heels, let cool air rush into the humid space between their bodies.

"Statistical outlier?" Abbot asks. His breath hitches as his knuckles bump Ned's stomach. Ned mouths at the bob of his Adam's apple, his hips moving frantic and quick.

When Ned comes, he groans through it into Abbot's neck. Shakes with that hot, rushing release, his hips still pumping and his toes curled. He breathes damply, kissing the taut tendon in Abbot's throat, the soft underside of his jaw.

"Yeah," he whispers when he can catch his breath gain. His fingers shake as he pushes Abbot's hair back. "Look at you, you're—" Ned kisses his lips once, twice. "Jesus, Abbot."

His breath skitters and he bites at his lip, wincing through taking off the condom. Then, he leans over Abbot again, moving down the stack of his abs and the faint, thin line of hair leading down from his navel.

"Gorgeous," Ned murmurs. This is what Ned wants as he takes Abbot's cock in his mouth. That heady scent of Abbot's skin, the thick shape of him against Ned's tongue. Abbot's fingers shift through Ned's hair, brushing it back from his forehead, and then resting lightly on the back of his head.

He wants to bottle this moment up. The last licks of pleasure through his own body and the soft noises he pulls from Abbot's throat, the way those slim hips start to shift against the bed. He tongues the tip of Abbot's cock and rubs his palms up his legs, tickling at the inside of his thighs where the skin is soft and thin. He could do this all day, lick at the ridge of Abbot's cock, suck the tip and then swallow him down until Abbot gasps. Feel the moment his legs start shaking and his breathing turns from the quick rhythm of building pleasure into a rougher, more desperate cadence.

When Ned looks up, Abbot's stomach is clenched, his head pushed back, and his eyes screwed shut. There's nothing placid on his face now, his mouth working silently and expression caught in the twist of pleasure. His hand clenches in Ned's hair, his hips rise off the bed, and a caught, choked noise finally leaves him. Ned wraps his hand around the base of Abbot's cock and works him through his orgasm, warmth flooding Ned's mouth.

Abbot relaxes slowly, his breath ragged, and Ned kisses the bump of his hipbone, the soft crease of his thigh. Gently, he takes Abbot's hand, limp where it's flopped to the mattress, and kisses his palm.

Abbot thumbs his jaw. He pulls clumsily at Ned's arm until he crawls back up. It's a fucking sight, Abbot lying there flushed and breathless, the ripped condom wrapper lying by his hip, the mess of the bedspread. Against the headboard, a pillow is knocked askew. Ned wonders which one of them did that. Slowly, he lies down on his back, shoulder to shoulder with Abbot.

"Goddamn," he says into the silence. So good. With both palms, he scrubs at his face. "Need anything?"

Abbot just lays there, his breath still rough.

Ned knocks his toes into Abbot's ankle. "Yeah? Water?"

"I'm fine." Fingers touch to Ned's hip. Rub there lightly and slip away again.

Ned rolls over onto his stomach. He could run ten miles. Knock his dissertation defense out of the park. Climb onto the roof and holler to the city that getting laid is the absolute fucking best. Let them all know that Ned's got a naked, beautiful man in bed next to him.

"Hey." Ned lays his chin on the nearest part of Abbot's shoulder. His skin is damp, sweaty. Ned kisses it. "Can I see your presentation?"

Abbot's stomach flexes with his breath. "Now?"

"Yes, now."

"It's on my laptop." Abbot scratches at his chest. He looks like he's about to let out an enormous yawn.

Ned snags the computer from the desk, flopping back down onto the bed again. It's cold against his belly. "You've got a typo."

Abbot sits up. "What?"

"Relax." Ned laughs and the computer moves with the motion. "It's perfect, of course it is."

Abbot lies down again. "Very funny."

Neck clicks through the slides, a hand behind his head. "What're you doing to celebrate after your presentation?" he asks.

Abbot's eyes slip closed. "Delete Louis's number from my phone."

"Brutal," Ned says. "I approve."

"I don't want to talk about him," Abbot says.

The laptop folds closed, Abbot's hand pressed to the back. He pushes it away and they're kissing again. Slowly and sweet, and outside the window, Ned can hear the rain drumming down again. Abbot's knuckles brush over Ned's cheek.

Ned wants to be a teenager again. To do this all night. He rolls onto his side and hooks his leg over Abbot's thigh. He feels like one, actually. The thrum of blood in his body, the urge to touch all that skin laid out for him.

"One thing though," Ned murmurs. He catches Abbot's lips again, kisses him once, twice. "I do know your name."

"What?"

"'Abbot'," Ned parrots back in Louis's tone from dinner. He kisses Abbot's lower lip gently. "Is it okay that I call you that?"

Abbot's hands fit to his, their fingers lacing together. God, he feels so good. So warm and strong and responsive when Ned kisses him again and then again.

"I like it," Abbot whispers when Ned lets him speak again.

"Good. I do too." Ned rolls onto his back, pulling Abbot with him so he can feel his weight. He frees a hand, smoothing down the long line of Abbot's back as they kiss, and feels up Abbot's ass, the firm curve of it, the hollow at the small of his back. There's softness where the jut of his hipbone ends and before his ribs begin. Abbot flinches and Ned grins. "Ticklish?"

"No."

"Hmm." Ned brushes his fingers over the spot again.

Gets his hand grabbed and his mouth kissed, hard enough Abbot rocks him back into the pillow. Ned lets himself be pushed down into the bed, smiling into their kiss. "You sure?"

"Quite."

Ned plays at freeing his hand, but doesn't do much more than loosely twist at Abbot's hold. It feels good, strong fingers around his wrist like that. *Stop*, Ned could tell him, and Abbot would immediately.

"Insufferable." Abbot kisses him again. Their legs thread together, their feet brushing, eagerness already building in how they move together. Abbot smells so good. Ned presses his nose into Abbot's cheek, kisses at the hinge of his jaw and up over his ear.

"Can I stay tonight?" Ned asks in a whisper.

"Of course."

"Good." Ned nestles closer. "Come here."

Abbot sinks farther into him, letting Ned take his weight. "I am here."

"You're warm," Ned says.

"Turn up the heat."

"Mmm, no." Even Abbot's hair smells nice. Ned needs to text his dad, so he won't worry. It can wait, though. He folds his arms around Abbot and bites at the lobe of his ear. Keeps at it until Abbot squirms, and Ned grins around the hold he's got with his teeth. "Wiggly, aren't you?"

"I'm not ticklish."

"No?" Ned asks. Abbot could pull away if he wanted to. Doesn't, though. Just turns his head so that Ned can lick up the curve of his ear. Lets Ned rest his hands on his waist again too, just over that spot that made Abbot flinch. Ned presses with a finger and Abbot's back flexes.

Ned smiles into the hollow behind Abbot's ear and pulls him even closer.

CHAPTER TWENTY-ONE

ABBOT KNOWS HIS SHIT.

It's fun to watch him from the last row of the auditorium, Ned's legs kicked under the seat in front of him and arms crossed over his chest. Abbot's shirt Ned borrowed this morning pulls tight across his shoulders and the sleeves are slightly too long. Ned rolls the cuffs back, trying to be as neat as Abbot would.

He gives Abbot a grin when he glances his way. Ned's ignored. Typical. Doesn't stop Ned from doing it again a minute later.

The last time Ned sat in the audience and listened to Abbot click through a presentation, he'd been scrambling to take notes he didn't understand. Maybe he still doesn't, but at least this time he's free to simply listen. And watch.

Ned gives Louis a grin too, and the guy does a much poorer job of glancing away. Ned can't bring himself to feel bad for breaking Louis' concentration. He let the way Abbot can fill out a suit walk right on out of his life. For a guy who can get up there and keep pace with Abbot and the brain he's got in that handsome head of his, Louis is apparently none too smart.

"As findings clearly indicate," Abbot says, clicking to yet another slide. His jacket pulls against the shape of his body as he gestures to a graph. Ned rubs his palm down his thigh. Louis is an idiot. A really lucky idiot for getting Abbot in his life for as long as he did.

Ned blows out a quiet breath. Well, he's been lucky too, in his own way. Waking up this morning to Abbot's arm draped across his waist, the warm press of him against Ned's back. Spending last night together, when Ned's gotten so good idling away his time by himself.

Though Abbot's had that with someone, a permanent fixture in his life. Ned would do well to remember that he's not exactly looking for it again.

Which will be easier to keep in mind when Ned's back in Boston for good. He won't be reeled in again and again by the temptation to tease him, that goading that has slid precipitously into flirting. And he won't have to catch sight of him, the way his jacket drapes over his frame and how his pants fit him, just slightly hugging the shape of his thighs. Ned won't have to be constantly reminded that he's funny. And smart. And—and sweet, in his quiet sort of way.

Ned tugs at his pants, pinching a fold of fabric in his fingers and straightening them. He shouldn't be sitting here thinking about that soft strip of skin above Abbot's neatly ironed collar, or how his eyes light up as he talks through his work, one hand gesturing to the presentation, his long legs carrying him around the stage. Ned's been here before, his heart tumbling over the precipice of deep, lasting interest, and his life fell apart because of it.

Though enjoying the sight of Abbot in a suit is different than Ned wrenching his life back open again. *It's nothing*, he tells himself, the little spark that lights in Ned's stomach when Abbot's eyes cut toward him. He and Abbot will drift apart, and that smoldering ember will surely fade, no matter how slowly.

Afterward, Ned waits in the back of the auditorium. "Nice job," he says when Abbot finally works his way free of the knot that had formed around him and Louis. "You did great."

"Are you suggesting you might have actually enjoyed it?"

"Oh, no, it was horrible, but you did good." Ned grins. He gestures with his chin to the front of the room. "Need to say goodbye?"

"No." Abbot tucks his laptop up under his arm and Ned follows him to the door, glancing back. Louis and Abbot slept together. For years. *Don't*, he tells himself, though jealousy itches through his chest anyway.

"Really," Ned says in the hallway. "That was good. You're a good speaker."

"Thank you."

"I'm serious. I don't know why you don't like teaching."

"You're the one who thinks I don't like teaching."

"No, I'm the one who knows you don't like teaching." They're at a conference. The hallway is full of other professors in their field. Ned shouldn't touch him. Still, he taps Abbot's elbow with a finger. "Don't worry, I won't tell."

Ned's smiling. He should probably stop. Instead, he leans closer, letting himself pretend it's the crowd pushing him toward Abbot. "You staying for the rest of the day?"

"I was going to."

Ned might do well to stick around himself, mingle a bit. There are plenty more presentations. A dinner too, Ned's pretty sure. He pushes his hands into his pockets. Though he's got grading to do before Peggy shows up this evening. And he should be preparing for his dissertation defense. He can't be hanging around with Abbot all day.

Someone brushes an inch too close to Ned's shoulder. Abbot's jaw tightens, that familiar tic at the corner of his cheek.

Ned doesn't have to turn to guess who's there. And sure enough, Louis walks by them, deep in discussion with some guy Ned doesn't know. He and Abbot give each other a short, crisp nod. Ned knows that one, has felt that same look on his own face, though it was at a conference-room table in Jen's lawyer's office.

"No, I'm not going to stay," Abbot says.

"You okay?" Ned asks.

"No."

Ned maybe shouldn't be touching him, but all the same, he squeezes Abbot's arm. "Let's go, then."

In the hotel room, Ned unbuttons his borrowed shirt and takes off his slacks too, the ones he wore yesterday to teach in, and trades them for jeans creased from being in the bottom of his backpack. Abbot packs his computer, unknots his tie, and lays his jacket neatly in his garment bag. It's a certain sort of domesticity. *Odd, but nice*, Ned figures as he stuffs his feet into his sneakers and buttons his jeans.

"Headed back home?" Ned asks.

"Portland? Yes." Abbot unfastens the cuffs of his shirt and then his collar. Ned watches his fingers work as Abbot flicks open the rest of the buttons in a line down his chest and stomach. "Thank you for coming today."

"Of course." Ned pulls his sweatshirt on over his head. There's no need to watch. Abbot leaves his undershirt on and pulls on a sweater. It's a nice color, a pale sort of tan, and soft looking. Abbot steps out of his suit pants too, and Ned swallows. *One for the road*, he could suggest, as if he doesn't still feel the heavy sort of looseness last night left him with. Abbot steps into a pair of khakis and Ned pushes his fingers through his hair.

"Would you like a ride?" Abbot asks.

"My folks' place isn't exactly on the way to the highway."

"It's no trouble."

Don't, Ned tries to tell himself. *Get a cab. Hell, walk, it's not exactly that far.*

"Yeah, I'd love a ride," he says.

Outside, the clouds haven't cleared, though the rain's not much more than a heavy mist. He sets his backpack next to Abbot's bag in the trunk and shuts it, watching Abbot fold his long body into the driver's seat.

"Take a right." Ned points out of the parking lot as Abbot turns the car on and shifts into gear. "And left here."

"That's a sign for downtown," Abbot says.

"Ignore it." Ned points. "Sharp left."

"Boston is unmanageable."

"This isn't even Boston, the actual city is tiny. Sharper left—nope, that was it, you missed it. Take a right."

"A right?"

"Yes, a right."

"But you had just said to take a—"

"That right, right there." Ned taps at the window. "C'mon, aren't Swiss roads all cow paths?"

"No." Abbot spins the wheel sharply. "No, they are not."

"If you keep going, you can take a right, and then your first left. Oh, just pull over and let me drive. Peggy'll be graduating high school by the time we get there."

Abbot glances over, a quick cut of his eyes behind his glasses. "Can you drive a manual?"

"I can handle a stick," Ned says. Abbot's not Pat. He's not already grinning at the low-hanging fruit that is the joke that could be made. *Thought you'd know that by now*, Ned could say. Would say, with anyone else. Abbot's not exactly Ned's normal speed, not at all.

Though the person Ned chose for himself was Jen, and look how far that got him.

Abbot pulls into a gas station with a sigh. "Fine."

In the driver's seat, Ned adjusts the mirror, his tongue between his teeth. "Sweet," he says, smoothing his hands over the fine leather of the steering wheel. "Is this what I have to look forward to when I graduate?"

"Please be careful."

"I'm careful." Ned eases the clutch out. "I drive my precious child around. I'm super careful."

Abbot grips the door as Ned pulls onto the street. "More careful than that."

"Aw, why own it if you're not going to enjoy it?" Ned lets the engine rev before he shifts into third. "This is the left you should've taken. Don't you ever drive around Boston?"

"You just said this isn't Boston." Abbot shakes his head. "As you can perhaps imagine, only under duress."

Ned lays his wrist over the steering wheel and points, his other hand still on the gear shift. "That's where my first job was. Well, my first job not working at my dad's shop. I bagged groceries, and by bagged groceries, I mean I squished loaves of bread and broke more than my fair share of eggs."

The car is smooth as all hell. Ned used to ride his bike down here, bumping along the uneven pavement, his teeth jarred every time he hit a pothole.

"And that—" Ned points again "—is where Pat drove his mom's car into a fence. See how that part of it is a different color?"

"Please don't repeat the incident."

"Oh, we were maybe fourteen. Fifteen, tops."

"We?"

"It was, what did you say? Under duress. I wasn't involved."

"Really?"

"Well, still got my ass grounded for a week." Ned nods out the window. "My elementary school."

"Where Peggy will go?" Abbot turns to look.

"No, they changed the zoning, and Jen doesn't live around here." Their house—her house—is on the other side of town. Ned shifts his grip on the wheel.

"What about this block? The site of more escapades?" Abbot asks.

"Oh, uh—" Ned glances out the windshield. "The park. One of them. Peggy doesn't like those swings. The good park's down the other way."

Ned taps his fingers against the wheel. It's weird having Abbot here, all these pieces of Ned's life laid out like this.

"My dad's shop is a block that way." Ned nods to a street they drive past. Maybe Abbot's not even interested, though he turns to look. "And here we go—that's Pat's parents' house, the blue one. And this is my folks'."

Ned pulls into the driveway. The garage is shut and his dad's truck is gone. He clears his throat. "Want to come in for a second, before you drive back?"

Abbot looks up at the house. Ned pulls on the emergency brake and rubs his palms down his thighs. He wonders what Abbot sees in the clapboard front, the lawn with leaves scattered across it, his mom's garden. Ned'll get the rake out tomorrow. Peggy always makes a mess of any attempt to actually clean up the yard, but she loves it all the same, and at least his folks won't have to do it themselves.

"Is anyone home?" Abbot asks.

"No." Ned glances at the house again. "My mom, maybe."

Slowly, Abbot unhooks his seatbelt. "I don't want to intrude."

"It's fine, it's a long drive back anyway." Ned gets out and grabs his bag from the trunk. The side door to the garage is unlocked and Abbot trails him to it. Inside, his mom's car is parked, a sprinkling of rain on it.

"You've always lived here?" Abbot asks.

"They bought it before I was born," Ned says. Peggy's bike sits next to the door to the house, training wheels still on and the frame plastered with dinosaur stickers. Ned had bought them for her, and two ended up on Baxter, and a third on his car keys. The stickiness is still there on the back of his key fob, though the sticker long ago wore off, jangling around in his pocket and his thumb working over the shape of it.

"Um, come in." Ned pushes open the door to the kitchen. "Mom?"

"That you, Ned?" she calls from upstairs.

Ned steps out of his shoes. "Want anything?" He drops his bag on the floor. "Hey, I'm back!"

"Hi, sweetie."

"Hi," he yells. There's a glass sitting on the dish drainer. Ned fills it and quickly drinks half of it. "Water, tea?"

"Water," Abbot says. He's got his keys in his hand still. He holds them for a moment longer, then tucks them into his pocket. Ned tries to follow his eyes as Abbot looks around—the refrigerator, layers and layers of Peggy's drawings on it, the calendar tacked to the wall, a plant on the windowsill above the sink, and the small yard beyond it.

Ned fills a second glass. "You don't have to stand there, you can sit."

Ned's mom comes in and stands on her toes to kiss him on the cheek. "Ned, hi, honey." She rubs his arm and he shuts off the faucet. Maybe Abbot wanted ice. Ned can't remember now if he has a preference. "I thought you were coming down last night."

"Hi, Mom." Ned sets the glass on the counter. "This is my mom, Cheryl."

"Henry," Abbot says, taking a step forward, his hand held out.

"Hi, Henry." His mom holds Abbot's hand in both of hers as she shakes it, smiling up at him.

"From Callahan," Ned says.

"Oh, from Callahan, it's so nice to meet you." She holds Abbot's hand for a second longer, squeezing it as she smiles at him. "You're in Ned's class?"

"I'm a professor," Abbot says. Ned takes another long sip of water.

"Oh, how nice." She lets Abbot go finally and pushes his glass toward him. "Sit, sit, it's always so nice to meet Ned's friends. You're down here for the weekend too? Do you know Patrick?"

Ned wipes at a drop of water on the counter. "He was giving a presentation, Mom."

"I do know him." Abbot perches on the very edge of a stool, one of the ones pulled up to the other side of the counter.

"Are you boys hungry? I made cookies." Mom squeezes Ned's shoulders. "I'm also starting dinner. Peggy's on her way? We'll eat early, then. Pat's just so lovely, isn't he? We miss him around here. How's he doing up there these days?"

"I'm all set," Ned says. They ate breakfast late. Because they slept late. A hell of a lot later than Ned's slept in a while, though also a hell of a lot later than he's fallen asleep, too. He scratches at the side of his neck. He still feels amazing after last night. "You want anything?"

"I'm fine," Abbot says.

"Pat's doing good." Ned grabs the stool next to Abbot and pulls it out enough to sit.

"We're having spaghetti and meatballs." Mom opens the fridge. "You're staying for dinner, Henry?"

"I have to drive back," Abbot says.

It's not an answer. Ned hooks his foot around a rung of the stool. "He doesn't eat meat, Mom."

He does have to drive back, Ned should've said. He kicks at the rung.

"Hon?" The front door of the house opens and closes again. "Whose car is that out there?"

"Well, you can have spaghetti," his mom says.

"Who's having spaghetti?" his dad asks. "Hi, hon. Ned! You're back."

"Hello," Abbot says. He stands and holds out his hand.

"Hello, again, to you, too," Dad says, his face split in a grin. Abbot gets a handshake, and with a long lean over the counter, Ned gets his hair messed up.

"Don't." Ned smooths it back down again.

"We're all having spaghetti," his mom says. "Henry here doesn't eat meat."

"Doesn't eat meat," his dad repeats slowly. He looks Abbot up and down. "You know what, you're tall."

Ned frowns. "I'm tall."

"Come here, I just need you for a second." Dad nods his head toward the living room. "A lightbulb, Ned, look alive. Now tell me, Henry, have you had issues with the camshaft tensioner? We had three Audis in over the last month, changed each one of them out."

"No," Abbot says slowly.

The lightbulbs are in the pantry, where they've always been. Ned grabs one and pushes it into Abbot's hand. Abbot looks at him, and then over at his dad again, before following him into the living room.

"Well, you should check for oil leaks. How long have you been parked there? I'll take a look later. It's better to catch that early, it can really be a pain." Dad points up at the ceiling. "That one up there, can you reach?"

Abbot can. Ned crosses his arms and leans against the doorframe between the kitchen and living room, watching Abbot stretch on his toes to unscrew the bulb over the mantel. It pulls his sweater up a bit, and his shirt with it.

Behind Ned, the faucet turns on. "He seems nice," Mom says.

"Mom."

"I'm just saying." She shuts off the sink. "Chop this, dear."

"Huh?" Just beneath the hem of Abbot's sweater there's a strip of pale skin and the prominent bump of Abbot's hipbone. "Oh. Yeah, sure. Can you make Dad stop?"

"Absolutely not, there's another bulb out on the stairs, and he's been using book club as an excuse to not change it." She pushes two tomatoes and a cutting board toward him. Her head tips, eyes narrowing. "Is that the door?"

Ned looks at the clock. It's definitely not five o'clock yet. In the living room, Dad asks Abbot about his spark plugs. It sure as hell is the door, and then the fast patter of small feet.

"We saw the T. rex!" Peggy shouts, arriving at a run and crashing into Ned's thighs.

Ned's mom puts down her knife and puts on a smile. "Jen. Hello."

Ned scoops up Peggy, a hand underneath each of her arms. Abbot's watching them. Ned can feel it pricking his skin. For a long moment, he presses a kiss to the top of Peggy's head, his cheeks hot. "Hi, shorty."

"We're early," Jen says from the door to the garage. *Letting the heat out*, Dad would say if Ned stood like that, the door hanging open. "Oh. Hi."

Mom raises an eyebrow. "You are early, aren't you?"

"Hi." Ned shifts Peggy to his hip. Her tiny shoes drum against his thigh, and he hitches her up higher.

Jen stares past him at Abbot. "I didn't mean to interrupt."

Mom slices an onion in half. "We were expecting you later."

"I'm Jen," she says.

Abbot glances over. "Henry."

Ned smooths Peggy's hair back from her face. "This is Peggy," he says.

"Hello," Abbot says to her, his voice soft. Ned's chest does something funny, something thick and warm, and he leans his cheek on Peggy's head, hugging her warm familiar weight.

"Did you have fun today?" Ned asks her. "Say hi, sweetie, this is one of my friends from school."

Peggy buries her head in his shoulder. Ned bounces her lightly and rubs at her back, craning to see her face.

"Where'd you see the T. rex?" he asks. "The science museum?"

She nods, her forehead bumping against his collarbone.

"Well, you must need to be getting going. Have a nice weekend, Jen," his mom says.

Ned bounces her again. "Say bye to Mom."

The door snicks shut behind Jen. Ned lets out a breath and kisses Peggy's head again.

"Feeling shy?" Ned asks. Peggy nods again and he rubs a circle on her back. He catches Abbot's eye. "Takes a minute, sometimes."

"I can go," Abbot says. He's still watching them and that thing in Ned's chest won't quit, just spreads to his stomach, warming him straight through.

"No," he says quickly. "Stay, if you want."

"While you two are here, we're moving the couch, we have to turn the rug," Dad says. "Plus, there's a cache of dino eggs under there."

"Isn't," Peggy says, finally lifting her head up. She needs her hair brushed. Ned pushes it back from her forehead with his palm.

"Is," Dad says. "The pterodactyl laid them. I saw it happen."

"That's not a dinosaur." Peggy's peeking over his shoulder now. She'll lose interest soon enough, forget altogether to be nervous around Abbot. "Where's Baxter?"

"With your Uncle Pat," Ned says.

"Lays eggs, though," Dad says. "Come look."

Peggy squirms and Ned lets her down. Butt in the air, she peers under the couch. "My knees," his dad groans and joins her there. "Ned, your phone."

Ned puts the flashlight on for him and hands it over. "Stay for dinner," he says quietly. Abbot's still got a lightbulb in his hand, his eyes on Peggy and Ned's dad. There are dust bunnies under there, in all likelihood. Maybe a stray ball or two.

"Something to drink, Henry?" his mom asks. "A beer?"

"He doesn't like beer," Ned says.

His dad peers up at them. "Doesn't like beer? Best news I've heard all day, more for me."

"We need to make a nest," Peggy says and then is dashing upstairs, sneakers clomping up the treads.

Dad sits back on his heels and sighs. "And that's why the lights are constantly going out."

"I don't want to impose," Abbot says.

"You're not." Ned licks at his lips. He can feel his parents watching them. "And anyway, you're the only person I know who could possibly eat spaghetti with zero mess, so I kind of gotta see how you do it."

Abbot looks down at his sweater. "Okay," he says.

Ned's father climbs back to his feet, a hand braced on the arm of the couch. "Do you like baseball, at least?" He claps his palm to Abbot's shoulder. "We've got wine too, and a really great vintage of apple juice."

"We went to a game," Ned says. "And he's going to say yes, just to be polite."

"Football?" Dad asks.

"I'm not very familiar with it."

"He's a professor," Mom says.

"I know." His dad swats Ned on the back of his head. "Nice, Ned."

"Dad, c'mon."

"Hockey, Henry? No?" His dad rummages through the fridge and comes up with two cans of beer. "Where the hell did you find him, Ned?"

"Diced," his mom says and pushes the cutting board and tomatoes toward Ned again.

Upstairs, there's a thump. "Peggy?" Ned calls.

She bounds down the stairs again, dragging her comforter, a stuffed owl, and a triceratops held by its neck in the crook of her arm. "We have to get the eggs."

"I'll chop those." Abbot's hand covers Ned's and slips the knife away. "I know the Bruins are trading their second-line right wing to the Panthers."

Ned looks up, surprised. "Where'd you hear that?"

"The paper." Abbot starts slicing. God, he has nice hands.

"Didn't know you read about sports," Ned says.

"I began to."

"Huh."

The floor lamp in the living room teeters. Ned keeps staring at Abbot as he backs toward it, catching it with one hand before it can fall. At his feet, Peggy arranges the blanket, and then sticks her arm beneath the couch.

She's going to be a mess, soon enough. She'll emerge dusty and dirty and probably ready to steal the tomatoes Abbot's already halfway through for a snack. Ned's still staring. When his dad catches him at it and grins, Ned's cheeks burn.

He kneels next to Peggy. But he glances back again all the same, Abbot there in the kitchen, his dad setting a wineglass in front of him, and his mom humming to herself as she turns on a burner.

His chest still feels funny. Though it might for the rest of dinner, and maybe that's just something Ned will have to try to get used to.

CHAPTER TWENTY-TWO

ABBOT PICKS UP ANOTHER PICTURE. "And this one?"

"Okay, that's just unfair." Ned grabs the frame and sticks it back on the mantel. "Either go for the ones where I was a cute kid, or anything more recent. None of this zeroing in on awkward adolescent school pictures."

"Awkward is a misnomer," Abbot says, and damn him, he picks up the photo again and tips it toward the lamp.

"I think awkward is generous."

"At least you didn't have glasses." Abbot replaces the frame and picks up the next picture.

Ned sighs. The drawback of being an only child: there are no siblings' pictures to hide behind in his parents' collection. And Peggy, the only child of an only child—there are enough framed photos that his folks really should've just bought stock in five-by-seven-inch frames.

Abbot moves onto those next, Peggy—wrapped in a blanket at the hospital, seated in her high chair and chin smeared with mashed peas, bundled in a snow suit with pink cheeks, practicing walking with Jen holding onto her tiny hands. Ned took that photo in his old living room in

Portland. Abbot probably doesn't know it's Jen helping Peggy, who's captured mid-step and off-balance.

"She really looks like you," Abbot says. "Your father, too."

"Good old Coppola genes."

Peggy was so damn cute. Still is. He glances at the stairs. She's hopefully asleep after his mom finally got her down and isn't about to come dashing downstairs again in her footed pajamas, asking for a story, a cup of water, another story, two, three, four of them. A day will come all too quickly when Peggy'll be buried in her cell phone, entirely too cool to launch herself at Ned and be swung up into the air, giggling. He sighs and puts the picture back.

Upstairs, a floorboard creaks and a sink runs. It's his parents bathroom, though, not Peggy helping herself to the faucet.

"I should go," Abbot says.

Don't, Ned nearly tells him. "Course," he says instead. It's late. Getting late, at least, and Abbot has a long drive.

The night's settled into an autumn crispness when Ned opens the front door. He should've found something warmer to wear if he's going to say goodbye out here, not just his sweatshirt. And whatever coat Abbot might've packed is still in his car. Ned eyes it, parked in the driveway, a far cry from any other make or model on this street.

"Thank you for dinner," Abbot says.

Ned nods. The top step of the stoop is cold through his socks. He's shorter than Abbot like this, who's wearing his shoes.

"Well, thanks for the ride."

"And for today," Abbot says. "For coming."

"I'm glad I got to see your talk." Ned's heart thumps too strongly in his chest. *Back up*, he tells himself. He should shut the door and get to work.

"Don't worry about your defense," Abbot says.

Ned snorts out a soft laugh. "And here I wasn't planning to sleep all night because of it."

He won't sleep at all. There'll be no Abbot pinned under him and pressed into a mattress, working out the spark of excess energy, no body to curl against, no legs tangled with his.

"When it's over, you'll be done with your doctorate."

"If I pass."

"You will."

"Yeah." Ned scuffs his heel on the stoop. It'll be fine. He lets out a long breath. Because otherwise . . . "I think I'm waiting for Chris to email again and tell me I need another set of revisions that's going to take a whole other semester."

"He won't," Abbot says. "You'll do well."

Ned clears his throat. "Thanks."

"Goodnight, Ned," Abbot says softly.

"Um, goodnight."

He touches Abbot's sleeve. His sweater is soft. And it is clean, isn't it? Not a speck of sauce. Ned's kissed plenty of folks on this very step, after an entire adolescence in this house. He could kiss Abbot now. Lean right in and let this moment between them stretch out, elastic and warm. But he hesitates, and when he doesn't move, Abbot draws back slightly.

"Goodnight," Abbot says again, and Ned lets his hand drop.

Ned sits on the couch, listening to the rumble of Abbot's car fade. Grading. He has grading to do. Slowly, he rubs his palms down his thighs. He should stand up, grab his bag, and get to it, before the clock keeps on moving toward midnight, and then toward morning. He tips himself backward, his legs hanging over the edge of the couch, and his head in the middle of the cushion.

No, he's going to have a hell of a time focusing on work, when the only thing swimming through his mind is the gentleness in Abbot's eyes.

"Dammit," Ned groans into his palms. His stomach's still flipping. Beneath his fingers, he can feel the soft weft of Abbot's sweater.

———

IN THE MORNING, he blearily pours cereal into a bowl for Peggy. "Sit," he tells her, tapping her chair with his fingers. "On your bum, like you're supposed to."

"Dimetrodons aren't dinosaurs either."

"Yeah?" One more tap and she shifts onto her butt, her feet dangling clear above the floor.

"Or plesiosaur." Her fist is tight around her spoon. Jen'd be after her to hold it correctly and after Ned for not caring. He sips at his coffee.

"What're those, then?"

"They swim." She shifts back onto her knees.

Ned rubs his thumb and forefinger into his eyes. There's a piece of toast on his plate. He should eat it. Nothing like running after Peggy all morning, and doing it on an empty stomach is all the harder.

"Swim?" Ned asks. "Or swam? Think they're still out there?"

"No," she says, her mouth full.

"Swallow, champ. How're your pterodactyl eggs doing?"

"Intubating."

"Incubating." He taps her chair. "Peggy, sit."

"M'gonna go check," she says and she's off, a clatter of her spoon in her bowl, and her chair left shoved out from the table.

"Peggy," he sighs. He wipes up a drop of milk from the table with his thumb.

"Bran flakes versus dino eggs, not exactly a fair choice, is it?" his dad says, settling across from Ned with his own coffee and the newspaper.

"Is that what this is?" Ned peers into Peggy's bowl, moving her spoon around. It's mushy already.

Mom pulls out the chair next to his dad. "It's good for you," she says.

Ned picks up a spoonful, and lets it plop back into the bowl. "Mom, I'm not so sure about that."

"So, your friend." Dad grins into his mug. "Henry."

"Dad." Ned tips his chin toward the living room.

"What?" His dad shakes out the front section of the paper. "Peggy's not listening."

"Yeah, but . . ."

"Did he stay late?" Mom asks.

"Did he stay—no, Mom, Jesus." Ned stands and opens the garbage can, dumping Peg's cereal into it. "I'm making pancakes."

Not a peep from the living room. Peggy's got her owl in one hand and her blanket still on the floor, pushed into a rough circle.

"See? She's not listening to us," Dad says. "I liked him."

"I did too," Mom says. "He's very nice."

"Stop," Ned says. There's flour in the cupboard. He roots around. Chocolate chips, too. "Do you guys want some?"

"You never bring anyone over," his mom says.

"He was giving me a ride. I invited him in. I was being polite."

"I want some," Dad says. "Tell us about him, we want to know."

Mom sips at her coffee. "We do want to know, we're very curious."

Ned sorts through the fridge, like it's really that hard to find the butter and milk. "There's nothing to say."

"Ned," Dad says.

"There isn't." Ned pulls a bowl out of the drawer. A pan, he needs a pan. And for his parents to lay the hell off. "It's not like that."

"What's it like, then?" Dad asks.

"I have to go outside," Peggy says from the living room, her owl held in both hands. "We need sticks."

"No sticks in the house," Ned says.

"Rocks," Peggy says.

"Let's bring the nest outside, hmm?" His mom stands. "I heard sunlight does wonders for dinosaur eggs."

Peggy frowns. "Pterodactyl."

"Your coat, miss." Mom holds out her mug for Ned to pour more coffee into. "There's blueberries in the refrigerator, Ned, and I bought some syrup, too."

When the door shuts behind them, his dad lays the newspaper down. "Ned."

"I don't know what you want me to say." Ned dumps a cup of flour into the bowl. "Can we talk about anything else?"

"Your dissertation defense?"

"No."

"You like him. Maybe that's complicated for you, but you do."

"Dad . . ."

"Go on, tell me that you don't."

"He's . . ." Ned shakes his head. "It's not that simple."

His dad shrugs. "Seems pretty simple. You like him, he clearly likes you."

"Well, I don't want to."

"Oh? You gonna just up and stop?"

"Dad." Ned cracks open an egg. "He's not—" he sighs.

His dad's smiling. "He's not what, Ned?"

Ned shakes his head. "He doesn't like sports."

"So?"

"And he's not . . . I don't know. Like Pat."

"So, then you'd be wanting to date Pat." Dad leans his elbows on the table, steepling his fingers. "We don't choose who we fall for, hate to break it to you, kid."

"You and Mom met in high school, you didn't have to—" Ned waves a spoon around the room. "Do this."

"Ned . . ."

"No, I'm serious, it's such a mess." Ned measures out a splash of milk. "I don't want anything. And he doesn't either, he's said."

"You know, when your mom and I met, we were, what, sixteen?"

"I know," Ned says, sharper than he meant to. Their story is really cute. Homecoming, prom, the works. He clears his throat. "Sorry."

"I didn't think I was going to marry her," his dad says. "We broke up, what, four times?"

"You did?"

"Sure we did. You two aren't putting a ring on it, moving in together, tying the knot. You like him and like I said, he likes you. Sounds simple to me. Go with that, Ned, don't worry about what comes next."

Ned turns the stove on, his back to his dad. He lets out a breath. "He wants kids."

"Convenient."

"Dad." Ned scoops out half of the batter and sticks his head back into the fridge. Maybe he can just crawl in here and avoid this entire conversation, but no, the blueberries are right there in front. "And he lives in Maine."

"So? Is he going to stay there forever? He can drive down, he's got a hell of a car. Unlike yours—it's still at the shop, but it should be good to go by tonight."

"Thanks." Abbot's not going to stay in Maine. That's what he said, wasn't it? He's wanted to move to Boston for a long time now. Ned pushes the door to the fridge shut.

"It's okay to try again," his dad says. "Are you going to stay single for the rest of your life?"

"It's working okay so far." Ned dumps chocolate chips into one bowl of batter.

"Is it? 'Cause that's the happiest I've seen you recently. In a long, long time, kid."

"I told you, he doesn't want anything serious."

"People change their minds. You've asked him?"

"I'm moving," Ned says.

"Then say something before you do," Dad says, like it's just that easy.

"I can't—we agreed—" he shakes his head.

"What're you waiting for, exactly? You going to date when you move back here?"

"I don't know. Maybe."

"What, online? Hit up the bars?"

"Dad, I don't know."

"Stumble upon someone smart and good-looking, with a steady job, who's looking to start a family, and isn't going to run for the hills because you come with a daughter?"

"Dad, please."

"You can spend the rest of your life looking for something perfect." His dad stands. Ned could probably duck away, but he lets his dad put a hand on his shoulder. "You didn't see all those years of me and your mom figuring everything out. Growing up, jobs, moving . . . he likes you and you like him. That's all you need, Ned. Real life doesn't look all that pretty up close."

"It's complicated between us," Ned mumbles.

His dad ruffles his hair. "It's okay to try again, kid."

"I'm not ready."

"If you weren't ready, he would've never been over here last night."

"Stop," Ned says, trying to pat down his hair. "You're making this worse."

"It's hard to watch your kid be unhappy," his dad says. "Listen to me, Ned. Get out of your own way."

"You're the one not listening to me."

"What're you more scared of? That it doesn't work out with him, or that it does?"

Dad lets go and starts tapping a pat of butter into the pan. Outside, Peggy and his mom collect dried flower stalks, their hands full of them. They'd been blooming only weeks ago, and now as fall closes in, they've given up to the frost that's settled. Peggy plops a handful down on her blanket, under the watchful eye of the owl.

"You trust him?" Dad asks.

Ned stares down at the butter melting in the pan. "Yeah."

"To not do what Jen did?"

"He wouldn't."

"Good. Now watch this. I saw it on the YouTube. I'm going to make a triceratops pancake."

Peggy picks up a handful of leaves and adds them to her collection. Any other weekend, and Baxter would be out there too, adding to the ruckus and noise. Ned tries to picture it, Abbot there as well. He wants kids. Wants . . . this, maybe. A life like this. The two of them, living in the same city. Someone for Ned to be with on the days and nights he doesn't have Peggy. And maybe, eventually, when he does. Liesl here too, now and again. Ned's stomach flips at the thought. Abbot . . . Abbot'd be good at this. With kids. With Peggy, in his own quiet, calm way.

He bought Ned dinner. Invited him to spend the night. Came over and spent an evening with his family.

That's still different, though, than anything long-term.

Peggy tugs the door open, her cheeks flushed and hair sticking to the corner of her mouth. "We need a bucket."

"A bucket," Ned says. "Pancakes, first."

"Pancakes!" She leaves the door open and runs inside. His mom follows behind, shutting it against the chill of the wind.

"One triceratops," his dad says, plating the pancake with a flourish. It looks like a hippo, maybe.

"Syrup, Peggy?" Ned asks.

"I want to pour it."

"Right," he says. "Let me just get the mop. A fire hose, maybe."

"I can do it." She takes the bottle from him, holding it in both hands.

"Sit, Ned," his dad says. "I got this."

Ned pulls out a chair for himself and one for Peggy. She climbs into it, already up on her knees.

"Sit," he says and taps the chair.

He'll have a house of his own, someday. They'll only be over here for visits. He taps the chair again and she plops down on her butt. Soon enough, she's hardly going to need the reminder. Ned tries to rearrange the picture to have Abbot there, too. Nerves flutter through his chest. *Maybe*, he thinks. Maybe.

CHAPTER TWENTY-THREE

NED OPENS his eyes to the gray cotton of his pillowcase and his heart racing. He squeezes his eyes shut. In the kitchen, Pat putters around, and at the end of Ned's bed, Baxter snuffles, sneezes, and starts scratching his neck.

"Bax," Ned mumbles. He gets a nose nudged into his calf.

How much easier it would be to simply pull the pillow over his head and avoid the day waiting for him outside of his cocoon of blankets. Tempting nearly, if he thought the jumble of nerves lodged up under his rib cage would let him.

In his office, he paces.

"Stop," Sameer says and reaches to bat the notecards out of Ned's hands.

Ned yanks them away. "Don't mess them up."

"Don't have an aneurysm. Take a deep breath, and for all of our sakes—mine, mostly—stop practicing."

Ned turns at the door and walks back across the narrow room again. "I'm not going to have an aneurysm." He flicks to his next notecard.

Sameer snorts. "Says the guy wearing a hole in the carpet."

Midafternoon, Ned heads back to the apartment. He's mumbling to himself, he knows, going over his conclusion again and again. He jogs upstairs and pats at Baxter's head.

"I'm okay," Ned tells Bax. "I'm okay."

"You're not." Pat trails Ned into his bedroom. "You look like you're going to throw up."

Ned's jacket lies on his bed, carefully picked clean of dog hair. His tie, too. He pulls on a clean shirt. "I'm not going to throw up." He loops the tie under his collar. His hands are shaking. "Okay, I might throw up."

"Did you eat?"

Ned quickly knots his tie. Then he frowns at his reflection and tugs at it. "No."

"You hungry?"

He adjusts the length, fiddles with his collar, and starts pulling at the knot to untie it. "Hell, no."

"You're going to ace it, Ned." Pat bats Ned's hands away and pulls the tie loose. "Oh, just stop, I can't watch this." Quickly, he drapes it over his own head, ties it, and then loops it back over Ned. "There. Stop fussing, it's fine."

"You're going to walk Baxter."

"I'm going to walk Baxter. And I've got a bottle of bubbly on ice, my dude."

"Don't jinx it," Ned says, groaning. "C'mon, man."

"Go knock 'em dead. Please. I can't suffer through any more of you like this."

Ned smooths his palms down his shirt. "Okay," he says. He's got his notecards. And a copy of his dissertation, both printed out and on his laptop. *You know your material better than we do*, Chris had told him just yesterday. *It's a formality, at this point, you've got this.*

Ned swallows. He's definitely going to throw up. Baxter

thumps his tail from his sprawl on the couch, and Ned sucks in a breath.

"I can't," he says, turning toward Pat.

Pat lets out a sigh. "Oh my God, Ned."

Ned pushes the heels of his hands into his eyes. "They're going to send me back for another six months of research."

"They are not."

"I did the entire analysis wrong."

"Right, and the lovely Mr. Abbot's going to let you walk in there and make an idiot of yourself. No way, you know that."

Ned's mouth is dry. "Abbot came over this weekend. He met Peggy."

"Okay," Pat says and gently shakes Ned's shoulders. "Okay, Ned, this is maybe not the time for this."

Good luck, Abbot had texted just that morning. Ned had sat with his coffee cooling, staring, his thumb tracing the screen of his phone.

"I think . . ." Ned takes a deep breath. "I think I'm not ready for all of this to be over between us."

He tries to suck down more air. His heart's beating too fast. And it has been, for so long now.

"Oh my fucking God, Ned, breaking news." Pat throws his hands up. "Jacket. Backpack. You have your wallet and phone?"

"Pat."

"You're not doing this now. You're defending your dissertation now. And you're going to be on time, and calm, and less purple in the face than you currently are."

"Pat, it wasn't supposed to be like this. With him. I wasn't—"

"Of course it wasn't supposed to be like this, you

doctoral fuckwit." Pat throws Ned's coat at him and it catches him in the face.

Slowly, Ned reaches for it before it can hit the floor. "My dad thinks I should go for it."

"Well, your dad doesn't have to live with you and listen to you pace and watch you twitch and wonder if you're going to just keel over." Pat grabs Ned by the face. "Ned. Go. Now, please, before you have to run there."

"Okay." Ned takes a breath. Pat holds out his backpack for him. On the couch, Baxter yawns. "Okay," he says again.

It's cold out. Pat locks the door behind him. Throws the deadbolt, too. "Go!" he shouts through the wood.

Ned should've worn a heavier jacket. The sky's a steely gray that feels somehow appropriate as he starts across campus. They wouldn't let him defend his dissertation if he wasn't going to pass. In his pocket, he closes his hand around his phone. *Good luck.* Ned's still sure this is going to be one giant joke, the rug pulled out from under him. Start again, he'll be told. Nice try, but not even close. *Good luck, good luck.*

His hands shake as he pulls open the door to the conference room. Chris is there, and a few laptops are set near his. The rest of Ned's committee is here, then. Milling around somewhere, getting coffee. They're busy with minutiae of their days, this hour just another appointment they have to keep among the rest of their work.

"Ready?" Chris asks. He's smiling.

Ned makes himself nod. He's as ready as he'll ever be. He hasn't texted Abbot back. His hands were already clammy, reading those two words on his screen. He should've, he thinks now. Typed out something blasé, as if he could've summoned up that casualness. But his stomach was twisting too hard, then—and it still is now. His guts probably won't unravel until well after this is over.

When he's finished presenting, his committee asks him to wait in the hall. His mouth is dry from so much talking. He should've brought some water. Slowly, he lowers himself onto a bench set against the wall. Normally, undergrads are sprawled across it with their book bags and ubiquitous phones stuck to their hands like Velcro.

Ned doesn't have that company today, and he lays his forearms on his knees, trying to keep his legs from bouncing as he waits. *They're talking about me*, he knows. Reviewing his presentation, the copies of his dissertation he sent. Ned blows out a breath, wiggling his toes in his socks and trying to stop clenching his fingers.

Shoes appear at the edge of his vision, neatly polished and the laces carefully tied. Abbot settles next to him on the bench.

"How did it go?" Abbot asks.

He's got on a light blue shirt, and he's studying Ned from behind his glasses. Ned's stomach somersaults in a whole new way. He presses his fingers to his breastbone. "Hi."

"Hello."

"I thought you were teaching."

"I am. They're reviewing each other's proposals for their final projects and providing feedback."

Ned squints. His stomach flips over again. "Is that just timed to give yourself a coffee break?"

"I don't drink coffee."

"Shut up." Ned wants to rest his shoulder against Abbot's. Wants to find out how soft that shirt is, and how it feels where it hugs the curve of Abbot's bicep. Wants to lean over, tuck his face into Abbot's neck, sigh into his shoulder, and breathe back in his rich, clean scent.

Ned's leg starts bouncing. "Can I—" He clears his

throat. Maybe he will vomit, do it right here in the hallway. "I want to talk to you later."

Chris sticks his head out of the door, and Ned's stomach pitches downward.

Abbot nods. "Of course."

"Doctor?" Chris asks, smiling.

Ned doesn't move, just sits there, rubbing his hands down his thighs. Abbot watches him, and gently, he touches his fingers to Ned's knee.

"That's you," Abbot says. He's smiling too, a soft, quiet curve to his lips.

"What?" Ned asks. "Oh my God."

"Congratulations," Abbot says.

Ned covers his mouth with his hand. "Oh my God."

"Come on in." Chris pushes the door open wider. He throws a grin toward Abbot. "We'll have him back to you soon."

"I'll see you after my last class," Abbot says.

"Yeah," Ned says dimly. "I want to—yes, later, okay?"

Ned gets his feet to move toward Chris. He's numb. Or not numb. The opposite of numb. Vibrating, every inch of him, his pulse hammering in his ears with a dull roar. Carefully, he lowers himself into a chair.

Chris is still grinning. "You did great," he says.

"Thank you," Ned hears himself say over and over again. "Thank you so much."

"Really, you worked hard on it, and it shows." Outside, the bell rings. Classes are changing over. Ned can hear them, students spilling into the halls and out onto the quad. How wild, that life can just continue to go on, when something so momentous has occurred.

"Thank you." Ned's hands tremble and he pushes them into his lap, gripping his fingers together. He's breathing too fast, he knows.

"Wherever you land, they'll be lucky to have you," Chris says. He claps Ned on the shoulder. "Hell, I'd try to keep you around these parts if I thought I could."

"I'm going home," Ned says, and for the first time in so long, it's going to be true.

"Yeah, you are. Keep in touch." Chris waves a hand, as casual as everything Ned doesn't feel. "Course you will, with Henry and all. We'll be seeing plenty of you."

Abbot.

Ned's stomach twists all over again. Though, this time that jump sparks with a sharp, clean happiness. God, Abbot, yeah. Ned wants to find him. Tell him about the defense, the handshakes, the feedback Chris will email over, the fact that Ned's done. Finally.

He stumbles through the rest of the meeting, and when it ends, Ned jogs down the stairs. His hand still shaking, he texts his dad. His mom, too. Abbot's classroom is empty. That's right, Ned's late enough that Abbot's got another lecture. Over across campus. Ned peers in the door again, like maybe that class has been cancelled and Abbot's actually here. That the entire rest of the day has been called off, the university grinding to a halt because Ned's life is actually able to move on. But the corners of the seminar room don't turn up a silent, austere, bespectacled professor with that hint of a grin playing at his mouth, and Ned steps aside for the students trying to get past him as they head to their next class.

So???? Pat texts.

Passed, Ned writes back. It can't be real, that word staring back up at him, typed out by his own thumb.

Baxter's waiting for him outside the bar, and for once, Pat lets him come inside. "Fuck yeah!" Pat yells and lifts Ned off the ground with his hug.

"Get off," Ned says, Baxter barking and Pat thumping Ned on the back.

"I love you, man," Pat says and squeezes tight enough Ned grunts. "Drinks, yeah? A round for everyone!"

When Ned fishes his phone out again, there's a series of texts from his folks. And word must get around fast, 'cause there's one from Pat's parents too, and Jesus, one from Jen.

Congrats, she's written. And below that, a picture of Peggy appears, cute as all hell at the park. That's right, isn't it, she'd be out of school by now, and Jen would've picked her up after work. His thumb hovers over the keyboard for a long time before he types out Thanks and sends it back.

Baxter pushes his head into Ned's hand, and Ned kneels on the sticky floor, letting his face get licked. "Did it," he tells Baxter. He gets a face full of dog breath and another lick.

The cork pops out of the bottle of champagne and Pat fills two glasses. "Damn, Ned. Well done."

Ned laughs. Sits himself on his favorite stool, kicks his bag under the bar, and reaches for his own glass. "Right?" He has to laugh again. "Right?"

Sameer comes, pushing through the door and letting in a rush of cold air. Aliyah, Lee, and Minori too, with smiles and arms slung around Ned's shoulders. Baxter jogs around the bar, the tags on his collar jangling and his tail waving back and forth.

"How's it feel?" Aliyah asks. "Chris emailed, he said you did great."

"I can't believe it," Ned says. He's still buzzing, energy coursing straight through him. Done. Done, done, done. So many damn years in the making.

"Doctor Coppola," Lee says. He gets a sweet kiss on his cheek. "Be a bear about it, make everyone call you that. No shame, Ned."

"I just might," Ned says. Pat pours more champagne into Ned's glass and it fizzes up right to the rim, bubbly, effervescent. "I think I just might."

I'm at Pat's, Ned types to Abbot. He deletes it, flicking his thumb against the edge of his phone.

"We're so proud of you," Minori says.

"Thanks," Ned says. Come to Pat's, he taps out and erases it too.

"Just the rest of the semester and you're gone?" Lee asks. "Getting on out of here, good job."

"Yeah," Ned says. What're you up to? he writes. "I'll be back in Boston."

He deletes that as well. I want to talk to you, he sends.

I know, Abbot writes back.

The door opens and Baxter trots over in a jangle of tags. Fresh, crisp air blows into the bar, and there's Abbot, a newspaper tucked under his arm and his eyes searching the crowd until he finds Ned.

Ned stands. "Hey."

"Well done," Abbot says.

"I was going to call you." Ned's tongue is too thick in his mouth.

"I was already on my way." Abbot leans down and scratches the top of Baxter's head. "Hello, there."

"I want to talk to you."

"As you've said." An eyebrow lifts behind those glasses. "What if I wanted a beer, first?"

"You don't." Ned catches Abbot's arm. Steers him right around. "Come here, with me."

Outside, evening's slipping into the city with its pale purple shadows and the glow of sunset. Cars have their headlights on, and the streetlamps are shining down, pale gold circles on the sidewalk. Students walk past them, on their way home from their last classes, and Ned draws Abbot into the recess of the door to his apartment.

He cups Abbot's elbow and Abbot doesn't pull away. And when Ned tugs, he takes a step closer so willingly, Ned's heart swells in his chest.

"You wanted to talk," Abbot says.

"I did." God, he did. He does. He works his mouth over words that don't come. *Just start*, he tells himself.

Gently, Abbot touches the front of Ned's shirt. "I'm proud of you."

"I wanted to thank you," Ned says. That's right. A place to begin, at least. He takes a deep breath and it shakes. "This fall, your help—"

"It was nothing."

"It wasn't." Ned steps closer. Abbot's warm against the chill of the autumn air. That spark of nerves is back, flittering through Ned's gut. "I'm—I'm glad we did this."

Pretending to date was wild. And—and better than anything Ned's done in a long, long time. "I want . . ."

I could love you, Ned thinks.

Abbot's watching him with soft eyes. Ned could grow to love him and a life together. Might already. Does already. Damn, now he's really going to puke. Or just burst open with the force of it all.

"You're incredible, you know that? You just keep pushing forward in life no matter what happens and I—" Ned shakes his head, his voice catching too tight in his throat.

"Ned," Abbot says softly.

Ned swallows, reaches out to bring Abbot closer to him. In a voice far clearer than he might've guessed, he says, "I know, this fall, we weren't really together. But I want to be. If you—if that's something you want, too."

Ned meant that to be more eloquent. His cheeks are on

fire. His entire body, really. He's holding Abbot's arm way too hard, and God, Ned needs him to say something. He's not going to breathe until he does. Not going to be able to, the way his throat is clenched up too tight.

"How fortunate," Abbot says. "I was intending to ask you to dinner this weekend. To celebrate."

"You were?" Ned leans in closer, swaying toward Abbot. Or maybe it's Abbot leaning, his fingers closing over the front of Ned's shirt. "You were going to take me out?"

"I had thought to." Abbot rests his forehead on Ned's. And oh, that's nice. Their noses brush and tension coiled in Ned's chest tears loose at the touch in a short breathy laugh.

"Really?" Ned asks.

Abbot kisses him. Gentle as anything, his lips pressed so softly to Ned's.

Come back, Ned wants to say when Abbot pulls away. It was just a tease of what he wants, just the brush of the very idea of it. In Ned's chest, his heart starts up a new beating thump, a too-fast rhythm he hasn't felt before. His head is spinning. And Abbot, Abbot reaches for him, a hand cupping the side of Ned's neck, his fingers warm and his thumb stroking back and forth. His touch is grounding. Solid. Something to lean against, and when Ned takes a breath, it's shared with Abbot's.

"Really," Abbot whispers and kisses him again. And this time, Ned curves his arm around Abbot's shoulders to hold him there, and kisses him back with a slow firmness, a confidence that makes his stomach flip over.

"Then it's a date," Ned whispers. And he ducks forward for one more kiss as the city continues on around them.

CHAPTER TWENTY-FOUR

On Friday evening, Abbot takes Ned down to the water, a briny breeze blowing off the harbor and the last of the season's boats still bobbing at their moorings.

"Where are we going?" Ned asks, campus left blocks behind as Abbot keeps walking.

"This way."

"Funny." Ned loops his hand through Abbot's arm. He meant to slow Abbot down, but doesn't bother to pull at him, just squeezes the crook of his elbow. "Very funny."

Ned wants to kiss him again. More than the peck Abbot had given him when he'd knocked on Ned's door. Really kiss him, no Baxter nosing at their knees, no Pat grinning and calling for Abbot to have Ned back by ten o'clock sharp, *no excuses, young man.*

They have all night. The weekend, too. Maybe it's better like this, anticipation building in Ned as they walk. Certainly better than trying to teach, staring at his notes and an empty whiteboard, marker in hand, as if he could possibly be able to explain anything with the hours ticking down until tonight, until now. Ned slips his hand down

Abbot's forearm so he can lace their fingers together, and when he squeezes, Abbot squeezes back.

Abbot finally stops in front of a restaurant, one of many that line the water. Even holds the door open for Ned. They could skip a nice meal out and grab a pizza after thoroughly making a mess of Abbot's bed, for all Ned cares. He unzips his jacket as Abbot loosens his scarf. That would be easier, in its own way. Ned knows that well enough, the simplicity of slipping into bed, rather than really . . . doing this. Dinner. Dating. A real relationship, after all this time.

Excited, happy nerves dance through him.

"Here?" Ned asks.

"If it's okay." There's a note in Abbot's voice that maybe —well, maybe Ned's not the only one riding high on a prickle of delight, of an actual night out together being nearly entirely too much to begin to grasp.

"Nice choice," Ned says. There's a hell of a beer list on the chalkboard hanging on the wall. This can't be a place Abbot would ever come on his own. Ever has come, and ever would, if not for Ned. "How'd you find it, run a non-parametric correlation analysis?"

"That was hardly necessary. Multiple regression was sufficient."

Ned snorts. "Good to know."

Ned settles into his chair, letting his grin spread over his face. On the TV above the bar, the Bruins game is on.

"I've got something to show you." Ned reaches into his pocket.

"Thank you, I've already seen that."

Ned kicks him under the table. Laughs too and lets his foot rest there, right up against Abbot's. "Later," he says, grinning. He fishes out his phone and opens his email. "Here."

Abbot reads while Ned plays with his menu, flicking his

fingers over the sides. He can't stop looking at Abbot. Doesn't want to, either.

"Something to drink?" the waiter asks.

"The IPA." Ned's going to have a beer, and a burger, and a plate of fries, and then he's going to take Abbot back to that gorgeous house and nail him in that bed of his. Ned's still grinning. "You going to get something?"

"Whatever's least unpleasant." Abbot scrolls down Ned's phone.

"He'll have the Kölsch," Ned says. "And fried pickles."

Abbot closes his eyes. "Americans."

Ned leans over and taps the side of his phone. "What d'ya think?"

"Congratulations." Abbot slides it back across the table. Ned locks it again, a picture of Peggy staring up at him.

"It's next week," Ned says. "I'm nervous."

"You've met Steven."

"Not for an interview." Ned drums his fingers on the table. A job interview. He's taken to reading Steve's email over and over again. Last night, Pat up and smacked the phone out of his hand. "And they specifically want a qualitative researcher."

"I would tell you good luck, but you'll hardly need it." Abbot turns Ned's phone toward himself again and pushes the button to wake the screen up. "When was this taken?"

"Last spring. May, I think." At the park near his parents' house, Peggy grinning at him from the swings. She already looks older than that picture, and she's long since outgrown the jeans she's wearing in it. Her shirt still fits her though, a big purple triceratops on it. Ned traces his thumb over the screen. "I'm not, um . . ."

Abbot waits. He's so patient.

Ned taps his fingers on his phone, his lips pressed together.

Gently, Abbot covers his hand with his own. "You're not?"

"Um." Ned wrinkles his nose. "I didn't really love that Jen told Peggy so much about her and Jeff. That he was—I don't know. Around, like he was."

It was confusing as all hell for Peggy. Moving back to Boston, Ned not there much at all, and Jeff half-living in what had been their house. Ned's forehead pinches. And Ned'll be moving back again now, shifting things up yet again.

Abbot's thumb moves over the back of Ned's hand.

"So I don't want to tell her anything. If we're really—"

Abbot's watching him.

Ned wants to clear his throat. "Doing this. For a while, at least. Sometime . . . later."

"That's fine."

"It is?"

"Of course it is."

"Obviously, my parents know."

"I like them." Abbot leans back in his chair, making room for the waiter to set down their beers.

"Good." Ned smooths his hands down his thighs. *There's more to say*, Ned's sure. That if Abbot wants to come down to Boston, Ned's only got his childhood bed and his parents always in the house. At least, until he finds a place of his own. That Ned's life always revolves around Peggy, and at a moment's notice everything else he's got going on can—will—get dropped. That there is no Ned without Peggy, and that building anything with Ned is to do it with both of them. He spins his glass of beer in a circle. "You're sure it's fine?"

"Ned." Abbot's foot taps against his. "We'll make it work."

"Okay." Ned nods. He takes a sip of his beer and sets it down again.

"Peggy is important to you, and you're important to me." Abbot's hand covers Ned's again. He feels better with Abbot's strong touch on his fingers, tracing over his palm. "I have no intention of inundating Liesl with details right away. She was entirely too taken with you. And with Baxter."

"Well." Ned sniffs. Blinks too. His eyes are stinging. "Baxter's always the favorite."

Ned lets Abbot trace his fingers over his wrist, up under the cuff of his shirt, and back around his knuckles. He has such nice hands. Ned tries to remember him back when they first met, handing out the class syllabus that first day, but it seems like another life, not hardly the same man sitting at the table across from him.

Ned sniffs again. "Drink your beer."

He doesn't let go of Abbot's fingers though, so Abbot raises his glass with his other hand, holding it up to the light and taking a small sip. "It's fine."

"A resounding review." Ned squeezes Abbot's fingers. "I haven't, you know, dated in—in a long time."

"I haven't either."

"I'm not . . ." He holds on tight, rubbing his thumb against Abbot's. "I'm not entirely sure I'm really ready."

"Me neither."

Ned lets out a small laugh. "Good. I guess we're in the same boat, then."

Another squeeze to Ned's hand. "We are."

"Well . . ." Ned takes a drink of his own beer. They should've just gone to Abbot's place. Then, Ned could do what he wants to, which is crawl over there and tuck his face into the crook of Abbot's neck. Hold him and be held.

"Well, maybe it's a good thing that we already had a chance to work out the hiccups."

Abbot smiles. Really, actually smiles. The corners of his eyes crease behind his glasses, his lips part, and he's got a fucking dimple that Ned wants to touch a finger to. "Maybe it was."

Ned leans across the table. "Do that again."

"Do what?"

Ned nudges his ankle. "You know what."

"I don't." Abbot takes a drink of his beer. He shifts their hands to the side so the waiter can set down a basket of pickles and takes a second sip.

"C'mon," Ned says.

Abbot neatly picks up a pickle, holding it in his fingers and turning it, as if examining it in the light. "I'm looking forward to you being in Boston. Frankly, the local cuisine leaves much to be desired."

"Smile again." Ned traps Abbot's foot between his, kicking lightly at his heel.

"I'd work on improving your sense of humor, if that's what you want."

"I will do whatever it takes. Once more."

Abbot holds up the pickle. "I'm eating."

"You're a total ass," Ned says, grinning. "Have I told you that?"

"I believe it was noted in the margins of one of the exams you took for me."

"Nah, I called you way worse." He's staring at Abbot, he knows. And he's not entirely sure he could stop, even if he wanted to. "I can't actually believe this."

"That someone thought it was a good idea to deep-fry sliced pickles?"

"What're the odds that this would've worked out?" Ned waves between them. "You and me."

"Had you learned anything this fall, perhaps you could calculate them."

"I didn't even think it was possible," Ned says. "That we could do all of that and end up actually dating. That it was even . . . that when we started, being together for real was even an option."

Abbot chews slowly. God, Ned wants to kiss him, those lips of his. And he can. The thought warms him right through, the thrill curling his toes in his shoes.

"I admit a certain amount of surprise," Abbot says.

"It was—" Ned has to laugh. "Pretending to date—that was wild."

"Quite."

"And fun." Ned taps his fingers lightly over Abbot's palm.

"You made me tea. I—I appreciated it."

"Well, we certainly had a fun night." Ned raises both eyebrows. "Minus the interruptions."

Abbot lightly traps Ned's index finger with his thumb. "You didn't have to do that. It was . . . kind. And unexpected. I thought you'd want to be rid of me, after that weekend at Chris's."

"I thought so too." Ned squeezes Abbot's fingers. "Good thing I was wrong."

After dinner, the wind's picked up, tossing dried, crunchy leaves onto the sidewalk. It's a gray sort of evening, the type that brings the reminder of the coming winter. Ned grins up at the sky, his head tipped back and the chill of the breeze on his cheeks. Hands tucked into his pockets, he bounces his elbow into Abbot's arm. "Invite me over."

"You're entirely too sure of yourself."

"I like it when you ask me to come up." Ned knocks Abbot's arm again. "You're so cute and awkward."

"And you look, I believe the phrase is, like a deer in the headlights."

"C'mon." Ned bumps his arm into Abbot's again. "I'll even listen to you wax poetic about the superiority of wine and living the pescatarian life."

"I love you."

Ned stops walking. Abbot does too, turning to face him.

"You don't have to say anything," Abbot says. "I just wanted you to know that I do. And that I have, for some time now."

"Okay." That's panic flaring through him. Or excitement, maybe. A deep-seated thrill of agitation that takes hold of him, and under that is a slow-burning, smoldering fire. One that's building, and which he doesn't quite know what to do with. He steps forward and Abbot's there to hold on to, to wrap his arms around and lean against.

"Very much so," Abbot says and softly, he kisses Ned's forehead.

Ned grips Abbot's jacket in both hands. "Yeah?"

"Yeah."

Against Abbot's collar, Ned has to smile. *It's not real*, he thinks. But Ned has a bad habit of doubting anything good in his life, and Abbot pressed up against him is the realest thing Ned's ever felt.

"For a while?"

Ned can feel Abbot nod.

Impossible, it has to be. Ned tightens his grip. "For how long?"

"I hardly know."

"Are we actually going to date?" Abbot smells good. Ned lets himself nestle closer, Abbot's chin brushing over his forehead. He must've shaved. There's no scratch of his cheek, just the soft press of it.

"I have every intention."

"And we'll figure it all out?"

Abbot's lips touch to Ned's temple. "We did once before."

"So we're really going to do this all over again?"

Abbot's hold on him tightens. It feels so good. Safe. Like they fit together. "I believe we already are."

"Okay," Ned says again. It's easier like this, to not look at him. Though, if Ned had wanted easier . . . he leans back in Abbot's grip. Abbot's eyes are soft behind his glasses. "I love you too."

Another smile. Smaller this time, but all the sweeter for it. "Convenient."

Ned closes his eyes. Breathes. His chest is too tight. Thick with the weight of his life slipping into a new shape. A better one.

"C'mon," he says, taking Abbot's hand in his. Ned tugs him up the street. "Let's get started."

A PLACE TO GO

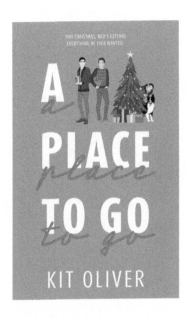

Falling in love was a long, bumpy, wonderful ride.
Now, they just have to figure out the rest of it: family,
holidays . . . and what to get each other for Christmas.

Read for free at:
www.kitoliver.com/aplacetogo

ACKNOWLEDGMENTS

This story grew into itself through the support, love, and enthusiasm of its original readers. You were all cheerleaders and friends through the many years of writing, and I hope that I've done this version justice deserving of all of your encouragement. Thank you all, so very much.

In bringing this book to publication, I can't thank Elle Maxwell enough for her beautiful art. She created the perfect Ned and Abbot for the cover and working with her has been an absolute joy. Sarah Calfee and Jules Hucke did a wonderful job editing the manuscript, and to them I owe deep appreciation for dinosaur research and the hard work of wading through my dubious use of commas.

Erin, thank you so much for all the emails, answering my panicked messages with love and encouragement, and your unending support through this foray into publishing. Having you in my corner has made all of this so much more possible.

Sam. Reader extraordinaire and friend above friends. From mailmen to Guernsey, you've been the best partner for so many literary adventures across the years. You've read every version of this story and have met them all with encouragement and enthusiasm. So much of the delight of this story stemmed from our long, winding conversations, and I can't wait to see where the world of books take us next.

And finally, the husband. You're pretty cool and I like you lots.

ABOUT THE AUTHOR

Kit Oliver's days are spent writing, thinking about writing, having just written, or preparing to write. When not mulling over plot points and dialogue, Kit can be found reading or outdoors - or reading outdoors - often with one or more of the family dogs for company.

Kit writes contemporary m/m romance novels full of bantering, bickering, pining, and kissing (and then some) that always end in Happily Ever Afters. Kit may take writing seriously, but believes that above all else, books should be fun to both create and consume. Kit's stories are based around a strong sense of humor, a deep love of complex characterization, and the joy of two people finding each other and falling in love.

ALSO BY KIT OLIVER

A Place to Go

Another Shot

Cattle Stop

Coming soon:

While the Sun Shines

Roll in the Hay